Ram-2050

A Ramayana Epic for the Future

JOAN ROUGHGARDEN

Art by Gwenn Seemel
Music by Trudy Roughgarden

KAUAI INSTITUTE, Kapaa, HI 96746

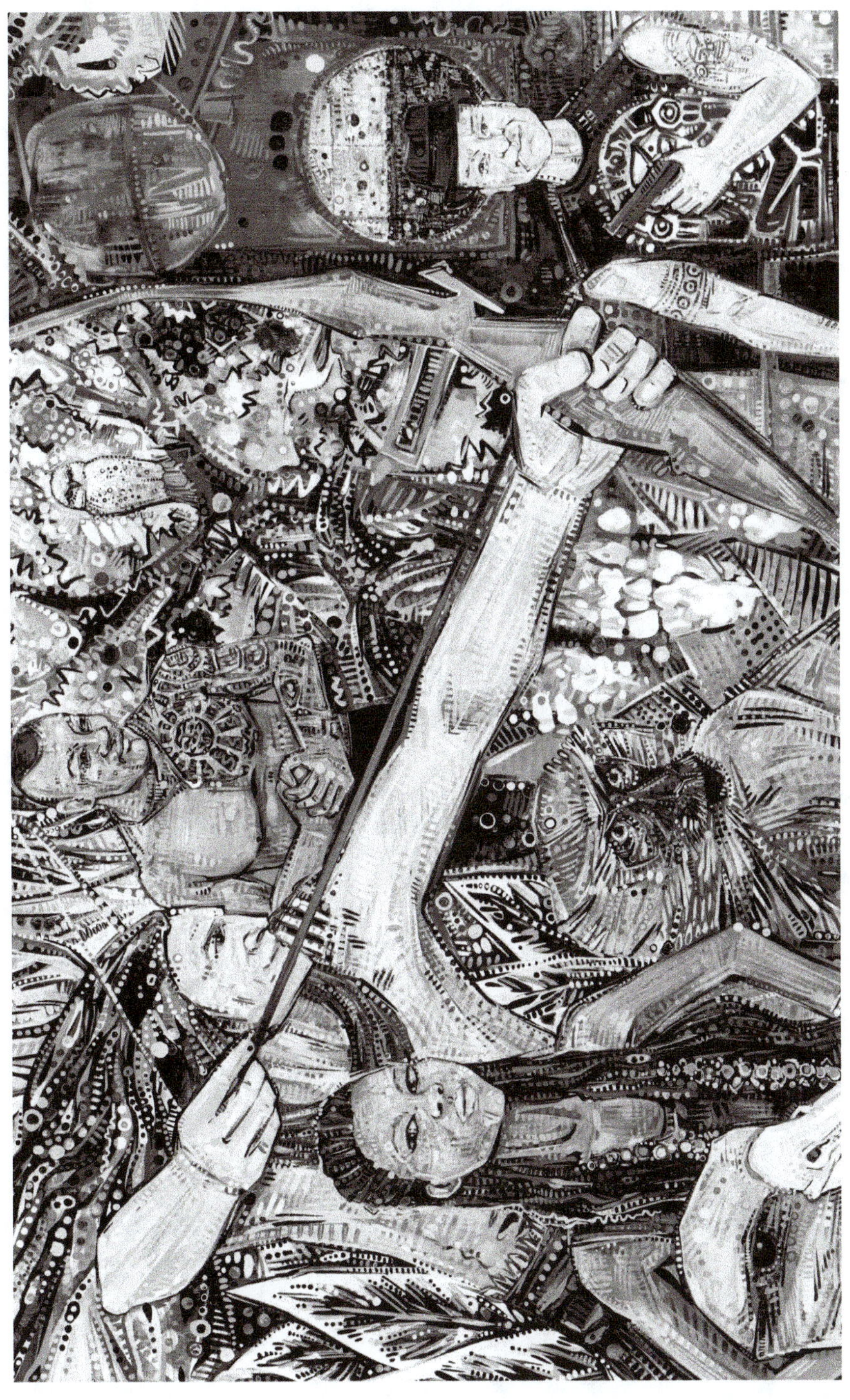

Readers are invited to a free download of the book's full-color art and recorded music at Ram-2050.com.

Contents

Characters

Agast	chief of Milolii Beach natural history encampment
Akam	Khar's lieutenant
Aks	Ravan's son, killed early by Hanuman
Anasuya	wife of Atri, gives shell lei to Sita
Angad	Val's son, a howler, Sugriv's nephew
Atik	Ravan's son, bodybuilder, killed by Lak
Atri	chief of Kalalau Beach encampment for hybrids
Barat	Das's second son
Bhad	chief public relations geek at Apple
Bhar	chief of Hanakapi`ai Beach jewelry-making encampment
Ceroc	iMonkey robot tutor
Das	CEO of Apple in Silicon Valley
Devant	Ravan's son, killed later by Hanuman
Dhum	syndicate boss from Colombia
Dundub	bushmeat hunter killed by Val
Durd	syndicate boss from Vatican
Durmuk	syndicate hit man from Northern Ireland
Dush	Ravan's other brother on Kauai
Dwivid	tamarin, Maind's brother
Elaros	iBird robot translator
Gaj	howler warrior
Gand	howler warrior
Garud	fish eagle, osprey, aids Ram and Lak

Gav	howler warrior
Guh	CEO of software company on Kauai
Hanuman	green (vervet) monkey, executive assistant to Sugriv and devoted ally of Ram
Ind	Ravan's eldest and most powerful son
Jamb	spectacled bear, escaped from Grenada Zoo
Jambu	Ravan's chief of security, killed by Hanuman
Janak	CEO of IBM/Microsoft in Seattle
Jat	Hawaiian hawk of Awaawapuhi Valley
Kaband	former banker, selfish Na Pali hoodlum
Kaila	Das's youngest wife and Barat's mother
Kamp	syndicate hit man from Miami
Kausha	Das's senior wife and Ram's mother
Khar	Ravan's brother on Kauai with helicopter
Kuber	Ravan's half brother, deposed by Ravan
Kum	hit man, Kumb's son, Ravan's nephew
Kumb	Ravan's muscular brother, a heroin addict
Kus	one of Ram and Sita's twin sons
Kush	Janak's brother, CEO of software company in Bangalore
Lak	one of Das's youngest sons, Shat's twin, Ram's companion
Lara	young albatross friendly with Elaros
Lav	one of Ram and Sita's twin sons
Mahap	Ravan's half brother living in Sudan
Mahod	Ravan's half brother living in Hollywood
Maind	CEO of tamarins
Malay	Ravan's maternal grandfather
Manda	Barat's wife, daughter of Kush
Mandara	Ravan's first wife
Mantha	Kaila's embittered chief of staff
Marich	Ravan's henchman, escapes from Ram and Lak
Matal	Vibish's assistant, pilot
Matang	late leader of tropical medicine geeks, Bocas del Toro

Nal	CEO of spider monkeys, architect
Nalak	Kuber's son, Ravan's half nephew
Naran	Ravan's son, killed by Angad
Nikum	hit man, Kumb's son, Ravan's nephew
Nil	CEO of night monkeys, warrior
Pragast	most powerful syndicate boss from Crimea
Praj	syndicate hit man from Syria
Pratap	syndicate hit man from Corsica
Ram	Das's first son
Rambha	Kuber's wife, raped by Ravan
Ravan	chief gangster
Rik	deceased howler, father of Val and Sugriv
Rish	howler warrior
Ruma	Sugriv's wife, a howler, Val's second wife
Sabara	chief scientist of tropical medicine geeks
Sampat	Jat's older brother, hawk in Grenada
Samud	police officer in St. Eustatius
Sarab	chief of Honopu Beach mahu encampment
Sarama	Vibish's wife, comforts Sita
Saran	security guard, spies on monkeys with Suk
Sard	security guard, spies on monkeys
Sharab	syndicate hit man from Nigeria
Shat	one of Das's youngest sons, Lak's twin, Barat's companion
Shurpana	Ravan's sister from Vegas
Sita	Ram's wife, adopted daughter of Janak
Sonit	syndicate hit man from Uganda
Subah	Ravan's henchman, killed by Lak
Sugriv	original CEO of howlers, restored by Ram
Suk	security guard, Ravan's emissary to monkeys
Suman	Das's valet, limousine driver and pilot
Sumitra	Das's middle wife, mother of the twins, Lak and Shat
Supar	syndicate hit man from Pakistan

Sush	CEO of capuchins, surgeon
Suta	Shat's wife, daughter of Kush
Sutik	chief of Nualolo Beach robotics encampment
Tara	Val's first wife, a howler
Tata	Chechen gangster, mother of Marich
Trijata	Sarama's maid, attends to Sita
Trishir	Ravan's son, killed later by Hanuman
Urmila	Lak's wife, daughter of Janak and Sita's stepsister
Vajrad	syndicate boss from Yemen
Vajram	syndicate hit man from Chechnya
Val	temporary CEO of howlers, killed by Ram
Valmiki	chief of Hanakapi`ai Falls human history encampment
Vasis	Das's genome manager and chief palace geek
Vibish	Ravan's brother and counselor, defects to Ram's side
Vidyu	Ravan's chief counterfeiter
Vidyumal	syndicate hit man from Los Angeles
Virad	former banker, greedy Na Pali hoodlum
Virup	syndicate boss from North Korea
Vish	chief algorithm geek, combat arts instructor
Yupak	Ravan's physician

Preface

The Ramayana is the most famous epic of South Asia. In 500–400 BC the Indian poet Valmiki composed a manuscript that consists of 24,000 verses spanning seven books. Over the years, many priests and sages have translated, amended, or retold the Ramayana, with versions appearing in more than 300 languages and dialects. Artists and sculptors have depicted the story in paintings and statues. Dramatists reenact the epic every day as plays, dances, and puppet shows in countries from India to Indonesia.

The Ramayana's impact can't be exaggerated. In 1987, over eighty million people watched a Hindi television series depicting the Ramayana. Because TVs were scarce, viewers gathered with family members in the few homes or local shops with a TV, hoping electricity didn't quit midway through the broadcast. Years later, in 2008, Indian television showed another serialization, this one consisting of 300 episodes of one half hour each.

I first encountered the Ramayana while traveling in Bali and Thailand. I was intrigued by how the epic depicts a blurred separation between humans and animals. In the West we police a strict boundary between human and animal. Much of Western philosophy and theology attempts to define what is uniquely human—what sets us apart and above other living creatures. Yet contemporary biotechnology produces transgenic hybrids every day. When extended to humans, this technology will dissolve the clarity of a human/animal boundary. What does this new reality of human/animal mixtures portend? The Ramayana offers a vision.

The Ramayana features an enlarged community of moral agents that includes humans and animals. The story is about a heroic prince from India who rescues his kidnapped wife with the assistance of animals. Humans and animals work together as allies to promote virtue and fight evil. During the epic the characters face physical danger and moral dilemmas. They succeed in spite of their own moral imperfections.

For *Ram-2050* I've recast the Ramayana's plot as taking place several decades from now, in the absence of magic or divine intervention. Where the Ramayana speaks of flying chariots, characters in *Ram-2050* take an airplane. In *Ram-2050* corporate empires and CEOs substitute for the kingdoms and kings of the Ramayana. Sects of professional experts, called geeks, replace sects of Brahman priests. I've set *Ram-2050* outside of India—in California, Kauai, Panama, St. Eustatius, and the Saba Bank. The character names are contractions of those used in the Ramayana. *Ram-2050* is science fiction, at times whimsical, an extension of today's science and society.

In addition to being a magnificent epic, the Ramayana is a sacred text. Rama is an incarnation of the great Hindu god Vishnu. This divine origin supplies him with physical power and moral integrity. In *Ram-2050*, Ram's power and integrity arise from how his genome is synthesized as well as how he's raised—both in the home and through encounters with social norms. The Ramayana contains moral instruction on what it means to be good. In *Ram-2050* I've honored these teachings by exploring naturalistic incentives for the Ramayana's virtue ethics.

Writing this book has been great fun. Please enjoy!

Das's Despair

Das had no son. He was dying prematurely. The gaunt CEO of Apple was despondent in his black turtleneck, jeans, and sneakers. He said to himself, "I've three wives. I've enjoyed their intimacy. Still no son. What am I doing wrong? Is my line going to end with me?"

Das's despair infected the Apple insiders. Their despair leaked to CNBC, provoking a sell-off, shrinking the distribution of returns from Apple stock to widows and retirees.

The citizenry became alarmed. Advice tweeted in. "Maybe you didn't want a baby enough." "Maybe you were in a hurry for a board meeting, a staff meeting, an architect's meeting, a yacht-builder's meeting." "Maybe you pulled out too soon." "You need to show you really, really want a son. Else it won't happen." "You need to sacrifice, sacrifice."

So Das called his chief geek, Vasis, and said, "I want to host a convention. Rent Moscone Center, all of it. Lease its hotels, even the lavish ones. Hire chefs, pay overtime to Tenderloin street cleaners, grease the cable car gears. I want the city of San Francisco to shine."

Das continued, "Contact our app coders, chip stampers, bean counters, our whole constellation of accessory makers. I want to make a sacrifice. So I hereby open up some proprietary code to the public. I increase our royalty payout on apps, books, and tunes."

"Yes, sir," replied Vasis, "will do."

Das added, "And invite everyone, the whole world, to attend. They can come in person or online."

And they came, they came from love. They loved Das for his brilliance, his fashion. It seemed he spoke with God, that his direction was God's direction. He brought prosperity to all.

Das held a press conference at Moscone Center for his attendants and bloggers, as well as CNET and MarketWatch. Das walked onto the center stage. He said, "We're the envy of the world. Our creations define civilization as the pyramids of old once did."

All who heard stood on their seats to applaud. They hollered and yelled. They were satisfied that Das's grand convention, his public recognition of their talent, his opened code, and his new payout rate added up to a generous sacrifice.

Then Das said, "One more thing." The murmuring ceased. Into the silence Das announced, "The time has come to create my successor." You could hear a pin drop.

He continued, "I will convene my product developers to conceive a creature worthy of your love and devotion. Your future will be secure."

All were elated. They had grieved for the CEO's frustration. They had prayed his wives could be delivered from the sorrow of their emptiness. They had worried about the future. Now, at last, they had hope for a worthy heir.

The conference attendants returned home. The media covered the announcement of a successor. Bloggers claimed the birth of Das's successor would, in effect, be the ultimate product launch. The stock soared. A relieved citizenry tweeted their optimism.

Ram's Genome

Das returned to his palace at 1 Infinite Loop in Silicon Valley. He started planning the capabilities his successor would have. He assembled his chief geeks—his material wealth manager, his genome wealth manager, and his phenome wealth manager. They joined Das in his executive suite, a west-facing sector, one degree of arc wide, carved from his spaceship-like toroidal palace. The light inside was golden from the afternoon sun. The mahogany conference table glistened.

Das first called on his material wealth manager, a middle-aged financial geek in a black motorcycle jacket. Das asked, "What's the shape of our financial assets?"

The financial geek replied, "Great, lots of cash." The geek continued to review the stock portfolio, as well as the buildings and yachts Das's son would inherit. Das yawned and cut him off, saying, "Fine."

Then Das called on Vasis, the palace's chief Geek. The geneticist was in his sixties, clean shaven, with a shaved head, and always dressed in a white shirt and slacks. Das said to him, "I want you to manage the portfolio of genes my son will possess, his genome. Any ideas?"

Vasis replied, "Yes, lots of 'em. Do you want just the bottom line or the reasons too?"

"I want nitty-gritty," said Das.

"Okay," Vasis said, "start with allocations. What fraction of your son's genome should be genes that come from you, what fraction should be genes from your son's mother, what fraction from other people, and what fraction should be genes from animals? And then there is the matter of which people and which animals to supply the genes."

"Keep going," Das said.

Vasis replied, "We've got computer simulations of life outcomes for people born with different genetic allocations."

Das gave him a reassuring nod, so Vasis continued, "At least 35 percent of your son's genome has to come from you, otherwise your son will owe you no loyalty. With less than 35 percent, your son will regard you as a stranger and have no special love for you. But with more than 35 percent of your genes, your son won't be sufficiently different from you to face the novel contingencies that will arise during his reign. Although your genes worked during the past, they are not guaranteed to be right for the future."

Das persisted. "Okay, now what about the remaining 65 percent?"

"Well," Vasis replied, "in days of old, half of every child's genes would automatically come from you, the father, and the other half would automatically from your son's mother."

"Yes, I remember those days," said Das.

"But now we can synthesize a child's genome in the laboratory. The synthesized genome doesn't have to have a fifty-fifty mother/father allocation. We're no longer locked into that."

"How do you use the synthesized genome?" Das asked.

Vasis replied, "The whole synthesized genome is dissolved in a special fertilizing potion that gets applied to an egg that has had its genes removed. The egg with its genes removed becomes the substrate for the fertilizing potion. That way the fertilizing potion provides the whole genetic makeup of an egg. I should add, though, that we don't control for the composition of the organelles remaining in the egg's protoplasm after the egg's genes have been stripped out of its nucleus.

Vasis continued, "Although your son's genome won't be fifty-fifty your genes and the mother's genes, there's an advantage to having your son possess an equal number of genes from both parents. This ensures that the mother/son bond is as strong as the father/son bond. That way, each of you will care equally for your son, and in return he'll love each of you equally. Neither of you will abandon your son to the sole care of the other. Nor will your son reject one of you for the other. Therefore, I recommend that 35 percent of your son's genome come from your son's mother."

"Okay," said, Das, "the genes from both parents combined account for 70 percent. What about the remaining 30 percent?"

Vasis replied, "If 10 percent come from animals, then your son will possess enhanced senses of smell, vision, and hearing that humans do not possess by themselves. Also, your son will be less susceptible to a human pandemic, although at the cost of being a bit more susceptible to the diseases affecting animals."

Vasis continued, "Moreover, if your son carries animal genes, then animals will feel a special friendship with your son. They will be his allies and come to his aid. Otherwise, the animals will see him as another human who has stolen their habitat and threatens them with extinction."

"Hmm…" Das said as he stroked his salt-and-pepper beard.

"But on the other hand," Vasis added, "possessing more than 10 percent animal genes risks a genetic incompatibility with the rest of the genome. Furthermore, he won't qualify for human rights under the UN Convention of 2030. You recall that convention?"

Das gestured with his hand to suggest he was a bit hazy about the 2030 convention.

Vasis said, "It defined the difference between humans and animals. Your son can't be a human, or entitled to human rights, if his animal genome content is over 10 percent."

"Yes, I remember now. It's okay with me if 10 percent of the genome is from animals," said Das. "So that leaves 20 percent of the genome still unaccounted for. What about that?"

Vasis replied, "Those genes can come from other people."

Das said, "Okay, which people should we tap for the remaining 20 percent of my son's genes?"

Vasis answered, "This decision involves subtleties. One possibility is to select genes from someone you admire whose qualities you wish your son to embody. You might choose a famous statesman like Mahatma Gandhi, a famous athlete like Mohammad Ali, a famous singer like Elvis Presley, or even your predecessor, Steve Jobs. You could also select someone from the *Wall Street Journal's* current list of the ten most admired people. The only requirement is that you select either someone alive, someone whose body has been exhumed to extract a genome sample, or someone who has deposited their genome in a sperm or egg bank. And even that requirement isn't absolute because you might be able to pay for exhuming the body of someone whose genome hasn't been determined yet."

Das thought for a few minutes and declared, "I don't know of a single individual I admire enough to replicate in 20 percent of my son's genome. Is there another possibility?"

"Yes," the genome manager replied, "instead of focusing on any particular individual, you could choose a genetic sector and include a sample from that sector as the final 20 percent of your son's genome."

"Which genetic sectors would you recommend?" asked Das.

Vasis answered, "You could choose a sample of all people of African descent, Aboriginal descent, Asian descent, or European descent if you wanted to use geography as a criterion. Or you could choose a sample of musicians, poets, scientists, priests, chefs, or laborers if you wanted to use occupation as your criterion. To choose a genetic sector for your son, you have to gamble on which sector is likely to prosper most in the coming era when you son rules."

Das mulled this over and said, "My son's genome is too valuable to play roulette with. Is there still another possibility?"

"Yes." Vasis hesitated. "Although it hasn't been tried before. You could choose a sample from all of humanity for the final 20 percent of your son's genome."

"Ah, that's exactly what I want," Das immediately exclaimed. "I want every man and every woman to identify with my son—I want everyone to see him as one of their kin, as a cherished member of their family. Then my son will feel a bond with all of humanity. He will act for its benefit, and conversely, all of humanity will love him and trust his leadership."

At this point Das said, "Let's break for half an hour. I'm ready for some coffee."

Das walked outdoors among the oak trees. Again scratching his beard, he felt he needed a second opinion.

So after the coffee break, Das summoned both his lawyer, a middle-aged legal geek in gray tie and jacket with small, well-trimmed mustache, and Vasis.

As soon as the legal geek arrived, Das told him, "I want your feedback on Vasis's plans for my son's genome."

Vasis then quickly briefed the lawyer.

Das asked him, "Sound okay?"

The lawyer said, "No, I have some issues with what I just heard."

Das was surprised. He said, "You've looked out for my interests in the past, and I trust your opinion. What concerns you here?"

"First," said the lawyer, "I wonder why your son won't have 100 percent of your genome. If your son were a clone of you, wouldn't that be best? I think the case could be made that you yourself can't be improved upon."

Vasis rose to defend his plan. "It's perhaps true that our Das's genome can't currently be improved upon, but the value of his genome has been proven in the past, not the future. Our simulations show that 100-percent clones don't fare well in scenarios of economic cycles and climate change. Under my plan, Das's son will be a 35-percent clone of Das. Our simulations show that such offspring survive and prosper much better than 100-percent clones do. So our CEO is expected to benefit more by hitching

35 percent of his genome to a mixture of genes from others than by going it alone with a 100 percent of his own genes in his son."

"Do you have other concerns?" asked Das.

"Yes," said the lawyer. "Why are you using samples of genes rather than specific genes? If you want your son, say, to have a gene for the high cheek bones and chiseled jaw of the biblical David, or if, say, you want him to have immunity to malaria, why not place the specific genes for these features in your son's genome?"

"Because," replied Vasis, "no one can predict exactly which trait a particular gene will produce. How a gene is expressed depends on the other genes in the genome as well as all the ingredients in the plasm the mother contributes to the fertilized egg. The best route to genetic design is statistical—using samples of genes from the populations whose typical traits you wish to propagate rather than bothering with individual genes."

"Any more concerns?" asked Das.

"Yes sir, my final concern is this," said the lawyer. "I suppose some of your own genes have indirectly come from animals in the past, maybe from a time before humans split from their animal ancestors. When the 35 percent of your genes, including your distantly derived animal genes, is combined with 10 percent genes drawn immediately from animals, the total your son will wind up with will exceed the 10 percent threshold. Exceeding that threshold will endanger his human status, according the 2030 UN Definition of Human and Animal."

"Good point," said Das. "What do you say to this, Vasis?"

"Well," Vasis answered, "the truth is that we humans already share many genes in common with animals, so we don't bother to classify these universal genes as belonging to either human or animal stock. What we do is only count the genes exclusive to humans and those exclusive to animals. Your son will inherit from you only universal genes plus your uniquely human genes. Therefore, he will have no more than 10 percent of a uniquely animal genome."

"Okay," declared Das, "I'm satisfied. We'll go ahead with the plan as originally outlined."

Addressing the lawyer, he said, "Thanks for your skeptical questions. Good job."

The lawyer bowed and was turning, about to leave, when he suddenly remembered that no one had yet selected the type of the animal to be used for 10 percent of Das's son's genome. He asked Das, "Have you chosen the animal for your son's 10 percent?"

After pondering awhile, Das announced, "I think I'll choose the monkey for 10 percent of my son's genome. I don't know why, but I have a premonition that my son may need the assistance of monkeys sometime in the future."

Das turned back to Vasis and asked, "How would you go about including monkey genes in my son's genetic portfolio?"

Vasis replied, "As you know, I like working with a sample of genes rather than specific genes when possible. I therefore suggest a sample of genes from many primates—bonobos, gorillas, mandrills, monkeys, lemurs, and bush babies. From the bonobos your son will inherit a loving disposition; from gorillas, great size and strength; from mandrills, colorful natural tattoos of blue and red; from monkeys, both agility and colorful hair; from lemurs, stealth; and from bush babies, night vision. With these features animals will discern your son to be a friend and relative and not an enemy."

"Wonderful," concluded Das, who added, "We've discussed lots of genetic issues. I want a record. Someday historians may want to know my son's pedigree. I'd like a diagram to summarize exactly what's been decided here."

So Vasis parted the bamboo curtains that covered a large touchscreen wall and diagrammed what Das's son's genome would consist of. He said, "The parental genes, with 35 percent from both Das and his mother, will comprise 70 percent of the genome. Genes from all of humankind will comprise 20 percent of the genome and be composed of matching paternal and maternal samples independently drawn from the aggregate gene pool of humanity. Finally, 10 percent of the genome will come from primates and be composed of separate paternal and maternal samples drawn from the aggregate gene pool of primates."

"Looks good," said Das. "Now it's my turn for some technical questions. Can you prevent the collection of genes from different sources from being no more than a random grab bag of genes?"

Vasis replied, "Good question. We make sure we don't have redundant genes coding for some functions while omitting the genes for other functions. So the genes we put together for your son's genome will be a well-thought-out orchestra with each gene playing its note in the symphony of life, not just some random grab bag. And not only that, we'll be splicing the genes into the right place on the twenty-three human chromosome pairs to make sure the cells can divide safely. Some deep technical work is needed to synthesize you son's genome. Frankly, I'm excited!"

Ram's Genome

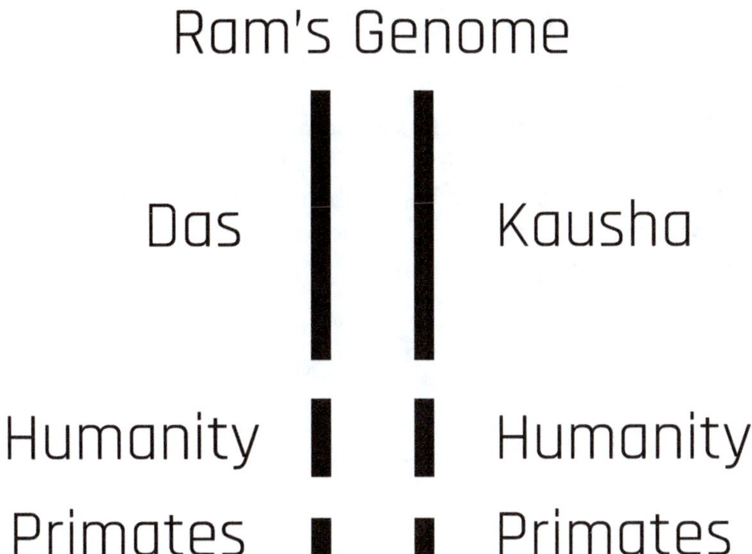

Paternal DNA on left, maternal DNA on right. Paternal genes come from Das (70%), from diverse humans (20%), and from various primates (10%). Maternal genes come from Kausha (70%), from diverse humans (20%), and from various primates (10%). Ram's total genome is 35% from Das, 35% from Kausha, 20% from other humans, and 10% from primates.

Das then said, "I have some further questions as well. How long does a gene have to be in the human lineage to count as human?"

Vasis said, "Here the answer is political, not scientific. By the 2030 UN Definition of Human and Animal, any gene found only in humans as of the year 2030 is a human gene, regardless of whether it derives originally from monkeys, donkeys, or sea slugs. If a gene's human in 2030, then it's fully human, period. Bit arbitrary, I'd say, but then, that's what the UN lawyers came up with."

The lawyer gritted his teeth at this seeming disregard for his profession.

Das said, "And as a follow-up question, when exactly is a gene considered to be present in a population? Is being present at a frequency of one in a billion enough?"

Vasis replied, "Again, a good question. There is a threshold marking a balance between how often a gene arises by mutation from other genes and how fast it disappears by random chance as the population progresses from one generation to the next. If the gene is commoner than this threshold, say around one in a million, then we assume the gene is permanently in the population."

Das replied, "Okay, works for me. One final point. Be discreet about the presence of animal genes in my son. Everyone may know that he includes genes from a sample of humanity, but keep his connection to the animal world close to your vest. Now let's get some lunch."

Vasis nodded and replied, "Mum's the word."

The somewhat chagrined lawyer then waved good-bye, leaving Das and his wealth managers to move to the cafeteria in the center courtyard of the toroidal Apple palace.

Ram's Phenome

Das and his wealth managers entered the cafeteria for lunch. They found a buffet set up with the world's most popular cuisines—Indian, Thai, Mediterranean, and Hispanic—along with an ice cream and yogurt bar. Small plates discouraged overeating, and a view of exercise equipment through the window of the palace gym further inhibited gluttony.

The seating was open. Das and his group grabbed a table for themselves.

Das called upon his phenome wealth manager, a young sports geek in white shorts and a white T-shirt. He was responsible for the totality of physical traits Das's son would possess, the phenome. The task was to determine Das's son's optimal portfolio of organs.

Das asked for suggestions. The phenome manager replied, "I recommend that we engineer soft tissues seeded with stem cells to permit ready regeneration in case of emergency."

"Yes, go on," said Das.

"If stem cells are preloaded into your son's heart, brain, liver, and kidneys, he can quickly recover from a heart attack, stroke, or lesion to the head, and from internal damage due to food poisoning. If his skin is laced with stem cells, he can recover from severe burns. If his face is provisioned with stem cells, he can retain a youthful appearance indefinitely. These engineered soft tissues can be injected or grafted into your son soon after birth, and they will grow as he grows."

"Excellent," said Das. "Anything else?"

"Oh, yes," said the phenome manager, "lots. Soft tissue is limited to biological materials. Your son should have access to the non-biological materials of hard tissues too. I recommend a subcutaneous layer of high-density acrylic that makes him hard to detect with X-ray snooper scopes and protects him from radiation. I also recommend bulletproof boron nitride shields to surround his heart and brain for protection during combat. These hard tissues can be inserted into your son after puberty, when he's stopped growing. With both engineered soft and hard tissues, your son should be nearly immortal and invincible."

"Good, make it happen!" Das clapped his hands.

The phenome manager added, "We're being careful not to add any components that might interfere with your son's cognitive functions. The UN convention of 2030 also outlawed intelligence-enhanced cyborgs—human/machine hybrids with implanted memory chips, CPUs, array processors, Bluetooth, or Wi-Fi receptors that could control the thinking and emotion loci of the cerebrum, cerebellum, and hypothalamus. We want your son to be in complete control of his own facilities, with the free will to devise his own strategies for dealing with future adversities."

"I approve," said Das. As an afterthought, he asked, "Is there anything my son will not be able to do?"

"Yes," the three geeks, speaking in unison, replied, "Your son will never escape obsolescence."

"Obsolescence?" asked Das.

One of the geeks explained, "Although he might live for over a hundred years, perpetually young and excelling in mental and physical prowess, undefeated in any combat or challenge, he'll still not be able to stay relevant for all of eternity. In time, his guidance and his aspirations for the people will lose their appeal and the people will yearn for another CEO. Your son, like all of us, cannot escape what you might think of as nature's product cycle."

By now lunch was over, and Das concluded the meeting. That afternoon Das authorized a press release describing his son's specifications. The citizenry was elated and tweeted their excitement. Blogs quickly filled with speculation on when Das's son would be born.

Das wished to reward his wealth managers for their good work. He offered them stock options and retirement packages. Vasis, as the senior geek, replied, "Thank you, but we are geeks. We don't aspire to riches. Our communities provide for us in retirement."

Das felt it was important for his geeks to accept some gift of thanks; otherwise, the citizenry would think him unappreciative. So, at Das's request, the geeks conferred with Vasis, who relayed their desires by whispering in Das's ear.

Upon hearing their requests, Das awarded to his phenome wealth manager, a sports geek, his choice of seats at both the Super Bowl and World Series, his material wealth manager, a financial geek, a promise to backstop any loan to fund a start-up company, and to Vasis, his genome wealth manager, a prototype of Apple's new product, the iGene, a pocket DNA sequencer and gene detector.

When the public heard of these awards, they tweeted their happiness—they thought the recognition the CEO had bestowed upon his geeks was fair.

Ram's Birth

Das wanted action. He drove from Silicon Valley to visit his senior wife, Kausha, at her palace near Skyline Drive in the Santa Cruz Mountains. From her palace Kausha could gaze upon the blue Pacific Ocean through a clearing in the coastal redwood forest. Her palace was made from redwood lumber, accented with Monterey shale, and featured large picture windows and a balcony. Outside the palace, steps led to a lookout in the redwood tree canopy where she could see the Steller's jays and their nestlings up close. Middle-aged, Kausha had soft features and long, mahogany-colored hair and brown eyes. She wore earrings of dark, polished wood and was dressed in forest-green slacks with a matching wool turtleneck sweater—the weather at her palace grounds was often chilly, and in the winter, the area occasionally received snow. Her bookcase contained ancient classics from around the world.

Kausha welcomed Das with a hug and kiss, and he asked, "Will you bear my firstborn child?"

Kausha was not surprised at the request. She had heard about the plans being made for Das's successor. She replied, "Yes," as indeed she had many times before.

So Das returned to his home and instructed Vasis to prepare the fertilizing potion containing the mixture of genes they had agreed upon.

Vasis then contracted with laboratories around the world. Genes from Das and Kausha were harvested from their bodily fluids and duplicated in the US. The genes from primates were obtained from numerous species and duplicated in India. The genes from the totality of humanity were obtained and duplicated in a collaboration among all the laboratories. After a month the potion containing all the genes from both parents plus the genes from other sources was ready.

Das also asked Vasis to prepare separate potions with genes from his two other wives for creating additional sons so that his firstborn would not be alone. He told Vasis to use his judgment in deciding which genes to include in these potions.

For both wives, Vasis prepared potions using independent samples of genes from many kinds of mammals rather than solely from primates as he had for Kausha.

For Das's middle wife, Sumitra, Vasis used genes from the legendary boxer Mike Tyson, reasoning that Sumitra's son would need to be an aggressive fighters to defend his brothers.

For Das's youngest wife, Kaila, Vasis selected genes from the American politician Lyndon Johnson, reasoning that Kaila's son would need to be a skilled negotiator and deal maker to bring a complementary skill to the brothers' leadership team.

Vasis summarized on Das's touchscreen wall the genomes for the sons to be born to his other two wives.

Once all the fertilizing potions had arrived from the laboratories, Das began by visiting Kausha at her palace in the woods.

Kausha welcomed him and asked, "Now?"

Das nodded and they slept together. She willed herself to ovulate. She invited Das to make love, saying, "The egg is ready."

So Das replied, "Just a minute."

As Kausha watched, he lodged a tiny capsule containing the fertilizing potion into a tiny pocket at the tip of a sheath for his male organ. The sheath contained a salve that suppressed male discharge while permitting sensation.

As Das murmured, "I hope this works," he entered his wife.

The capsule burst and the egg absorbed the capsule's contents. Substances from the potion dissolved all the genes originally in the ovum and substituted all the replacement genes from both parents together with genes from other sources.

The fertilized egg was now endowed not only with all the genes from the fertilizing potion but also with the living substances contained in Kausha's egg's plasm, including her mitochondria, ribosomes, and other organelles.

Kausha then said to Das, "It feels different this time. I think we may have struck gold at last."

Within hours, the fully fertilized egg divided. Within days, the early-stage embryo implanted in Kausha's womb. Kausha felt the embryo grow. In nine months Kausha delivered a baby boy at her palace.

Barat's Genome

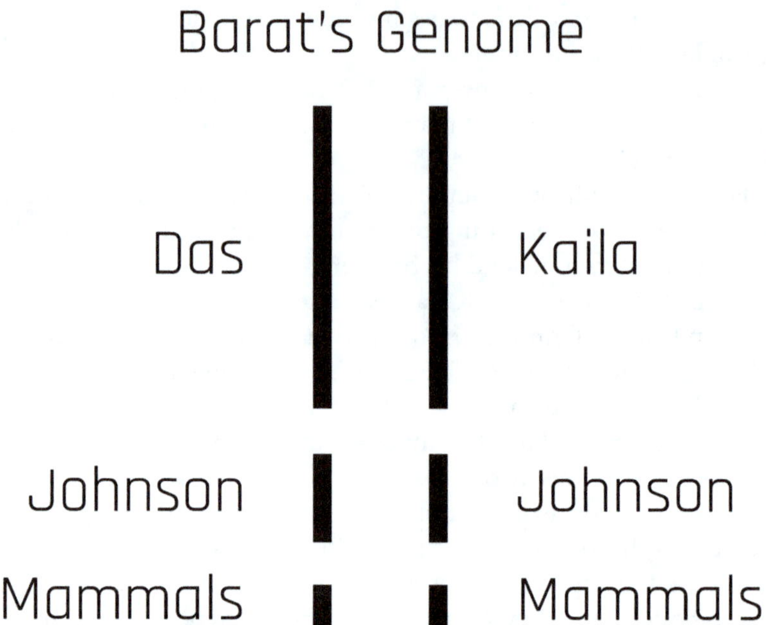

Kausha said to her new baby, "I name you Ram in honor of the hero and saint of the great Indian epic, the Ramayana. I will always love you with all my heart."

Meanwhile, Das also wished to sleep with his other wives, and they too wished to be with child.

Das was especially attracted to his youngest wife, Kaila, who lived with him in his Silicon Valley palace. Still young, her complexion was fair, with short, vanilla-blond hair, blue eyes, and a winning smile. She wore small diamond stud earrings and a diamond cross broach.

Das approached Kaila, who said, "I've been waiting for you, and I know how to make you happy." With her hands, lips, and eyes she seduced him onward.

Kaila then made herself ovulate. She said to Das, "Go on, I've released an egg."

He then put some of the potion formulated for her in a capsule for the pocket on his sheath and entered her.

The egg implanted, and soon thereafter Kaila called Das to her quarters, embraced him, and stroked his body, saying, "I am with child."

In time Kaila delivered a baby boy in her quarters at Das's palace whom she named Barat.

Lak's and Shat's Genome

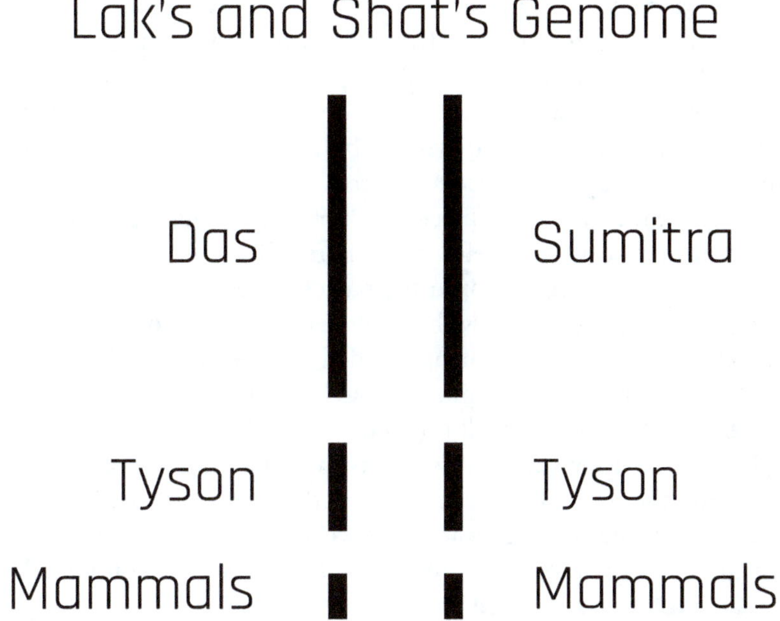

Das's middle wife, Sumitra, lived in the desert. Her palace was made of sandstone overlooking the grand, colorful, and stark vista of Death Valley. Her panoramic view extended over dry, white salt lake beds bordered on the east by snowcapped mountains. Sumitra was approaching middle age. Her face was weather-beaten from the sun, and her body lean and wiry. Her eyes were gray, and her hair was gray as well, highlighted with streaks of white. She wore earrings of polished beige granite with rusty red flecks.

Das helicoptered to her palace, bringing the potion with him.

When he arrived at her side, Sumitra said, "Welcome. It's been a while."

He said, "I know. I'm sorry. I've come so that you may be with child."

Sumitra said, "Should we make love now?"

"Yes," he said.

So Sumitra ovulated, saying, "My eggs are now ready. Please use enough potion for more than one egg."

Das then placed a large amount of the fertilizing potion designed for her into a capsule. He placed the capsule into the pocket on his sheath and entered her.

In nine months Sumitra delivered fraternal twin boys at her palace. She named them Lak and Shat.

Medical geeks were present when Ram and his brothers were delivered. They extracted stem cells from blood remaining in their mothers' umbilical cords. They also retained the surrounding placentas.

While the boys were under sedation with regional anesthesia, the medical geeks seeded each boy's heart, brain, liver, kidneys, and skin with stem cells for ready tissue regeneration.

Then the medical geeks placed each boy's placenta together with his remaining stem cells in labeled containers. These were stored in liquid nitrogen in a basement room in the palace of each boy's mother. These stores provided the brothers with a reserve of stem cells for use later in life as a backup to the stem cells already seeded into their skin and vital organs.

Das was ecstatic. Where once he had been childless, now he had four wonderful sons. His wives felt fulfilled.

Das called upon his creative geeks to prepare an interactive movie celebrating the birth of Ram and his brothers. He streamed the movie for free across the communication networks of the world. The citizenry tweeted its joy, unemployment dropped, the stock market boomed, and widows and retirees received bonuses.

Whereas Das was ecstatic, Vasis was proud.

Vasis knew he had to review for his apprentice geeks how reproductive technology had changed over recent decades. They would need this knowledge in the future. But his apprentice geeks were boys and young men whom he knew had not given much thought to human reproductive biology. So Vasis vTexted his staff to say that the agenda for their weekly staff meeting would be postponed one week to allow a special topic to be discussed instead.

The next day Vasis's staff poured into their conference room wondering what the day's special topic would be.

Vasis opened the meeting by saying, "I'll bet none of you have given much thought to human reproductive technology or to how you yourself were conceived and born."

Some of the young geeks coughed nervously.

One said, "No, sir, after all, we're geeks. Speaking for myself, although I try to stay in touch with my mother and father, I've always been too embarrassed to ask them how I came to be."

Vasis nodded and continued, "Can anyone define what a mother and father is and how those definitions have changed over the years?"

No one spoke up. They looked a little bored.

So Vasis said, "Here are today's definitions. Your mother is now called the initiating parent because this parent supplies the egg with its plasm.

The initiating parent is necessarily female because only females produce eggs. She is also the one who carries the embryo in her womb."

The youngsters still looked bored, as if to say, "Tell us something new."

Vasis continued, "Your father is now called the consummating parent because this parent delivers the potion containing all the genes to the egg."

Vasis looked around inquiringly and received a half-hearted nod to continue.

Vasis said, "The consummating parent can be either male or female because only the delivery of genes matters, not where the genes came from.

"The consummating parent's genes are included in the fertilizing potion along with the genes from the initiating parent, plus that of any desired third parties.

"By delivering the fertilizing potion to the egg, the consummating parent becomes a father. The act of delivering the fertilizing potion to the egg generalizes the traditional role of a father, which was to deliver a sperm ejaculate. Got it?"

Vasis looked around. His staff was starting to pay attention.

Vasis continued, "Socially, the father is also the one who supplies the pedigree. The father places the child on a family tree of legitimacy, a tree of authorized descendants. Our society remains patrilineal even though both males or females can be counted as a father. These roles are now spelled out for all the world in the UN Convention of 2030 Definition of Mother and Father."

One of the young geeks spoke. "Both my mother and father are women. I've always wondered what decided who was to be known as my mother and who was to be my father. Now I know. My father was the woman who delivered the genes that fertilized the egg made by my mother."

Vasis continued, "The technology of conception has also come far. Not long ago, to configure a child's genes before conception, our medical geeks had to violate the mother's body to harvest her eggs. Then the medical geeks would spread the fertilizing potion over her eggs in a petri dish, external to the mother's body. Surgically collecting the eggs was invasive and also wound up wasting many eggs. Now the eggs remain in the mother's body and the fertilizing potion is delivered directly to them by the father. This internal fertilization avoids egg wastage."

One of the young geeks muttered, "Obviously much better now."

Vasis nodded and continued, "There's more. Long ago women had no control over their ovulation. They experienced an involuntary egg release each month. Now any woman can elect to have a tiny hormone receptacle permanently embedded in her voluntary musculature at a body location of her choice. Then she can open the receptacle's hatch and insert a small capsule of egg-releasing hormone if she anticipates wanting to ovulate in the near future. When she wishes, a woman can flex her muscles to break the capsule, releasing the hormone that causes an egg to move into her fallopian tubes. Universal health insurance pays for the simple implantation procedure."

One of the young geeks spoke up to say, "If I get what you're saying, women have escaped the tyranny of biology's control. Now a woman controls her reproductive destiny to the same extent we men do. Sounds like an improvement over the birth control regimen of previous decades."

Vasis replied, "Yes, that's true, but what's even more important is the enormous social impact of this new reproductive technology. Now every pregnancy can be deliberate. No pregnancy accidental. Every baby wanted. No abortions. No riots at abortion clinics. No murders of the medical geeks who perform abortions. Now a woman exercises her right to choose before a baby is conceived, not after. I know that as young men, women's reproductive rights may seem a remote concern for you, but think: Now each of you can know that you were wanted. Your own personal presence on earth is not accidental. Tell me you don't find that comforting."

Vasis could see that early boredom had given way to sustained interest. He continued, "Have you ever wondered why twins are born sometimes? Well, a woman can vary the quantity of egg-releasing hormone in the capsule she places in her hormone receptacle. A lot of hormone releases enough eggs so that two or more progress to implantation after fertilization, yielding twins or triplets. That's why Das's middle wife, Sumitra, was able to give birth to her twins, Lak and Shat. She must have placed an extra large amount of egg-releasing hormone in her hormone receptacle before making love with Das."

Vasis went on to ask, "Bored, or should I stop here? Our regular time slot is nearly over."

A young geek spoke up, saying, "No one's ever talked to us about human reproduction before. Keep going."

Vasis then said, "You may take for granted that women today can control the timing of their menstrual cycle. But have you ever wondered how they do it? The answer is, they vary the type of capsule they place in their hormone compartment. Women place one type of capsule between ovulations and another type during ovulation. Women now time their cycle to fit their schedule. Going for a vacation? Just postpone the cycle for a couple weeks."

The young geek's attention was complete.

Vasis continued, "Although a woman may decide not to have any cycle at all, most want to regularly exercise their reproductive system to keep it fit. Their choice of timing can even be shared on social media. Clubs now exist for all women who choose to synchronize with the first day of the month for their period. Others choose a rotating schedule, honoring the birthdays of female pioneers like Susan B. Anthony, Betty Friedan, and Simone de Beauvoir."

Another young geek spoke up. "What you've just told us makes me wonder. How have women actually exercised the choices they now have available?"

Vasis replied, "Some women have become tired of using their reproductive organs. Either they don't want to give birth to any children at all or consider the children they have sufficient. These women elect to take a menopause and set their own date for it. Others elect to forgo menopause altogether."

Another young geek then said, "I've heard of a trillion-dollar biotech company called NewEgg that advertises menopause-eliminating technology."

"Right," replied Vasis. "The company's name had been used decades ago by an electronics retailer. A startup biotech company offered the retailer a billion dollars to change its name to NewGeek. Then, after paying for this name change, the newly minted NewEgg went on to produce technology to eliminate menopause. Want me to tell you how they did it?"

Heads around the table nodded. The young geeks loved hearing about anything techie.

Vasis continued, "NewEgg started with the fact that voluntary ovulation meant follicles weren't automatically being used up each month, but only on demand. That alone could postpone menopause, because the supply of follicles lasts later into life. But the problem remained that even if a supply of follicles persisted into old age, the fraction of those follicles that were viable declined each year."

Another young geek, all ears now, piped up to ask, "So what did New-Egg do?"

Vasis answered, "NewEgg's first technique was to harvest 10 percent of the egg follicles from a newborn girl—that's the time when she has about 700,000 of them, from both her ovaries combined. They stored these follicles in liquid nitrogen until she was middle aged. Then New-Egg medical geeks re-implanted the stored follicles back into the woman's ovaries, restoring her supply of the viable follicles. But, as you can see, this procedure is invasive, and so they developed another technique."

Vasis looked around. The young geeks were rapt.

Vasis continued, "NewEgg's second technique was to synthesize a growth hormone targeted to ovarian cells. The growth hormone reactivated the genes in those cells to make them start regenerating follicles. This special growth hormone can be taken as a dietary supplement. This way, the follicle supply never runs out because the supply is continuously being regenerated, postponing menopause indefinitely. This newer method has become their preferred and most profitable approach. Now, who do you think is making money from this menopause self-regulating technology?"

The young geeks looked at each other and shrugged.

Vasis said, "The chief investors, the CEO, and the science geeks in the NewEgg venture were all women. The existing biotech companies at the time viewed menstruation as a disease. They focused on marketing drugs to treat its side effects. Women, in contrast, regarded menstruation as just one more aspect of a body, all of whose parts need care and exercise to stay healthy. These women took the initiative, got some crowd-sourced funding, and now have become among the richest people on the planet."

Some of the young geeks whistled in admiration. They wondered if they would ever have an idea that could turn a huge profit someday.

Vasis continued, "Although the technology itself is neat, it also produced societal change. On one hand, some women didn't want to bother having children after middle age. Others, however, took the opposite tack. They wanted to ovulate forever. As of 2050, some women have produced three generations of children while outlasting three husbands. They are keeping their multi-generational extended family with them as they run a family enterprise, a family firm."

The young geeks were shaking their heads in amazement.

Seizing the moment, Vasis said, "I had to brief you on today's reproductive technology. Das, our own beloved CEO, has employed this technology with his wives to create his successor. Many years from now, after Ram retires from life, you too may be called upon to design a successor, just as I was. At that time, you'll need this knowledge. If I'm alive when Ram's life has ended, I will convene us again to review how well we've done in our efforts to manufacture a perfect person."

The young geeks filed out of the meeting room, murmuring to one another.

Vasis reflected on his own mother. He recalled how she fought so consistently throughout her life for equal pay and recognition. Vasis felt his mother would marvel at the diversity of reproductive choices that women had now created for themselves.

Ram Grows Up

As Ram and his brothers approached manhood, their distinctive traits increasingly emerged.

Ram was born with blue and red striped tattoos on his shoulders, endowing him with natural epaulettes of leadership, colors inherited as repositioned expressions of his mandrill genes. He had deep-tan skin and streaks of amber hair rippling through his thick black mane. His face befitted a god incarnate, with high cheekbones and a chiseled jaw, yet his eyes were soft and attentive.

Ram's twin brothers, Lak and Shat, had brown hair and a still darker shade of glistening tan skin and handsome features.

Ram's other brother, Barat, had blond hair and skin that was a light shade of tan.

Ram's brothers lacked tattoos because distinctive body markings dissolve when the products from genes of many types of animals are averaged together.

When Ram was a boy, Kausha brought him to play in the forest surrounding her palace. Pointing to a black-headed Steller's jay foraging on the ground and a black-coated squirrel scurrying on a tree trunk, she said, "See the animals. They are your community. You must get to know them."

Young Ram walked, tentatively at first, into a grove of coastal redwood trees. The animals sensed a kindred spirit and they showed themselves to him. Ram saw the birds—the sparrow hawk, horned owl, kingfisher, woodpecker, phoebe, meadowlark, goldfinch, sparrows, junco, jays, towhee, warblers, shrike, wren, wren-tit, thrushes, and robins; the amphibians and reptiles—the salamanders, toads, frogs, fence lizards, whiptail lizards, alligator lizards, skinks, garter snakes, and rattlesnakes; the mammals—the bats, mice, skunks, raccoons, gophers, rabbits, squirrels, deer, bobcats, mountain lions, coyotes, and feral dogs and cats. And Ram witnessed the insects—the butterflies, moths, dragonflies, grasshoppers, fruit flies, mosquitoes, beetles, roaches, ants, bees, wasps, and termites. And he saw the spiders, the banana slug, and all the creatures of the woods. Ram understood that he was surrounded by living things of many kinds. He synced to their rhythms, grasped their body language, sang with the tenor and pitch of their calls. He noticed the groups in which the animals occur, whether they were gregarious or solitary, and if social, with whom each was sharing conversation.

Kausha could see her son bonding with the animals in the woods. She asked him, "Would you like to sleep in the wood to be close to your friends?"

Ram replied, "Oh, Mother, I'd love to do that."

So Ram learned to sleep overnight in the forest, to find food and water, to keep warm, and to hear the forest talking to him. Ram became a citizen of the forest.

Once Ram's growth spurts stopped, the medical geeks reappeared at Kausha's palace to insert the hard tissues.

Kausha explained to Ram, "Once the medical geeks have placed you under mild sedation, they will inject an X-ray- and radiation-shielding acrylic at multiple spots across your body. The acrylic will solidify into a thin, pliable layer underneath your skin. They will also inject an epoxy solution containing boron nitride into your heart and brain cavities. They will be careful to extract a matching volume of fluid from the cavities to make room for the injections. The boron nitride epoxy will solidify into a pliable bullet shield harder than diamond to protect your heart and brain."

Ram took a deep breath and said, "I trust you that I'll really need all this someday."

Kausha replied, "Yes, I suspect you will."

Then the medical geeks began their procedures.

When Ram awoke, Kausha asked, "How do you feel, my son?"

Ram replied, "A bit stiff and sore. Also a bit heavier."

Kausha replied, "That's from the new materials you're now carrying, although the weight of the new materials should be mostly offset by the weight of the fluids they withdrew to make room."

While Ram was joining the forest community, Sumitra brought her twins, Lak and Shat, into the desert community surrounding her palace in Death Valley. They became lean and wiry like their mother.

Pointing to a hawk soaring in circles above the valley floor, Sumitra said, "You must get to know the animals. They will be your friends."

The twins soon synced with the desert's rhythm of dawn and dusk activity bracketing the midday period of rest. They learned to conserve water, how to find shade in the day and warmth at night. They walked among the birds—the red-tailed hawk, quail, roadrunner, wrens, robins, thrushes, starlings, warblers, blackbirds, finches, sparrows, juncos, flycatchers, ravens, swallows; amphibians—the toads and tree frogs; reptiles—the desert tortoise, banded gecko, desert iguana, chuckwalla, zebra-tailed lizard, fringe-toed lizard, collared lizard, desert spiny lizard, sagebrush lizard, side-blotched lizard, western skink, blind snake, boas, red racer, gopher snake, king snake, rattlesnakes, and sidewinder; mammals—the bats, gophers, pocket mice, kangaroo mice, harvest mouse, deer mouse, canyon mouse, desert wood rat, squirrels, rabbits, porcupines, coyotes, foxes, skunks, mountain lion, bobcat, burros, horses, deer, sheep; as well as pupfish, butterflies, spiders, and scorpions.

Like Ram, the twins learned they shared the earth with a multitude of living creatures. They became citizens of the desert.

Sumitra also watched as the twins sparred with each other for fun. She bought them a boxing ring and hired a coach to visit regularly. She knew they had been born with a boxer's instincts. She didn't want to thwart their development.

Barat's mother, Kaila, introduced him to activities in the urban habitat between Silicon Valley and San Francisco. Kaila brought her son to the playgrounds and gyms of Silicon Valley. She showed him where the stadiums were, where the professional athletic teams played, where the symphony, opera, and pool halls were. She showed him how to take the shuttle train to San Francisco and around the Bay Area.

Kaila said to her son, "People will be your life. Learn what they do, what they want, and how to navigate their conflicts, their prejudices."

Barat grew to play a mean game of squash, made music with both the violin and Moog, and mastered the Xbox and PlayStation while attaining international renown with online gaming. He gleaned street smarts as he traveled by himself to rock concerts in San Francisco, Oakland, and around the Bay Area. He could scalp a ticket with the best of them and hustle into a club ahead of the queue. He knew the gangs, their tattoos, their neighborhoods, and walked casually among them. He was a natural dealmaker. He became a citizen of the city.

When the brothers came of age to prepare for adulthood, Das summoned them from their mothers' quarters to join him in his Silicon Valley palace. There Das and Vasis conferred.

Das asked Vasis, "How do I raise my sons to cooperate with each other? I want them to work together as a team. I don't want them wasting their effort and my resources in sibling rivalry."

Vasis replied, "Your request is challenging. Your sons don't share the same genetic relationship to each other that brothers of old often did. Back then brothers and sisters born of the same parents shared 50 percent of their genes in common. That genetic relationship provided an evolutionary incentive for brothers to help one another."

Das said, "Yes, I know. In helping each other they indirectly increased their own genes in future generations."

"But the genome we've designed for your sons requires a new genetic calculus," said Vasis. "Only 35 percent of your sons' genes come from you. Of that, only half will be shared in common among them. So instead of 50 percent genes in common among the brothers, there's only 17.5 percent, which doesn't supply as much incentive for cooperation as in monogamous families of the past. The fraternal twins, I might add, have a higher genetic relationship to each other, 35 percent, because they have in common both you as their father and Sumitra as their mother. So they are incentivized to cooperate more with one another than with either Ram or Barat."

Das said, "Yes, my sons will see each other more like strangers than like kin as compared with the past."

Vasis continued "Exactly. You need to take special steps when raising them to foster sibling cooperation."

"Any suggestions?" asked Das.

"Yes," said Vasis. "You have to incentivize cooperation during your sons' upbringing. You have to figure out a way to make your sons enjoy cooperating more than competing with each other."

So Das insisted that his sons join the teams their school had to offer. Das was not interested in track and field sports, which emphasize solo competition—he wanted team sports for his sons. During the winter, playing basketball, the brothers learned combination plays, how to rotate coverage, and how to play zone coverage disguised as man-to-man coverage. They learned the joy of coordination in plays like the alley-oop pass.

Das spent time watching his sons as they played. And whenever they made an alley-oop or other combination basket together, he rewarded them with credits that could be cashed in with a trip to a favorite restaurant, with a sneak peek at a new Apple product. If the boys simply made foul shots, no extra reward. The extra reward came only if points were scored by the brothers via a combination play.

Das continued this training with other sports. During the spring, in baseball, the brothers learned to turn a double play, run a double steal, to execute a hit and run and a suicide squeeze. Das would give them extra rewards for putouts and runs scored with these combination plays but not for any home runs they might hit.

During the fall, in football, Ram played quarterback and learned to execute run-and-pass options under pressure. His brothers learned to read his eyes and to catch acrobatic passes. They learned to block together while anticipating each other's moves. For every successful combination play the brothers pulled off, Das heaped an extra reward on top of the ordinary rewards that winning itself provided.

Beyond the skills they learned in sports, Das taught the boys about teamwork in negotiation. Barat learned to work with his brothers in coordinating offers while bargaining, how to make joint offers, and how to purchase a large item or piece of property with good–cop–bad–cop tactics and high–low bids. Das offered extra rewards to his sons when they showed teamwork in negotiation.

After years of using rewards to encourage teamwork, Das called his sons together in their Silicon Valley quarters and told them that their extra rewards should no longer be needed. "Now," he said, "you've learned to enjoy teamwork for its own sake, and you shouldn't require further inducements from me."

And so it came to pass that the mutual enjoyment of teamwork itself propelled the brothers to act to each other's benefit. Even though each profited individually from their teamwork, this profit was not the motivation for their working together. They worked as a team for the sheer enjoyment of it. In this way, the relationship among the brothers developed into sibling cooperation instead of sibling rivalry. And because of their teamwork, Lak and Ram especially grew to become fast friends, bound by loyalty like that of soldiers bonded through combat, and similarly Shat bonded with Barat, making them a special team as well.

At times, Das educated his sons in business matters including Apple's policies. He taught them about the need for corporate secrecy, especially about new product developments. He described how a code of secrecy had come to replace the last century's primitive codes of sexual purity. Das explained that a citizen suspected of being under the influence of a rival corporation would be subject to enhanced interrogation to ascertain their trustworthiness.

Ram was surprised and asked, "Isn't torture unreliable? Isn't a statement obtained through waterboarding useless?"

Das replied, "But its value for deterrence cannot be underestimated. Enhanced interrogation protects the widows and retirees who depend on returns from our stock from the collapse our company would suffer if our latest products under development were leaked to competitors."

Shaking his head doubtfully, Ram said, "I hope I'll never have to employ such methods when my time to lead Apple arrives."

At other times, Das instructed his sons in how the biosphere worked, in how the forests of the world were the lungs for the global system of life. He showed them how the forests of the earth inhale during the North American spring and summer as the trees photosynthesize to lower the air's CO_2, only to exhale again in the fall and winter when the leaves fall and photosynthesis shuts down, allowing the air's CO_2 to rise back up again. He showed them how the winds blowing from the north along the California coast causes an upwelling that brings waters rich in nutrients to the surface. He explained that these nutrients fertilize the algae that is food for little shrimps that in turn are food for fish that then are food for birds and people. Das taught his sons how the peoples of the earth had grown so numerous that their activities all together could change the earth forever, changing its air and rerouting the currents of the oceans.

Ram grieved that the peoples of the earth had become so powerful that they might prevent the planet from supporting his own children, future generations of people, and the plants and animals he had grown to love.

Das asked his son, "Why do you grieve for human progress?"

Ram replied, "It's not the progress I grieve. I grieve the responsibility this power of mankind now places upon me."

Das asked, "Why upon you? Why do you take a personal responsibility for human welfare?"

Ram answered, "Father, I don't know why I personally feel so responsible for humanity's good and for the good of the plants and animals we share the planet with, but I do. I do feel this responsibility so very deeply, in the deepest marrow of my bones, in my genes."

Das was moved by Ram's response. Das knew that his son had been born with these most moral of instincts for the protection of humanity and all living things because he was, in truth, related to all of humanity and to the many animals on the earth.

Das cried out to all who would hear, "This is my beloved son with whom I am well pleased."

Ram's Mission

Now that Das's sons were maturing, the citizens began to tweet their greatest anxieties and hopes.

The most dangerous international crime syndicate was led by Ravan, a tall, handsome, swarthy, and charismatic man who lived on a secret island. The citizenry lived in fear of Ravan's exploitation. They hoped his influence could be tamed and dared to wish he might be killed. From his island headquarters Ravan directed all manner of crimes rendering the various casts of geeks powerless.

Financial geeks tweeted that Ravan enticed naive young couples and old retirees to take loans that they could not repay. He directed ambitious stockbrokers to waste clients' money, leaving bankruptcy in their wake. He manipulated international borrowing rates to inflate the costs of mortgages. He counterfeited currency. His machinations made repairing the international and domestic financial systems a continual struggle for the financial geeks.

Genetic geeks tweeted that Ravan introduced Trojan genes into gene banks. He then seeded the gene pool with genetic diseases for which he sold proprietary cures. The genetic geeks had difficulty removing the steady stream of harmful genes he continually placed into repositories of the human gene pool.

Information technology geeks tweeted that Ravan launched denial-of-service attacks against the websites of universities, power-generating stations, banks, brokerage houses, corporations, and governments, shutting down their services. He launched viruses that stole passwords and compromised the bank accounts of widows and retirees. Ravan's ransomware extorted payments from unsuspecting users. The geeks worked incessantly to keep the web's lines of communication clean.

Sports geeks tweeted that Ravan undercut international sports by enticing athletes to cheat with money from gamblers and tricking them into thinking that performance-enhancing drugs were harmless. The geeks were kept busy pruning official sports records of games whose outcomes had been fixed in advance.

Legal geeks tweeted that Ravan corrupted the rule of law by buying and selling influence in state and national legislatures. He conspired to prevent legislators from ever reaching a compromise. He found candidates to run for office who would obstruct the legislative process and stall interminably on appointments, making governments dysfunctional. He packed school boards with candidates who watered down the curriculum and introduced biased history and science texts. Legal geeks reported working tirelessly with elected officials and the judiciary to weed the legislative record of misleading and counterproductive laws and to identify and impeach corrupt legislators.

Creative geeks tweeted that Ravan plagiarized their works to sell as his own, sabotaged their concerts with power outages and counterfeit tickets, distributed watered-down paints to painters and defective mixes to DJs, and destroyed writers' reputations by interjecting inappropriate words and scenes into children's novels, scripts, and cartoons. Creative geeks worked endlessly to protect the integrity of their artistic creations, to call out counterfeits, and to defend artists from spurious lawsuits.

Ravan not only disrupted the geeks upon whom society depended, he sowed mistrust in the general citizenry. He floated false rumors about each race, religion, gender, and sexuality, fostering hatred and bigotry. He trafficked in women, buying low in impoverished areas and selling high in regions with a shortage of women.

Ravan underwrote programs to breed human soldiers who were immune to ricin, sarin, and other chemicals used in warfare. He introduced a new form of warfare called tactical weeding: Ravan's poison-immune soldiers were sent to fight against poison-sensitive soldiers. Then Ravan applied the poison to kill off the poison-sensitive soldiers, allowing his own soldiers to triumph.

Ravan prospered from global poverty. He won bids for construction projects by paying exorbitant bribes while recruiting workers from slums. He housed his workers ten people to a tiny room, held their passports, kept them as slaves, required them to pay off bogus debts, and charged a finder's fee for employment. Ravan believed the poor were genetically destined to their lowly status even as he was genetically destined to rule.

Ravan's henchmen kidnapped journalism geeks, holding them for ransom. His henchmen often killed their hostages and posted videos of their executions on YouTube, trying to provoke war.

Ravan was a bad man.

The citizenry tweeted their prayer that Ravan would someday be eliminated from the face of the earth. They hoped that Ram would be the one to lead them successfully in a campaign to rid the world of this hated demon.

But Das didn't understand. "Why," he asked Vasis, "are the citizens tweeting their problems about Ravan to me? I agree he's bad and something should be done to rein him in. But I am the CEO of a multinational company, not the king of a country. It's the job of government to prosecute criminals. Our company pays hefty taxes to sustain the police and armed forces."

"Sir, you forget," replied Vasis, "although Ram is still young, never before has a boy been born of man and woman whose genome has been synthesized to foster kinship with all of mankind. The people know this and look to Ram as a future protector of the whole human family—indeed, his family. Meanwhile, Ravan is the single most feared and dangerous source of evil in the world. If Ram can't somehow, someday deal with Ravan, then no one can and the future of humanity will be a bleak dystopia of conflict and deceit."

Das considered what Vasis had said. He then shrugged with resignation, saying, "The future will unfold in the fullness of time."

Ravan's Immunity

Das was trying to put in a day's work at his office with its splendid view of the California oak woodlands in the late spring. The wind blew the hay-colored grass that was soon to be mowed. The sky was blue, the weather crisp. It was hard to keep his mind on work. Das was oh so happy with Ram and his other sons. Now that they were growing into strapping young men, he was musing on how they might marry. He was lost in these thoughts while he should have been pouring over the design for a pending product announcement, revising an offer to settle with antitrust lawyers, and dealing with a volley of complaints about this year's version of the company's map app.

His reverie was suddenly broken by Vasis, who entered to say that an old friend from his college days was being admitted directly to his office.

Surprised, Das rose to greet Vish, a buddy who had gone on to head a sect of algorithm geeks. They were responsible for devising new procedures for coordinating the millions of computers interconnected across the global Internet, finding ways to harness their collective power to predict changes in the weather and climate and ways to isolate individual computers that had become infected with a virus before it spread to become an Internet pandemic.

Vish was lean and tanned, with shaved head and no facial hair. He lived with his team in the oak-forested hills on a breathtaking ridge overlooking the Pacific Ocean in Montecito, California, 1,250 feet above sea level, near Santa Barbara. They occupied buildings that once had been a gorgeous Spanish-style religious monastery before its decimation in a chaparral fire started by partying college students.

Vish and his sect of geeks bought the old monastery ruins and built in their place a simple yet functional habitat for algorithmic innovation. Vish was important to Das's company, and it was right that he be ushered into Das's presence immediately. Das knew Vish would not have come if the matter weren't vital.

Das said to Vish, "It's wonderful to see you after so many years." Das meant every word of his greeting. He recalled their enjoying late-night pizzas together, food that his doctor wouldn't allow him to touch now. "What brings you here?" he asked.

"Oh, my old friend, I've biked for four days all day long just to reach you," said Vish, who was committed to travel by low-carbon means. "I'm deeply troubled and have come for your help."

Das replied, "Anything, just ask, I owe you so much from our time together in college, and I depend upon your team for the algorithms we code into our products. What's the problem? How can I help?"

Vish said, "Bullies regularly come to our camp—big men with big beer bellies. They drive across our lawn with four-wheelers sporting gigantic tires and blaring stereos to park on our gardens, destroying our crops and flowers. They terrorize us. They yank rifles off their gun racks, and just for the hell of it, they shoot birds and squirrels and any other animal in sight. They trespass into our building and tromp through in muddy boots. They pull the plugs on our computers and servers. They ruin everyone's work for the day. They make fun of my people, their eyeglasses, their ever-present coffee cups. They call my algorithm geeks names it pains me to repeat."

"Well," said Das, "it does sound horrible, but you guys aren't wimps. If I recall correctly, you were even an expert in martial arts when we were in college and then you spent some time as a Navy Seal. Why not ambush them the next time they roll in to your camp and teach them a lesson they'll never forget?"

"True, we're not wimps," agreed Vish, "but physical fights are not our calling. When we signed on to be algorithm geeks, we vowed to live a life of thought and contemplation. We lose our concentration and blur our focus when we physically defend ourselves against such idiots. My fellow geeks live in fear. But fear is the enemy of creativity. Furthermore, others are just as capable as we are, if not more so, of putting a stop to this intimidation."

"Okay then, what do you wish me to do—send some of my private militia?" asked Das.

"Well, the problem is deeper than it first seems," said Vish. "These bullies are not garden-variety rednecks having their fun at our expense—they have connections. They are henchmen from Ravan's syndicate. If you take them out, you cross Ravan, and he's certain to follow up."

"Ah," said Das, "that does cast a new light on the matter. What, then, do you specifically request?"

"Well, here it comes." Vish hesitated. "I'd like you to lend me your eldest son's services for ten days—eight days for the journey both ways and two days at my team's compound."

"What!" exclaimed Das. "You must be kidding. No way. I'm not going to send you my son so he can get roughed up and make a powerful enemy as well. Ridiculous!"

Vish replied, "I will instruct him in the techniques of combat. Have no fear for his safety. I have an arsenal of military gear mothballed in a barn at our encampment. I can teach him how to use the weapons he'll need someday."

Das replied, "Ram is barely sixteen years of age, no match for bullies twice his age and size."

Now Vish was angry. He said, "Just minutes ago you promised 'Anything, just ask,' and now you're going back on your word. You leave me no choice but to find another company—say, Samsung—to offer our algorithms to, provided they, unlike you, will guarantee our safety from bullies."

At this point Vasis intervened, saying to Das, "It seems your son will have to tangle someday with Ravan. How else will he be able to serve all of mankind? If Ram is to serve mankind as you have wished, and if the biggest threat to mankind's welfare is Ravan, then a confrontation between them is inevitable. Perhaps this request from your old friend, Vish, is actually an opportunity. It's an opportunity for Ram to experience firsthand how to defeat evil—not the greatest evil he will ever face, but the childish evil of bullies and young punks."

Das said, "I hear you, but I can't come around on this so quickly. Let me talk with Ram and then sleep on it. Please take my old friend to a five-star hotel here in Silicon Valley so he can rest up after his arduous journey."

To Vish he said, "Please forgive me and give me time to think about your request."

Vish replied, "Of course I forgive you, and do take your time so that you're sure about this."

So Das called his son to discuss the matter.

Ram had seen the citizens' tweets and was puzzled. He asked, "Father, who is this Ravan? And why haven't the cops or some other law enforcement folks chased him down and locked him up?"

"Well," Das replied, "it isn't that easy. First, no one actually knows where his island hideaway is. He has layer upon layer of firewalls, text encryptors, URL anonymizers, and metadata scrubbers so no one can trace him. Well, at least no one has so far—I think with serious effort he probably could be tracked down."

"Well then, why hasn't such serious effort been deployed?" Ram followed up.

"Here's the rub," Das replied. "Even if Ravan is caught, he'll get off scot-free. Therefore, no one really bothers to find him and put him out of business. Occasionally some of his henchmen do something dumb and get caught, but apart from that, Ravan can do what he wants and get away with it."

"Why? This is doesn't make sense. Why can Ravan get away with whatever he wants?" persisted Ram.

So Das told him, "It pains me to recall what was, shall I say, a particularly stupid time in our country's history. At that time, our country was supporting rebel militias in one of the oil-producing countries. If the rebel militias were successful, they promised that our country could buy some large oil fields outright. They promised that we could place our own oil wells on the land. The rebel militias were promising our government a land deal like the Louisiana Purchase or the purchase of Alaska. If we went ahead, the thinking then went, we could add to our sovereign territory. In this case we would be buying land containing oil fields somewhere in the Middle East. The government loved the idea. It would get us oil and would increase the size of our country. There was even talk back then of creating our fifty-first state on these newly acquired Middle Eastern oil fields."

"Okay, so what does that have to do with Ravan?" asked Ram.

"I'm getting there," replied Das. He continued, "Well, this militia that our government was backing needed to have arms smuggled in to them—bombs, rocket launchers, rifles, ammo, and so forth, right?"

"Okay so far," said Ram.

"So the problem was how to get these arms to the rebel militia without directly involving our country. It shouldn't look like we were taking sides in a foreign civil war. So Ravan offered to handle all the logistics and transport all the weapons for us. The government asked his price. Rather than money, Ravan asked for immunity from prosecution for any crimes he had already committed plus any he might commit in the future. He argued that he would have to break some eggs to deliver the arms to the rebel militia, that he couldn't simply airfreight the arms by UPS to the rebels because of customs inspections. He would have to smuggle the arms, and to do this he would have to hire some unsavory characters to do the legwork."

"I'm with you so far," said Ram.

So Das continued, "Well, amazingly, the government bought in to Ravan's pitch."

"But why did they agree to immunity for all past and future crimes?" asked Ram. "Wouldn't any crimes he committed solely in connection with his smuggling operation have been enough?"

Das answered, "Congress was then controlled by people whose only priority was to reduce government spending. Ravan was smart enough not to ask for any money, only blanket immunity from prosecution. He further argued that he couldn't estimate how long into the future he'd be called upon to resupply the rebel militias. He was, after all, being asked to smuggle for the government indefinitely as an open-ended commitment, so he felt it was fair to ask for an open-ended commitment of immunity in return. Unbelievably, the government went for it. And now look at the mess we're in. And to make matters worse, the rebels never succeeded in their rebellion and we never got the land that was promised."

"Or a fifty-first state in the Middle East," added Ram.

Das continued, "Right. Meanwhile, Ravan was given license to operate a crime syndicate with impunity. It's a disaster."

"So what's to be done?" asked Ram.

Das replied, "The only solution is for a private militia to take him out on their own. The immunity doesn't apply to private militias, only to official government-sponsored security forces. And that's where we come in—or, I should say, you come in. The citizens are tweeting their hope that you will lead a private army to conquer and eliminate Ravan and his crime syndicate."

"That's a big responsibility to lay on me!" exclaimed Ram.

Das replied, "Yes it is, but there we are."

Then Ram said to himself, in terms very mature for someone his age, "I suppose this outcome was to be expected. Good and evil originate with the populace, not the government. If government doesn't do its job, the populace must take over and replace the evil with good. But having private militias function as police can easily degenerate into vigilante rule, so we'll need to restore policing to the proper government authorities as soon as possible."

"So," continued Das, "I have a proposition for you. An old friend, leader of a sect of algorithm geeks in the Santa Barbara hills, has come to ask me for your assistance. His encampment is being terrorized by some of Ravan's henchmen. This friend, Vish, has been an expert in combat arts since college. He says that if you join him for ten days, you could learn techniques of combat and then employ them to dispense with a few of Ravan's henchmen. This, he says, would be a good warm up for going against more of Ravan's syndicate in the future. I said I could not bear the thought of your leaving and possibly returning injured or even dead, for surely I would then die myself from grief. But I also said I would leave the decision to you. So, what would you like to do?"

Without any hesitation, Ram said, "I'll do it for the reason Vish suggests, but even more, I wish to do a favor for you by doing a favor for your friend. I ask only to have my dear brother Lak accompany me."

Das agreed and then sighed. "Well, so be it, the matter is settled. I'll tell Vish, who will be overjoyed. How soon can you both be ready? You'll need to travel with him by bicycle. You'll be getting a bit of a workout."

"Tomorrow," replied Ram, and then added, "we must tell our mothers about this and obtain their blessings."

The next day, having obtained their mothers' blessings, Ram and Lak joined Vish by mounting their bicycles and riding away together on a beautiful sunny summer's day.

Ram Defeats Tata

The threesome headed south, sticking to bicycle paths. They peddled through the residential sections of San Jose and on into the Santa Clara Valley. They soon approached the small town of Coyote, just south of San Jose. Something looked amiss. Drunks and derelicts sprawled on public benches, and the local park was bare of vegetation, with shriveled brown stems where flowers had once flourished.

Vish said to Ram, "Does anything look wrong here?"

Ram replied, "Looks like pictures I've seen of war zones. What's happened?"

Vish explained, "This is the turf of a Chechen gangster named Tata who runs a drug and prostitution racket. She was once a beautiful woman. A run of bad luck at the gambling tables in Vegas turned her into a nasty, abusive, and dangerous woman. She has a son, Marich, who follows in her footsteps, having been abused himself. Tata beat her son. She left him chained up at home for days while she went crawling back to Vegas to continue gambling. Marich eventually broke free. He wound up joining Ravan's gang, which offered him protection from his mother's clutches. Meanwhile, Tata expanded her drug and prostitution business. She has connections in eastern Europe that supply her with a steady stream of kidnapped girls whom she entraps as prostitutes. She has connections with Mexican dealers that keep her customers supplied with crack, cocaine, and the latest boutique drugs."

Vish then glared at Ram and Lak and said, "I want to arrest her and take her out if necessary."

Ram glanced at Lak, received a confirming nod, and said, "Whatever you say, boss. We're here to help."

The three of them strode into the center of town. Vish pulled an emergency flare from his pack and tossed it into the middle of the main street. The flare hissed and let out a cloud of smoke. Everyone in town dropped what they were doing and went to the nearest window.

Vish shouted out, "Tata, we've come to arrest you."

Tata, wearing blue jeans, a denim jacket, and a black T-shirt emblazoned with a curious insignia resembling cave art, emerged from her office. She walked to the street curb and shouted back angrily, "Who dares to challenge me in my town? Go to hell."

Then she pulled a gun and fired a few shots in the general direction of Vish and the brothers.

Vish and the brothers ducked and scattered. The bullets whizzing past Lak, making him furious.

Lak said, "If I get my hands on her I'll tear the arms from her body and stomp her to death."

Ram interjected, saying, "Cool it. Killing a woman is wrong, and mutilating her before doing so is wrong twice over."

Vish then declared, "Our social norm has it that a woman should always be protected. But taking out this woman is necessary for the social good. To protect the exploited, we must sometimes perform a seemingly wrongful act. This is the your divine duty as a CEO, Ram. You should not hesitate."

Ram replied, "My father told me to follow your teachings. But you argue that the ends justify the means. Doesn't each generation need to learn anew that fighting evil with evil serves only to make one evil himself?"

Vish rejoined, "What, then, would you recommend?"

Ram answered, "I'll call my father and summon our helicopter to take her to Moffett field. Then our plane can fly her back to Chechnya and dump her off there."

So Ram called his father with FaceTime from his iPhone, and asked, "Dad, we have an emergency. Can you send our helicopter to collect a gangster we're about to capture and then deliver her back to her homeland? She's from Chechnya."

Das replied, "This is sudden. Can you put Vish on the line?"

Ram handed the phone to Vish. Das asked him, "Is this okay?"

Vish replied, "Yes, the gangster is Tata from down here in Coyote. I wanted to take her out, but your son prefers this route instead. Can you arrange this?"

Das replied, "Yeah, our helicopter will be there in thirty minutes."

"Thanks," said Vasis.

He handed the phone back to Ram who added, "Thanks from me too."

Vish then said, "We have only thirty minutes to capture Tata before the helicopter arrives. Circle around her, and I'll mount a frontal attack."

With lemur-like stealth, Ram went to the right, and Lak to the left. The brothers approached Tata from the rear as Vish stood facing Tata, shouting out insults. Both brothers sprang like cougars and took Tata down. They removed her denim jacket, ripped off its long sleeves and pockets, used the sleeves to bind her hands and feet, and stuffed the pocket material in her mouth to keep her quiet.

In a few minutes the helicopter arrived, collected Tata, and began a journey that would deliver her back to Chechnya.

The mayor, sheriff, and school principal then emerged to thank Vish and the brothers for saving their town. They could now restore the buildings fronting the main street to their former appearance, which resembled the quaint set of an old Western movie.

Before getting back on their bicycles, Ram pulled Lak aside and asked him, "Would you really have pulled off Tata's arms and stomped her to death if I hadn't intervened?"

"Yes," said Lak, "I would have, but your solution was best, and I'm glad you stepped in."

"Why would you have mutilated and killed her? Because she was a criminal or because she was a child abuser?" asked Ram.

"Because she was an abuser," answered Lak.

Ram did not reply because he doubted that even being a child abuser warranted mutilation and torture as a prelude to death, however well deserved that death might be.

Ram Beats Marich

Vasis and the brothers mounted their bicycles and continued cycling through the farms of Santa Clara Valley to Morgan Hill, Gilroy, and Hollister, by the truck farms of Salinas Valley, past the prison at Soledad, the fields of Greenfield and King City, then past ranches, pastures, and oil wells to the hills of Paso Robles, past San Luis Obispo, until reaching the ocean a few miles north of Pismo Beach. Then they continued back inland through farmland by Santa Maria and Solvang until they reached the ocean again at Gaviota, where they cycled east along the blue ocean's shore through Goleta and Santa Barbara, until finally reaching Montecito.

The last pull was up from the ocean to the site where Vish's sect lived in the oak woodlands at an elevation of 1,250 feet. Ram and Lak had enjoyed their four-day workout along Vish's winding bicycle route and the chance to see countryside invisible from a speeding car. Knowing that Vish was the same age as their father, the brothers were especially impressed with his stamina.

Upon arriving at Vish's encampment, the algorithm geeks greeted Vish and the brothers with cheers. They were desperate to be saved from further harassment and viewed the brothers as their saviors.

The geeks showed the brothers to a cabin where they were to sleep. Ram opened the window during the night to let the crisp air blow through the room. The pungent fragrance of the trees, the call of the crickets, and, when they awoke, the songs of the birds, reminded him of living at his mother's palace in the coastal redwoods.

After breakfast, the brothers were anxious to start their training. Vish began his instruction by teaching the brothers techniques of personal defense and offense, how to use an opponent's strength against him, how to sidestep, to misdirect, and to chop at lethal points on the body. He taught them how to work as a team, to fight with each covering the other's back.

Vish showed the brothers his arsenal of military hardware stock-piled in a barn left over from his martial arts days. Using his supply of weapons, Vish taught the brothers how to handle a carbine, pistol, sniper rifle, machine gun, rocket-propelled grenade launcher, shoulder-launched surface to air antiaircraft missile launcher, a fire-and-forget light antitank weapon, as well as how to wear level five zircon oxide ceramic plate body armor.

Vish taught the brothers how to move flat against the ground, how to creep up and surround an opponent. He also taught them how to throw a knife from different distances, find a target with digital thermal-imaging scopes, and other techniques of personal combat.

Vish was impressed at how quickly the brothers learned—a month's worth of training in a day—yet he suspected such speed was no less than necessary, as the hoodlums were likely to arrive tomorrow. He told them both to carry a knife at all times while they remained in the compound, anticipating the imminent arrival of Ravan's gang.

Meanwhile, Ravan's henchman had gathered in the evening at a local bar in Santa Barbara. The two leaders, Marich and Subah, chuckled that they hadn't been up to visit the geeks recently. Marich was a muscular man of medium build; he had black hair, was clean-shaven, and wore a black leather jacket with black jeans and gold ear studs. Subah was a tall, heavy weight lifter with a black beard and shaved head who wore a black sleeveless T-shirt. Marich, Subah, and the rest of the gang sported clothes or tattoos with the same cave-art insignia that Ram, Lak, and Vish had seen on Tata's jacket back in Coyote.

Marich asked his gang if they felt it was about time to pay the geeks another visit and have some fun. "Sure, great idea" was everyone's response.

So the next morning, eight members of Ravan's band piled into two big four-wheelers with Marich and Subah driving. They motored on up to the geeks' compound, driving over the lawn and flower garden with their music blaring. The gang piled out of their vehicles whooping and shouting.

Ram and Lak had just finished breakfast when they heard the noise, and they went out to see what was going on. As soon as Marich and Subah saw the brothers, Marich shouted, "Oh, great, two new wimps have just joined the pointy-headed geeks. Extra fun today."

Lak then walked directly up to the huge Subah and delivered a sudden uppercut to the jaw. Subah's head snapped backward. He fell to the ground.

Marich was stunned. This was the first time one of the geeks had ever fought back. Marich bent down over Subah and said, "Get up."

Subah twitched but didn't speak or try to stand. A moment later he stopped moving altogether. Marich bent down even closer to Subah's face and felt for a pulse. The color drained from Marich's face as he shouted, "He's dead!" He growled to the brothers, "This changes everything. I'll kill you for this!"

Then to his gang Marich said, "Fall back behind the four-wheelers. Get the guns. We're gonna kill us a few geeks. We're gonna avenge Subah's death."

Ram and Lak immediately split up. With cheetah-like speed they ran to the woods. With their lemur-like stealth they circled around the members of Ravan's band, who had gathered behind their four-wheelers to load their guns.

Ram and Lak each pointed to one of the band. In unison, they threw their knives and killed two of the gang. The rest of the gang stood frozen in surprise. They couldn't adjust quickly enough to how serious the encounter had become. This trip to the geeks was supposed to be easy pickings, the way it had been in the past.

The brothers charged the remaining members of the gang, knocking the guns out of their hands. Ram put Marich in a headlock and said, "Get outta here, now. If I hear any of you has bothered my friends again, I'll personally hunt you down. And just so you know, I'm Ram. Got it?"

Marich nodded and waved the rest of the gang into the two vehicles. They sped off down the hill. Marich promised the surviving members of his gang that Ravan himself would get a full report on this outrage. Still, Marich absorbed the importance of what he had just experienced. He resolved to avoid further conflict with Ram if possible.

With standard-issue trenching tools, Ram and Lak dug a burrow into the ground. They unceremoniously threw the three dead bodies in it, covered the burrow up, and left the ground as an unmarked grave in the woods.

Ram knew they had just murdered three persons—evil persons, but persons nonetheless, and possibly not beyond salvation. Ram's pride of triumph over evil was tempered by realizing he hadn't managed the encounter well. He hadn't provided Ravan's gang with a different path, one leading to reform and redemption rather than condemnation and death.

The geeks were shocked at the violence they had just witnessed but were grateful nonetheless. In their wonderment they asked Vish if he thought this conflict could have been avoided somehow.

Vish replied, "No, this violence was inevitable. Ravan is above the law, and his henchmen think they are too. This clash is not the end, although for us personally, we're safe at last."

To the brothers, Vish added, "Nice work, but don't rest on your laurels. When you deal with Ravan himself, you'll be in another league. Anyway, we're eternally grateful. In return, we look forward to your calling on us for help sometime in the future."

Ram replied, "Sir, we're grateful for all you've taught us about combat techniques and for giving us the chance to see firsthand the sort of people Ravan employs. We're beginning to get a sense of our life's mission."

The next day, Vish and the brothers began their four-day return journey to Das's palace.

Ram and Sita

When the brothers arrived back home, Das was overjoyed to see that his sons had returned in good health. He thanked Vish for his successful supervision of their safety.

Meanwhile, Das had continued to ponder the question of marriage for Ram. He shared his concerns with Vish.

Vish suggested visiting Janak, the CEO of IBM/Microsoft, who lived near Seattle and had a daughter of legendary beauty and grace.

Although Apple and Microsoft had been competitors in the ancient past, the two industrial kingdoms had made peace many years ago. Apple served consumers. IBM and Microsoft had merged to serve industry and the government. By occupying different niches in the same industrial guild, these commercial kingdoms now avoided competition. They frequently were allies when lobbying Congress for tax breaks and waivers to immigration restrictions.

Moreover, Das liked Janak personally. He thought it would be wonderful if Ram and his brother were to visit his old friend near Seattle and strengthen the warm personal ties between their families.

Vish offered to guide the boys during the two-week bicycle journey north to 1 Microsoft Way, Redmond, Washington. Das agreed and asked him to consult with Vasis before leaving to see if any private messages needed to be conveyed to his old friend.

After visiting with their mothers and assuring them that all was well, the brothers headed out.

With Vish they peddled out of the Bay Area to Sacramento in the Central Valley and north through Red Bluff and Redding. They camped near the towering, snowcapped Mount Shasta.

Around the campfire, Vish told the brothers the geologic history of the landscape they now inhabited. He told them that the continents of the earth were perched atop giant plates that floated on a bed of hot molten rock called magma in the center of the earth.

Vish explained that three of these plates collide on the ocean floor near Cape Mendocino to the west, creating a triple junction where earthquakes occur almost daily. He explained that lava leaks between the cracks that separate the giant plates. The lava then bubbles up to make the volcanoes and hot springs they could see around them to the east.

The trio pressed on through Oregon and came to rest at the shore of the great Columbia River. After crossing the river into Washington, they continued north to Redmond, the home of IBM/Microsoft. Every night on their journey, Vish explained the history of the landscape where they camped. The brothers marveled at his knowledge.

Vish and the brothers visited Janak's palace on Microsoft's sprawling campus. After their presence was announced, Janak went to the lobby to personally welcome them as emissaries from an allied corporate giant.

Vish introduced the brothers to Janak, who was dressed in casual slacks and a dress shirt with an open collar. Janak was overjoyed to meet the sons of his friend Das.

Vish explained that Das had heard of Janak's beautiful daughter and wished his permission for Ram to be introduced to her.

Janak grinned and said, "Not so fast. Anyone who wishes to court my daughter must first pass a test of strength before I will introduce my daughter to him."

Addressing Ram, he said, "Do you want to take the test? Many suitors have come before you only to be turned away by the test's difficulty."

Ram replied, "Yes, sir, I do wish to take the test. But first, may I ask why you're asking for a test of strength rather than a test of intelligence and competence? I don't wish to offend you, but a test of strength sounds like nothing but a useless, macho symbol of manhood. Surely your daughter deserves to be courted by someone whose capabilities exceed those of mere weight lifting. Why don't you test me instead on some advanced knowledge—like, say, the proof of Gödel's incompleteness theorems and their importance in computer science?"

Janak chuckled. "You do have spirit, I must say. My reason for the test is that I have around me many people who are mathematics geeks and many who are weight-lifting geeks, but finding someone who is both is rare. Yet that is whom I seek. I take it as given, knowing your father, that you understand Gödel's theorems. What I don't know is your strength. Yes, the test is symbolic, but whether the skill set needed to pass the test is useless remains to be seen."

Ram said, "Okay, then, what is the test?"

Janak replied, "It is to string a special recurved bow with a 200-pound draw. The draw strength of a recurved bow is rarely over fifty pounds, and the maximum draw of a bow any human has used before is 150 pounds. And after you string the bow, you have to use it accurately. Do you think you can do all that?"

Ram replied, "Yes, of course. I will ask Vish to teach me archery tomorrow. I will return for the test the day after tomorrow."

"Fine," said Janak, "I await your return."

As Janak sized up Ram and his brother, he fervently hoped one would be able to string the bow that had defeated all the previous suitors.

Meanwhile, Janak's daughter, who lived with her parents in the palace, surreptitiously peered at Ram from behind a one-way mirror in Janak's office. She couldn't help notice his size and poise. She saw the hairs on his chest. She took a deep breath. She hadn't been attracted to any of her previous suitors. Sita immediately sensed that Ram was different. She wanted him.

Janak and his wife maintained a tradition of philanthropy extending back to their kingdom's ancestral founder, Bill Gates, and his wife, Melinda. When inspecting hospitals in the Upper Nile many years ago, Janak and his wife met an orphan child whom they eventually adopted and named Sita. While touring the countryside, they saw her from a distance gracefully walking, almost gliding, along the dirt furrows of a newly planted field.

Sita was a dark-skinned young Nubian woman with brown eyes, a long, slender neck, and statuesque bearing, like Queen Nefertiti of old. Today she was wearing a broad red-leather choker necklace with golden cowry shell accents, matching dangling earrings, and a red turban hat.

Sita was stunningly beautiful, and regularly received offers to model. She turned these offers down and stayed true to her studies as a biology major.

Ram and his brother retired to guest quarters in Janak's palace.

Vish set about acquiring a recurved bow for practice and found one with a 110-pound draw at a shop in Seattle. He also obtained some armor-piercing carbon arrows, as well as a practice target.

The next day they set up at an empty field on the Microsoft campus and Vish taught the brothers archery. And as with other types of weaponry, the brothers were immediately proficient, learning in only one day what would ordinarily take months.

So, after a good night's sleep, the brothers awoke. Ram was anxious to take the notorious test of strength. They both dressed themselves in loose garments. Then Vish and the brothers went to see Janak.

Janak led them to the special high-security chamber where the bow was stored under lock and key in a decorated mahogany chest. Janak opened the chest to reveal a seventy-two-inch bow with laminated limbs, a carbon riser, and a twisted string possessing high tensile strength. Arrows were also in the chest.

Then Vish, the brothers, and Janak joined up with the palace geeks, and all went out together onto the field where a target had been set up at 200 yards away. Sita too went to the field to observe quietly in the background. She brought with her a colorful handbag into which she had placed a wedding lei that a Hawaiian friend from college offered her as a token of good luck. Sita hoped to have the occasion to use it.

Ram took off his shirt, and Janak handed him the bow. Without hesitation and with gorilla-like strength, Ram quickly strung the bow to the 200-pound draw. Janak gasped. Sita saw Ram's muscles ripple and the natural epaulettes on his shoulders quiver.

Then Ram placed an arrow in the bow, pulled the arrow back, and released. Everyone watched the arrow speed to the target, hit the bull's eye, and burrow deep into the target's backing.

Ram then asked if there was a tennis ball around. A palace geek procured one. Ram asked Janak to toss it into the air. With another arrow, Ram shot the tennis ball, hitting it at the top of its trajectory. The arrow passed completely through the ball and fell harmlessly in the distance.

"Done! Congratulations!" exclaimed Janak. "As I promised, I will now introduce you to my daughter."

He called Sita forward and said to Ram, "I present to you my daughter, Sita, whom I love with all my heart. The rest is up to you and her."

Ram was stunned speechless at the sight of Sita's beauty. He approached her and said, "My name is Ram. I am from Apple. May I spend the afternoon with you? May we walk together and talk?

Sita dropped her eyes bashfully, took a deep breath, and said, "I'd like that. The Cougar Mountain Park is a short drive from here. We can talk in private there."

Ram and Sita climbed into her car, a four-wheel drive Subaru sedan. Ram remarked, "This car looks pretty rugged."

Sita replied, "We need it for the snow." Then, smiling, she added, "You're not in Silicon Valley anymore."

Ram grinned.

Sita drove into the park's parking lot near a trailhead. They exited the car and started to stroll along a paved trail.

Ram said, "I don't know how to begin. When I saw you, I felt I was gazing at the most beautiful woman the world has ever seen."

Sita replied, "I was taken by you as well. I saw how you passed my father's test, a test I had thought would be impossible for any human to pass. I have little experience with dating. A school prom, little more. My father has guarded me like a hawk."

Ram replied, "I too have little experience dating. My father's health is failing. He's been grooming me and my brothers to take his place at Apple when he's gone. That's left little time for socializing."

They strolled a bit more down the path in silence. After a while Sita said, "I would like to have children."

Ram took a deep breath and said, "I would too."

They strolled some more.

Ram couldn't stand it anymore. He turned to face Sita and pulled her close to him, his body against her body. He could feel her breathing. He looked into her face. She looked up at his and did not pull away. Ram then kissed Sita on the lips.

Ram and Sita held their embrace. Eventually each felt the other relax.

Then Ram fell to one knee, and said simply, "Will you be my wife?"

Their eyes met, both knowing they were bonded in love.

Sita reached into the colorful bag she was carrying, pulled out the large-leafed Hawaiian wedding lei, placed it around Ram's neck, and said, "I accept you as my husband."

Ram and Sita walked back to the parking lot. They drove back to Microsoft/IBM and sought out Janak to tell him the good news.

Janak's first inclination was to send word immediately to Das and to begin planning a wedding. But he then reflected on Ram's success.

He asked Vish, "Can you tell me a bit more about Ram? He has passed my strength test, he has proposed to my daughter, and she has accepted. Still, I am troubled. Is Ram actually human? No human could pass the test because I selfishly set up the test so that Sita would remain by my side indefinitely. I did not want her to depart to some distant place with a husband."

Vish replied, "Ram's genome was engineered by Vasis together with Das. Ram was raised initially by his mother and later by his father with input from Vasis."

Janak persisted, "How, then, was Ram's genome engineered?"

Vish replied, "Well, what you probably want to know is whether there are any nonhuman genes in Ram's genome. Vasis disclosed the details to me. Confidentially, I can tell you the answer is yes—one tenth of Ram's genome was drawn as a sample from nonhuman primates."

Then Janak said, "Can you set my mind at rest that my daughter is not being married off to a transgenic halfbreed between man and monkey?"

Vish replied, "Yes, I can set your mind at rest. Don't let prejudice cloud your judgment. See the magnificent capabilities that Ram possesses because of his engineered genome—capabilities not limited to strength but that permeate all his senses and intelligence. Furthermore, you must be true to your word. You set the strength test, so now you are bound to live by the test's results."

"Yes," sighed Janak, "I'm indeed bound by the test's results. I'm sure I'll come to accept Ram as a son-in-law worthy of my daughter, but this news will take some time for me to get used to."

Vish then added, "And remember, according to the 2030 UN Human/ Animal distinction, Ram is human and entitled to all human rights without exception, including the pursuit of happiness, which in this case is clearly his desire to marry Sita. But to set your mind at ease, why not ask Sita how she feels about Ram's genome?"

So Janak called Sita aside and whispered to her, "I've just learned from Vish that Ram is not 100-percent human—that 10 percent of his genome comes from primates like monkeys, gorillas, lemurs, and so forth. Do you still want to marry him, knowing this? It's not too late to back out."

Sita replied, "Oh, I could tell right away there is more to him than any ordinary man. What do I care that his father had to reach out to the rest of the animal kingdom to acquire the genes needed for his son to turn out so spectacularly? The genes themselves don't come with little flags of origin on them. They're just chemicals to be judged by their effects, not by the history of their synthesis. I love him because of who he is and want to marry him."

Hearing this, Janak then said, "Your marriage to Ram has my blessing."

Janak sent some messenger geeks in his private jet to tell Das the news in person. The news was too important and too personal to entrust to electronic communication.

When the messengers arrived at his palace, Das knew immediately that something was up. From the look in the messengers' eyes he guessed the news was good. After being told of Ram's success in passing the strength test and that Janak's daughter had accepted Ram's proposal of marriage, Das asked for more information about his soon-to-be daughter-in-law.

The messengers told Das that Janak's daughter's name was Sita. They told him that Sita was a beautiful, statuesque Nubian princess whom Janak and his wife had adopted while touring farmland in the Upper Nile many years ago. Das did not know what to make of this and resolved to consult with Vasis.

Das then assembled his other sons, his wives, and his palace geeks, including Vasis, and they boarded their private jet to fly to Seattle. When they arrived at Janak's palace, he welcomed his old friend and ally. He gratefully accepted gifts of Ghirardelli chocolates and Napa Valley wines that Das had brought with him from San Francisco.

Then Janak proudly presented his daughter to Das, who exclaimed, "My dear, it's a pleasure to meet you. I can see the beauty and charm that has captivated so may suitors. My son Ram is lucky indeed if you are to be his wife."

Sita replied, "It's my pleasure as well to meet you. I thank you for your compliment, but it is I who am the lucky one if Ram is to be my husband."

After these introductions, Das and his entourage retired to the guest quarters in Janak's palace to freshen up before dinner.

When Das had reached the guest quarters, he pulled Vasis aside to express his misgivings about Sita.

Vasis asked, "What exactly troubles you about this match?"

Das said, "It's just that I wasn't expecting matters to turn out as they have. Sita is Janak's adopted daughter. She's not from Janak's actual lineage."

"And why is that a problem?" asked Vasis.

"I don't know if Janak's commitment to an adopted daughter will be as unshakable as it would be to a daughter born of his own flesh and blood," replied Das.

"But it's clear, in fact, that Janak does value his daughter every bit as much as any father possibly can. His devotion to his daughter equals or exceeds that of fathers to their natural-born daughters."

"Yes, I can see that," said Das, "but still, I have reservations. Furthermore, I am concerned that Sita does not originate from a culture with expertise in the technologies of today's world. Although the Nubians had a well-developed ancient culture, that was two thousand years ago. I'm not sure she'll prosper in our contemporary culture. Moreover, the part of the world she originates from is religiously hostile to modernity."

"But she has prospered in the environment that Janak provides, which is certainly a contemporary technological culture. She has enthusiastically assimilated Western modernity. Not only that, she has committed herself to the study of science, at which she excelled," replied Vasis.

"Yes, I see that too," said Das, "but still, I remain somewhat unsettled about the marriage."

"Then," said Vasis, "I suggest you allow your son himself to resolve the matter. If he's convinced, then the die is cast, for better or worse. In the final analysis, the marriage is his choice alone to make."

"Okay, said Das, "I will speak directly with Ram about this." Das then called for Ram.

When Ram arrived at the quarters where Das was staying, Das took him aside and said, "I have learned that Sita is Janak's adopted daughter and she's of Nubian descent. I'm worried she may not be comfortable in our world. She may even be hostile to our values and to the role of technology, free-market economics, and secular democracy in our lives. If she were hostile to the life we lead, there would be domestic conflict and an unhappy marriage. Think about this. It's not too late to back out of this marriage."

Ram unhesitatingly replied, "I have seen her here in Janak's palace that is itself a testament to Western modernity. I have seen how much she's loved here. If she were unhappy with our values and the way we live, she would have left Janak's circle long ago and the love between her, her father, and her extended family would not have developed. Moreover, she is already an accomplished young biologist. I see no cause for alarm. The bottom line is that I love her and my decision comes down to faith and trust. I believe and trust that Sita will make the best wife I could possibly wish for."

"Okay, then," said Das somewhat skeptically, "the marriage has my blessings."

Dinner was a modest banquet, with meat, vegetables, fruits, and wines from California, Oregon, and Washington. The two CEOs of ancient computer kingdoms, Das and Janak, sat together as old friends along with Vasis, Vish, and the rest of the company.

After the meal, as coffee was being served, Vish leaned over to the CEOs and said, "I believe there can't be too much of a good thing. May I suggest some more marriages might be in order."

Das replied, "I didn't know you were such an ardent matchmaker. What do you have in mind?"

Vish replied, "Hasn't Janak mentioned he has another eligible daughter?"

Janak jumped in. "Indeed, I do, but I was hoping to keep her secret so that I wouldn't be facing an empty nest if she marries and leaves with her husband. But now that Vish has let on about her, I must say that my other daughter, Urmila, is indeed eligible and a great treasure to me. Perhaps your son, Lak, the one who is a faithful companion to Ram, would consider proposing to her."

"Perhaps he would," said Das, "and what about my other sons, while we're on the subject? They too need wives."

"May I suggest the two daughters of Janak's brother, Kush," said Vasis.

Janak added, "That is an interesting idea. My brother lives in Bangalore and heads an industrial kingdom supplying software support and specialized manufacturing. If your sons marry my two daughters and my brother's two daughters, their bonds will weld our families together for a long time to come."

Das said, "I agree this does sound promising. Now it's up to our sons and daughters to find these arrangements appealing from their points of view."

So, Janak Skyped his brother to present the idea.

Kush agreed the idea was interesting and approved of his daughters traveling to Seattle to meet Das's sons. He said, "And I'll follow in my own jet with my wife and family if it looks like a wedding is about to happen."

"Great," replied Janak.

When Lak met Urmila the mutual attraction was immediate. And although seemingly too good to be true, when Barat met Kush's daughter, Manda, and when Shat met Kush's other daughter, Suta, the mutual attractions were also immediate.

The next day, after some private time together, marriage proposals were made all around and immediately accepted. Meanwhile Kush gathered together his wife and family and flew in their jet to Seattle to join the wedding festivities.

Janak and the four couples consulted with their etiquette and entertainment geeks about the ceremony. They settled on a private and secluded cove on Puget Sound as the setting for the weddings and for a ceremony that was part traditional and part unique. For clothes, the brides and bridesmaids wore white gowns and the men dressed in black suits with ties. The wedding service drew on a liturgy from the New Zealand Anglican prayer book with a female Roman Catholic priest presiding, accompanied by a neoclassical string quartet with a newly composed wedding march. Meanwhile, each bride and groom contributed their own individual wedding vows.

On the morning of the marriage, the fog lifted as the weather turned crisp and sunny with dew glistening on the leaves. The air was fresh and filled with the fragrance of pine and wildflowers. The four couples said their vows and exchanged wedding rings of gold with inlaid platinum that gave the appearance of a flowing mixture of metal alloys.

After the ceremony, the reception featured one of Bruce Springsteen's grandchildren, who sang, among other songs, his grandfather's cut, "Part Man, Part Monkey." The catered food included Californian, Pacific Northwestern, Indian, and Ethiopian cuisines with French wines, Scotch whiskeys, and Caribbean rum, along with nonalcoholic punches. The guests included emissaries from the former Google, Amazon, Intel, Adobe, Facebook, Netflix, and Pandora kingdoms as well as a few DC politicians of both parties who promised to talk to one another collegially on this special occasion.

When the reception was over in the wee hours of the morning, the guests overnighted and returned home the next day to their kingdoms scattered around the world.

Barat and Shat with their new wives joined Kush and the rest of his family in his jet and returned to Bangalore. For their parts, Ram and Lak with their wives returned with Das, Vasis, and the other palace geeks in Das's jet to Silicon Valley. Ram brought his bicycle and bow along with him as baggage in the jet. Meanwhile, Vish set forth on his bicycle on a path to a bungalow in the High Sierra, where he planned to think for some months on a particularly difficult algorithm problem he was determined to solve.

Throughout the entire festivities, Janak's PR geeks blogged about the wedding ceremony and the reception, as well as the arrival and departure of guests. The citizens responded with euphoric tweets. All was well in the world—the market bulled forward and retirees and widows received bonuses.

Kaila's Deceit

Life at Das's palace in Silicon Valley returned to normal. The brothers and their wives went camping in the Sierra for a honeymoon together and afterward set about developing how to live their daily lives as married couples.

After the marriages, Das's health improved somewhat, and he was able to spend some months occupied with strategic decisions at Apple. Then the months stretched on, adding up to ten full years. During this time, Das worried about all manner of issues, from devising new product concepts and categories to marketing and dreaming up commercials that subtly mock the users of rival products—from managing stockholder motions for upcoming conventions to consulting the board of directors about financial prospects, raising lawsuits against competitors, defending against lawsuits Apple's competitors had brought against it, lobbying DC politicians (and appearing before useless panels), and deciding whether to support social causes (the latest being to extend voting rights to people with more than 10 percent animal genomes)—from ensuring that new product announcements were not leaked prematurely to maintaining an engaged and healthy work force and so forth. In all these activities, Das brought Ram and his brothers along, tutoring them over the years in the tasks expected of contemporary entrepreneurial captains of industry. And all this while he continued grooming Ram as his eventual successor.

The various geeks and ordinary citizens of Apple were impressed, especially with Ram, with his even temperament, quick grasp of technical detail, appreciation for innovation, enthusiasm for new ideas, and eye for strategic planning. The citizenry often tweeted their admiration for Ram. MarketWatch regularly featured columns identifying him as the heir apparent to rule the Apple kingdom.

During the ten years Das lingered on, Sita and Ram discussed having children. Despite the luxury at their disposal in the Apple palace, Sita felt the time wasn't right. Ram had not yet been appointed as Apple's CEO. Moreover, each passing day brought a subtle loss of Das's facilities. Sita felt that it was premature to place an egg-releasing capsule in her hormone chamber. Sita and Ram decided to postpone having children until their situation stabilized.

Das was no fool. He knew his health was slowly failing. He was losing weight, getting short of breath, and sleeping fitfully—he sometimes awakened to nightmares portending death. His regular bodily functions were often strained and painful and his skin was becoming jaundiced.

Das wanted to pull back from his responsibilities. He wanted Ram to succeed him as CEO of Apple while he lived his remaining years in an advisory position as chair of the board of directors. So he convened the board and placed before them the proposition that Ram become CEO. The board was enthusiastic. Das asked Vasis to plan a formal installation ceremony.

Das called Ram to his office and explained the situation. He said, "You've now reached the age of twenty-seven. Your health is vigorous, but my health is failing, and I'm tired. I'd like you now to assume the CEO position as my successor. I know this is a large responsibility, but you are ready, and I hope very much you will answer this call. I've spoken with Vasis, the other geek leaders, and the board of directors. They have assured me of their enthusiasm, both for you personally and the opportunity to prevent a hiatus in the kingdom's management. Will you do it?"

"Yes," replied Ram without hesitation. "I feel it's my duty to serve, and if your judgment is that by accepting the CEO position at this time I will be serving our citizens, then I will do so. My one reservation is that I don't feel my education is complete enough. Although I've watched and learned from you, I'm not confident that I have enough breadth and depth of knowledge to lead our kingdom as it develops in ways we can't predict. My present reservoir of knowledge seems too shallow."

"I appreciate your feelings. But we can't choose the time of our calling. We must respond whenever it comes, however untimely," replied Das, who added, "Meanwhile, you can continue to call upon the advice of Vasis and the other denominations of geeks. I'm sure that with advice from them all, you'll be fine."

"Okay," concluded Ram, "I'll do my best."

So Ram then retired to join Sita in their quarters in the palace, and together they pondered their future.

Because his health was failing so quickly, Das invited only the CEOs of the nearby kingdoms in Seattle and Silicon Valley—IBM/Microsoft, Amazon, Intel, and Adobe. In the haste to move ahead, the CEOs of distant kingdoms, and particularly Kush (with whom the brothers, Barat and Shat, were staying), were not notified of Ram's impending installation.

Now, Barat's mother, Kaila, had a chief assistant named Mantha. She was a powerful presence in the Apple palace owing to Kaila being Das's favorite wife and the only wife who lived and regularly slept with him in the palace.

Mantha demanded and received lots of perks: a reserved parking space, a reserved spot in the dining hall, and another reserved spot outside in the palace grounds where she could be by herself, as well as a handsome salary with a travel allowance, entertainment allowance, company car, and a medical insurance policy that covered all manner of elective cosmetic procedures. Still, Mantha was not a happy person—she rarely smiled or laughed, and she had a calculating and manipulative personality.

Mantha was, however, devoted to Kaila. Kaila in turn trusted her completely. Mantha had been attending Kaila since she had been a little girl. Mantha had shielded Kaila from many suitors, and as a result, Kaila was eligible to marry when she caught Das's eye, which eventually lead to Kaila becoming Das's third and youngest wife.

Mantha recoiled at the news of Ram's pending installation as Apple's CEO and grew angry. She reasoned that she would lose the perks and status she enjoyed if Das were to die and install Ram as his successor because Kaila would then become a has-been. Instead, Ram's mother, Kausha, would inherit the status Kaila now enjoyed, as would Sita, Ram's only wife.

When Mantha heard that Ram was about to be installed as the new CEO of Apple, she panicked. She rushed to Kaila, who was in the exercise room doing calisthenics, and cried, "Have you heard the horrible news?"

"No, what is it, Mantha?" replied Kaila.

"Ram is about to be the new CEO of Apple. If that happens, you're doomed!" she wailed.

"What do you mean? It's great if Ram becomes the new CEO. He's always been as loving to me and Sumitra as to his own mother. He's been a perfect son to all of us wives. It's good for us if he's the new CEO. In fact, I think we'll prosper with Ram as CEO and the value of our stock portfolios will rise," replied Kaila.

Mantha retorted, "You're still so young and naive. Don't you see what Das is up to? He's going to cut you and your son out of the family entitlements. He's sent Barat and Shat with their wives away to Kush's palace in India. Now that they're gone, Das is springing Ram's installment before Barat and Shat can hear about it."

"Well," replied Kaila, "that theory seems far-fetched to me. Das has shown no lack of vigor in bed with me, nor any sign of pulling back on his affections. I think we're as much in love as ever. I don't think there's anything to worry about. I'd be able to detect any duplicity or double cross on his part."

After Kaila showered and dried off, Mantha persisted. She followed Kaila back to her quarters in the Apple palace. She pleaded with Kaila to open her eyes and see the possibilities. She urged her not to be so trusting.

Gradually, Mantha bent Kaila to her point of view. Eventually, Kaila asked her, "What would you have me do?"

Mantha replied, "I know that as a condition for lying with your husband on your wedding night you asked him for two favors. I know he agreed to grant you the two favors whenever you chose to ask. So now, demand that Das honor his word and grant you the two favors he once promised."

"What favors would you have me request?" asked Kaila.

Mantha answered, "Favor number one is to call off the installation of Ram as CEO and install your son Barat as CEO. Favor number two is to demand that Ram be banished from Apple for fourteen years, after which time he may return to the Apple palace or wherever he wishes to live."

Mantha reasoned that if Ram were anywhere nearby, Barat would not be able to govern independently, but would always be looking over his shoulder for Ram or Ram's people. If Ram remained nearby, he and Barat would form rival power centers.

Kaila replied, "I feel your course of action will do more harm than good. The citizens of Apple will blame us for preventing the person they most want from becoming the CEO. They will see us as promoting our favorite to benefit ourselves at their expense."

"Yes, they may think that for a while, but you have no choice if you wish to survive. After Barat has ruled for a while, people will become happy again and will forget about Ram if he is far away," argued Mantha.

Kaila sighed, "Okay, then, I'll do it because you've guided and protected me since I was a child. I've always trusted you and your judgment. I'll persevere and get Das to grant me these two favors to fulfill his promise even though I know it'll break his heart."

That evening when Das came to Kaila's quarters to lie with her, he found her sprawled out on the leopardskin rug in her quarters. She had been crying and her face was blotched and tearstained. He placed her head on his lap, stoked her hair, and covered her face with kisses as his passion grew.

He asked what the matter was. "You were so full of joy and verve yesterday. What has happened, how can I help?"

Kaila rolled over and moaned, "Oh, I feel I have no future. I know you're not well, but what am I to do after you have passed on? I will be left a pauper on the street. I'm close to panic," she wailed.

"Of course you won't be left homeless on the street. I have endowed a trust in your name to provide for you for the rest of your life," Das said soothingly.

"I know you've been generous, but once you're gone, sharp-eyed lawyer geeks are going to test every provision you've made and try to take it away. I won't have any lawyer geeks of my own to prevent my trust from being plundered," Kaila persisted.

"Oh, my dear, what would you have me do to reassure you?" asked Das alarmed.

Kaila replied, "Do you remember that on the night before we lay together for the first time you promised me two favors that I could ask at any time in the future?"

"Yes," said Das.

"And if I asked two favors of you now, would you grant them as you promised?" she continued.

"Yes," said Das, growing a little uneasy.

"And would you vMail to Vasis and the other chief geeks to reaffirm that you had given your word to grant me two promises when you took me?"

"They already know that I made you two promises, but if it will make you happy, I will surely confirm the promises in a vMail to my palace geeks," said Das, wondering where this was going.

"Then here's my iPhone, please dictate a vMail to them now," said Kaila.

Seeing he had no choice by this point, Das took Kaila's iPhone and recorded a video reaffirming that he had made two unconditional promises to Kaila and sent the vMail to his geek distribution list, knowing this surely guaranteed the existence of the promises as public knowledge.

Then Kaila asked, "Can I ask my two favors now?"

Das replied with sinking heart, "Yes. What do you wish, my love?"

"First, I wish that you cancel the installation of Ram as CEO of Apple and install Barat instead. Second, I wish that you send Ram to the jungles of Hawaii, away from the West Coast, for fourteen years. If you keep your word, you will grant me these promises," stated Kaila.

Das pushed her head from his lap none too gently and got up angrily. His head was spinning.

"What a bitch!" he thought. "How did I go so wrong? How did I not see this vicious streak in her? She's been so constantly sweet and loving for the many years we've been together. This is so out of character."

"Oh, my lovely Kaila," Das cried, "what has come over you? It is so unlike you to be so mean. And why do this to Ram? He's been devoted to you even as to his own mother. Why would you want to hurt me? Why hurt Ram too? I can't believe you really understand what you've asked me to do."

Kaila replied, "Oh, my love, I do know how painful these requests are, but I have my own survival at stake, along with that of my son, whom I have to protect too. Please don't be so angry. Barat will be a good CEO in his own right, and after the fourteen years are over, Ram may return to the palace and Barat will find a place for him in Apple's management at that time. All will be well, and the future of all us wives will be secure."

"Oh, Kaila, my love, you have sentenced me to death as if you had knifed me through the heart with your own hand. I won't survive the grief of Ram's departure. I will worry constantly about him while he's gone. I won't live to see him return. This is cruel beyond belief," wailed Das in anguish.

Kaila replied, "I will comfort you and lay with you as always and soon your grief will dissolve".

"Oh, your heart has turned to stone, I don't want to lie with you any-more during the few remaining days I have to live," gasped Das.

Das wanted to remonstrate with her. He wanted her to see the hurt she was causing. He said, "How can you benefit from this? Ram would ensure that sharp lawyer geeks don't steal your trust. And would Barat accept the CEO position under these conditions? No. He and Ram are friends who grew up together and participated in many cooperative sports together. They have fun together and enjoy each other's company. Barat is loyal to Ram. And their skills are different. Barat will enjoy an important place in the kingdom with Ram in charge."

But Kaila's face was hard. She set her jaw, clenched her teeth, and declared, "My mind is made up. Oh Das, my husband and CEO, if you do not honor your word, I will tell the world. I will tear my clothes into tattered rags. I will stay in a homeless camp under the Bay Bridge in San Francisco. I will call out to bloggers from CNET and MarketWatch, and journalists from the *San Francisco Chronicle* and the *New York Times*—the whole world will know you do not honor your promises. Your power and Apple's prestige will be finished. They will wonder if Apple can stand by their products and honor their warranties. The full faith and credit of Apple will become as worthless as the government's bonds. Apple's stock will crater, and the citizens will tweet their rebellion when widows and retirees don't get their checks and are cast out by the banks to join the homeless and starve on the streets."

Das was defeated. He knew he had to keep his word even if it cost him his life.

Das trudged out of Kaila's quarters and returned to his own. He tossed and turned all night, and the next morning he returned to Kaila's quarters in the desperate hope that she had changed her mind. A glance at her face proved otherwise.

Meanwhile, Vasis was searching for Das to consult on the plans for Ram's installation. Vasis encountered Das's personal valet and limousine geek, Suman, to ask if he had seen where the CEO was at the moment. Suman told him that Das was last seen going to Kaila's quarters.

Both Vasis and Suman proceeded there, thinking that Das and Kaila might be safely interrupted during their breakfast together. When they arrived, they saw that Das looked horrible, pale and drawn.

Vasis immediately asked, "Sir, is there a problem? Are you all right? Should I call the palace doctor?"

But Kaila jumped in to say, "Das has had a sleepless night, that's all. It's the excitement." She went on to demand, "Get Ram and bring him here."

Vasis was puzzled. Shouldn't Das himself be the one fetching Ram on this auspicious day?

He glanced over to Das, who said, "Go ahead, please find Ram and bring him here." So Vasis dispatched Suman to find Ram.

Ram Banished

When Suman arrived at Ram's quarters, he found Ram and Sita sitting together. He said, "Your father wishes you to visit with him now in Kaila's quarters."

Ram was surprised. He looked at Sita and said, "I imagine they want to work out some last-minute details. I'll be back soon."

Sita replied, "Go with my love. I await your return."

On the way to Kaila's quarters, Ram passed many of the palace geeks and citizens of the Apple kingdom who congratulated him on his pending installation and wished him well.

Ram arrived at Kaila's quarters and immediately felt apprehensive. His father looked deathly ill. Das remained seated and would not meet Ram's gaze but stared intently at the floor, and with a gulp uttered only, "Ram."

Ram was aghast. His father always stood up to greet him with an embrace and often a bear hug.

Ram turned to Kaila, who was sitting some distance from Das and asked her directly, "Oh Kaila, why is my father so upset? Why doesn't he greet me as usual? Have I committed some offense? Have I failed to offer respect? If I have, then I apologize for whatever I've done wrong."

Kaila was silent. Ram began to sense the tension between Kaila and his father. He ventured, "Could there be some disagreement between you both that involves me? Can I help in some way to restore peace during what should be a joyful occasion?"

Kaila replied, "Your father is reluctant to tell you something that he feels will hurt you. He's made a promise to me that he now hopes he can renege upon. If you will do whatever your father has promised on your behalf, then I will disclose to you what he has promised. Otherwise I will reveal to the world that he is not a man of his word, which will bring insufferable damage to your father as well as to the Apple kingdom and the many people depending on it."

Ram than declared, "Shame on you for doubting whether I will carry out my father's promises. Since my birth I have always followed his advice and bidding. I would do so now as well."

As Ram's temper began to rise, he added, "Furthermore, you do not need to threaten me with the consequences of breaking a promise. I value keeping a promise for its own sake, not for the sake of its consequences. I am an honest man, absolutely and without compromise. My word is not a commodity to be negotiated, it is the essence of my character, my very being."

Kaila was relieved to hear what Ram said, knowing that she now had him trapped. He was now bound to execute the promise his father had made.

She said, "Very well then, here is the situation. On the night that your father first took me, he promised he would fulfill two wishes of my choosing whenever I should request them. I have chosen the two wishes now. They are, first, that Barat be installed as CEO of Apple and, second, that you retire to the geek encampments in the jungles of Hawaii for fourteen years. Barat can be installed with the ceremony that had been planned for you. You should live in the Hawaiian Islands—or any other remote tropical island—with your hair in matted locks and wearing homespun clothes."

Das groaned, and Kaila cried out, "See, your father cannot even look you in the face. Oh, Ram, save your family's reputation and carry out your father's promises!"

Ram replied, "Oh, Kaila, you needn't have gone to such lengths. All you had to do was ask. I would have gladly relinquished the CEO position to Barat, and would gladly have parted with the perks of the office. In any case, I'm happy to honor my father's promises to you. I'll gladly matt my hair, dress in homespun clothes, and live among the geek encampments in Hawaii and elsewhere on tropical islands."

Ram looked at his father, who was still staring at the floor and now beginning to cry.

Kaila said, "Word will be sent to Kush in India so that Barat and Shat can fly here for the ceremony. In the meantime, you should leave for Hawaii immediately."

Ram replied, "Reassure my father that I willingly carry out the promises he made to you. But for now, I wish only for time to take leave of my other mothers and to get the agreement of my wife, Sita. For your part, I ask that you help Barat protect the kingdom and promote the welfare of its citizens."

Then Ram approached his father, raised him up, put his comforting hands on Das's forehead, and embraced him.

Turning back to Kaila, Ram said, "I have no desire to live in this world as a slave to material gains." Ram then strode out of Kaila's quarters.

Meanwhile, Lak had heard through the palace grapevine that an important conference was taking place in Kaila's quarters and he went to its entrance. As Ram exited Kaila's quarters, Lak fell into stride with Ram and asked what had happened. Ram was adept at keeping his self-control, and he calmly brought Lak up to date, explaining that Barat was now to become the CEO of Apple—that he would soon leave for Hawaii and would remain living on tropical islands for the next fourteen years.

Lak was dumbfounded and becoming furious as he began to wrap his mind around this new reality. They both quickly grabbed a company car and drove up to Kausha's palace in the coastal redwoods.

When they arrived, Kausha welcomed them with open arms. "You're both a sight for sore eyes. I'm so glad to see you both."

They went inside, and Ram sat next to her, holding her by the hands, and said, "Mother, I have some difficult news to tell you."

"Yes, my son, what is it?" she asked.

Ram calmly said, "I will not be installed later today as the CEO of Apple. Instead, I leave later today for the jungles of Hawaii and will remain living on tropical islands for the next fourteen years. In the meantime, Barat will be summoned back from Kush's palace in India to assume the CEO position here as soon as he arrives. All this is to fulfill two promises that my father made to Kaila when he first slept with her."

When Kausha heard the news she became confused and distraught. She knew the news must be true because Ram's style was not to be flippant, nor to joke about something so serious.

She blurted out, "In your absence, what should I do? You're my love and reason for living. Before you were born I spent many years craving a child, and your birth brought me such joy. And now I am back to being childless again. I cannot bear this."

Kausha reflected too on how she was continually overlooked by Das in favor of Kaila. With Barat in charge of Apple, she would feel entirely abandoned. She wailed, "Oh, my son, now I will be useless here. I want to follow you to the jungles of Hawaii."

Lak stood nearby. He felt the situation was intolerable and wondered how Ram could accept it.

Unable to repress his anger any more, he spoke to Kausha, saying, "I too cannot accept this. My father has been overcome by lust and senility. What has Ram done wrong? Nothing! What man who respects virtue would double-cross his own son as Das is about to do? Surely he's lost his moral authority. Why should a son obey a father who has fallen so far?"

Lak continued, "If at Kaila's bidding our father has lost the ability to tell right from wrong, he should not be allowed to control who inherits the power he has wielded as CEO of Apple. I will kill my aged and depraved father!"

Kausha picked up the thread, saying, "Your brother has raised valid objections to your departing. You shouldn't obey the unjust command that comes from Kaila, leaving me here to grieve all alone."

Ram replied, "Oh, mother, I hear you and grieve with you. But I cannot undercut my father's promise, which would tarnish our entire family's moral standing. My father has not asked me to do anything sinful—unjust, perhaps, but not wrong. By obeying his command I am following the path of morality that's always been followed by good men."

Turning to Lak, Ram said, "I know that with your strength you could easily kill our father and take down his security guards with him. Please don't. In her grief, my gentle mother does not deeply appreciate the importance of the moral imperative to honor a promise. I myself have now given my word to follow Kaila's command and thus to honor my father's promises. So now it's my own word too that I must keep. And I will keep it. Please don't lose yourself to anger. Please accept that I am resolved to go to the jungles of tropical islands."

Ram continued explaining his position: "Only fools think a person can be fulfilled with sensual pleasures, whose enjoyment always turns out to be transient. Real satisfaction comes through living a moral life. Moral goodness is eternal, and the perks of power and the sorrows of deprivation are temporary, like sticks floating on a river briefly thrown together but soon to be parted by the swift currents of time. I choose goodness over ephemeral perks, knowing that any present grief will in time be stilled."

Ram placed his hand on Lak's shoulder and added reassuringly, "Kaila must have been truly terrified to demand these favors from our father. I have known her to be gentle, and she has treated me as her own son ever since I was born. She is kind and must be forgiven. Something is amiss that will emerge in the fullness of time."

Turning to Kausha, Ram then said, "Please don't ask to go with me. Please stay with my father. He needs you now more than ever before. He was betrayed by Kaila and is now seeing me exiled. I fear for his life. The moral path is to tend to his needs and forgive his weaknesses. He has the greater need. Please remain here and assuage his grief. Wait until I return, and then we'll be reunited."

Kausha replied, "I see there's no changing your mind. Then go with my blessings. My misery will end only when you've returned."

Ram and Lak then piled into their car and drove back to the palace in Silicon Valley. They went to the quarters where Ram and Sita lived so that Ram could break the news to Sita.

Sita hadn't heard a thing, and she was expecting to welcome a jubilant Ram returning from his meeting. Instead she was greeted with a husband who arrived holding himself rigid, with his teeth clenched.

She immediately exclaimed, "What's wrong? I know something is wrong. What is it, my love?"

Ram answered in a controlled and measured voice, "I'm not going to be installed today as Apple's CEO after all. Instead, I am being sent to the jungles of Hawaii to live as a geek for fourteen years. I will mat my hair and live austerely in homespun clothes. Barat will be returning from India, and he will be the one installed as CEO."

Sita was dumbfounded. She listened in horror as Ram continued, "I wish you to remain here and assist my father and Barat. Perhaps you can pursue your interests in conservation and other charities when I'm gone."

Sita gathered herself, took a deep breath, and replied, "No way! Absolutely not! I will not remain here without you under any circumstances. It's my right to accompany you wherever you go, and I insist on exercising this right. There is no place for me here with you gone. And I have no problem with the thought of living in the company of geeks in the jungles of Hawaii."

Ram was doubtful. Sita had been raised in privileged circumstances and with the best facilities. He feared she was romanticizing what it would be like to live full-time in a tropical jungle.

So he replied, "I don't think that would be a good idea. It's no fun sleeping night after night in the cold rain."

Sita replied, "Oh, come on—I've camped in the cold and snow of the temperate rain forests of the Olympic Peninsula. Surely you're not trying to tell me that the jungles of Hawaii are more uncomfortable than that. I can take the jungles of tropical islands, easily. It's your companionship and love I need. Loneliness in the Apple palace is a horrible alternative to the joy of your company, even if only around a campfire."

Ram said, "Life together at a campfire might be fine for a short time, but fourteen years?"

Sita replied, "Yes, fourteen years of loneliness would be worse than fourteen years at a campfire."

Seeing there was no dissuading her, Ram finally said, "Okay, my dear Sita. Please do come with me. I will love you, respect you, and protect you all my life. Thank you for being willing to sacrifice so much to live with me in the jungle."

Sita went off to gather her personal camping supplies. She included inter-ovulation capsules to place in her embedded hormone receptacle. She anticipated not wanting to bear and raise children with Ram while they were living in unpredictable and primitive conditions.

Now Lak's turn came, and he said, "Since you are determined to accept the bidding of our father, I too wish to accompany you to the jungles of Hawaii. I'll be at your side should any danger arise."

And Ram again resisted, saying, "But Lak, you have a future here at Apple. Barat is certain to find a useful and challenging position for you."

But Lak was firm. "Not a chance. There's simply no way I will remain here, where I would be redundant, while I can be of service with you. I'll be separated from my wife, a major sacrifice for both of us, but I'm definitely not staying. My bond to you, forged during our childhood as we shared the physical joy of cooperation, is my life's organizing principle. If I can't go with you, I'll find something else to do with my life, but staying here at Apple? Nope, won't happen."

Seeing that Lak was determined, Ram sighed and said, "Well, then, please do come with me. I'm deeply honored that you want to join us in our austere life in the woods. I will do my best to be a good and faithful companion."

With Sita's and Lak's decisions settled, Ram asked Lak to go to Vasis and fetch the weapon that Vasis was storing. Lak returned with Vasis, bringing the great bow and arrow set.

Vasis said, "Here is your bow—you might be needing this. I'm sorry to see you go. All I can say by way of consolation is that when you return, you'll be over forty years of age and better experienced than you are now, which means you'll be better able to guide Apple's strategy in the future. And while in Hawaii you'll visit the encampments of geek sects with different specialties. You'll meet sects of history geeks, human/animal hybrid geeks, mahu gender-variant geeks, robotics and big data geeks, and animal behavior and conservation geeks, among others. By learning from them you'll be in a better position to defeat Ravan and his syndicate. And if you need resources, remember you have online access to your financial accounts

Ram asked, "I know I have Apple stock. Do you know its worth?"

Vasis answered, "Many billions. If you need to buy or rent some facilities, log on to your account, sell some securities, if necessary, and send the funds directly by wire to the vendor."

Ram replied, "That's good to know. I'm not anticipating the need for any funds soon, but thanks for letting me know. Also, I was thinking that I might need more than money. Remember the stem cells that you preserved when Lak and I were born? They've been stored at our mothers' houses, correct?"

Vasis nodded.

Ram continued, "Can you have some of our stem cells transferred to a tissue culture laboratory with a link on my assets page to where they are so we can obtain them, if needed? If we're badly hurt in any upcoming battles with Ravan we might have to regenerate parts of ourselves beyond what is possible with the stem cells already implanted in our bodies. We might need a large supply several years from now if the going gets tough."

"Will do. That's thinking ahead," said Vasis.

Ram replied, "Vasis, thanks for everything. Thank you so much."

Vasis nodded in acknowledgment.

Ram then said to Sita and Lak, "Okay, let's get going. No point dragging out the farewells. Let's go to my father's quarters, say good-bye, and and then we're out of here."

So they went to Das's quarters. Das had been joined by Ram's mother, Kausha, who drove down from the redwoods, and by Lak's mother, Sumitra, who had flown in from her palace in the desert.

Ram said to Das, "Father, we'll go now."

Das just nodded. He couldn't bring himself to speak.

Ram embraced Kausha, Lak embraced Sumitra, and both of them then embraced their father.

Das asked Suman if the company plane was fueled to fly to Hawaii. Suman replied that it was and the luggage had been loaded. Das nodded sadly.

Then Ram, Sita, Lak, and Suman made their way out the front entrance to the Apple palace where the palace geeks and many citizens had assembled to witness their departure. The people looked grim, some with tears.

Suman drove the trio to the Moffett Field airport where the company plane was waiting. Their luggage including camping supplies had already loaded.

They boarded the plane. Suman went into the cockpit and assumed the controls, and they all jetted off to the island of Kauai. Vasis, meanwhile, contacted the guests to Ram's installation to say that the ceremony had been postponed until further notice.

Ram to Kauai

When the Apple company plane arrived in Kauai, the CEO of a local software company, Guh, met the trio at the Lihue airport. He was a wiry man with blond hair, deeply tanned. He wore shorts and a green T-shirt with Kapaa Warriors stenciled on it and had a tattoo glistening on one shoulder.

He placed flower leis over the head of each guest and introduced himself to Ram, saying, "Aloha, I'm Guh, and I've long wanted to meet you. We've supplied programs to your app store for decades. How can I be of service?"

Ram replied, "Thanks for meeting us. We're about to leave for the jungle on the North Shore. Could you possibly take us to the trailhead?"

"Yes, I'd be happy to show you where it is," replied Guh.

Meanwhile, Suman refueled Apple's company plane for the return flight.

Seeing that Suman was about to depart, Ram said to him, "Suman, you've been wonderful. Thank you so much. It's important you return to Apple and reassure Kaila that we have in fact disembarked and are about to enter the jungle. She should not fear any deceit. And when you return, please give your support to Barat. He'll need your help too, even though you may not feel inclined to give it. But the company and its citizens will be better off if Barat is not opposed at every turn. Please try to work with him, and before you know it, we'll all be back together again."

Suman nodded unhappily, climbed into the plane, and flew back to Silicon Valley.

Guh had driven to the airport in a Land Rover with a surfboard tied to its roof. The trio loaded their luggage in the back, including Ram's bow, and squeezed into the front and back seats.

Guh headed north from the airport, driving along the island's east coast, with the ocean on the right and remnants of volcanic mountains on the left. They drove along Wailua Beach, past dikes that protected the road from the ever-rising sea's pounding surf, then through Old Kapaa town with its boutiques and on to the bypass around the recently flooded Kealia Bay. Heading north, they continued past Princeville, and after bearing left, they crossed a reinforced one-lane bridge over the Hanalei River. They ended up at the tiny, funky town of Hanalei on the North Shore known for artists, movie stars, and wealthy hippies.

As Guh approached Hanalei, Ram noticed a banyan tree by the side of the road. He said, "Please stop here, I must mat my hair with the sap of a banyan tree."

"Are you sure?" asked Guh, adding, "It's messy stuff and uncomfortable in the heat."

Ram replied, "Please, it is my vow."

So Guh pulled off to the side of the road and the trio went to the base of the banyan tree. There they reached up for a branch, broke it open, and harvested drops of the milky white sap. They two brothers sat down, and Lak worked the sap into Ram's hair and braided it into dreadlocks. Lak's hair remained shaved on the side with a brush in the center, vaguely suggesting a Mohawk.

Guh said, "You'll be mistaken for a Rastafarian."

Ram replied, "I'll be wearing homespun clothes with no sign of Jamaican colors. I hope people take a second look and recognize me as a geek on pilgrimage and not as a Rasta wannabe."

Guh then said, "I had hoped to treat you to one of our best restaurants and then put you up at one of our luxury hotels, but I sense that would not be a good idea."

Ram replied, "You're right. Can we simply stop in a local store and buy some bread and fruit? We'd love to sit by the shore and eat there while watching the sunset."

"Okay, we'll stop at our local independent grocery store, the Harvest Market, and grab some organic produce. Also, you can try some of our local spicy ahi poke from their deli—that's our Hawaiian version of tuna sushi," said Guh.

They also bought supplies that included a machete for Lak and two inflatable Sea Eagle kayaks. Lak then shimmied up a coconut tree and knocked down a few coconuts. After Lak chopped a hole in the coconuts, they all sat on the shore on a log and together ate their meal while watching the sunset.

Ram then said, "This is absolutely wonderful. I think we're going to be just fine here."

Guh said, "You may pitch your tents nearby in the Hanalei Beach Park. I've just called in to make reservations for you. Tomorrow I'll pick you all up and bring you to the trailhead, which is only a few miles or so away."

"We're looking forward to it. In the meantime, can you vMail my father to say we've arrived safely and are very happy? Please say he shouldn't grieve for us. And speaking with you, his old colleague, will lift his spirits too."

"Okay, I'll give him a shout," said Guh, "and see you tomorrow."

The trio pitched their pup tents and slept inside them to avoid being rained on during the night. The next morning they awoke to the ocean breeze and took a deep breath of the clean air. As they were finishing their granola and milk, Guh pulled up and asked how they'd slept.

Lak replied, "Like a rock," while Ram and Sita nodded in agreement.

Guh asked them to load up their gear. They went a few miles west along the road to the trailhead for the Kalalau trail.

After thanking Guh for the lift, the trio started up the trail. The path took them along the edge of rugged cliffs with gorgeous views of the Na Pali coastline. After a brief two miles, the trail dropped down to a beach prominent during the summer. The trail sign read, *Hanakapi`ai* Beach.

In the surrounding jungle the trio came upon a geek encampment flanking some taro ponds fed by a mountain stream. Ti and banana plants were growing near the pond. An apprentice met them and guided them to meet their chief geek, Bhar, a large man with a long braid of thick, dark hair.

These geeks were known for making extremely expensive necklaces of tiny shells from dove snails. Most of the geeks with Bhar were of Native Hawaiian descent, and many originally hailed from the nearby island of Niihau.

Bhar looked up from his meticulous work. When he saw the visitors he rose.

Ram introduced himself, Lak, and Sita, and said, "Sir, we have admired your shell leis for many years and are honored to have the opportunity to meet you."

Bhar replied, "And I, of course, have heard of you. Welcome. You may stay with us as long as you wish."

Ram replied, "Thanks, but we'd like to find a location more remote. If we were to stay here, so close to the trailhead, then visitors from Apple would come by regularly, and it would be all too easy to become reengaged with Apple's decision-making. By my vow I can't allow myself to become entwined with Apple and its issues. Can you suggest a more remote loca-tion where we might settle down?"

"Yes, of course," replied Bhar. "Hike up the stream here until you come to a waterfall called Hanakapi`ai Falls. There you'll find an encampment of history geeks headed by the historian Valmiki."

"Perfect," said Ram.

Valmiki's Camp

The trio turned left and began to clamber over the slippery rocks in the stream-bed up to the waterfall. After about a mile, a trail appeared next to the stream-bed. The trio climbed out of the stream-bed and began walking up the mountain trail.

Rows of mustard plants were thriving in dark, organic-matter-laden soil on both sides of the path, soil that contrasted with the red dirt elsewhere on the mountain slope. Where the path was shaded, the trio could see that the plants glowed.

"These plants are bioluminescent!" Sita exclaimed. "This path is lit in the dark."

Lak added, "I can't wait to see the whole encampment. Probably the whole camp is illuminated at night with bioluminescent plants."

After walking up the path for an additional mile, the trio came to Valmiki's encampment. It was near the base of a tall waterfall that spilled from a cliff a thousand feet above into a lovely pond below.

As Lak had anticipated, the camp was illuminated during the evening by bioluminescent plants. The mustard plants had genes spliced into them from dinoflagellate algae, as well as bioluminescent mushrooms, bacteria, fireflies, and jellyfish, making for plants that gave off different colors of light.

Lak sidled up to one of the geeks and asked, "Why don't the plants invade the surrounding vegetation and wind up covering the hillside?"

She answered, "The light-making plants don't invade because the light they make consumes some of the energy they produced through photosynthesis during the day. Diverting energy away from growth puts them at a competitive disadvantage with regard to the local plants. The light-making plants can't spread on their own into the surrounding habitat. Instead, we need to help the light-making plants survive. We're always watering them, giving them our compost as fertilizer, and weeding away competing local plants."

"I see," said Lak. "I gather then that these plants don't work well in California because they need to be given so much water and labor that they're not economical there. But I can see they're perfect here."

Sita then asked, "But what if there is a mutation that eliminates the drain of energy put into the expensive light-making? Wouldn't a plant carrying that mutation invade the surrounding habitat?"

"Almost surely not," replied the geek. "The ground is occupied by the plant species that are already here, so merely eliminating the light-making ability in the plants we're raising wouldn't make them competitively superior to those already here. To be better than those already here would require two mutations—one to knock out the light-making capability and another to make them somehow more competitive than the plants we already have. And that's just too improbable to bother worrying about."

"Okay," replied Sita, "good point."

The geek continued, "The people living here in Kauai initially opposed light-making plants as part of their overall prohibition against genetically modified plants. But when it became clear that light-making plants couldn't be invasive, and that they're not only harmless but useful, the sentiment changed. Local opposition to genetically modified plants was intense because of hostility to Monsanto's hooking farmers on their pesticides. But the light-making plants were developed by do-it-yourself bio labs in Silicon Valley, not big companies, so the local county council made an exception because they didn't feel manipulated. And then the citizens tweeted their approval, so the matter was settled."

As the trio walked around, they came across other geeks who were combing pet cats with special combs that had a thick handle and what looked liked little USB sockets in them.

Sita approached another geek and asked what the big-handled combs were for.

The geek replied, "These cats generate bioelectricity. The combs harvest the electricity and make it available for recharging our iPhones and MacBooks."

Sita asked, "How does this work? I've never seen it before."

The geek replied, "These cats have had genes from electric eels spliced into their genomes. The genes express themselves only in the muscle cells underlying the fur. When a bioelectric cat is stroked with the comb, it feels a little tingle and purrs. Bioelectric cats develop big appetites because of all the metabolic energy they use when producing electricity. So each geek who owns a bioelectric pet has to catch fish daily to provide enough food for it. The bioelectric cats do not wander off because their appetites are too large to be satisfied with food they can catch by themselves. Also, they want to stay near their owners for the enjoyment of being regularly stroked with the rechargeable comb."

"Wow." Sita grinned. "So petting a cat is not only fun but productive."

The geek continued, "We also have some solar cells to generate electricity—and we have solar hot water too, with a solar pump—but obviously, these only work during the day. We keep away from big, heavy, and toxic batteries. We live by the motto that if you packed it in, you pack it out. We can't pack big storage batteries up here so we won't use them. We do use solar cells with a few batteries at our Internet relay tower, but that's pretty much the only use we have for solar electricity."

Sita looked surprised and asked, "Internet?"

"Yes," the geek replied. "We're isolated, but not marooned. We're here to work on our various history projects. We're still part of the real world. We're not trying to go back to the Stone Age or anything; we're just living close to nature."

"I see," said Sita. "Can you possibly take us to your head geek, Valmiki? We'd like to discuss staying here for a good long while."

"Sure, follow me," said the geek as she led the trio to Valmiki's hut.

The geeks in Valmiki's encampment lived in huts recessed into the cliffs as protection from the increased number of hurricanes visiting the island, a result of global warming.

Valmiki, a heavyset man with a white beard, was in his hut working at his laptop when the trio arrived.

He rose to greet them. "Would you be Ram, his wife, Sita, and his lieutenant, Lak? I've been waiting for you. Word has spread by the coconut wireless that you had arrived and were looking for a place to stay."

"Yes, we are," answered Ram, "and your location is absolutely beautiful. I can also see astonishing innovation in your encampment."

"Indeed, we're unabashedly proud of our little setup here. I gather you've already encountered some of our unusual biotechnology assets. Also, let me show you our old-fashioned garden," Valmiki said as he led them to groves of trees and rows of vegetables.

Valmiki explained, "We're harvesting all sorts of tropical fruits that thrive here—papayas and bananas, of course, and also mangoes, avocados, guavas, sweet sops, sour sops, dragon fruit, rambutans, mangosteens, and longans. For vegetables, we're harvesting cherry tomatoes, lettuce, green beans, corn, and many types of herbs. Kauai's nickname, the Garden Island, is well deserved."

He continued, "The waterfall flows year round, and the stream supplies us with ample drinking water, plus water for cooking and washing. For the people who are not vegetarians, we harvest fish from the waters offshore of Hanakapi`ai Beach. Those wanting meat can trap the wild chickens in the jungle. They were originally released when Hurricane Iniki demolished the cages holding cockfighting roosters and hens. Also, wild pigs whose original release dates back to the first occupation of the islands by the Polynesians can be trapped and prepared for a traditional Hawaiian luau."

"Truly wonderful," said Ram, and he continued, "Would it be an imposition if we stay here for an extended period? We'd love to join your encampment if you'll have us."

"Certainly, you may join us for an extended period," replied Valmiki.

Gesturing to the cliff walls bordering the encampment, he continued, "We'd be honored. Here's a vacant area of the cliffs where you can excavate and build a hut for yourselves. The cave houses at Mesa Verde, the Loire Valley, or Cappadocia can give you some design ideas. Our community of geeks will help, of course. As you've gathered by now, we're not a commune but a work community. People come to stay to work on a history project, which is feasible now that the collections from all the world's libraries and museums have come online. Our community participants leave camp when their projects are complete. They're basically taking a sabbatical among us for a few months to a couple of years. You'll fit right in."

"Oh, thank you so much," Ram said enthusiastically as Sita and Lak nodded in agreement.

Then Valmiki added, glancing from Ram to Sita, "By the way, we have only limited facilities for children, although some members have brought their families for as long as a year's stay. School-age children could hike out to the trailhead, where they would pick up a school bus to Hanalei, but the hike takes about four hours each way and is not practical, so children here are usually homeschooled."

That evening Valmiki invited Ram and Lak to join him sitting on a circular bench lining the perimeter of a conversation pit. In the center of the pit was a circular table on which was sitting a bouquet of plants that glowed in shimmering shades of red, orange, yellow, and blue.

Valmiki explained his own personal history and how he had come to be the chief geek of a history encampment.

He said, "I used to write pornography for X-rated websites and ebooks. I used the earnings to support my family. But although my wife and children were perfectly happy to spend the money I earned, they weren't willing to tell their friends what I did for a living. They were ashamed. I found this discouraging. I paid my taxes, I voted, and I was a responsible citizen. And my occupation was legal. Still, what I was doing was not right. So I renounced what I was doing and decided to enter an order of geeks dedicated to historical narrative and analysis."

Ram was surprised. He said, "Well, I didn't expect such a background. I thought you came from a family of history geeks and were carrying on a family tradition. What you do now is valuable to civilization."

Valmiki replied, "Thanks, though I wasn't pulling for a compliment. I'm just telling you where I'm coming from. Now, may I ask a favor of you?"

Ram said, "Yes, I'm at your service."

Valmiki then said, "With your permission, I'd like to record your biography. In return, I can tell you the recent history of Google, Amazon, and the other industrial kingdoms that Apple contended with decades ago."

Ram replied, "Yes, of course you may chronicle me in whatever format you think best. I know I can speak for Sita and Lak too when I say we'd be happy to cooperate. And I can't wait to learn more about the recent history of the industrial kingdoms that are so much a part of our lives today."

Valmiki replied, "Wonderful! After your dinner tomorrow come by the conversation pit here and have some historical questions ready for me."

"Great, see you tomorrow," replied Ram.

The next day, at Sita's direction, Lak and Ram excavated a cavern and constructed rooms in it with a front porch at its entrance. They could see the blue ocean through the green leaves of the jungle trees.

When the hut was done, Sita was overjoyed. She said, "I can think of no better place to spend the next fourteen years."

She went to the gardens where the bioluminescent mustard plants were being cultivated, gathered some seeds, cleared some ground, added compost to the soil, and planted the seeds, saying, "Now our house is complete."

She then prepared a dinner, and the three ate together on their newly constructed front porch.

Valmiki's Lesson

After dinner, the trio went to the conversation pit. Valmiki was waiting and asked, "Which industrial kingdom do you want to hear about?"

Ram replied, "Google was a powerhouse decades ago, what's become of it?"

Valmiki replied, "Once Google was a huge kingdom because of its search engine and linked advertisements. But decades ago many thought our national government had become too big. This antigovernment movement then morphed into a general anti-organization movement."

"Yes, I know," said Ram. "What's the connection to Google?"

Valmiki continued, "The reasoning that finds government as too big can be applied to a firm too. Maybe firms have also become too big. So Google had the courage to ask themselves whether they should continue to exist as a huge corporate empire and if not, what they should become instead."

Ram said, "Yes."

Valmiki went on, saying, "The alternative was to devolve into smaller pieces, to reorganize, with their former employees becoming a network of independent contractors."

Ram asked, "What's appealing about that? Google could simply break into several divisions without bothering to make each of its many thousands of employees into independent contractors."

Valmiki answered, "What appealed is this: if all their workers could directly negotiate with each other about what jobs to do, the net effect would be a more efficient deployment of their workforce—labor would go where the demand for it was and not be wasted where it wasn't needed. This tactic theoretically would be better than relying on a manager to assign tasks."

Valmiki continued, "Google figured it could set up a clearing house for its workers to buy and sell contracts with each other for labor, parts, and access to big equipment. They could use software from an online brokerage to manage buying and selling contracts among their workers."

"This sounds risky," said Ram.

Valmiki replied, "Yes, but Google has always had a libertarian streak. So Google bought out their stockholders and took itself private. They deeded a prorated share of the company's assets together with an office at their Silicon Valley facility to each employee as a nest egg. Each employee then became a single entrepreneurial agent, free to buy and sell labor and parts to other agents on their contracts exchange. Google adopted a new name, Google Matrix. It named their main trading floor the Rand Paul floor in honor of a libertarian politician of the time. Google always supported an open-source software philosophy. A consortium of independent contractors was the culmination of its open-source philosophy. Google Matrix became the world's first open company."

Ram thought for a while and then asked, "Has this move by Google been successful?"

Valmiki replied, "Well, yes and no. Google is no longer recognized as a powerful centralized industrial kingdom like Apple and Microsoft/IBM still are. But the aggregate productivity and wealth accumulated by all of Google Matrix's independent contractors remains extraordinary, probably larger than those workers would have achieved if they had remained under a central management. Google Matrix's contractors produce lots of innovative products because new ideas don't have to be cleared with a firm's management. And Google Matrix's contractors collectively are responsive to changes in the market. But Google Matrix has no overall direction, theme, or identity."

Ram then asked, "Is that a problem?"

Valmiki replied, "I don't know. That's a matter of personal preference. A worker can choose to work as a contractor within Google Matrix or as an employee for a centrally organized firm like Apple or Microsoft/IBM. Someone who is personally risk averse and enjoys team thinking can choose to be an employee of Apple's industrial kingdom. Someone who prefers flexibility and self-directed pursuits can join Google Matrix as an independent agent."

Ram then said, "Well, maybe it's just my coming from Apple and preferring our way of doing things, but I wouldn't have disaggregated Google if I had been in charge."

To bring the lesson to an end, Ram said, "Thanks. When I return to Apple, your historical perspective will help."

Valmiki replied, "Tomorrow night we'll continue, and we'll do this night after night until you've had enough."

Ram yawned and said, "It's been a long day, and I'm tired now. It's time for us to go to bed."

After the trio retired to their new hut, Ram said to the others, "I do worry about my father. His health wasn't good before we left. Our departure may have weakened him further."

Lak replied, "There's nothing we can do about it, so let's get some sleep."

Lak retired to his room, and Ram and Sita to theirs.

The next evening Ram, Lak, and Sita resumed their spots on the benches around the conversation pit.

Valmiki was waiting for them and asked, "Where does your curiosity lead this evening?"

Ram replied, "I've been thinking about Google Matrix and have a question."

"Fire away," said Valmiki.

Ram replied, "Google Matrix works for developing and producing products, but what about basic research to create knowledge prior to developing and producing products? I can imagine a basic scientist posting a contract to work on animals in the ocean's deep Mariana Trench. But who would buy the contract? I can imagine a mathematician offering work on a theorem about topology in n-dimensional space. Who would buy that? Is there a market for basic research?"

Valmiki replied, "Good question. Not only Google Matrix but all the industrial empires, even your Apple, agreed they needed to grow an open commons of basic knowledge. So they agreed to tithe their annual gross income to fund two government-operated foundations that would buy labor contracts for basic research."

"Why two?" asked Ram.

Valmiki replied, "To encourage competition between the foundations. Congress allocates each foundation a proportion of the monies raised by the industrial tithing in accordance with their success in identifying innovative scholarship. The old system of relying on peer review at one foundation led to funding only projects that promoted the beliefs of the foundation's reviewers. We used to have only one funding agency, the National Science Foundation, or NSF for short. Now we also have the American Science Foundation, or ASF. The tithing money is split between the NSF and ASF depending on how well each did during the previous year relative to the other in finding high-impact scholarship. This new system has been generating knowledge at a faster rate, and probably with more innovation than the previous one-foundation setup."

Ram said, "So far, so good, but I feel you're missing something. Personally, I'm curious. For me, learning is exciting. I feel a sense of pleasure when I grasp a new idea or see a connection I hadn't noticed before. Just as I enjoy music, I enjoy learning, and I'm willing to pay for scholarship just as I'm willing to pay for a concert or a painting."

"Well," said Valmiki, "when you return to Apple, perhaps you'll become more engaged in philanthropy than your family has been. If you set up a private foundation whose objective is to promote basic scholarship and not just policy goals, then you could make a lasting difference to our civilization."

Valmiki then asked Ram, "How do you think the various encampments of geeks here are funded? How is your friend in Santa Barbara, Vish, funded? How am I funded?"

"I don't know," replied Ram.

Valmiki answered, "It's by the very system I just described. Vish offers a contract to work on the theory of algorithms and the NSF or ASF bid for it if they think it's important scholarship. Vish has been successful in feeding his disciples this way. I too offer a contract for my historical analysis. The NSF and ASF both have small sections devoted to the history of science and technology. They bid for the contract I offer on behalf of this encampment here. Like Vish, I too have been successful so far. Furthermore, many geek encampments are also funded by the private foundations whose objectives coincide with theirs. I do sincerely hope you use some of your own enormous personal resources to set up an Apple Philanthropic Foundation to buy contracts for basic scholarship in the arts and humanities."

"Will do. That would close the circle, allowing me to reciprocate the support I've received from you and the wider community of geeks," said Ram.

Ram then yawned and said, "Thanks yet again for the lesson. However, I'm finding it hard to concentrate when I'm still awaiting word from my family and wondering if everything there is okay."

Lak and Sita also thanked Valmiki before the trio returned to their hut for the evening.

As Ram, Lak, and Sita were settling in and making a home in Valmiki's encampment, life back at the Apple palace in California was heading downhill fast.

Das Dies

When Suman landed back at Moffett Field he immediately went to Apple's palace in Silicon Valley. He met up with Das, who had become pale and emaciated. Kausha was with him, looking grim.

Suman told Das, "Ram, Lak, and Sita have now taken up permanent residence at an encampment in the jungles on the North Shore of Kauai. They are well and ask you not to grieve for them."

Das gulped and cried out, "Couldn't you convince them to return home?"

"No," Suman replied, "Ram was definite about remaining in the jungle. He said in no uncertain terms that upon my return I should relay to you that he wanted Barat to be installed immediately as the new CEO and that I and the rest of the Apple citizenry should respect and obey Barat's directions thereafter."

Das recovered his composure and asked Suman whether his flight back home went smoothly.

Suman replied, "The flight itself was fine. But my arrival here at the palace was unnerving. Everyone here is sullen and depressed."

Das relapsed into grief, crying, "I feel lost."

Then Kausha turned against Das and cried out, "Oh, Das, my husband, you were so famous for compassion and kindness. How could you thoughtlessly banish an innocent son? How will Ram, Lak, and Sita, who herself is little more than a child, survive in the jungle as ascetic geeks with matted hair?"

She became more angry as she spoke, shouting at Das, "And after returning, Ram will not assume the CEO position once Barat has made a mess of the company with his senseless policies. A tiger won't eat food brought by another animal. Ram has been ruined by his own father—it is as though a fish brooding eggs in his mouth had swallowed his young. I believe you can no longer tell right from wrong! You've ruined your whole kingdom, all from your lust for Kaila."

Das groaned and pleaded, "Please don't turn against me."

After a while, Kausha relented, saying, "Forgive me. I spoke from anguish." She went to Das, held him, and comforted him even while she cried uncontrollably.

And Das sobbed too, saying, "I'm reaping what I have sown."

Das was still crying as he recalled a story from his youth. "A long time ago, I was hunting deer in the gold country of the Sierra and I heard a sound. I was certain that it was the buck I had been scouting all day. I took a shot and heard a scream. I ran through the vegetation. To my horror I saw that I had shot a young man who was gathering food and water by a stream. He looked up at me and said, 'What have I done to you that you should shoot me? I'm harmless. I'm gathering food for my parents who live in a log cabin nearby. My parents are invalid and can't fend for themselves. They depend on me for their lives.' And the boy died."

Das continued, "I then searched and found the cabin where his parents lived and went to it. His parents heard me coming and the old man said, 'Oh, my son, how wonderfully you tend to our needs, bringing us food and water. We're so hungry and thirsty.' And I then said, 'Oh, sir, I'm not your son. I'm a hunter, and I've committed a great tragedy. I've shot and killed your son by mistake.'"

Pressing on, Das said, "The old man gulped, and I went on saying, 'Oh, please tell me what I can do now in any way to rectify my dreadful error.' Then the old man and his wife asked me to describe in detail how their son had come to die and what his last words were. The man then said, 'Take me to where his body lies.' And I did, and both of them caressed the body of their dead son, and shed tears on his face as his body lay on the ground. The old man then said to me, 'Gather my son and bring him back to the cabin.'"

Das rubbed his eyes as he continued his recollection. "So I gathered the boy in my arms and guided the old man and his wife back to the cabin. I laid the boy down upon a bed. The old man brought out a dog-eared copy of the Bible and read a funeral rite. The old man and his wife then settled themselves in their well-worn chairs and cried."

Then looking up, as though talking to the sky above, Das said, "After a while, the old man said, 'You have come to me in honesty to admit your error and ask forgiveness. So I will not press charges against you. Bring me some paper.' I then rustled around in the man's desk and found a pad of paper and a pen and brought them to him. He said, 'The sheriff is an old friend, and I will write him a letter.' The old man then scrawled out a note saying that I had killed his son by accident and that he had forgiven me and did not wish to press charges. He said the tragedy was not a crime and that the matter was to be forgotten. Knowing he and his wife were about to die, he asked the sheriff to arrange for the three of them to be buried together beside their cabin in the woods."

Das continued, "The old man then said to me, 'Perhaps some day you too will lose a son and will die of grief as my wife and I are both dying ourselves. We will now join our son in heaven.' With that the old man and his wife passed away."

After a pause, Das resumed by saying, "I trudged out of the woods and found the sheriff's office at the edge of the park. I told him what had happened and brought him to the cabin, where he read the old man's letter. The sheriff mulled the matter over and decided to honor the old man's wishes. He said I was free to go. I returned home deeply shaken by the experience. I followed up by sending a large anonymous donation to both the sheriff's and county prosecutor's reelection funds, as well as to the funeral home to cover the burial costs. I see now by awful coincidence that I too shall soon pass away in grief at the separation from my own sons."

Das gathered himself to say, "I must leave a message for Ram, Lak, and Sita to be played when they return. Take me to the hologram studio."

Kausha ushered Das to the studio. Das asked her to leave so he could dictate a message in private. When the recording was over, he called Kausha, who walked him back to his quarters.

After a while, Das uttered his final words, "This grief dries my vitality like a summer sun sucks water from the ground. Blessed are those who live to see Ram, Sita, and Lak when they return."

Kausha asked Das's permission to return for the evening to her palace in the redwoods. Das nodded approval and she drove home.

Then Das dozed off, exhausted, and died during the night.

Barat Returns

The next morning Kausha drove back from her palace to 1 Infinite Loop in Silicon Valley. She went to Das's quarters and discovered he had died. She called Sumitra on the voice line to break the sad news. Sumitra helicoptered from her home in Death Valley to the landing pad at Apple. Meanwhile, Kaila began to suspect that something was amiss, and she came from her quarters at the Apple palace to Das's bedroom.

When Kaila arrived, Kausha shouted to her, "You cruel bitch! Now your son assumes command of Apple, and you enjoy the glow of his power. I hope you're satisfied."

Vasis then entered Das's bedroom and took charge. He ushered Das's wives from the bedroom and called an undertaker to remove the body. Vasis directed the body to be embalmed and preserved for however long was needed for Barat to return and preside over the funeral.

As word of Das's death leaked, the citizens tweeted their despair. Apple's stock tanked. Widows and retirees tightened their belts, gave up morning coffee at Starbucks, and wondered if their homes would be foreclosed on or if their landlords would evict them. Citizens tweeted insults to Kaila demanding her banishment or even a painful death.

The next day, Vasis summoned the palace geeks to discuss the succession.

One of them said, "Obviously, we need to get Barat here immediately. The company needs a CEO now. Otherwise our engineering and marketing divisions will be at each other's throats, our efficiency will dissolve, our strategic vision will blur, and we'll all be out of jobs."

Another geek added, "And the stockholders will be outraged. They'll demand that management get its act together."

Vasis replied, "Yes, I agree completely. Let's bring Barat and Shat back immediately from Kush's palace in Bangalore. But I don't think we should tell them of the developments here. I hope they've been wrapped up in their own affairs and haven't been following our news here in California."

Suman then departed in the company jet for the long flight to Bangalore, where he landed at Kush's private runway. Kush's palace was a 650-foot skyscraper, comfortably taller than the palace once built by the oil magnate Mukesh Ambani in Mumbai.

After freshening up, he was ushered into the executive suite on the thirtieth floor, where Kush, Barat, and Shat were waiting.

Suman said to Kush, "Das asked me to convey to you in person how highly he regards you and how deeply thankful he is that his sons have married your daughters. However, he also sent me because of some decisions that need to be made in person concerning Apple. He would like Barat and Shat to accompany me as I fly back now to California."

Kush replied, "It's great to hear from my old friend, but I wonder what is so important."

Suman lied. "I don't know either. I'm just the hired help."

Barat and Shat glanced over at each other. Barat said, "I don't like the sound of this. Can you give us some clue as to what's going on?"

"Nope, that's beyond my pay grade," said Suman. "My orders are to take you back with me pronto. That's all."

"Well," said Kush, "then so be it."

Then to Barat and Shat he said, "Come back as soon as you're done. I'm sure I speak for my daughters when I say that your wives anxiously await your speedy and safe return."

Upon arriving back in California, the brothers went immediately to Das's executive suite at the Apple palace. They passed some of Apple's citizens on the way who looked despondent. Once at Das's suite, Barat saw an empty chair behind Das's desk. Kaila was sitting nearby on the couch next to a coffee table in the room.

Kaila rose and said, "Oh, my son, it's so wonderful to see you. I've missed you so much." She went and embraced him, and he hugged her in return.

She asked, "How was your flight?"

Barat replied, "Long, but okay. Anyway, where's my father? Why have I been summoned? What's going on?"

Kaila replied, "Your brilliant and loving father has just passed."

"What?" exclaimed Barat. "When did this happen, and why wasn't I contacted immediately? And where is Ram, my dear brother? Shouldn't he be here in that chair, preparing to assume the responsibilities he's been trained and groomed for? Can you call him here to join us? I want to ask him what to do next and how I can help him."

Kaila replied, "I cannot bring him here. He, along with Sita and Lak, have gone off to live for fourteen years as geeks in the jungles of the Pacific."

Barat was stunned. He said, "What? Is this some sort of joke? Tell me you're not serious."

Kaila replied, "It's true my son. It's true."

Barat replied, "But why? Not only do I return to face the tragedy of my father's death but to learn that I've been abandoned by two of my brothers. This is unbelievable. Again I ask, what's going on here? Did my brother somehow do something wrong?"

"No, no," Kaila replied, "Ram did nothing wrong. I asked your father to send him away. And after he did, your father died of grief, I'm sorry to say. He was not well in any case, and his death was not unexpected."

"But why do such a thing? Why ask Father to send Ram away? I don't get it," said Barat.

Kaila explained, "With Ram gone, now the deck is cleared for you to become the CEO of Apple."

Barat was shouting now. "What? Why would I want such a thing? I can't believe my ears. Ram is far better qualified than I for the role of CEO. He's a natural leader with a special bond to all of mankind. My skills are different than his. I'm a natural negotiator, not a leader. I was looking forward to assisting him someday in the tasks that I enjoy doing, that I'm prepared for and good at. Why did my father agree to your absurd request?"

Kaila then explained that Das had agreed on the night they first made love to give her two favors. She said that she had asked first for Das to arrange for Barat to be his successor and second for Ram to be sent far away, to the jungles of islands in the Pacific for fourteen years.

Kaila pleaded with her son, saying, "Don't be angry, my love—I've done this for you."

But Barat replied, "You must be mad. I can't possibly go along with this wild scheme. I want no part of it."

He continued, "Your explanation still doesn't make sense. I get how you were able to manipulate my father by calling in the promises he made to you, but why did you ask for these favors specifically? Why not ask for something else instead? Why this?"

Then Kaila went on to describe how Mantha assumed that Das was conspiring to deny Barat his rightful chance to become the CEO and was maneuvering to put Ram in charge of the Apple kingdom instead. She said, "So, I did this with your best interest at heart."

Barat shouted back, "You've been duped by that evil woman you consider your devoted assistant! She only wants this for herself. She thinks she'll indirectly benefit if she is the chief assistant to the mother of Apple's CEO. You fool. I'll have no part of this. You should have checked with me first to see if I wanted to be the CEO, if I wanted to be deprived of the companionship of my dear brother. You forget, we grew up together. We played on teams together. We take pleasure in cooperating with each other. Along with my other brothers, he's my best friend. I was looking forward to renewing the pleasure of working together once Apple became our responsibility."

Vasis was alerted to Barat's return. He called Kausha to let her know. She then drove down from her house in the redwoods. Vasis meanwhile went on to the executive suite himself to watch and to be of assistance, if needed.

Barat dragged a large chair from near the coffee table to face a window. He sat there sullen, staring out the window at the hills. Vasis didn't try to disturb him.

When Kausha arrived, she was dressed in a black outfit that set off her pale face, emphasizing its lines of grief.

Kausha strode up to Barat and said sarcastically, "Well, Mr. CEO, I hope you're happy now. Enjoy your power and don't worry about my son. Ram can take care of himself. I want to get out of here. My lovely house in the redwoods gives me no joy now. I want to find my son and join him in the jungle."

At that, Barat awoke from his melancholy daze. He rose to face Kausha, looked into her bloodshot eyes, and said softly, "This is not my doing. I didn't know anything about my father's death or my brother's banishment until now. I'm outraged. Please believe me. I had nothing to do with this. My love for you and my brothers is unbounded. I would never double-cross him. Please know that I am innocent in this whole affair."

Kausha returned Barat's gaze and saw the calm in his eyes. In her heart she always had trouble believing that Barat was aware of what was supposedly being done on his behalf. She said, "I'm sorry I spoke so bitterly. You don't deserve my anger, which should be reserved solely for your mother. Have you found out why she did all of this?"

"Yes," murmured Barat, "she was put up to it by Mantha, an evil woman if ever there was one."

"Ah!" said Kausha. "At last I see it all. Your mother is to be pitied. Sexy plus naive is a tragic combination."

Barat then said, "I know what I'll do. I'll go find Ram, wherever he is, and bring him back. I won't be party to this injustice. Perhaps I can undo some of the damage. I can't bring my father back to life, but I should be able to bring my brothers and Sita back home."

Vasis intervened to say, "Before you can leave to search for Ram, I'm sorry to tell you that you must attend to your father's funeral. There's no getting around it."

Barat groaned. "Vasis, what do you want me to do?"

Vasis said, "Here's what I recommend: your father should lie in state here at Apple tomorrow so people can pay their respects in person if they wish. Others can participate remotely over the web. We'll stream the service and provide interactive commentary. Tomorrow evening we can have the funeral service and a small reception afterward. Now I suggest you retire to a guest suite here, try to collect yourself, get some rest if you can, and be prepared mentally for the funeral service to come."

"Okay, I'll go to my room now. I know where it is. By tomorrow I'll be all right."

"Good," said Vasis, "I have faith in you."

Early the next evening Barat, Shat, and Das's three wives dressed in black and visited the rotunda at the Apple palace where Das's body lay attended by Vasis.

When Barat saw his father in the casket he blurted out to the corpse, "What will become of us now? Your vision, your initiative—I don't have those qualities. How can I possibly continue your legacy? If only you hadn't sent Ram away, then you'd still be alive and my dear brother would not be far away in some distant jungle. Couldn't you see what banishing Ram would lead to?"

And when Shat saw his father's body, he growled loudly. "Mantha has released a sea of grief. Where was my twin brother Lak? How could he stand by and let this happen? If I were here I would have stopped this outrage. I'm so furious I could strangle her."

Vasis pulled the brothers aside and whispered, "Get a grip. People are watching. We need you both to remain calm and respectful during the funeral service."

Then Vasis added, "The body is lifeless dust. A person is born of dust and returns to dust. A fool grieves for what can't be avoided. The wise understand that all living creatures die someday. Since the beginning of time this has been nature's cycle and will always be. Peace."

The funeral lasted from eight in the evening until midnight. Many spoke lovingly of the former CEO's accomplishments, how he inspired and, yes, sometimes cajoled and intimidated others to achieve more than they had thought possible. Das's sons recalled his love and support while they were growing up and how he taught them the pleasure of cooperation. Das's wives recalled his earnest charm and how he sustained their independent interests and activities. By the end of the service, everyone was exhausted from grief. The public who watched online tweeted a historic number of condolences to Das's family.

After the reception following the service, Barat and Shat were on their way back to the guest rooms with a security guard when they stumbled upon Mantha in one of the hallways. The guard grabbed and restrained her, then spat his words to the brothers, "This bitch is responsible for Ram's banishment and your father's death. Do with her what you will!"

The sight of Manta inflamed Shat. He hissed, "Ever since I heard what you did, I've wanted to tear the limbs from your body, one by one." He grabbed her and started dragging her down the corridor.

Mantha screamed and kicked, which brought Kaila running to see what was happening to her treasured assistant. Seeing Kaila, Shat also unleashed a barrage of insults at her.

But Barat intervened, saying, "Don't attack Mantha. And don't abuse my mother. Don't add our mistakes to theirs. If we demean these women, it won't restore our father to life. And Ram is sure to disapprove. We want him back. If we compound the errors of others with our own, we lose our moral authority to ask him to return once we find him."

Shat then released his grip on Mantha. She dropped to the floor, wailing. Kaila ran to Mantha to calm her. She reassured Mantha that she was safe. Barat's wisdom and calm demeanor reminded her of his brother Ram. Kaila remembered how kind Ram had always been. She wondered how she could ever have doubted her welfare under his management. Kaila knew Mantha had wrongly manipulated her. Although Kaila knew she would eventually forgive Mantha for her deviousness, she was pained to consider how grave the injustice was that she had inflicted on Ram.

Everyone then retired to their rooms for the evening.

Barat Seeks Ram

The next day Vasis polled Apple's board of directors and assembled Apple's principal geeks in the CEO's executive suite. He then went to Barat and asked him to join them for a meeting.

When they arrived at the suite, Vasis said, "On behalf of Apple's board of directors and principal geeks, we are all agreed that you should be Apple's next CEO. We'd like you to take control immediately now that your father's funeral is over."

Vasis then gestured to the head of the conference table and said, "Please assume your position there."

Barat replied, "No way. I decline. While Ram is alive I will never sit in that chair. It will remain empty. What I want to do now is fly to wherever Ram is and persuade him to return home."

Everyone was surprised but happy. One of the geeks asked, "Do you really think you have a chance of persuading Ram to come home?"

"I'm determined to," replied Barat.

At that, the assembled geeks murmured their approval. It was no secret they preferred Ram as their CEO and were accepting Barat as their next best option.

To the assembled group Barat said, "I would like to take a delegation from among you, along with my brother, my father's three wives, and Vasis."

And to Vasis he added, "Please have Suman ready our jet for the flight to Hawaii. We'll take a total of twelve people."

"Will do," Vasis replied.

The next day they flew to Kauai. Guh met them upon their arrival and bestowed a lei on each. Guh was suspicious. He looked for signs of weapons that might be packed in the luggage.

Barat asked, "Is it true that my brother Ram has come to this island? Did you assist him in getting settled?"

Guh replied, "I did meet him at the airport." Cautiously he added, "I don't know for sure if he found a place to settle or even if he's still on the island. Why, may I ask, are you looking for him?"

Barat replied, "I want to persuade him to reconsider. Although I've been asked to assume the CEO at Apple, I don't want to, and hope to convince Ram to return."

At hearing this, Guh was relieved, saying, "Well, okay then, I do think I can help you find him. I believe he's in the jungle on the North Shore among the Na Pali cliffs. I can bring you to the trailhead, but from there you're on your own. With so many of you, I'll have to enlist some extra drivers and cars."

After a few phone calls, a couple of other men showed up with their vehicles. The caravan containing everyone and their luggage then sped off to a hotel in Hanalei.

Guh said, "I'll send my cars in the morning to transport you to the trailhead. From there you should hike out to the encampment of Bhar, a chief jewelry-making geek. His encampment is at Hanakapi`ai Beach."

Then Guh added, "I think you should know, Ram matted his hair with sap from the banyan tree. During his time with Bhar, he and Sita and Lak all slept on the ground. They were getting themselves used to living close to the land and sea. They were clearly planning on staying here for the long term."

Barat sighed. "I hear you. You're telling me that bringing Ram back is a long shot. But I have to try anyway."

Guh closed by saying, "All right then, good luck."

And Barat responded, "Thank you for all your help."

After overnighting, the large party piled into the cars that Guh had sent. Once at the trailhead, they began to trudge along the trail in search of Bhar. When they reached Hanakapi`ai Beach, they paused and waited. They didn't see anyone. Meanwhile, Bhar and his fellow geeks had melded into the jungle to watch. They were wary of Barat and his party.

Vasis said to Barat, "I suspect Bhar is watching us from the jungle. He's casing us out before deciding whether to show himself. Let's go into the jungle and see if we can meet up with him."

Barat nodded, and together they started making their way into the jungle.

After they had gone about one hundred yards into the thicket, Bhar partially showed himself at the edge of the jungle.

Barat called out to him, "Sir, my name is Barat. I am the brother to Ram. I wonder if you could kindly tell me whether he has passed here. Would you know where I might find him?"

Bhar replied, "I know who you are. What brings you such a long way from your home, leaving your duties at Apple?"

Barat replied, "I've come to visit with Ram and entreat him to return with me back to Apple."

Bhar asked, "Why? Aren't you now the CEO? I've heard of your father's death and Ram's banishment. Surely you have all the power you need now. How can Ram be a threat to you now that he's so removed from your sphere?"

"But sir, you mistake my intentions," said Barat. "I wish my brother no harm. To the contrary, I want to persuade him to return and become the CEO himself. I don't want the job."

Hearing this, Bhar moved out of the shadows of the jungle and came right up to Barat. He stood face to face with Barat and looked him in the eye. Barat held his gaze.

After a while, Bhar said, "Okay, I believe you. You may camp here for the night before heading farther into the jungle to find Ram. In the meantime, we'll prepare a luau to welcome you to our island."

"Oh, that would be wonderful. But we've done nothing to deserve such an honor," said Barat.

Bhar replied, "You're an honest and generous man. That's enough."

At this, Bhar gestured to the men and women who were hiding in the foliage. They emerged, grinning and laughing. One said, "It's been a long time since our last luau, bro, and I'm hungry."

Several of the men went to their tents, picked up rifles, and then peeled off to head up the canyon. Other men dug a pit and started coals in the bottom. Some women harvested banana leaves, along with bananas, papayas, breadfruit, ti, and taro leaves from nearby ponds. Still others went to the beach to fish and harvest delicate seaweed.

Later everyone heard a gunshot, and some time thereafter the men marched back down the canyon supporting on their shoulders a wild boar tied to a pole.

One of them said, "This one here was caught in our traps, so all we had to do was collect it."

The men dressed the pig, seasoned it with salt, placed it in the pit over the coals, covered the pig with ti leaves, covered the whole assembly with earth, and then allowed the wild boar to cook for several hours.

After the pig was done, teams of men and women uncovered it. They drew out some meat and wrapped portions in taro leaves, which they let steam for several hours. Others took a tuna that had been caught offshore, cleaned it, and diced the fillets into bite-sized pieces, which they marinated in sesame oil with salt, sweet onions, and the delicate seaweed. Another team prepared desserts with coconut and banana.

Meanwhile, some other men hauled out some drums and prepared a space for dancing surrounded by logs for people to sit on. After the meal was prepared and everyone had eaten their fill, women and men danced the hula to the sound of drums, ukuleles, and slack-key guitars. The graceful shapes of the hula, with its hand gestures and gentle swaying, evoked the spirits of the wind, nature, love, and aloha.

Near midnight Barat approached Bhar and said, "Sir, this celebration is over the top, beyond what I could ever have dreamed possible here along a hiking trail to the Na Pali jungles. I'm so grateful, but also so undeserving. I wish to say, in your language, *mahalo.*"

Bhar replied, "*E komo mai*—you're welcome, come in to our encampment. You all may sleep here." He gestured to some spots where Barat and his group could pitch tents and settle down for the night.

The next morning Barat asked Bhar, "Again, I thank you so much for your hospitality. May I also inquire as to where I can find my brother?"

Bhar replied, "Follow the stream that runs through our encampment up the mountain until you reach a waterfall. There you will find Valmiki's encampment. Your brother Ram, his wife Sita, and Lak now live there."

Barat replied, "Thank you so much. We're off now and don't wish to delay."

At this point, Kausha and Sumitra also approached Bhar. Bhar said, "I'm honored to have met you at our luau last night." The women replied that the honor was theirs and thanked him for his hospitality.

Then Kaila approached Bhar too. Barat growled an introduction, "I regret to say this is Kaila, my mother, the person responsible for all the trouble we're now in—for my father's death, my brother's banishment, and the crisis that Apple now finds itself in. I can't stand her anymore."

Then Bhar admonished Barat, saying, "Do not disrespect your mother. It solves nothing. Be kind instead. Take aloha into your heart. It will bring you peace and happiness and eventually prosperity."

Hearing Bhar's admonishment, Barat felt chastised and remembered he had himself given the same advice to Shat. He stiffened his resolve to move beyond his current predicament.

Barat and his company then gathered their tents and supplies. They started trudging up the stream bed to find the encampment where Ram now lived with his wife and brother.

Ram Remains

Sita was content. She was overjoyed to be living with her husband near Hanakapi`ai Falls. She'd grown to love the sound of geckos chirping in the evening, the trade winds blowing through the jungle's canopy, the gurgling of the stream, the sight of whales spouting offshore, the occasional glimpse of a whale's tail fluke, and the subtle but real change of seasons as the North Pacific's wind and ocean circulation waxed and waned from winter to summer and back again.

She enjoyed Ram's attention. She found him more available than when they were living in the Apple palace. There, Ram always seemed preoccupied with Apple's affairs.

Despite the simple surroundings, Sita felt this time was the happiest of her life. She wished it would never end.

Ram too was happy, proud to have married such a beautiful and devoted wife, waking each morning carefree to enjoy nature's bounty of diversity and never-ceasing wonders.

One day Ram said to Sita, "Let's take our afternoon bath in the spring. I feel so free. Our life together now seems timeless."

As they bathed, Ram and Sita heard people clamoring up the path next to the stream. Ram called to Lak to ask him to investigate.

Lak scrambled up the nearby cliff to check out the noise. He called out in hushed tones, "Looks bad. I think I see Barat and some others making their way over here. I don't think it's safe to remain. I suspect he's come to do away with you somehow so you can't challenge his authority at Apple."

As Ram looked up at him, Lak continued, "But don't worry. I'll kill him rather than stand by while he harms either of you."

Ram replied, "Relax. I'm sure Barat wants me to return to Apple and take the responsibility off his hands. I doubt he wants the job. Anyway, I'm going to stay here. It would make no sense to renounce my vow. That would subvert both my reputation as well as Apple's."

At this, Lak cooled down somewhat. He also began to remember the good times he had with Barat as they were growing up. He said, "Okay. It may be premature to assume he's become a pawn to his mother."

The trio gathered their clothes and went to sit on the lanai at their house. They watched the trailside by the stream waiting for Barat and his company to arrive.

Barat came around a bend and burst into the clearing below the waterfall. He saw his brothers and Sita sitting on their porch at the side of the clearing and ran over to them.

He gasped, then said, "Oh, my dear brother, it's so wonderful to see you."

Ram rose and embraced his brother. "I'm so glad to see you too. What brings you here to the jungle to see me? How was your journey? You've come so far! And I see so many from Apple's court have accompanied you. What would lead you all make such a long trip?"

Before he could answer, Lak and Shat ran to join in and all four brothers embraced.

"I'm amazed at how you've taken to the local surroundings," Barat said. "That does not bode well for the request I've come so far to make. I see your matted hair, your homespun clothes, your healthy tan. I see Sita radiant, looking lean and fit. Still, will you consider what I have come to ask?"

"No harm in asking," replied Ram, "but before you do, let me ask, where is my father? Why would you come such a long way without him despite having brought so many others?"

Barat said, "Let me say first that I had no part in my mother's scheme to have me installed as CEO of Apple instead of you. She was wicked to ask my father to have you banished. The position is rightfully yours, not mine. Please come back with me and assume the position of CEO yourself. You're better qualified for it. It agrees with your natural talents, whereas I would enjoy assisting you in whatever negotiations you need carried out on Apple's behalf."

Ram rejoined, "But Barat, you are perfectly competent to carry out the CEO's duties, especially as advised by Vasis and the other skilled palace geeks. For me, I'm content to remain here for what's left of my term of fourteen years. I'm happy here—I really am. But where is my father? He can surely continue to help you as well?"

Barat replied, "I can see you haven't been wasting any time on the web and so you haven't heard. Our father has passed."

"What! How?" Ram asked.

Barat replied, "Well, you know he was in poor health. But frankly, what pushed him over the edge was his grief at your leaving. It's just tragic. What can I say? I'm devastated too. That's why I need you to return. I need your companionship, and Apple needs your guidance."

Ram said, "Let's not talk about this anymore. I need to tell Sita right away."

Ram then went to Sita and broke the news.

Sita burst into tears. Then she collected herself and said to Ram, "We must have a ceremony in his honor right away. We must bring this tragedy to closure somehow."

Ram said, "Yes."

He asked Lak to show Shat what a ti tree is and to gather some ti leaves. They returned, bringing some ti leaves and some banana leaves as well. Sita fashioned the leaves into the shape of a small boat. Ram, Sita, the brothers, and each person in Barat's group then placed a different token in the boat—a short homily on a piece of paper, a locket with a picture of Das, a US coin engraved with an old iPhone's image, a fragrant plumeria flower, a seed from a sweet sop fruit—and cast the boat off to travel downstream to the ocean. Ram said to everyone that they would observe an evening of silence in memory of his father. They would reconvene in the morning.

Barat and his group laid out their sleeping bags, some on the lanai of Ram and Sita's small house, some in pup tents that Lak and Shat pitched near the house.

Before turning in for the night, Barat sidled up to Vasis and whispered, "Tomorrow let's try our best to get Ram to return. Let's put all our arguments before him in a full court press."

Vasis nodded his approval.

The next morning after a breakfast of papayas with lemon and water from a spring-fed stream, Vasis and Barat approached Ram.

Barat began, "My brother, please consider again returning to Apple. As I've said, I don't want the job and would prefer to work with you as your negotiator. But more importantly, I can't do the job, I really can't. I can no more emulate your capabilities than a donkey can emulate a horse or a sparrow an eagle. Your not returning hurts the many people dependent on Apple. Remaining here is irresponsible, short-sighted, and, if you'll permit me to be frank, selfish."

Ram replied, "I hear you, brother, and in some respects I'd love to return to take the reins of the position for which I was training. That would be pleasant indeed. But no one is free simply to do whatever seems pleasant all the time. As I speak with you, I've come to feel you're still in grief and shock over our father's death. You're also resisting the burden placed on you by my banishment."

Ram continued, "Here's what I advise. Do not grieve for our father any more. Think of it this way. All gains end in loss, every meeting ends in separation, and all life ends in death. Death is our constant companion. It walks with us, sits with us, goes the distance when we travel, and eventually returns with us. The simple passage of time during our lives consumes our life spans as the summer sun sucks the water from a vernal pond. Oh, brother, grieve no more. Our father passed after a long, honorable, and productive life. Throw off grief. Let's now dedicate ourselves to continuing on his path. For your part, do his bidding and guide the Apple kingdom. For my part I shall remain here in the jungle until the fourteen years have expired. Under no circumstances should we jeopardize the integrity of Apple's leadership or undermine in any way the full faith and credit of Apple's commitments to its citizens, customers, or bondholders."

Barat replied, "And I hear you too and respect what you've said, but there are principles to consider beyond merely protecting Apple's good name. Were it not murder, I will have killed my mother for what she did. How did my father allow himself to fall under her sway? Whether from infatuation or just foolishness, our father acted wrongly in sending you away and anointing me as his successor. Isn't it also our duty to correct our father's mistake, his obvious injustice? Look at all the people who depend on Apple. Do you consider their welfare too? They will not prosper with my leadership as they would with yours. Nowhere is it your duty to cavort in the jungle while shirking your calling to serve as Apple's head."

Ram countered, "No, whatever the reason for our father's promise to your mother, a promise made is a promise to keep. In the long term, far more harm would come to Apple and the people dependent on it if I return now, even assuming, which I doubt, that I could manage the company better than you. You underestimate yourself. Moreover, the fundamental principle at stake is this: do nothing to subvert the full faith and credit of Apple's commitments to others. That's the ultimate principle I stand for."

Barat accepted what Ram said and remained silent. Then Vasis took his turn, saying, "Ram, please consider another argument for why you should return." He called forward a geek from the Randian sect of libertarians, disciples of the philosopher Ayn Rand.

The Randian said, "Alone we came into this world, and alone we shall leave it. Each of us should work to further his or her own individual interests. Then the collective welfare prospers from the sum of the prosperities of the individuals comprising the whole. You shouldn't suffer for a dead father who doesn't matter anymore. Take your CEO position and enjoy it. Doing so will further your own personal interest. And furthering one's own interest is, after all, the most that anyone can realistically accomplish in this world."

Ram sat down on a large rock to listen further. He looked unconvinced.

The Randian continued, "I feel sorry for those who become ascetic geeks, those you now try to emulate. Geeks live in discomfort, hoping for some spiritual inspiration in this life or even imagining a reward in some nonexistent later life. It's ridiculous. Geeks are nothing but the victims of sophisticated crooks who make a living preying on young idealists. They acquire cheap research for their own projects by conning the naive. Oh, Ram, please renounce this useless self-deprivation and return to civilization where you can become a job creator, where you can acquire wealth that will trickle down to the citizens of Apple, making them better off than they now are."

Ram then stood up, fire in his eyes, and said, "If I followed your path, then chaos would result. No one's word would be worth anything. Trust would disappear, and people would live their entire lives just to lie, cheat, and steal from one another."

Ram continued, "Personal gratification is not the path to happiness. In time our senses dull and the objects of our material lust break, become lost or obsolete. And so the quest for personal gratification becomes endless, never resulting in happiness. Go away, you idiot. Don't speak this way again. Misleading people so profoundly is a sin in my eyes."

Ram then calmed down and said, "My father was wedded to the truth. Following his instruction is the only path to happiness. I am remaining here for the fourteen years that he promised. That's final. Do you all understand?"

Barat wasn't done, however. He said to Ram, "I will stay here in your place. That will fulfill my father's vow."

"Oh, come on," said Ram. "You must be kidding. Obviously, my father's vow applies specifically to me and not to some arbitrary person who might wish to take my place or whom I could pay to do so."

At this Barat turned to all the people in his group who had accompanied him to Hanakapi'ai Falls. He said to them, "Will you all try to see if you can change his mind?"

But Vasis intervened, saying, "It's clearly a waste of time to try to change his mind. We'll only make him angry, and that will lessen the chance that he will actually come back even once the fourteen years are up. Let's leave the matter alone."

Everyone then stood to embrace Ram, Sita, and Lak prior to departing.

As Kaila was embracing Ram, she whispered to him, "I'm the cause of all this hardship. I am deeply sorry. Will you forgive me?"

Ram replied, "Yes, I do. Now please return to Apple and live there peacefully."

Hearing this, she gratefully joined up with Kausha and Sumitra for the hike back to the trailhead.

As Barat and Ram stood together for the final time, Barat asked Ram if he might have a worn pair of sandals as a symbol to remember the meeting. Ram went to his house, found an old pair that was about to be discarded, and brought them to Barat.

Barat said, "I will place these sandals in your chair in the executive conference room back at Apple as a constant reminder to all that I am not the permanent CEO of Apple but am serving only as your stand-in until your return."

Ram then said, "I'm confident you'll do just fine." They embraced and Barat joined the others for the trek back to the trailhead.

When the party reached the trailhead, they met up with Guh, who drove them to the airport. Suman had fueled the plane. They took off and returned to Silicon Valley.

The day after the group arrived back at the Apple palace, Barat went to the executive conference room. He placed Ram's sandals in the chair at the head of the table and placed a photographic portrait of Ram printed on canvas on the wall behind his chair. Thereafter, the chair remained empty while business was conducted in the room.

Barat was determined to live as an ascetic himself during Ram's absence. He moved into one of the guest suites, leaving the quarters for the CEO vacant until Ram's return. His wife, Manda, agreed to return to live with her father, Kush, in Bangalore until Ram and Sita's return from banishment.

Atri's Camp

Ram, Sita, and Lak continued enjoying their days together at their cabin in Valmiki's camp. They found themselves becoming familiar with the island's subtle seasons. At times the trade winds out of the northeast weakened or stopped altogether, giving way to winds from the south that brought warmer temperatures, higher humidity, and the possibility of rain. These southern "kona" winds also brought airborne soot from the erupting Kilauea volcano on the Big Island, Hawaii, creating a haze that islanders called "vog," short for volcanic fog. And in winter months the southern winds brought torrential downpours even as the weather stayed warm and fragrant.

The trio also spent time at Valmiki's campfire leaning history. And they accompanied the geeks of Valmiki's encampment into the fields to learn organic farming techniques. But as they stayed on, all three increasingly sensed tension. Valmiki's geeks began looking over their shoulders frequently and were wary of venturing away from the site of their camp in Hanakapi`ai Falls.

So one morning Ram approached Valmiki and asked, "I sense a growing fear among you all. Am I right about this? Is there a problem?"

He replied, "Yes, our group has become increasingly afraid."

"Why?" asked Ram. "Perhaps we can help."

"We hope so," replied Valmiki, "seeing that you are trained in martial arts, whereas we are have taken vows to avoid conflict and live lives devoted to thought and contemplation."

"Okay, so tell me, what is the problem?" Ram demanded.

Valmiki replied, "Ravan has two brothers, Khar and Dush, on this island. Khar runs a helicopter service for fat-cat tourists. He flies them illegally into the state park's remote hanging valleys for private picnics. They come with hoards of food and wine, plus guns and sometimes a band too. They wander along the trails shooting wild boar and goats, leaving their carcasses to rot while spreading litter everywhere."

Valmiki continued, "Now, I know of Ravan's animosity toward you. I know you eliminated some of his henchmen back in California. It makes sense that, since learning you're staying with us, Khar has been retaliating by guiding drunk trigger-happy tourists down from their partying and into the lands where we grow our crops. They've been destroying our gardens and wrecking our phone, Internet, and utilities infrastructure. They've been harassing us and even sexually harassing our women. We're increasingly terrorized. We're even thinking of leaving and finding somewhere else to pitch our encampment—say, over the mountain in Waimea Canyon or even somewhere on Maui or the Big Island."

Ram was deeply disappointed to hear this and said, "Okay, I can see the time has come for us to move on so that you can return to your activities in peace. Then I'll find Khar and put an end to this."

Valmiki replied, "We'll all be so sorry to see you leave. Thanks for staying with us. You and your wife will always be welcome to return. And thanks too for anything you can do about Khar. I believe you're likely to meet up with him if you stay in the area. I suggest you head back down the path by the stream until you hit Kalalau trail and turn left. Then you'll come to a series of beaches. You may meet Khar along the way or maybe sometime later. In any case, each of these beaches harbors an encampment of some sect of geeks and you'll be able to meet them and learn of their specialities as you did ours."

Ram replied, "On behalf of my wife and brother, thanks so much for your hospitality all these months we've stayed here with you."

When Ram returned to his cabin, he called Sita and Lak and said, "I'm sorry to say the time has come to move on."

"Why?" asked Sita. "I'm happy here."

Ram replied, "So am I, but there's a problem. Our presence is attracting harassment to the geeks here. It turns out that Ravan has a brother named Khar living on the island who runs a helicopter service and who brings drunken gun-toting tourists to areas where the encampment grows its food and has its infrastructure. We have to move on to allow our hosts to live in peace and get back to their work. So we really have no choice. If we move, we may encounter Khar on our own terms and then I can take him out. I was told he has another brother, Dush, on the island too. We might have to deal with him."

Lak nodded.

Ram continued, "And a side effect of moving on is that we can find a place more isolated so that visitors like Barat, however well intentioned, cannot stop by after what amounts to little more than a long day's hike. We need a place where we can't be as easily disturbed if we're really to disengage from Apple as pledged."

Sita nodded her reluctant approval. So Ram, Sita, and Lak gathered the possessions they could carry with them, including Ram's bow and Lak's machete, and started to move out.

As their friends from the encampment waved good-bye, they headed down the two-mile path from Hanakapi'ai Falls to Hanakapi'ai Beach and then turned left.

They hiked all day, fording streams, clamoring over rocks and around boulders. After nine difficult miles, the trio approached a beach with a signpost saying *Kalalau Beach.* As they sat down on a log to rest and drink some water, they felt eyes watching them. They caught glimpses of faces behind bushes in the forest and heard the pitter-patter of footsteps in the brush.

Eventually, a man emerged from the forest. He tentatively approached the trio and looked them over.

Ram stood up, saying, "Greetings. I'm Ram. This is my wife, Sita, and brother Lak. May we camp here for the night and then continue by kayak tomorrow morning? I promise we'll not inconvenience you."

The man replied, "I am Atri, chief of this encampment. Are you Ram, outcast from Apple in California? I've heard you might be coming our way."

"Yes, I am," replied Ram.

"Since you're not from around here, let me explain," said Atri. "Our encampment is different from those you've experienced until now. Hawaii has always had places where outcasts could live in peace. In the 1860s Saint Damien ministered to lepers on the island of Molokai. And right here at this beach, Jack London wrote of Koolau, who in the 1880s founded a small leper colony after he was denied the right to have his wife accompany him to Molokai. Today we continue this tradition of offering refuge to outcasts. We too are a colony of outcasts. And why, you are wondering, are we outcasts? Are we diseased? Do you have to worry when talking to us that you might catch something? No. We are not diseased. Our problem is this: we're not allowed to be human. Most of us are unnamed because we are banned from having proper names ourselves."

"I don't understand," said Ram. "Have you or your people committed some crime?"

"No," replied Atri, "we have committed no crimes, nor is there anything wrong with us in any way. So why, you ask, are we prevented from being considered human? Well, I'll tell you why. Because most of us have a fraction of our genomes that come from nonhuman animals, a fraction larger than the 10 percent allowed by the UN Convention of 2030 that defined what it means to be a human. I myself have 10.4 percent of my genome from animals. I was originally assigned as a nonhuman when born. I sued the hospital to reclassify me as a human because the UN Convention allows the decimal to be rounded down. The court ruled that my 10.4 percent could be rounded down to 10 percent and then, voila, I became human. Sounds arbitrary doesn't it? Oh, and do I sound somewhat embittered?"

Ram replied, "You sound no more embittered than I would be if I were in your place. How many, what should I say, 'folks' are living here with you?"

Atri replied, "At present, we're at two dozen. And what makes you think you couldn't be in our place? I sense that you have a few animal genes in you as well. I can clearly see the mandrill-blue in the patrician epaulettes inscribed in the skin on your shoulders."

"Well," said Ram, "I've been told that my birth was planned and my genome designed by Vasis, but I haven't been told the details. Perhaps I do have some animal genes in me. Do you know how to tell?"

Sita was listening. She knew the answer, but she didn't know that Ram had never been told.

Atri said, "Yes, we have the latest version of your own company's new product, the iGene, which is a pocket DNA sequencer. Let me scrape a few cells from the inside of your cheek, and we'll see."

So Ram opened his mouth and allowed Atri to scrape some cells with a tongue depressor. Atri placed the cells into a little chamber at the front of the iGene, closed the cover over the chamber, selected the options *Species Detect* and *Single Pass*, and then pressed the *Analyze* button.

Atri said, "This takes a long time if you want to know the identity and function of the specific genes it finds, but if we're just checking for species of origin, the results come in pretty fast with just a single pass."

Atri kept talking while a colored circle swirled on the iGene's screen to signify that it was analyzing. He continued, "We need this device because individuals keep coming to us not knowing if they are human or not. We need to be able to tell them right away what their situation is. If they're human but have been misclassified the way I was, we can advise them to challenge their classification and get their birth certificates changed. If they're not human, we can counsel them about how to fight the restrictive legislation used to persecute them. We advise them to join activist groups like the Nonhuman Rights Project. We also recommend allying with Greenpeace, which promotes conservation of all animals, and with the Humane Society, which promotes kindness to all animals—both these groups don't care if the animals they're protecting have some human genes as well."

The iGene beeped, the swirling colored circle disappeared, and the screen displayed: 89.1%: genus Homo unique; 10.1%: genera other Primate unique. (Choose multiple passes for more accuracy.)

"Hah," said Atri, "I guessed as much. You're 10.1 percent nonhuman primate. You're lucky, though. You would have been classified as nonhuman like I was if the hospital where you were born had not decided to round down. Many individuals here weren't so lucky. They've been scarred from years of litigation to get their status changed to human from nonhuman just because they were born with one decimal point more animal genes than the UN standard. So, just think, you could have been an outcast like us except for the luck of having a clerk who made out your birth certificate papers in your favor. Or maybe Vasis pulled some strings at the hospital to get you classified as human." Nearly touching his thumb to his index finger, he added, "You're this close to having had to live here as refugee yourself."

Ram took a deep breath, and Sita came over to comfort him. She said, "I've known this all along, and I chose to marry you anyway. It doesn't matter. Use your talents for the betterment of all, including the folks here, whatever their status."

"But how could this have happened? Did Vasis make a mistake?" Ram wondered aloud.

Sita answered, "I learned in college that these genetic engineering techniques are not exact. It seems to me that it would be very hard to get the genome mixtures perfectly right on some number like 10 percent. And also, Vasis was working with genetic data from years ago, when you were conceived, whereas the iGene is working with today's genetic data. If some of the genes that were thought be uniquely human back then are now known to be in animals too, then the uniquely human fraction of the genome drops and the animal fraction automatically goes up. That could account for the extra 0.1 percent beyond what Vasis planned. Anyway, as I already said, it doesn't matter."

Ram replied, "Thanks, Sita, that helps. I'm glad you were a bio major instead of a computer jock like me. Still, this revelation means I have much to discover about myself. What does this genetic link with other primates say about me? Because of this, do I have some special abilities or special liabilities? I wonder." Ram fell quiet, lost in his thoughts.

Sita then turned to Atri and defended Ram, saying, "You've been hard on my husband. He's done you no wrong. Now please let us rest."

At hearing this, Atri relented, saying, "I'm sorry. I didn't mean to be rude. Please stay the night with us, share our food, and meet the folks who live here. When you're ready, come and join us at the conversation pit."

Atri led them to a flat area protected from the wind, where Lak then pitched their tents.

Like Valmiki's history encampment, Atri's had a "campfire" circle lit by colorful luminescent plants.

Atri introduced Sita to his wife, Anasuya. They went off to sit together. Anasuya asked Sita, "Would you like to meet the other members of our encampment?" Sita replied, "Yes, of course, I'd love to. I wish to hear their stories."

The encampment members were shy and wary, but Sita looked non-threatening, and they gradually came out from the shadows of the forest to sit with the two women.

Anasuya said, "Let me introduce you to Number One, the first resident to join us."

Sita said, "I'm glad to meet you. You look lovely."

Number One replied, "Thank you, I am 15 percent feline. Like a cat, I keep my own company. I'm rather solitary. And I'm very quick. I can snatch a bird barehanded, and I can detect something moving in the bushes long before anyone else here can. And you should hear me purr when I'm happy. If you look closely, you'll see a thin layer of golden down covering my body, which makes my presence shimmer in the right light."

"Very nice," said Sita. "And why, if I may ask, are you called Number One and not by some other name more appropriate to a beautiful woman?"

"Because," said Number One, "I am not human. My animal fraction is too large to be rounded down to 10 percent like Atri. So I'm stuck being an animal. As an animal I have no rights, no rights at all."

Her voice began to rise as she continued, "I have no right to a name of my own, I have no right to freedom, or to own property. Instead, I am property myself. I can be bought and sold as someone's pet. I could even be legally bought and sold as a sex slave to breed, provided my owner fed me and did not physically mistreat me in ways forbidden by the laws banning cruelty to animals."

Sita replied, "I sense the injustice you experience. As I reflect on what you've told me, I feel myself becoming outraged. Thank you for your story, I'm honored and enriched to meet you."

Anasuya then said, "Now let me introduce you to Number Two, the second resident to join our encampment."

Number Two kissed, almost licked, Sita's hand and said, "I am 15 percent canine, and like a dog I'm gregarious. I love team sports, especially playing wide-receiver in our games of touch football and catcher in baseball. I love to play. I love to flop around and just lie down in any old place and read a book. I can also detect whenever anyone is coming down the trail to our encampment and warn the others to hide. And I can smell. I can identify each resident here by their unique smell. I can even tell their mood by their smell. And I can shout louder than any other resident. I possess lots of talents that a human doesn't have. And yet, like Number One, I can't use my talents for anything productive."

Sita said, "I'm honored and excited to meet you too. I can see your extraordinary energy. Now tell me, why can't you put your talents to a productive use?"

"Because," replied Number Two as he raised his voice, "being an animal and not a person, I can't enter into a legal contract. I can't be an employee or an employer either. I can't get a social security number. I can't pay taxes. I can't serve in the military except as a pet, or a service dog, or a guard dog. I'm condemned not only to be someone's property but also to be dependent on humans. I'm condemned to live on human welfare and prohibited from taking a job on my own. So I'm stuck being a drain on society, living off its largess, rather than taking a productive place in it myself."

Sita replied, "I hear what you're saying. The situation seems not only unjust but stupidly inefficient as well."

Anasuya added, "Most residents have primarily feline or canine genes in them. Their genomes were synthesized with genes from their parent's favorite pets. Their parents were hoping to get the best of both worlds—a son or daughter endowed with the lovable personality traits of their favorite pet. But because they went to a bargain genome synthesizer, the fractions weren't accurate and the parents wound up with the worst of both worlds. What they thought would be their son or daughter wound up being classified as a domestic animal."

Sita turned to Anasuya and asked, "You've studied this injustice during your time here. What is preventing the UN from widening the standard for personhood to allow 15 percent nonhuman genes instead of only 10 percent?"

Anasuya answered, "Well, I'm not really in favor of that because that wouldn't solve the problem. The problem lies with having any arbitrary cutoff, wherever it's put."

Sita asked, "What would you recommend, then?"

Anasuya replied, "I think the criterion for personhood should be the ability and willingness to participate in moral dialogue, to be able to discuss with others what is right and wrong and to act accordingly. Here, all our so-called nonhuman residents are articulate and well read. It's easy to see them as part of the human family. Those abilities might seem to be enough. But what I'm saying goes beyond that."

Anasuya continued, "I'm saying that even animals we can't yet converse with should be considered human too once we learn to talk with them. The animals all around us are talking all the time. Just listen to all the birds around here calling to one another. If only we could join their conversations. Then we could discuss with them what is right and wrong. We might not agree, of course, and in fact probably wouldn't agree much of the time. But at least we'd be conversing, which would create an enlarged moral community. That's what I think!" said Anasuya emphatically and added, "End of speech."

Sita replied, "Yes, I think that's a fabulous vision. I agree it would be better to define personhood on the basis of participating in a moral community rather than on the basis of some arbitrary genetic cutoff rule. I'll speak to Ram about this. Maybe something can be done."

Anasuya then spoke to the other residents that had gathered around them and asked, "Should we decorate Sita with one of our special leis to honor her visiting with us and hearing our stories?'

The group shouted, "Yes," and someone handed Anasuya a lei of colorful shells that she bestowed on Sita.

Sita stood up, saying, "I'm overjoyed with this. I feel so at home here. Before I was adopted by my parents, I lived among the furrows of fields back in Nubian Sudan where I was born. I was a daughter of the earth. I was outcast there as the illegitimate offspring of a chieftain and a girl from a different village. In Seattle where I grew up and went to college, I was always an outlier, a speck of black on sheet of white. I've had to deal with questions not about my genome but about my abilities. And it wasn't too long ago that my peoples were considered property too. So thank you for your welcome."

Anasuya replied, "And we are honored to have you among us. And by the way, you look stunningly beautiful in that lei of shells."

The women then joined the men at the "campfire." Atri hosted the meal. At the end he mentioned to Ram that his encampment was being harassed by Khar and his rowdy clients.

Atri continued, "Ram, although our residents are refugees, they are also geeks. Like other geeks we too have vowed to avoid physical conflict and strive to live in contemplation. Like the other encampments on the island, we ask your protection, and indeed all geeks depend on society's protection even as a fetus is protected by its mother."

Ram said, "Don't worry, I'll get Khar—it's a matter of when, not if."

At this, Atri said, "Mahalo, and now it's time for sleep."

The next morning Atri briefed the trio on how to proceed, explaining that the remaining beaches along the Na Pali cliffs were only accessible via water. He said the next beach toward the left was very close, so close that in good weather, a boat was not required—it could be reached by an experienced swimmer.

Lak went ahead and unpacked the inflatable kayaks as Atri spoke. Lak then loaded most of the gear into one of the kayaks, pushed it ashore, and jumped in. Ram and Sita climbed into the other kayak (a two-person model) with the remaining gear. The trio began paddling off from Kalalau Beach on the short journey to the next beach.

Sarab's Camp

As soon as Ram, Sita, and Lak rounded some huge boulders extending into the ocean at the left edge of Kalalau beach, a canoe darted out in front of them, blocking their route.

A muscular 300-pound man with gangland tattoos on his bulging biceps sat in the canoe. He demanded, "Who are you?"

Lak growled back, "Who wants to know?"

"I'm Virad," the man, seemingly a human monster, declared, adding, "Anyone who goes here pays protection."

"And what if we don't?" replied Lak.

"Then I'll club you and sink your boat. Have you heard of tourists who've gone kayaking and mysteriously never returned?"

Ram nodded.

Virad continued, "That's me. If only they'd paid up, they'd still be alive. Now, who are you? You're dressed like geeks. But you've got attitude, and you send out a physicality that geeks don't have."

Lak replied, "I am Lak, and this is Ram and his wife, Sita. We are sons of Das from Apple. Now get out of our way."

"Well, I'll bet you're worth a pretty penny. And I like your chickie here. So here's my price: ten million plus the woman and I'll let you live. I'll give you an account to wire the money to. I'll hang on to the chickie for a month while the funds clear. Then you can come back and collect her—that is, if she'll have anything to do with you wimps."

Lak was starting to seethe. "I don't think so, big boy. Get lost."

Virad grabbed for Sita and pulled her into his canoe. Ram recoiled, seemingly intimidated.

Lak said to Ram, "Why are you holding back? You can take him. If not, I'll kill him myself. I'm overdue for a fight. I thought I'd have one with Barat, but that ended peaceably. I'd like to mix it up with this idiot."

Meanwhile, Virad again spoke to the brothers, saying, "You still haven't told me why you're here."

Ram replied, "We agreed to leave Apple and live in the forest for fourteen years to honor my father's word."

Virad retorted, "You sound like obnoxious goodie-goodies. Go away. I'm going to enjoy your chickie for myself."

Ram finally lost his temper. He reached for his bow and fired an arrow directly into Virad's breast. Virad fell back, releasing Sita from his grasp. Then Lak jumped onto Virad's kayak and hacked at him with his machete.

At this point, Virad said, "Enough. I'm ready to die. I deserve it. Wanna know how I got here?"

Ram motioned Lak to stop slashing Lak.

"Speak up," said Ram.

"I'm cursed because of my crimes. I embezzled money from JPMorgan Chase, where I used to work—they're a sect that worships the god of wealth. I then killed my accomplice to avoid being caught. If I'm found, I'll die for premeditated murder. And that's not even counting the tourists I've drowned. So, kill me now—just bury me alive by the rocks over there," he said, pointing to a beach where they could land.

Virad continued, "That's Honopu Beach. Being buried there is a better way to die than by the electric chair."

"Are you sure?" asked Ram.

"Yes," Virad said.

Virad added, "After I'm buried, continue past the arch you see there in the middle of the beach. On the other side of the arch you'll find Sarab's encampment, and Sarab will treat you right."

So Lak guided Virad's canoe to shore, and Ram jumped into Lak's kayak and followed. Sita paddled the remaining kayak to shore as well. Once on shore the brothers dug a pit with their camp shovels and rolled Virad into it. After the brothers backfilled the grave with dirt, Virad suffocated for his past sins.

Following this incident, the trio finally had time to survey their surroundings. They saw steep cliffs over 1,000 feet in height lining the beach where they had landed. They saw an archway in the middle of the beach that opened up onto another beach nearby.

Rather than carry their kayaks and gear through the arch, they returned to their kayaks on the beach, pushed away from shore, and paddled around the huge rock that contained the arch.

The day was gorgeous. The trio saw seabirds flying over the ocean. They saw boobies, albatrosses, frigate birds, tropicbirds and the nene goose. And they saw the spouts of humpback whales and dolphins playing in the ocean. They saw marine turtles break the surface to take a breath.

Ram said to the others, "You see here the grandeur of creation. We are blessed to be alive." Both Lak and Sita nodded agreeably.

After about thirty minutes, the trio pulled up to the beach on the other side of the arch. An elderly person dressed in a skirt with a lovely shell lei necklace and black pearl earrings came out to meet them.

In a husky voice, the person said, "Welcome to Honopu beach. I am Sarab, the leader of the encampment here."

"Thank you," said Ram.

Sarab continued, "I know who you are, and I know you've just come from Atri's refugee encampment. We too are refugees. We have much in common with our close neighbors. You see, we are mahu, the ancient Hawaiian name for gender-variant people. Mahu live throughout Polynesia. Our counterparts live throughout south Asia as well as in the Americas. We are a refugee encampment for those persecuted for their gender expression or sexual orientation."

Ram said, "We're glad to meet you. We hope to get to know you better. If it's okay with you, we'd like to stay the night. Tomorrow we'll press on, looking for a permanent place to live until our time in the forest has ended."

"Yes," replied Sarab, "you're welcome to stay here. We're honored to have you."

The trio pulled their kayaks up high on the shore. Lak grabbed the tents and pitched them while Ram and Sita unloaded the rest of the gear.

Once settled, the trio wandered to the "campfire." There Sarab said, "Let me introduce you to some of our people. I'm a mahuwahine, which you can translate as a male to female transgender woman."

Other residents had lined up to shake hands with the visitors. As Ram moved down the receiving line, Sarab whispered in his ear a sentence about the background of each: "He is mahukane, a female to male transgender Hawaiian. And here is someone from India, a hijra, roughly translated as male to female transgender woman. Next we have another person from India, a kothi, a gay man who prefers the bottom or passive position in sex. And here we have someone from Thailand, a kathoey, who is a feminine boy. Next is a waria, a male to female transgender woman from Muslim Indonesia. And here is someone from North America, a Native American from the Crow nation who is two-spirited, similar to the mahuwahine of Hawaii. And now we come to someone from Central America, from the Zapotec culture of Oaxaca in southern Mexico, who is a vestida, also similar to the persons you've just met from Thailand and Indonesia. And here are some transgender women from New Zealand, and here is another from the U.S. We are the beautiful rainbow of humanity."

Ram paused from shaking hands. He asked Sarab, "How many people do you have here in your encampment? And how many countries are represented?"

Sarab replied, "At any one time we have about two dozen people staying with us. They don't stay long. They come to heal and then head back to their home countries to carry on there. Most have been disowned by their parents, spouses, and children, or have been castigated by priests, ministers, rabbis, imams, or bishops, not to mention politicians, police, and teachers, what have you—always people who use their authority to hurt others. But we have it easy compared to our brethren next door at Atri's refuge. Our people are all classified as human, so all of us can appeal to laws and ethics that guarantee our human rights when fighting discrimination against us. But our experience does give us a special empathy for our brethren next door."

Ram pressed, "How many countries do your residents come from?"

Sarab replied, "In the years I've been here, we've had residents from nearly every country in the world—I can't remember offhand. And even different regions of the same country—India, Mexico, or the U.S., for example—have their own names for the people who in some way cross genders or depart from strict heterosexuality."

"In my opinion," added Sarab, "the heterosexual gender binary is a myth. I don't know how the myth got started, but I clearly see throughout all of today's humanity worldwide—as well as in my readings in history—that a large fraction of the population doesn't fit into heterosexual male-female boxes and never has."

Ram asked, "What fraction?"

Sarab replied, "Well, at least 10 percent, probably more."

Ram then said, "Living near San Francisco, I've of course seen pictures of the gay pride parade there. I've have occasionally met someone who was gay, but my contact with your people is limited. Have I been missing something?"

Sarab replied, "Yes, you have. Did you know that your trusted advisor back at Apple, Vasis, is gay?"

Ram was taken aback. "No, that's news to me. I'm embarrassed I didn't know this. I should have noticed."

Sarab continued, "And not only that, did you know that one of your predecessors from Apple, Tim Cook, the CEO who succeeded your founder, Steve Jobs, was gay too?" Ram said, "No, I didn't know that either."

Sarab continued, "And the founder of computer science, Alan Turing, was too."

Ram sighed, "I see I've not given this matter much thought."

Sarab replied, "Most people haven't."

Sarab then added, "But what I wanted to say most is that we'll be happy to help should you need some people-power in whatever projects you dream up while living here in the forest. All of the encampments here keep in touch and help each other out."

Ram replied, "Thanks for the offer. I suspect we'll likely take you up on it. In the meantime, we're tired and need to turn in for the evening."

Sarab said, "I know you're tired, but how about a bite to eat first? We have our own eating area that we call 'home.' That way at evening time we can say to one another, 'It's time for dinner at home,' and then we all gather together at the tables as one big family. That eases the pain for those who were kicked out of their original homes by their families and had to live on the streets for a while."

"We'd love to join your meal. Honestly, we're pretty hungry," said Ram as Lak and Sita nodded enthusiastically.

After the meal Sarab said, "When you continue your kayaking tomorrow, the next beach you'll come to is Nualolo, where Sutik lives. Please give him my regards."

"Sure, I promise," replied Ram.

As the trio stood up and started to leave the eating area, some geeks from the encampment surrounded them and whispered to Ram in an air of desperation, "Oh, please do what you can about Ravan and his thugs. They have terrorized us too, along with everybody else around here."

Ram replied, "As I said to Atri next door, it's only a matter of time until we meet up and take them out"

Sarab then said, "I'm relieved. Though I'm getting on in years, I hope to see the day when Ravan and his thugs are defeated."

Sita saw someone from the encampment hanging back, not sharing in Sarab's evident relief. Sita walked up to a tall woman with strongly defined features and a husky voice.

Sita grasped her hand and asked under her breath, "Is there anything amiss? Is there anything you want to say to me privately?"

"Oh, yes," the woman whispered back. "I am always so upset, always on the verge of tears. I've enjoyed Sarab's hospitality for two years, but I still can't seem to break through my gloom. I once had a family—a wife and two children, a son and daughter. I once had a career and the respect in my profession. And then I transitioned. I just had to. I thought I was living a lie. I looked like a male, and I was given male privilege. I was admitted to clubs, smoked cigars, and sipped single malt scotch. But I couldn't stand it. I kept fighting the urge to transition. It was so irrational, and I was a rational being. But I had to give in—I just had to. I couldn't suppress the need to transition. It was on my mind 24/7. I was snapping at people, holding myself in check, hoping to rely on my self-discipline. I was drinking too much, too much of that single malt scotch I was so entitled to. Am I running on too long? Am I boring you?"

Sita squeezed her hand and said, "No, no, it's fine, you can talk to me."

The woman continued, whispering, "I thought I could manage my transition, the way I had managed so much else in my life. I thought I could make all the preparations, pave the way with endorsements, count on my abilities, and take ownership of my achievements. But I was wrong. Like everyone else who'd gone before me, brimming with confidence at the start, only to suffer despair in the end. There is no meritocracy. When you come out as transgendered, you're branded for life. No matter what you accomplish, that becomes your identity—you give up being known for what you achieve. It doesn't matter anymore."

The woman inhaled deeply and continued through her tears, "And then there's my family. I tried so hard to do the right thing by them. I raised my children the best I could, providing for them, sticking with them if they got into trouble, trying to be a role model for the rewards of hard work. Now they speak to me no more, are embarrassed to acknowledge my existence, refuse to invite me to their weddings, and don't call on my birthday. I tried to be a good person—I was a good person—I am a good person…"

Sita suggested, "Maybe your family felt you had rejected them, abandoned them when you came out as trans."

The woman replied, "Yes, maybe so. Everyday I grieve the hurt I have caused others."

The woman's voice trailed off, and Sita held her in an embrace. The woman then said, "And all I wanted was a job and respect. I wanted to belong—I wanted to work…" And again her voice trailed off.

Yet she continued, "And one night as I finished up on the graveyard shift in a call center—the only job I could get—I was robbed, kicked, and beaten on my way home. The thugs called me a slut, they squeezed my breasts, they grabbed the lipstick from my purse and wrote fag on my face, and left me in the roadside gutter. A passerby dialed 911. When the cops finally came, they just laughed. I don't know what to do next…"

The woman tried but failed to suppress her sobbing, and the sound caught Sarab's attention. The woman said to Sita, "I just don't know how I can go on."

At this Sarab jumped in and asserted, "Don't ever say that—not now, not never. You're doing fine. It's slow, but it gets better. The friends that have left you, well, that makes room for others."

And Sita said, "Yes, I am your friend. Now and forever. You must come and visit someday. You're always welcome to contact me. Here, let me take a photo of us, and I will send it from my direct number where you can always reach me."

Sita took a selfie with the woman and asked her to key in her phone number. With her number dialed in, Sita sent the photo to her.

The woman stopped crying and whispered to Sita, "Oh, thank you so much. You have saved my life."

Sita replied, "Call me when you need me. Be well. Now I have to go to bed. It's quite late."

"Yes, of course," said the woman. "I'm so sorry."

Sita replied, "Don't be sorry. Now let's get some sleep. This has been emotionally draining."

The woman nodded, Sita pressed her hand, and they went their separate ways—Sita to her sleeping bag, and the woman back to the encampment.

The next morning the trio awoke to the sight of the encampment's residents all gathered around Sarab's cabin. He was not well and had nearly died during the night. Relieved at Sarab's recovery, the trio folded their tents, gathered their items, and quietly piled into their kayaks. Then they respectfully bid good-bye to some residents who saw them about to leave, and quietly paddled out to sea, whereupon they turned left to continue along the Na Pali coast.

Sutik's Camp

The trio paddled on along the coast. Over the next mile and a half they saw waves crashing against the walls of sea caves at the base of cliffs that bordered the ocean. They paddled as close to the cliffs as the surf would allow. Along the way they entered a cave with light shining up from below, making a grotto. Cormorants and other seabirds lined cavities on the cave's walls. Lak whistled in appreciation of the beauty they were seeing as they continued along the coast.

After a half a mile more, they passed a narrow inlet with a small rocky beach abutting some low cliffs. Flocks of seabirds flew overhead. Ram, Sita, and Lak could see nests in the cliff walls. They paddled closer to the beach but could find no sign of human encampment, so they paddled back out to sea.

Before continuing along the coast, Lak looked back at the inlet and said, "I wonder what's beyond those low cliffs. Maybe a valley."

Ram looked back too and said, "Yes, that must be a hanging valley that just ends as a low cliff rather than as a gradual descent to sea level. Lots of birds seem to be flying out of the valley too. Maybe we'll come back someday to explore."

After another mile they came to a large sandy beach fronted by a coral reef. As they headed toward shore through a passage in the middle of the reef, they saw a sign saying *Nualolo*. Some people had gathered along the shore.

As the trio beached their two kayaks, a man walked up to greet them and said, "I am Sutik. Welcome to our encampment. We are a sect of geeks specializing in robotics."

Ram introduced the trio and then said, "Please forgive my asking, but this seems an unlikely place for the study of robotics."

Sutik replied, "I know it seems unlikely, but isolation from commercial pressures allows us to resolve the boundary between humans and machines for its own sake, without needing to generate a marketable product. That may come someday, but here we concentrate on how to endow a robot with human capabilities and deciding which capabilities it's useful to endow them with."

Ram asked, "Do you plan to make robotic humans?"

Sutik answered, "Our robots aren't humans, and we don't aspire to make humans with robotic technology. We'll leave the question of synthesizing humans to the bio geeks who are into cloning and tissue engineering. What we want to do is to make better machines—machines that are human friendly, that are endowed with just the right human capabilities to make them more useful to us."

"I see," said Ram, "but how do you fabricate your robots? I don't see any machine shops here."

Sutik replied, "No, we don't have machine shops, but we do have a solar-powered 3-D printer when we have to actually make something. Many of our robots are just software creations. They are computer programs that interact with one another. We write these interacting programs to explore algorithms for robotic learning. Our software robots discover the environment we program them to live in, and they go on to learn how to socialize with other software robots. On a computer you can actually watch software individuals learn to talk with one another, and learn to form software societies with one another, complete with self-government and other institutions that mimic how human societies have developed through history."

Ram pressed on, saying, "But don't you need a physical robot sometimes to test your algorithms?"

Sutik replied, "Yes, sometimes, and that's where the 3-D printer comes in handy. It's not only solar powered, it uses sand from the beach as its raw material and extrudes glass. Our robots are made of glass, not metal, but that doesn't matter. If we want them to have a certain look or feel we can always paint them or glue artificial fur on them. Also we use facial rubber—frubber, designed by the great robotics geek, David Hansom, to create a realistic skin complexion. But we usually don't bother with that because we don't need our robots to look particularly human. Still, if the robot's color or coating is important to its functionality, we'll do something about it."

Sutik added, "And we've based the software for our robots on ROS, an open-source modular operating system for robots that's based on the decades-old Ubuntu Linux. The library of contributed modules has grown to include thousands of modules that manage how a robot describes and discovers the geometry of its environment and how it navigates through that environment. It's wonderful what the community of robotics researchers has compiled over the years. And all from the power of open collaboration."

Ram replied, "I'm amazed. This is absolutely the last thing I'd expect out here on a tropical island on a beach that can only be reached by kayak. But here you are."

Sutik continued, "Yes, here we are, and we're thriving. And our encampment is quite large too. I'll take you around. We have a lot of space here bounded by those steep cliffs. You can see around the edges of our encampment."

"Great. Can can we spend the night before moving on along the coast?" asked Ram.

"Sure," Sutik replied, "and after you've pitched your tents and unloaded your gear, I'll take you for a tour before joining us for dinner."

"Wonderful," Ram replied, "we're grateful for your hospitality."

The trio pulled their kayaks up onshore away from the waves. Then they looked around. They saw easily accessible coral reefs right off the shore that would make for great spearfishing. Then they noticed a gigantic letter X scratched into the walls of one the cliffs.

Lak said, "I wonder if that was made by the ancient Hawaiians."

Ram replied, "We'll find out from Sutik shortly."

The trio then pitched their tents near the edge of one of the cliffs.

The trio met up with Sutik before dinner, and he guided them around the compound. The trio had by now discerned elements common to all the encampments they had visited—Internet infrastructure, luminescent plants, a central meeting pit for the nightly campfire, freshwater from a mountain stream, recycling and compost facilities, and so forth. This encampment had, in addition to such features, a cabin dedicated to robot fabrication where the 3-D printers were housed. Sutik took them in to see the fabrications.

Sutik pointed to some parts that looked like human arms and legs, human torsos, and human heads, both female and male.

He said, "Our current big project is to make robots who can communicate with emotive gestures. We've pretty much mastered the ability to make our robots speak convincingly in several languages. They can match the inflection of native speakers as well as use native-speaking idioms and slang. By listening carefully, the robots train their neural networks to become native speakers just like a baby learns a native language while growing up. But the effect with our robots still comes off as mechanical even though the voice itself can sound perfectly realistic. So we're now working on giving our robots the ability to have physical gestures—to communicate with body English, not just spoken English. I'll now take you to a part of our encampment where we're hoping to showcase the body-English abilities of our robots."

Sutik walked the trio over to the cliffs near the back of the compound and underneath the big X inscribed on the cliff wall.

Sutik said, "Our near-term goal is to program our robots so that they can perform traditional Native Hawaiian hula dances here. As a working assumption, we assume that if we can produce robots who can dance expressively, we're on our way to producing robots who can also gesture expressively and not rely solely on correct enunciation to convey their meaning."

Sutik pointed to what seemed to be relics of rock walls. He explained, "These are the foundations of what was once a multilevel temple, what the Native Hawaiians call a heiau. We'll have our robot dancers perform hula on the lowest platform of the heiau, with the upper levels and cliff as a backdrop. We feel this would honor the traditional use of this area."

Sita then spoke up to say, "This is fascinating. Do you plan to use this knowledge in some way?"

Ram added, "Say, in a product of some sort?"

Sutik replied, "Generally speaking, the robotics profession needs to make commercial robots that are more convincing. Say that we develop a robot with a heat sensor and we use it to monitor for fire. Suppose a fire starts and the robot warns people to leave. But there's always someone who doesn't want to leave, who wants to stay and retrieve some possessions. Well, we want the robot to convince that person they will die or be seriously injured if they stay. We want the fire-monitoring robot to persuade the person to actually leave the danger area and seek safety instead. It's not enough for a robot just to speak words—the robot will also need gestures, intonation, and body language to be convincing and effective."

Sutik then asked, "Would you like to see our progress so far in making our robots dance the hula? Though you'll have to promise not to be too critical, as this is a work in progress."

"Sure, we'd love to," said Sita as Ram and Lak nodded agreement.

"Each night before dinner," said Sutik, "we review the day's progress. It only takes about ten minutes or so."

As Sutik was speaking, several members of the encampment hauled a cart containing three robots to the edge of the heiau.

As the robots were being unloaded, Sutik explained, "We'll demonstrate a dance set where the three robots move in unison to an old song from the 1940s entitled 'The Hukilau Song.' It's about fishermen who are throwing their nets into the sea. It's a catchy tune and involves actions that lend themselves to expressive dancing."

Then Sutik called over to the people who had by now unloaded the robots, "Okay, ready?"

Altogether they replied, "Yup."

Sutik said, "Then let her rip."

The music started. The three robots began swaying in unison and soon were gesturing in unison to suggest throwing nets into the sea, fish swimming into the nets, and then hauling the nets back in.

Sita said, "Very beautiful," as Ram and Lak nodded.

Sutik said, "Doing this with robots is harder than it looks. This is not simply three robots independently running the same program. The three have to coordinate. If a wind blows in from the sea and hits one of the robots, slowing it down, the other two must wait for it to catch up. They must somehow actively resynchronize."

"And how do you do that?" asked Sita.

Sutik replied, "At first, we achieved this by letting the robots touch each other to help one another get back on track physically. But now we've programmed it so that each robot can simply look at the other. Each is always recording a moving image of the others, and they can change their own actions to match the average of the other two. Then, when one robot senses it's behind the others, it flashes a tiny green light to say it's speeding up, and if it's ahead of the others, it flashes a tiny red light to say it's slowing down."

"Interesting," said Sita. "Each catches the other's eye, so to speak, and signals its intention."

"Yes, exactly," said Sutik. "The trick has been to get this signaling process to converge rather than having the robots over correct and wind up oscillating around in a cacophony."

"Oh, could I see that too?" asked Sita.

"Sure," said Sutik. He shouted over to the people running the robots, "Increase the time lag on the sync and run them again."

"Okay, here goes," one replied.

The robots then did a herky-jerky modern-dance version of "The Hukilau Song" that would have made John Cage proud.

"Wow," said Sita, "that's art too. I wouldn't disparage it just because it's jerky rather than smooth. I think of it as a dance piece showing what happens when three people miscommunicate, a study in misunderstanding. Maybe anti-romantic, but art nonetheless."

"Well," said Sutik, "you've got a point. We've been focusing on the technology, not the art."

Sutik continued, "Getting back to regular, smooth expressive dancing, we're starting to work on getting two different roles to synchronize. The three robots you just saw were all dancing a female role. We're now working on getting a male-role robot and a female-role robot to dance together. Here the chance for miscommunication is even higher than with three female-role robots because each has a different program, a different agenda, if you will. We need to build in payoffs for each robot that depends on their both successfully cooperating in their dance steps."

"Yes," said Sita, "I can see this is much harder." She pressed, "But what do you mean payoffs? Does a robot actually want something that you can then reward it with?"

Sutik replied, "Right, I see I'll have to explain a bit more. We somehow have to build into a robot that it has desires of its own that we can then reward. The obvious choice for a desire to give a robot is a desire to stay alive. The payoff to a robot who does what we want, which in this case is to cooperate in dancing with another robot, is to let it live longer."

Sutik continued, "If a robot doesn't do what we want, we take it apart, recycle its pieces and recombine them with the pieces from other robots, and then manufacture a new one. Also, we discard the pieces that after a full month of trials have never been part of a successful robot. We then fabricate replicas of the pieces from the effective robots to replace the discarded pieces. Week after week—by selecting only the best-performing robots during that week's trial and recycling the rest, keeping only the components from the best robots—we slowly wind up with a collection of robots whose desires match what we want them to do. These final robots cooperate at dancing because, by doing so, they satisfy their desire to live longer."

Sita replied, "I see. You're using a kind of evolution to produce the robots you want."

Sutik replied, "Exactly."

Sita then said, "Very nice."

The two brothers were nodding in agreement.

Sita then asked, "Would you say that you have evolved your robots to be conscious?"

Sutik replied, "No, we have only evolved the illusion of conscious, purposeful behavior in our robots."

Sita pressed, "What do you gain by saying the robots are only conveying the illusion of conscious purpose when what your robots do is indistinguishable from what a conscious person would do in the same circumstances?"

Sutik asked, "Where are you going with this?"

Sita answered, "Well, it just seems to me to me that you have in fact succeeded in making conscious robots. What else could consciousness be other than an evolved bundle of mechanical parts in a particular configuration?"

Sutik replied, "Well, okay then, if you wish to consider my robots as conscious, go ahead. My taste would be to consider consciousness as a quality unique to humans, perhaps specially given by god."

Then Ram spoke up saying, "This is all fascinating. I can speak for all of us when I say we're looking forward to hearing more about this project as it develops."

"Thanks," said Sutik. "Now let's head over for some dinner."

After dinner the trio gathered with Sutik and the other residents of the encampment. Ram queried the algorithm geeks about the details of their programming, and Sita got to know the Hawaiian modern-dance geeks in the encampment who were present to critique and authenticate the hula moves carried out by the robots. Lak meanwhile sharpened his machete, performed maintenance on the bows and arrows, and tended to the gear. After a while, everyone wandered off, and the trio returned to their tents.

When Ram and Sita were alone, Sita spoke. "Ram, I've been thinking about what Sutik has just told us."

Ram replied, "Yes, my love, what is it?"

Sita replied, "To be convincing, I think Sutik's robot should communicate empathetic emotion."

Ram then added, "Yes, well, if Sutik's robots can be made to have empathy as well as the ability to communicate like a human does, then what's to prevent the robots from engaging in a moral dialogue with humans? And if a robot can teach a human what's right and wrong in some situations, then what's to prevent the robot from qualifying for human rights?"

Sita replied, "Yes, it's mind-boggling. If robots did have rights, presumably they wouldn't be all the rights of humans, only some of them, so they would always be second-class citizens. But then that would lead to them wanting to upgrade to full human rights. The UN would have to get involved again, just as it did when defining the cutoff percentage for animal genes in a human."

Ram said, "Let's ask Sutik about this in the morning before we leave for the encampment at the next beach. Meanwhile, I'm tired. How about you?"

"Me too," said Sita and they drifted off to sleep.

The next morning Sutik went to the water's edge to send the trio off.

Ram said to him, "Before we shove off, Sita and I were talking last night and have some more questions. What you're doing is so interesting. We were wondering whether your robots would ever possess a sense of empathy?"

Sutik answered, "Yes."

Ram replied, "Well, if a robot has empathy and the ability to talk, accompanied with realistic face and body gestures, then do you think a robot could participate in a moral dialogue with humans—could even instruct them on what is right and wrong?"

Sutik replied, "Yes, I think that would be possible someday."

Ram continued, "Well, wouldn't that qualify them for human rights, even if they were not defined as humans themselves?"

Sutik replied, "If there were a partially human robot capable of moral reasoning, it might serve as an ethics consultant in a law office or might help a jury in its deliberations during a trial. It might help in wading through volumes of law books on precedents. It could also help digest the precedents to see how they might be applied to a particular case. It would be an ethics specialist."

Ram muttered under his breath, "Replacing a lawyer with a robot—sounds good to me." Sita poked him in the ribs.

Sita added, "Still, this takes getting used to—robots with partial human rights. I gather that robots would be owned by humans as mechanical special-purpose slaves that could be bought and sold on an open market, and that a robot couldn't own another robot."

"Right," replied Sutik, "ownership would be reserved for humans."

Sita smiled and said, "Thanks for spelling all this out."

Sutik then said, "Sure, no problem. But look, we've just spent a lot of time talking this morning, and you folks need to get going. There's only one more main beach toward the west, along the Na Pali coast—it's called Milolii Beach. If you were to continue beyond that, you'd leave the forest and after a few miles be offshore of the towns on the west side of the island. The leader of the next encampment at Milolii is Agast. Please give him my regards."

"I promise," said Ram, "and thanks for all your hospitality."

"You're welcome," answered Sutik. "We hope to see more of you and your intelligent, beautiful wife now that you'll be living among us for a spell. Let us know if we can be of any help."

"Thanks. We look forward to it. Well, bye for now," replied Ram.

At that, the trio pushed off and continued their search for a good place to settle for the remainder of their time in the forest.

Agast's Camp

After paddling for a spell, the trio approached a long beach at the head of a narrow valley. The beach was rocky in the middle, with a stream running through the rocks, and was sandy on either side. The beach was fronted by a coral reef with a passage.

The trio threaded their way along the passage and soon arrived at the shore, where they were greeted by a man who announced, "I am Agast. Word has spread of your coming, and I'm so glad to welcome you."

Ram made the usual introductions, and the trio pulled their kayaks out of the water.

The trio looked around. Although the beach didn't receive as much rain as the beaches earlier in their journey, Agast and the other residents had a green thumb. Plants spilled over one another in wild abandon, showing flowers in every color of the rainbow. Colorful birds unique to Hawaii—including the orange iiwi with its long, curved bill and the orange apapane, with its probing bill—darted among the flowers. Nene geese wandered around the huts and tents of the residents.

Ram said to the Agast, "I see all your beautiful plantings and lovely birds."

Agast replied, "We are an encampment of natural history geeks. Our residents enjoy surrounding themselves with living things. It seems we spend every waking moment of our lives devoted to understanding the habits of plants and animals. And there's no better place to do this than here in the forests of Kauai."

Ram asked, "Is this only for personal enjoyment, or is there some project you and your residents are pursuing?"

Agast replied, "The overriding mission is conservation and the protection of biodiversity. And in the last fifty years we've seen progress here in Hawaii, even as progress has often been thwarted in other places of the world. Here we've seen expansions of populations of endangered and protected species. For example, our monk seal population has expanded, so you now often see them on beaches."

Ram nodded his agreement.

Agast continued, "There's still lots to do, however. We have endemic species that are found only here. We also have indigenous species that are found here and elsewhere as well. The indigenous plus the endemic we call native because they came here by themselves. The remaining species were introduced by people, starting with the Polynesians and followed by Europeans, Americans, Filipinos, Japanese, and other Asian nationalities."

"Well, how many species are you talking about?" asked Ram.

Agast answered, "A lot—let me check my notepad for the figures." He pulled out his iPhone and opened his Notebook app. "Here are some numbers. We've got over 240 native bird species, with over 60 endemic. We have two endemic mammals—the monk seal and a bat. We've got over a thousand native flowering plants, with over 900 endemic. We've got over 170 native ferns, with over 120 endemic. And no, I'm done yet. We've also got over 1,200 native mollusks, with over 900 endemic, and over 1,100 native fish species with around 150 endemic. Plus, we have over 5,800 native insect species here, of which over 5,400 are endemic. As you can see, it's a lot to keep track of and try to learn about."

Ram commented, "Those are big numbers."

Agast then added, "But beyond the numbers themselves, we realize that each species has its own story to tell. The business of simply staying alive is different for every species. Some depend upon and help others, while some prey upon and compete with others. Together, the species form a community of life replete with drama, love, triumph, and tragedy. When we conserve species, we're not aiming to fill a diversity quota. Instead, we're conserving nature's culture. We're preserving the stories and histories of living things that are every bit as important as human culture is. Surely the story of how the beautiful iiwi you see here among the red flowers came to the island—how it adapted and changed through time from its ancestors—is as important as how the pilgrims came to America, and how they adapted and eventually prospered in a strange land in the face of hardships. Animal epics are no less important and interesting than human epics."

Agast continued, "And we're not nativists. Although we feel a special responsibility to conserve our endemics, we don't really care how a species got here. All life is valuable to us. But if only we could learn more about how all the animals around us here see the world and what they've been through and what makes them happy and what their struggles have been—if only we could talk to animals directly…"

Agast's voice trailed off. Sita stared at Agast and then glanced over to Ram. So Ram stepped in, "Do you have any support for the kind of work you're doing here, if I may ask?"

"Yes," said Agast, "we're in constant contact with our colleagues at the Bishop Museum in Honolulu, who created the lists of Hawaii's original species to begin with. And then we have the wonderful iGene device that your company makes, which allows us to determine the species of an unknown specimen in a matter of minutes. This helps with our species identifications and in making family-tree genealogies for all the species. But deciphering animal culture is where it's slow going. We haven't had any technological assistance there."

Sita was again looking intently at Agast.

Ram replied, "Interesting. I had no idea our iGene gadget was so useful. It's not a big profit maker for us."

Agast replied, "Yeah, well, please keep the iGene product line going whenever you get back to Apple. Meanwhile, if I may ask, would you be willing to use some of your remaining time here to consider how tech might help to uncover animal culture? I know that ensuring everyone's safety from Ravan and his henchmen is your top priority, but maybe you will have some spare time."

Sita caught Ram's eye again. So Ram replied, "About keeping the iGene product line—I promise I will. But that won't be soon. I still have ten years left here in the forest. If Ravan and company stay out of sight, I also promise to give the matter of animal culture some thought. Maybe there's a new product line somewhere in there too. But turning to immediate matters, we'd like to stay the night and then continue looking for a place to settle down for the remainder of our stay. I'd love to hear your advice on where we might stay for a long while."

"Sure, you've already passed by it," said Agast. "Do you recall passing by an inlet with a rocky landing at the base of some low cliffs? That's the base of a hanging valley called Awaawapuhi Valley."

Ram replied, "Yes, we did see it and even remarked on it at the time. Why do you recommend it?"

Agast answered, "Awaawapuhi is a long pristine valley that is rarely visited because it's hard to land on the rock beach. Even if one does manage to land there, one still needs to scale the cliffs beyond the beach. These cliffs are not too high, about one hundred feet, but high enough to prevent casual tourists from climbing up into the valley. On the other hand, it's also hard to descend down into the valley from the top of the cliff walls at the sides and end of the canyon. Although the top of the cliffs is accessible by roads leading from town, tourists can do little more than look into the valley far below because the drop-off is nearly vertical. You'd be quite isolated there."

Ram said, "That sounds perfect."

Agast added, "I'll give you some climbing gear to scale the low cliffs at the mouth of the valley, as well as a rope ladder. That will allow all three of you to get yourselves up to the valley's entrance. You'll want to continue hiking inland to the head of the valley and pitch your camp there. There are lots of birds at the mouth of the valley. It's become a rookery for seabirds because it's protected from intruders. You'll want to avoid setting up camp too near the rookery. Then, after a few weeks, I'll arrange for supplies for a base camp to be helicoptered in to you."

Ram said, "Oh, that would be wonderful. I'll be forever in your debt."

Agast replied, "Sure, no problem. And for this evening, just pitch your tents over there." He pointed to a spot away from the beach, near a cliff wall not far from a stream.

Agast continued, "And later this afternoon, come on by for some food and visit with us some more. The residents would like to meet you."

After the trio pitched their tents, Ram and Sita sat together. Sita said, "I'm fascinated with the idea of animal cultures that Agast mentioned. It seems to me an animal's culture would have to be very different from ours. Animals have completely different sensory perceptions from us. If an animal can see wavelengths we can't, smell scents we can't, hear sounds we can't, well, then, they would have a different idea of what's actually in the world. But they'd also miss some of the things that we can see."

"Yes," said Ram, "their culture wouldn't be a sort of stripped-down version of our own culture. It would be a whole different take on reality."

Sita continued, "Right, and I don't know if animals have what we would call logic, but they must have some idea that a consequence follows from an action. After all, when a lizard, say, chases a bug, it must expect to catch and gobble it. So if animals have a primitive sense of action and consequence, they must also have a primitive sense of causation. And that would be the beginnings of a kind of logic, going from an 'if' to a 'then,' like if I chase that bug over there, then I will get to eat it."

"Yes, maybe," said Ram.

Sita continued, "Also, when animals learn through repetition with reward, it's like a primitive form of generalization. It's like, if I'm a lizard, and whenever I see a mango fall to the ground, I go to it and soon some bugs will come for me to eat. So, I'm thinking an animal could have both a primitive ability for inference and a primitive ability to generalize. They don't need to be thinking like we humans do—they could be behaving as though they were rational based on just these abilities. What I mean is, an animal's abilities lead to a kind of practical logic, an empirical logic."

Ram thought for a while and said, "Deciphering animal culture sounds like it might be a worthwhile project for us. We've surely got the time here. Let's work on this together, assuming Ravan and his henchmen don't show up."

Sita replied, "Yes, let's hope for enough peace to accomplish something before the hostilities begin."

Ram then said, "It's about time for dinner. Let's join Agast and the other residents."

The trio wandered over to the dining area. Several residents remarked that Agast had told them of his request to have Ram look into how to decipher the culture in animal societies. They too urged Ram to do this, as well as to keep a lookout for Ravan and his henchmen. They offered to help if called upon. Otherwise, the dinner was uneventful, and the trio returned to their tents for the evening.

The next morning the trio loaded up their kayaks and reversed course, paddling back in the direction they had come. Agast and the other residents waved from shore.

The paddling was difficult, as they were heading into the wind and surf the whole way. They paddled past Sutik's encampment until they came to the inlet at the base of the cliffs that marked the beginning of Awaawapuhi Valley.

Ram's Camp

The trio beached their kayaks on the narrow, rocky beach before the low cliffs fronting Awaawapuhi Valley.

Lak gazed at the low cliffs and said, "Looks doable."

He then reconnoitered a crease where the low cliffs fronting the valley joined the tall cliffs that dropped into the ocean. There he found a small trail, apparently once traversed by feral goats or boars. Lak strapped the rope ladder to his back along with a rope, a hammer, and some long steel pegs. He then slowly ascended the crease until he reached the top of the low beach-facing cliff. Once there he hammered the pegs into the ground, attached the rope ladder, and threw the ladder down the face of the cliff so that Ram and Sita could climb up.

Meanwhile, Ram and Sita removed all the gear from the kayaks then deflated and packed them up. They carried all the gear to the base of the cliff. Lak let the rope down, and Ram and Sita tied a small basket to the end of the rope. They loaded some of the gear into the basket, and Lak hauled it up. After five more lifts, Lak had accumulated all the gear at the top of the cliff. Then Ram and Sita climbed up the rope ladder to the top. Once there, Lak pulled the ladder back, rolled it up, and covered it with a tarp, ready for letting down again should any of them need to return to the beach.

The trio gazed at the blue white-capped ocean below, and then turned about and studied the entrance to the valley that was to be their home. A forest surrounded by 2000-foot high cliffs angled into the interior of the island. From where they were standing at the mouth of the valley, they saw birds all around them. They saw red-footed boobies and a dusty gray shearwater nesting in the cliff walls; white-tailed tropicbirds flying overhead, trailing long tail feathers; and forked-tail frigate birds—males, with inflatable red display sacs on their breasts—pirating food from the other seabirds.

Sita took a deep breath and exclaimed, "This place is absolutely gorgeous! It's like I've died and gone to heaven, and yet here we are alive, healthy, and on this good earth. I've read these seabirds have life spans of twenty to thirty years. They must have seen a lot in their lives."

Ram replied, "Yes, and even more birds may arrive soon. It is late summer now. I wonder if the albatrosses I've read about in seafaring novels will come. The abandoned nests all around us might belong to them."

Then Sita nearly shouted, "Oh, look, there's a pair of endemic Hawaiian hawks! I read they were once only found on the Big Island but are now expanding their range. These hawks must be patrolling our new forest home as their territory."

As Sita and Ram stared at the hawks, the male flew over to them and began flying in a tight circle. Then he shot upward and diving-bombed down upon them before swerving away at the last second.

Ram said, "Maybe he wants us to leave his territory."

But then the hawk found an updraft and hovered. He turned toward the forest and assumed an upright position, sticking his feet out, and dropped down as if to land, but then averted its course just in time to avoid hitting the ground. He flew toward the forest and then back up to his hover spot in the air.

After watching this maneuver two more times, Ram said, "Maybe he was originally just trying to get our attention, and now he's inviting us to go farther into the forest."

Sita replied, "That makes sense. But I wonder why he would be inviting us into his territory."

Ram thought for a while and replied, "Maybe he wants our protection. When Ravan's henchmen helicopter into these mountains, they probably try to hunt him. I hear some of Ravan's henchmen enjoy hanging stuffed specimens of endangered species in their trophy rooms."

"Yes," said Sita, "that's probably what's going on here. Perhaps the bird could somehow discern that you are a friend and not a foe because of the nonhuman genes you are fortunate enough to possess."

"Right," said Ram, "the bird must have some basis for his willingness to trust me rather than regard me as another dangerous intruder. If he can somehow sniff out that I am partly his kin, then that would be a possible basis for trust. After all, he's got no choice but to find an ally—otherwise, one of Ravan's henchmen will eventually kill him. Trusting me may be his only option to prevent that."

Sita replied, "It would be great if we could team up with him somehow. I guess he would be willing to patrol the forest on our behalf. After all, he's cruising the entire forest on his daily foraging rounds anyway."

Ram the said, "Yes, but to receive information from him we would need to talk to him better than we can now. I mean, these dive-bomb gestures are certainly attention getting, but figuring out what he's really trying to say amounts to no more than making an educated guess. I'd like to do better."

Sita replied, "The task of learning how to speak with animals is becoming more important to us than the academic exercise Agast originally suggested as a way to pass our idle time. We now have a real need to know, not merely curiosity."

"Okay," said Ram, "let's set up camp and start strategizing on how to proceed. Meanwhile, I want to give this bird a name. I name him Jat, in honor of the king of the vultures in Indian mythology."

To find a place to set up home, the trio pushed through the forest until reaching the head of the valley. They found a location at the base of 2,000-foot cliffs near a stream. Over the next two months, the trio set up their home there. Lak cut some trees, with which he made two cabins and fashioned rough-hewn tables and chairs. He also cleared a landing space in the forest. The supply helicopter Agast promised arrived with materials to set up an Internet link, luminescent plants for lighting at night, and solar collectors for electricity.

As the trio's home base was nearing completion, the long-awaited albatrosses began to arrive. They reminded Sita of giant seagulls. One by one they returned to their nests, until the entire base of the valley was packed with birds. Ram and Sita visited the rookery daily, walking slowly along a path at the side of the valley about ten feet above the valley floor. They found several spots where they had an unobstructed view of the birds while hiding behind some bushes. They saw several birds who had bands on their legs, indicating that they had caught and banded while visiting other locations.

"Look," said Sita, "I imagine the birds are talking to one another. Take that pair over there. The one on the left is shaking its head up and down, and the one on its right is nodding its head in synchrony. They're clapping their beaks together too."

"Yeah," said Ram, "and see the other movement too where a bird turns its head backward and buries its bill in its wing feathers for a few seconds. I wonder how many kinds of movements these birds have."

Sita replied, "When we're back at the cabin, let's see what we can find about their movements. Meanwhile, let's keep watching to see if we can recognize individuals."

Once back at their home, Ram searched the Internet for articles on albatross dances. He called over to Sita, saying, "There are lots of articles on albatrosses, many by someone named Harvey Fisher and his wife, Mildred. They're almost a hundred years old, from the 1970s and earlier. And here are a bunch of articles specifically on albatross dance moves. There's one by someone named Earl Meseth in 1975. He was Fisher's student and worked on Midway Atoll."

Looking at the article on his iPad screen, Ram continued, "He presents diagrams of, let me count them, eighteen different gestures that the birds make. He's also provided written descriptions of what's going on when the birds make these gestures, along with his guesses about what the gestures mean. Let me look into this some more."

After a pause, Ram continued, "And here are some fifty-year-old YouTube videos taken on Midway showing some of their dances. Look at the birds all packed in together. They might be even more numerous there than they are here. Oh, and look, sometimes when one pair is displaying, a third bird joins, and the three sometime briefly dance together. And then, oh, look here, the three birds dissolve into a pair with the third bird replacing one of the original members of the pair who just wanders off and, I guess, starts dancing with a bird outside of the camera view."

Sita said, "Yes, I see."

Ram continued, "I had simply assumed the dances were between two birds at a time, with each deciding, say, whether to form a pair with the other, but this video suggests something more like a nightclub mash than a classical ballroom dance."

Sita then said, "If we're serious about discovering how to talk with birds and even what culture is in an animal species, maybe we should start with these birds."

"Yes," said Ram, "good idea."

While Ram and Sita were discussing birds, Lak had climbed down the rope ladder and headed across the beach to fish. After catching the evening meal, he returned to camp, where Sita was peeling some fruits and vegetables and cooking rice. Over dinner the three talked about their plans.

Lak began, "I see you two have been scoping out the birds."

Ram replied, "Well, it's part of a larger problem of figuring out what we're actually going to do here for as much as ten years—if Ravan doesn't show himself in the meantime."

Lak replied, "I know what you mean. When we were going from place to place, we were fully occupied. And even when we spent some time with Valmiki's group, we were busy figuring out how they do things. But now that we're here and there's just the three of us and we've built our own camp, well, I don't know what we're going to do."

Ram replied, "Sita and I have a possible solution. Remember how that hawk, Jat, seemed to be trying to tell us something when we first arrived?"

"Yes," replied Lak.

Ram continued, "Sita and I were thinking it would be useful to enlist Jat as an ally to help patrol our valley and to reconnoiter the nearby cliff and hills for signs of Ravan. And to do that, we'd need to be able to converse with him. Also, there was the big push from Agast and the other members of his group to have us look into deciphering animal culture. Working on how to converse with animals could be a nice big project that would take years to carry out. What do you think?"

Lak replied, "Well, it's not really my thing, but sure, I also need to do something to occupy my time. What would you want me to do?"

Ram replied, "Sita and I were thinking of starting with the albatrosses because they're so numerous and they seem to be talking and dancing with one another all the time. So there's a lot of watching to be done. A lot of data can be recorded in a short time as compared with working on a rare species where you have to spend all your time just trying to locate the animals, leaving little time to actually watch them."

"I'm listening," said Lak invitingly.

Ram continued, "Right off, it would be really helpful if you could build us some blinds to watch the birds up close without disturbing them, little enclosed hutches with a window where we could sit to watch and photograph the birds up close. They're not very shy, and we already can get pretty close to them by just walking slowly and quietly, but I'd like to be sure that we weren't disturbing them, so studying them from an enclosed blind would be best. And one other thing—after you've built the bird-blinds, could you lay out stakes for a grid? The grid should be visible through the window in each hutch. The grid should be about fifty meters by fifty meters, with small stakes every odd meter, big stakes every even meter, and a colored stake every five meters. That way we can note the position where the activities are taking place."

Lak replied, "Okay, can do. I'm beginning to see that if you two are going to be busy taking in data on birds, you'll need someone to set up and maintain your observation site, handle logistics, tend the camp, and so forth."

Ram replied, "Exactly, that would be super helpful."

Lak replied, "Well then, it's agreed."

Albatrosses

Every morning for the next six months, Ram and Sita went to the blinds that Lak had constructed and watched the albatrosses. They learned to distinguish individual birds from one another by looking at tiny details such as scuff marks on their feet, nicks on their bills, flecks of color on their feathers, and slight differences in their tone of voice and the way they moved, all signs of varying personalities.

Ram and Sita watched returning pairs set up their nests for another breeding season. They watched long-term pair members display to each other, renewing their friendship from last year's breeding season. Then they noticed that eggs started to appear.

Ram and Sita had read articles about how to tell the sexes apart and found out that researchers usually caught the birds, took a blood sample, and analyzed for sex chromosomes—males having two of the same sex chromosomes and females having two different sex chromosomes.

Ram said, "I gather about 10 percent of the pairs we're seeing consist of two females. We won't be able to check that out because the male and females look the same and we're not catching them or taking blood samples to check chromosomes."

Ram and Sita continued to watch as the nestlings grew month after month. One of the parents would fly away for days and return with food to regurgitate into the chicks' hungry mouths. After communicating somehow with each other, the two parents would exchange roles—the one that had tended the nest would depart to search the ocean for food, and the other would take its turn at the nest.

Sita remarked, "I'd love to listen in on what the birds are really saying to each other. Is one of them telling the other where the fish are? Is the other giving a report on how much their chick has grown during the last few days, or on whether it was beginning to flap its wings?"

Ram said, "Yes, I'm curious too. I've been reading about bird signaling. Each is supposedly trying to convince the other about who would be the best mate, with males showing off their strength and females advertising their domesticity. But these birds have already pair-bonded and have no need to show off to each other. They've already mated and have a chick together. And yet they are still communicating a lot with each other. So it seems to me instead of showing off that they are coordinating what they should do to make sure their chick survives and flies off on its own."

Now that the adult birds were engrossed in their parenting activities, Ram and Sita's attention was increasingly drawn to the juvenile albatrosses, the ones who hadn't pair-bonded and who were gradually returning to Awaawapuhi after a year or more at sea. These teenage birds were in their social-butterfly stage, always talking and dancing. These were the birds that Ram and Sita had seen earlier on the YouTube video, the ones at a rock concert mash not a stately ballroom dance.

Sita remarked, "Oh, what I wouldn't give to listen in on their social lives. And even here, when the birds are looking for mates, the birds don't seem to be showing off to each other, advertising strength or domesticity. The way they put their beaks together and shake their heads in unison, the way they make clucking sounds in synchrony, all suggests to me that they are looking for compatible partners, partners they hit it off with and can sing the same tune with. That way, they will have a partner with whom they can coordinate when it comes time to raise a chick next year when they return to breed here."

Six months passed and the chicks were now nearly adult sized. They tried spreading their five-foot wings, gathering courage to fly off. Finally, one by one, each of the newly fledged birds went for a run, hurled itself off the cliff, and launched itself into the air, with wings slowly flapping.

Sita said, "Their takeoff reminds me of a giant cargo plane rumbling along until the runway ends. At the last minute, it goes airborne out of desperation because there's nowhere else to go but up. These birds are so graceful in the air yet so awkward on land."

When back at their home camp, Ram said, "Almost all the birds have left. It's time to take stock of what we've learned so far."

Sita replied, "Yes, let's do that."

Ram continued, "The birds have been here from November through July, which is eight months. Because we got a late start, we've been watching the birds for only about five months, but we have been watching during that time every day, nonstop. So that's about 150 days."

Sita flipped through the spreadsheet tabs on her iPad and said, "Actually, 134, because we had to miss some days because of weather. Also, I remember helping Lak gather some of the vegetables and fruit, as well as with processing a large haul of fish on a few occasions."

"Yes," said Ram, "and I pitched in on some of Lak's construction projects. Okay then, we have 134 days and about six hours per day. Now, how many individual birds were you following?"

After counting the spreadsheet lines, Sita replied, "One hundred and twelve birds in total, but some didn't stick around. I watched twenty-three pairs, which accounts for forty-six of the birds. I watched twenty-one of their chicks, because some pairs raised more than one egg and some didn't raise any. That's sixty-seven birds, and the remaining forty-five birds were non-breeding juveniles. How about you?"

Ram replied, "About the same. I watched at one time or another one hundred and eight birds in total. The breakdown is twenty-one pairs, twenty-three chicks, and forty-three juveniles."

Sita then asked, "And what did you find?"

Looking at his notes, Ram replied, "Well, here's how it seems a dance usually begins: an unpaired female strolls into an area where males have set up their home bases. The males who were sitting in the vicinity then stand up, thrust out their breasts, arch their necks, and bow toward the female while uttering what sounds like eh-eh over and over again. A receptive female then approaches one of the advertising males holding her head low while watching the male."

Turning to a new page in his notes, Ram continued, "Now that the female has chosen a male to dance with, she silently bobs several times and extends her bill to touch the male's bill. Then each bird turns its head down and backward to place its bill at its shoulder just in front of its wing. Then each bird begins snapping its bill open and shut, making a clapping sound, like two pieces of wood clapped together. The birds may break off these synchronous gestures to rub their bills together again. Also, they may pick at small sticks, stones, or debris on the ground. Finally, the female may just wander off to dance with another male."

Sita replied, "Yes, I've often seen variants of that same theme too. The birds string together these discrete gestures, making me think they may be constructing a sentence of some sort."

Ram said, "We're just scratching the surface of how these birds are communicating. We need some advice on where to go from here. I suggest we throw a party and invite our neighbors for some consultation."

Brainstorming

Ram took out his iPhone and vMailed the leaders of nearby encampments to invite them to a party at Awaawapuhi. Now that the winter had ended, the seas off the Na Pali cliffs had calmed and their guests could now paddle over to their beach easily. Everyone was glad to accept, as parties were rare among the residents of the secluded North Shore beaches.

The trio worked to gather the food and prepare for a luau. Lak went fishing, Ram hunted for wild boar with his bow and arrow, and Sita gathered fruits and vegetables. Lak also dug a large pit to bury the pig that would be covered with leaves on a bed of hot coals. The trio worked for a week preparing all the yummy food for the festivities while decorating the encampment with flowers.

On the day of the party, Atri and a group of his animal-human geeks were the first to arrive. After they rowed in to the pebble beach fronting the cliffs leading to Awaawapuhi Valley, Lak guided them to the rope ladder to ascend to the valley floor.

Next to arrive was Sarab with members of his refuge for gender-variant geeks. They were immediately followed by Agast with a group of natural history geeks. Lak led both these groups to the rope ladder.

Finally, Sutik with his robotics geeks straggled in. They had taken some robots with them that were supposed to help with the rowing, but the saltwater interfered with the joints on the robots' arms, rendering them useless. So Sutik's people had to do all the rowing by themselves, which was stressful because they weren't in great physical shape. Lak showed them to the rope ladder as well.

Before settling down for the evening banquet, the trio showed their visitors around their encampment. They showed off the small cabins they stayed in and the conversation pit they had built. They also showed off the hutches they used to watch the albatrosses. And they showed the infrastructure they had built, including the helicopter landing pad.

Lak pointed out where the visitors could pitch tents and stay for the evening.

Ram thanked Agast again for arranging to have the building and infrastructure supplies helicoptered in when the trio was first setting up camp.

Although it was still daylight, Ram said to the visitors, "I propose that we sit together and discuss plans before the festivities begin. I have a proposition for you to consider."

"Sure," the visitors replied as they gathered themselves in the seats around the conversation pit where the campfire would take place later in the evening.

Addressing the group, Ram began by saying, "We loved visiting your encampments last year when we were searching for our home base. We were fascinated by your activities and sense of mission. And at the last encampment we visited, Agast challenged us to develop a project that would keep us occupied for the ten years we'll be here—assuming, that is, that Ravan and his thugs don't show up in the meantime."

Agast acknowledged with a nod.

Ram continued, "Agast specifically invited us to figure out how to speak with animals, how to talk with them to find out how they understand their own sense of morality and culture. Well, Sita and I have reflected on this and agree this task would be worth a ten-year commitment on our part. So we'd like to tell you what we've found so far, hear your feedback on that, and engage your help in the next steps, if you'd be willing."

Agast replied, "I'm very interested, so fire away."

The other visitors nodded their approval too.

Ram continued, "We thought that the albatrosses would be a good group to begin with. They are numerous, relatively easy to watch, and actively communicate with one another. There's lots to see, no paucity of data. You've already seen the hutches Lak built to observe the birds from and the stakes marking out a grid for our observation sites."

The visitors gestured to indicate that they had seen the hutches.

Ram turned to Sita, who then spoke up, saying, "We've done a lot of reading on previous studies of the dance moves of albatrosses. For the most part, we've confirmed the earlier studies and can see that gestures are organized into sequences that suggest sentences. I mean, if each gesture is a word, then a string of gestures may be a sentence. Anyway, that's our thinking so far, and we'd like to show you our notes."

Agast said, "Great, I'd love to see them."

So Agast and his natural-history geeks bunched up around Ram and Sita while the rest of the guests looked over their shoulders. As Ram and Sita reviewed their observations, Agast and his natural-history geeks became increasingly excited.

Agast exclaimed, "This is a great start. You two are naturals at animal observation."

"Thanks," said Ram, "but we really can't take this very far. The observations we've made seem so old fashioned, so quaint. With what we've done, we can't say for sure what the birds mean when they're communicating, and while we can see some rough patterns—like some gestures used only in a territorial fight over a home base or used mainly by a young male to invite conversation with a female—we're just guessing. We need to ramp up this study to include some of today's technology if we're going to get serous about figuring out how to talk with animals."

Agast replied, "Yes, something more high powered will be needed for the quantum jump you're seeking. What do you have in mind?"

Ram said, "Well, I'm reminded of machine language translation. Years ago computer scientists figured out how to translate one human language into another. The early efforts were almost laughable, but by 2020 the translations were so good that professional translators always began with a machine translation that they would later edit to supply a more harmonious wording than the machine could provide on its own. Simultaneous translation, like at UN meetings, is now all done with computers. So I'd like to see us go about harnessing computers to translate animal language for us."

At this point, Sutik jumped in, saying, "But machine language translation went from one human language to another, with many words having a direct correspondence between the two languages. Of course, human languages have some differences between them, like whether or not to bother with the 'to be' verb or assign genders to nouns and whether the adjective is placed before or after the noun it modifies, along with various tenses and so forth. I'm not saying it's easy to translate between languages, but going from one human language to another is a piece of cake compared to going from an animal language to a human language. I mean, how do we know if there's any correspondence at all? We see a rock as distinct from say, a plant. How do we know a bird bothers to distinguish between rocks and plants? They may refer to them both as just solid things to sit on and not bother to separate them further in their language."

Agast replied to Sutik, "In our group we have been thinking about animal language for some time and wondering how we would go about communicating with them someday, if we ever got the chance to do so. Since we're just brainstorming here, how would you go about deciphering a bird's language?"

Sutik responded, "Well, I would try to extract the rules of grammar that the birds use. Do they require some gestures to precede others? I mean, do the gesture sequences always start with a gesture from a one class of gestures and always end with a gesture from another class? Do they have some gestures that are like verbs or nouns or adjectives? You see where I'm going with this?"

While Ram and Sita stepped back to watch the exchange, Agast replied, "Yes, that might be a way to go. However, the geeks in my groups are particularly drawn to how a philosopher named Wittgenstein wrote about language around a hundred years ago. Let me call on our resident Wittgenstein expert to pitch in here."

One of the geeks from Agast's encampment stepped forward to say, "Yes, I've got some quotations saved on my iPhone. Here's one: 'to imagine a language is to imagine a form of life.' I think he means that speaking is part of our lived experience and that just as we don't live our lives by following rules, we don't actually converse in a language by following rules either. Although grammar rules can't be neglected altogether, in a real language we're free to make up new words as we go along and to deliberately violate grammar rules for emphasis or brevity."

Sutik replied, "Yeah, I think you've got a Point. A human language is open-ended, and I'll bet the birds' language is too. They probably coined new words when people with their dogs, cats, and pigs began to show up in their habitats."

Agast's colleague continued, saying, "And Wittgenstein wrote, in another relevant passage, that the 'crystalline purity of logic' is not a reality. He wrote that the words exact and inexact are value loaded, just shorthand for praise and condemnation, even though, as Wittgenstein writes, 'no single ideal of exactness has been laid down.' What this means for us is that we're not looking for some hidden underlying logic to avian language. We must anticipate that avian language, like ours, is an imprecise and open-ended aspect of the birds' living experience."

Sutik replied, "I agree we should not obsess with finding out what the rules of logic are for albatross language. Does your Wittgenstein have any positive recommendations?"

"Yes," replied Agast's colleague. "Not explicitly, but he does bring up the idea of a 'rule by which he proceeds.' I like to focus on the word *proceeds*.

I think Wittgenstein is trying to say that we should try to understand the bird's experience surrounding its gestures—what goes before the gesture and what goes after it. In other words, we look for associations between gesture sequences and actions."

Looking around and finding no objection, Agast's colleague continued, "If we follow Wittgenstein's lead, it's not enough to keep track of what all the gestures are and what grammar they seem to contain. We also have to track what actions result from what is said. Sometimes a word will simply provoke another word—other times it will lead to a relatively immediate action, like glancing up for a predator or coming over to pick apart a food item, and still other times to a long-lasting action like flying off for several days to get food for a nestling."

Sutik replied, "Well, sounds like you're going to want the data to be recorded for a bird's gesture sequence to consist of four components. First you want a description of bird's gestures themselves. Second, you want links to the preceding gestures by it and its neighbors within its inter-active neighborhood. Third, you want links to succeeding actions by it and the birds in its interactive neighborhood. Finally, you want a context description consisting of the identity of all the birds at the site, including those beyond the interactive neighborhood, plus physical indicators of rain, sun, and temperature."

"Yeah, that's about it," replied Agast's colleague. "A bit of a tall order, I suspect."

"That's an understatement!" Sutik retorted.

At this juncture, Atri spoke up, saying, "Well, if it's people power you're looking for, I know my folks would be glad to join in. Many of our people have a good chunk of bird genes in their makeup, and they'll offer some intuition and context about what's going on. I'm sure my group could supply about two dozen folks to help work with the birds."

And Sarab added, "Me too. My folks have spent a lot of time thinking about courtship and family life, and can help interpret the language used in those activities."

Ram then entered the conversation to say, "It's great to hear this enthusiasm. Where should all this fieldwork be conducted? I'm not sure our site here is large enough or has enough birds. Many of the papers Sita and I consulted were from Midway Atoll, which seems to have a lot more birds than we do here. Agast, what's the scoop about Midway?"

Agast replied, "It's an atoll at the far end of the chain of Hawaiian islands. You can line up all the Hawaiian islands from Midway in the northwest down to the Big Island by age and height. The oldest are below water now or just touch the water's surface as atolls, and the youngest tower into the sky like the active volcano on the Big Island of Hawaii."

"And what about the birds?" asked Ram.

Agast replied, "All those atolls out there harbor lots and lots of albatrosses. There are over one million albatrosses on Midway Atoll alone. The Laysan albatrosses there are nesting near another species of albatrosses, the black-footed albatrosses. Although these species breed on the same atolls, they forage out to sea in different regions of the Pacific Ocean. The Laysan albatrosses mostly fly west out to Japan while the black-footed albatrosses fly east to North America. Both species eat lots of squid, fish, and crustaceans. We could easily do all our observations on Midway—but if we need even more locations, we can use some of the other atolls. We could even observe both species if we have time."

Ram asked, "How do we get there?"

Agast replied, "It depends on the atoll—boat, helicopter, and seaplane are all possibilities. Midway even has a runway left over from WWII battles."

Ram said, "That's great too."

Agast then continued, "One point to keep in mind is that the birds are protected. The Laysan albatross species that you've been watching is listed as vulnerable. One can't just walk up to one and attach a camera to it. You need a license and training to handle the birds. It's good you and Sita made your observations without capturing the birds or disturbing them. Fortunately for the project you're proposing, I and many of the geeks in my group are trained and licensed to handle the birds, so we're good to go on that front."

Ram then asked, "What kind of instrumentation will we need?"

Agast said, "Well, some critter-cams, which are little cameras we attach to the birds, some nest-cams that we place in their nests, and video cameras at fixed points in our observation grids. In addition to making a video recording of what the birds are doing, the critter-cams will record GPS, time, and environmental temperature data. Each critter-cam and nest-cam will be Wi-Fi connected, so we can continuously stream the data to our monitoring computers."

Ram turned to Sutik and asked, "What do you think? Is this doable?"

Sutik replied, "Yes, probably, but what I'm worrying about is what to do with all the data that will be coming in."

He then asked Agast, "How many birds do you want to follow this way?"

Agast replied, "How about a thousand, with each critter-cam reporting back once a minute?"

"What!" gasped Sutik. "That means a thousand birds reporting back video and location data every minute for nine months."

Agast replied, "Yup, can you do it?"

Sutik answered, "It's never been tried Before. But hey, why not?"

Ram continued, "Sutik, can you analyze this amount of data?"

Sutik replied, "Not me, but I can reach my friends at Google. They've been the big data experts for decades and still are. I can buy a contract on Google Matrix to adapt face recognition software to birds. I can buy contracts for classification software to pick up repeatable gestures and generate a vocabulary of gesture sequences. I would also want to classify bird actions to discover the connection between their words and actions. There's a lot of work ahead, but I'm sure the Google software geeks will be interested. After all, this is pretty out of the ordinary, and they like challenges."

Sutik then turned to Ram and asked, "I think we can put this project together if you really want to do it. So now it's back to you. Do you think you could fund a venture of this magnitude?"

Agast and the others now peered intently at Ram, who said, "Yes, without a doubt. I can't think of anything that would change our lives and the lives of all people everywhere more than developing technology for talking with animals. I say go for it. I will commit whatever is needed from my personal resources to support our efforts. Also, my friend Vish, the chief algorithm geek, and his group would pitch in too."

The assembled geeks excitedly clapped hands and slapped each other on the backs. It felt wonderful to be engaged in an ambitious and important challenge together.

Ram said, "The meal's ready, so let's move over to where the food is and start our feast."

After the feast the visitors bedded down for the night. The next morning, one by one the visitors joyously paddled back to their home encampments.

Listening

Agast took the lead in organizing the expedition to Midway while Sutik took the lead in contracting with the software geeks on Google Matrix and the liaison with Vish. Agast worked with Atri and Sarab to teach the geeks from their camps techniques for making avian field observations. Agast trained and licensed additional workers to handle the birds in order to attach critter-cams and individual identification bands around their legs. Agast also lined up biochemistry labs to receive blood samples drawn from the birds for determining their sex and genetic pedigrees. Sutik and his volunteers planned the study-site instrumentation.

As summer drew to a close, Agast reported back to Ram that they were ready to go to Midway to set up operations. Ram gave the thumbs up, and soon helicopters ferried the expedition to the Lihue airport in Kauai, where they boarded a chartered cargo plane for the three-hour flight over the Pacific Ocean out to Midway.

The expedition gathered data throughout the season. Ram and Sita, who remained in their Awaawapuhi Valley home, followed the work online and participated in weekly progress reports. Lak often joined in too as an observer. The face-identification and classification software adapted to work with albatrosses successfully distinguished the birds' moves and gestures. Video-game programmers took the face and gesture data and developed realistic animations of the albatross dances.

In late spring, at the end of the first year's season, the expedition returned to Kauai. Ram and Sita then invited all the expedition members to a luau to celebrate their successful first year of gathering data. The party this year was bigger than last year's, as the guest list had swelled with the addition of all the expedition participants.

As soon as everyone had arrived and was welcomed by Ram, Sita, and Lak, Agast waved to the conversation pit and said, "We're excited to be here and anxious to discuss what the data mean."

Sutik was his usual skeptical self and muttered, "I'm not sure it means anything. Lots of fieldwork, and all we've got to show for it are some slick video games of birds dancing around in guano."

Ram said, "Let's get some pupus first, and then we'll talk."

Lak had caught some fresh ahi tuna; Sita marinated some of it in lime as a tasty ceviche and diced the rest as a spicy poke. They sipped fresh spring water and fresh pineapple, guava, coconut, and orange juices as well as some mouth-puckering noni drink.

By this time Agast could not contain his bubbling enthusiasm anymore.

He said to Ram, "We've achieved an unparalleled data set on bird behavior. Nothing like this has ever been attempted before. For the first time, we've gotten a quantitative and purely objective picture of all the elements of a bird species' dance repertoire."

Sutik replied, "But you've lost sight of our objective. You're an animal behavior geek. I get that. I get it that just leaning about what the birds do is reward enough for you. But not for me. I signed on to this project with the goal of figuring out how to communicate with animals. I'm not satisfied with just making recordings of them. I want to know what their dances mean, what they are saying to one another, and someday, even how to talk back to them."

Atri then jumped in to say, "In my group we've talked among ourselves about what the dances might mean. Our members who are endowed with a large fraction of bird genes have suggested that although each chick lives with its parents for several months, they can't see any evidence that the parents actively teach their chick how to communicate. Sure, the chicks instinctively know how to solicit food from their parents and there's some chick-to-parent back and forth communication, but there's nothing that can be viewed as a parent teaching its chick how to navigate its way within albatross culture. Instead, each chick has to learn for itself how to join albatross society and how to go about finding the mate with whom it will breed for the next ten years or more."

Ram said invitingly, "Yes, go on."

So Atri continued, "Well, think of the one-year-old bird who returns to Midway for its first time. Last year it was a chick and lived in its parents' nest until it launched itself into the air and flew out to sea. Now it's returning to land and has to interact with other birds its age. But here's the problem. They don't know the language. They've individually got to develop their language. So, we're thinking, maybe all the back and forth between the young birds is their way of trying to teach each other how to talk. Maybe they're busy trying to develop the signaling system they will use later in life."

"How do you think they're going about this?" Ram asked.

"We think," continued Atri, "that the way the birds dance may be like playing a game with each other."

"How so?" asked Ram.

Atri replied, "Well, assume that the birds are genetically programmed to feel pleasure at each gesture they find a common meaning for. It's like two people singing in harmony. It just feels wrong when one is off key and feels right when both are in tune. So maybe the birds feel good when they hit on a common understanding of what a gesture means, and they're grumpy with one another when they can't converge on what their gestures mean."

"Yes, so where's the game in all this?" asked Ram.

Atri replied, "I'm coming to that. Now imagine one bird is trying to tell the other where to find a school of fish. The school can be, say, to the east or the west. Now the bird can try out either of two gestures, say, placing its bill at base of a wing or arching its neck. What the two birds must learn is to associate one gesture, say the neck-arch, with the direction to fly east and the other gesture—say, the bill-on-wing—with flying west. Or vice versa, of course, because which gesture becomes associated with which direction is arbitrary."

"Okay so far," said Ram. "Keep going."

So Atri continued, "Now suppose one bird, the sender, saw the fish in the east and it gives the neck-arch signal. Then the other, the receiver, flies off to the east and finds the fish there. It returns and they share the experience of success by, say, rubbing their bills together. This makes both of them feel pleasure. On the other hand, if the receiver flies off to the west and doesn't find any fish there, it returns and instead of rubbing the sender's bill, it just tosses some twigs and stones at its feet. Then neither feels pleasure. In this case the birds must do something different to pursue pleasure together, since what they just tried didn't work."

"Okay so far," said Ram.

Atri continued, "One possibility is for the sender to switch signals, hoping the receiver will not change what it does with each signal. Another possibility for the receiver to switch what it does when it sees a signal, hoping the sender does not change what it means with a signal. So they keep doing this over and over again. By chance, in some pairs the signal and response will line up correctly. In these pairs, the sender will display a signal that the receiver responds to successfully, and upon returning, they share the pleasure of rubbing their bills together. These birds can go on to form a pair bond. Other pairs won't be so lucky. They won't hit it off, and each will misunderstand the other. Then they won't feel pleasure when they reunite and will experience negative feelings at seeing twigs and stones thrown around. So these pairs dissolve, and these birds will move on, seeking others with whom they might communicate successfully."

"Maybe," said Ram skeptically. "This sounds like pure speculation on your part."

Atri replied, "Well, it is pure speculation. I don't deny that. But you can see for yourself that the young birds are spending a whole lot of time—many days each year, year after year—gesturing to one another, and they must be doing all that for some reason. If you have a better idea for why they're spending so much time in these gestures, let's hear it."

Ram sighed. "Well, can this theory of yours be tested somehow?"

"Yes," replied Atri, "we've been thinking about that too. Next year we would want to supplement the instrumentation we have by implanting little microelectrodes at the back of the neck of some selected birds to monitor for pleasure hormones like endorphins in their cerebrospinal fluid. When endorphins are released in the fluid surrounding the brain, we know the birds are feeling pleasure. That way, we can find out if successful communication is bringing a sense of reciprocal pleasure to the birds."

Ram turned to Sutik and asked, "Can this be done?"

Sutik replied, "Probably. It hasn't been done before but seems possible. I'll look into it."

Ram then turned to Agast and asked, "And would you be okay with this?"

Agast replied, "I would, but I don't have a license to conduct surgical interventions. I am authorized to attach critter-cams and other external monitoring gadgets to the birds and to draw an occasional blood sample to determine sex and genetic pedigrees. But I can apply to get this additional permission as well. It seems safe for the birds, though, so let's assume I can get the approval."

Meanwhile, Atri was becoming increasingly excited. "And remember, it's not enough for just two birds to learn to speak to each other. The gestures must be shared among all the birds, so they can understand what one another is saying. That's why the young birds have to gesture with so many different possible partners during the season and over several years before ever setting up to breed."

"Okay, okay," said Ram, "calm down. Let's see if we can establish whether the dances and gestures of the young birds amount to their learning how to communicate with each other. If that's true, then we could go on to parse the communication system in more detail."

After spending the summer gearing up to add the new remote micro-endocrine assays to the instrumentation package, the expedition set out in early fall for another season's fieldwork at Midway.

Soon the juvenile albatrosses began to arrive. Agast and Atri identified sixteen couples whose interactions looked especially promising because they were actively interacting for extended periods, as though they were trying really hard to get to know one another. The remote feeds from the critter-cams, nest-cams, and the remote micro-endocrinology assays were streamed back to Ram and Sita, who followed the results in their cabin at Awaawapuhi Valley. When not tending to the camp's infrastructure, making sure the Internet feeds were working correctly in spite of the humid tropical air, he too looked in at the progress with the albatrosses.

After two months, Agast vMailed Ram with a message: "You've got to watch this."

So Ram fired up his laptop and logged into the video stream from the Midway expedition.

With Sita looking over Ram's shoulder while Lak too looked on, Agast said, "Now let me turn the mic over to Atri."

Atri began by saying, "Look at pair 13. The bird called 13a does a neck-arch. Now the other, 13b, searches the atoll's lagoon. So let's wait a few minutes for this to occur."

After a brief pause, Atri continued, "Okay, so 13b has now found the fish in the lagoon. Watch it come back to the nest. Now the two birds at the nest will do a bill-rub. Watch the endorphin level in both birds jump."

Ram could see a graph at the top of his screen of the cerebrospinal endorphin levels in both birds spike up. At the bottom of the screen, he could see the birds bill-rubbing. When the rubbing stopped, the endorphin levels in both birds dropped down to their background levels.

Atri then rushed on to say, "Hang on, there's more. From yesterday, here 13a flies out to sea near Eastern Island. This time, the fish it finds are near Eastern Island, not in the lagoon. And what does it do? Well, it flies back to the nest and gives a bill-on-wing signal instead of a neck-arch. And what does 13b do? It flies out to sea near Eastern Island and finds the fish and then flies back to the nest. And yes, they then bill-rub, and the endorphin levels of each spike."

Ram said, "So this appears to confirm your theory. Successful signaling causes a pleasure sensation in both sender and receiver. For pair 13, neck-arch means there are fish in the lagoon and bill-on-wing means there are fish at sea near Eastern Island."

Atri said, "And we've got the flip side too, where they don't successfully communicate. In that case the birds don't bill-rub and don't show any endorphin jump. When this happens, the couple breaks up and the birds seek other partners."

Agast jumped in to say, "Well, it looks like we're on the right track. Now we want to increase our sample size and conduct more analysis. We'd like to get one hundred pairs. Based on these preliminary data, that sample size will give us statistical power for results that pass muster in professional e-journals."

Ram replied, "Great, do it," and then turned to Sita. He asked, "Is there anything you wish to add?"

Sita replied, "Yes. I notice, Atri, that you didn't identify the sex of the birds you were reporting on. Was there any difference in the communication being developed between birds in a male-female pair and in a female-female pair?"

Atri replied, "Not so far as we can tell. That might turn up later when the birds start using their communication skills to set up a family, but for now they seem preoccupied with simply getting the words and their meaning correct. I'll keep you informed."

"Great," said Sita, "I'm so excited about what you're doing."

The expedition returned from Midway to Kauai in the late spring after the albatrosses had departed for their life at sea. As was becoming their custom, Ram, Sita, and Lak prepared a luau to welcome its return from another successful season of fieldwork. The expedition participants all kayaked in from their encampments and were welcomed ashore by Lak.

By now everyone knew their way around the facilities at Awaawapuhi Valley. Before setting down for the meal, the four leaders of the expedition joined Ram and Sita and they gathered together at the campfire site for a parley.

Ram glanced over to Agast, who began, "As you know from Atri's briefing a couple months ago, we're in pretty good shape now to understand how the birds arrive at the signaling system they use to communicate with each other. In the time since then, we were able to double our sample size, but we're still a ways from having enough data for a professional journal. We need another season at least."

Sutik then interceded, saying, "That's all fine and good, but I still don't see us getting anywhere, at least in terms of where I want to go. I want communication with the birds—not just our listening in on what they're saying but us talking with them too."

Agast said, "Okay, I agree, we've been working on only half the task so far." Looking at the others, Agast asked, "Any ideas on how to move forward from here?"

Sarab said, "The problem as I see it is that even if we wave our arms and make clucking sounds and try to imitate the way a bird talks, we won't be convincing. I mean, we obviously don't look like birds, and our gestures just wouldn't cut it. You can evoke a response from birds by playing a tape recording of their calls or showing a movie, but they catch on fast and don't continue to respond. I'm frankly stumped about the next step."

Sutik said, "Well, if you want a more convincing actor, then I'd say— you guessed it—use a robot. We could make a robot that looks and acts like an albatross. The geeks who developed the albatross animations for computer games could adapt their software to operate a robot. We know from the gesture database exactly how to perform each of the gestures. You could imagine a new kind of robot that would be a translator robot. We speak to it in our language, and it speaks to the birds with their gestures and sounds. The birds speak back to it, and the robot relays what was said to us. What do you think?"

"Wow," said Sarab. "Could you really do that?"

"Sure. We would have to fabricate a suite of new robot parts and then evolve bird-robots that, in order to stay alive, would feel a desire to communicate successfully with birds. We've already done that sort of thing with our hula-dancing robots. We'd have to transfer that technology to our application here, but it should be possible."

Ram observed, "You make it sound easier than I'm sure it is. But hey, go for it. It's the only idea on the table. And speaking of the table, let's eat."

The expedition leaders then sauntered over to the tables where Lak and Sita were preparing to serve the feast.

After dinner Ram called the team leaders together for a few last words and asked, "How much longer will this project take?"

"Well, I'm guessing three years or so," said Agast.

Ram replied, "It's already been two, so that would make five years total."

Atri said, "We need another year to increase our sample size on how the birds develop their signaling."

Sutik added, "And we'll need next year to develop and build robots—then, say, two years to deploy and test them."

Sarab piped up to say, "And after the robots are working, we'll need a couple of years, at least, to interrogate the birds. We've got to ask them what they're doing and what they're talking about, to learn their culture. So that would add at least two years beyond the three that have already been mentioned."

Ram said, "Well, at that rate, this project will consume the entire time I have to remain here in the forest."

Sutik replied, "Well, at least you won't be going back empty-handed. If this project works, you'll be able to launch a new product line at Apple consisting of translator robots fabricated for different types of animals."

Chuckling, Sutik added, "You could even call the product line the iZoo and the first series in it iBird robots, with versions for albatrosses and other species like parrots and macaws that people want to converse with. There's a huge pot of gold that will go to any company that can market devices that allow people to have two-way communication with animals."

Ram grinned and said, "That has not escaped my notice. However, my real reason for pursuing this project now is to talk with the animals here so they can warn us if Ravan or his henchmen want to pull off a sneak attack on us."

Agast replied, "We've been fortunate to work in peace so far, and I hope and pray it continues."

The next day all happily kayaked back to their home encampments.

Talking

The next year's season passed uneventfully. Atri's geeks—working with Sarab's and Agast's—increased the sample size of bird observations as needed. Sutik's geeks fabricated the parts for albatross iBirds, including wings, feet, and feathers, and they assembled a dozen of them, retaining spare parts for two dozen more.

At the end of the season, at the now annual luau, the expedition leaders gathered with Ram and Sita around the campfire. Ram asked for an update.

Sutik brought a sample iBird with him and demonstrated it. Ram, Sita, and the others watched with amazement as the iBird went through a suite of gestures. They saw the iBird cooing in the air with its neck extended and then placing its bill into the feathers by its wing.

Ram said, "The iBird certainly looks like a real albatross to me, but we'll have to see if the birds think so too."

Sutik added, "We've programmed the iBirds with voice recognition so we can communicate with the iBird in ordinary human language."

Ram said, "Impressive."

Agast replied, "We're ready for the next phase. In the upcoming season, let's deploy the iBird translators and see if we can establish communication with the albatrosses."

Ram took a deep breath, glanced at Sita, and said, "This will be an anxious time. We'll be watching your video stream. Please keep us informed at every step."

Sita nodded.

Agast replied, "We promise. We'll set up daily video feeds."

Sutik added, "We have to transport the iBirds and their parts to Midway. We also have to transport facilities to repair and reassemble iBirds."

At that, the expedition leaders and participants commenced their annual feast. The next morning they kayaked back to their encampments.

When the next season came around, Agast chartered two small cargo jets that could land on Midway's runway to carry the supplies. The expedition members gathered at the Lihue airport and flew to Midway for another season of fieldwork.

Upon arriving at Midway, Sutik and his geeks set up their facilities and carefully unwrapped some iBirds for deployment.

When all was ready, Atri said, "I suggest we try to duplicate the basic interaction we first witnessed two years ago with pair 13—they were the birds who agreed that neck-arch means that fish are in the lagoon and that bill-on-wing means there are fish at sea near Eastern Island. Let's see if an iBird and an albatross can develop the same understanding with each other."

Atri turned to Sarab and said, "Can you locate an albatross that looks like it would be willing to engage with our translator robot?"

Sarab said, "Yes, I'll start with an unpaired juvenile who's been fully equipped with video and endocrine sensors."

Meanwhile, Agast accompanied the natural-history geeks, some of whom spread out along the edge of the lagoon and others on Eastern Island. The geeks immediately noticed fish nipping at small shrimp at the water's surface in the lagoon.

Agast called Atri to say, "We've sighted a school of small surface-feeding fish in the lagoon."

Atri replied, "Thanks, I'll relay that to an iBird."

Sutik gently cradled one of the iBirds in his arms and carried it to the neighborhood of the instrumented juvenile that Sarab had located.

Atri commanded the iBird: "Try to engage with the unpaired bird directly in front of you. Tell it that fish are in the lagoon."

The iBird strode directly up to the juvenile and bowed.

The juvenile clapped its beak making a rat-a-tat-tat sound.

The iBird then extended its neck in a neck-arch.

The juvenile repeated its beak-clapping.

Atri told the iBird to repeat the neck-arch.

After four such repetitions, the instrumented juvenile flew off to the lagoon. Agast's geeks stationed around the lagoon reported that the juvenile saw the school of fish feeding there, scooped up a couple of small fish, swallowed them, and flew back in the direction of the nesting site.

Then Atri reported that the juvenile returned to the nesting site, where it rejoined the iBird.

Atri and Sarab then saw the juvenile and the iBird rub bills with one another. The juvenile's endorphin level immediately shot up. At this, the juvenile sat down next to the iBird.

Sarab commanded the iBird to reciprocate by sitting down next to the juvenile. The pair remained together for the next hour.

That evening, Agast vMailed Ram, saying, "The preliminary results look promising. The iBird successfully communicated to a juvenile where to find fish. The juvenile flew off to where the iBird directed and caught some fish. When it returned, it conveyed its pleasure to the iBird for the successful directions. Do you want us to stream you today's videos?"

Ram excitedly called Sita, and they sat down together in front of their shared laptop.

Ram said, "Yes, start the stream, and we'll watch."

After watching a playback of the day's encounter between the juvenile albatross and the iBird, Ram exclaimed, "Phenomenal! What's next?"

Sarab stepped in to answer. "Next we need to ask questions of the birds so they will tell us about themselves. The geeks from my group with experience in relationship counseling can take the lead."

Ram replied, "Good, do it."

After the call Sarab turned to the rest and said, "I think the way to ask a bird a question—maybe any question, not just where to find fish—is to start with the bill clapping. The bill-clapping may translate to a human word like *why* or *where*. If that's true, the iBird may be able to interrogate a bird by starting with a bill-clapping gesture. That may evoke the juvenile to answer the iBird's question."

For the rest of the season, Sarab and his geeks taught themselves basics of the albatross language. They confirmed that the bowing gesture translated to *hello*; bill clapping translated to *why, what,* or *where,* depending on the context; tossing rocks and twigs translated to *I'm disappointed with you*; and mutual bill-rubbing translated to *I'm happy with you.*

As the season drew to a close, Sarab called Ram and Sita to say, "Beyond what we reported to you earlier, we've also figured out that any sound made during the neck-arch is a modifier, like an adjective. The neck-arch means something important is going on at the lagoon. But depending on whether a sound is made during the gesture, that something may be good, like where food is, or bad, like pollution from drifting refuse is clogging the lagoon."

Sita then spoke up. "Albatross language is beginning to look complicated, with the possibility of saying many kinds of things. The birds are clearly talking all the time, saying a lot to one another. There is apparently a rich culture here."

"Yes," said Sarab. "Their culture is painstaking to decipher because we can't automate the process. We have to imagine different social scenarios that might occur among the birds and try out different questions to tease out what's going on."

Ram said, "This season is coming to an end, and we're looking forward to welcoming you home to another luau so you can feast on food as well as share the joy of your discoveries. We can't wait to hear the full update once you arrive."

Once the expedition returned from Midway and had rejoined Ram, Sita, and Lak for the year's celebratory luau, Ram called the leaders together before the meal.

He asked, "When will I be able to use a translator robot to speak with the birds living here with us in Awaawapuhi Valley?"

Agast answered, "Give us one more year."

Ram gritted his teeth and said, "Seriously, you've got to deliver on this project. I appreciate the endless source of joy all this research is for you. And yes, that joy can surely continue in the future. But along the way, you've got to deliver. After all, it's been many years now."

Agast replied, "Okay, I promise. At the end of next year's season, we'll have a translator robot well developed enough to deploy as a first-generation model."

Ram concluded by saying, "Good. Now let's eat."

The next year at Midway, the expedition members investigated the albatross culture in much more detail. Sutik's group now deployed a dozen iBirds. Atri's group applied sensors to dozens of birds, who then served as candidates to take part in conversations with the iBirds. Sarab's geeks posed hundreds of different questions to probe the intentions, contexts, and meanings of the albatross conversations. Agast's group managed the data acquisition, analysis, and summary.

Halfway through the season, Agast vMailed Ram, saying, "We have lots to report. Although it initially looked like each pair was autonomous, we've pieced together that the pairs are members of clans and that there are clan elders. A cluster of pairs comprises a clan."

"How do you know that?" asked Ram.

Agast replied, "From our DNA pedigrees we know that neighbors are usually genetically related to one another, which is why we're calling a cluster of pairs a clan. Our translator robots have in turn told the birds that we too have elders, which are you and Sita, of course."

"Yes," said Ram, "continue."

Agast continued, "Not all of the birds we've been communicating with are particularly sociable with our iBirds and curious about us in return. But some are, and we've been able to develop a rapport with those particular birds. We asked one of them if it would be willing to engage with an elder, by which I mean you two, and answer some questions. It said yes, so we've arranged a real-time demonstration for you."

Looking through his iSight camera at Sita, Agast asked, "Sita, would you like to interrogate one of the birds?"

Sita looked at Ram and exclaimed, "Yes, I'd absolutely love to!"

"Good, I thought you might. Please wait while Atri sets things up," replied Agast.

Atri placed cameras and microphones in the habitat and turned them on. Sita could hear the wind blowing across the atoll and the sounds of birds in the distance. Sita then noticed what looked like two young albatrosses in the foreground.

Agast pointed to one of the albatrosses and said, "There, what looks like an albatross on the left of the screen is actually an iBird. It's the one we've selected to talk with you. Why don't you go ahead and speak with it?"

Sita asked Agast, "But how? The iBird looks like any other young albatross. Can it somehow hear me and speak through its bill? Can it form human words with its tongue?"

Agast replied, "We don't use audible sounds to communicate with an iBird. It's Bluetooth enabled and communicates by radio. It sends an MP3 signal to us when it wants to say something, and we then play that signal as a sound in our headphones. Conversely, the sound from our microphones is transmitted to the iBird as an MP3 signal that it can understand directly without having to hear a physical sound. That way the communication between us and the iBird is completely silent. We can't have an iBird talking to us with actual sounds and still be convincing to the real albatrosses."

Sita replied, "Okay, I get it." She then spoke directly to the iBird. "Hello, I'm one of the elders among the humans. Can you tell me your name and a little bit about yourself?"

Without making any audible sound or showing any movement of its own, the iBird responded over Sita's headphones in a pleasant male voice, "I call myself Elaros. I'm a translator robot. I've been talking with the albatrosses now for one and a half seasons. I've hit it off with one young albatross in particular. I call her Lara. She knows that I'm not a real bird like her, but apparently, I'm close enough to be worth talking with. She knows

I was brought by the human visitors and has noticed that I'm retrieved by the humans each night for maintenance. Shall I introduce her to you?"

"Yes, Elaros," replied Sita, "please do."

Elaros approached and bowed to the young albatross toward the right in the foreground. They both then arched their necks in unison while uttering cooing sounds together and then rubbed their bills with one another.

Agast whispered as an aside to Sita, "See how friendly they are with one another. Elaros seems well on his way to pair-bonding with Lara."

Elaros then communicated to Sita, "I think Lara is willing to converse now."

Sita said, "Thanks. If it's okay with you, I'll direct my questions directly to Lara through you."

"Exactly," said the robot. "Please begin."

Sita said, "Hello, Lara, I am with the visitors to your home and wish to ask you some questions. Is that okay?"

Sita saw Elaros arch his neck while uttering a long whistle followed by a staccato whistle and Lara responded with bill rubbing.

Over the headphones, Sita heard in a charming female voice, "Yes, welcome to our habitat. Go ahead and ask your questions."

Sita began, "I see you talking so much with other birds. What are you talking about?"

Lara responded, "I'm looking for a mate."

Sita said, "Well, we've all been there. A few years ago, I was looking too. Do you know what you're looking for?"

Lara answered, "I want a mate I can cooperate with. After I lay my first egg, I want my mate to share time sitting on the egg during the two months it takes to hatch. We'll need to alternate, and each of us will need to sit on the egg for one to two weeks while the other is out to sea. And after the chick hatches, we'll need to share in bringing food to the chick every couple of days until it can fly off by itself in five or six months."

Lara continued, "I won't lay my first egg until I'm eight years old, which is five years from now. That gives me lots of time to search for my mate. And I'll need that much time to be sure of making the right choice. I hope to live to a ripe old age of fifteen. I know of some elders who have lived twice that long. So my relationship with my mate must remain intact for many years."

Sita asked, "How do you tell if you've found a mate you can trust?"

Lara replied, "First, I experience whether we basically agree on a common vocabulary. Do we mean the same thing when we say where fish or squid are located? If we do, it makes me feel good. Second, do we have the same opinions? Do we feel the same way about places for our nest? Do we feel it's more important to have a nest protected from rain and wind or from predators? Then, if we feel the same way on these things, I try to see if there's trust. We play the game of finding the food together. We both go off to find food. Then the one who finds food first has a choice—to gobble the food and not tell the other or to go ahead and tell the other and wind up with less food after sharing. But it doesn't feel right when your partner is holding out on you. You can always just tell somehow once you have spent enough time together. And when you feel you're being played for a sucker, you bail and look for someone new."

Sita rolled her eyes and wondered who programmed the translator robot to use slang.

Lara continued, saying, "By playing with a potential mate repeatedly, each of us can experience that we can't get away with taking advantage of the other, because if we do, our deceit comes back to haunt us. Then our relationship would be over and we'd both worse off. I've made mistakes and lost out on some potential mates by not playing fair. And now I know better. It takes time to learn honesty—at least it did for me."

Sita replied, "Wow, I wish I were able to search for a mate so rationally. I just fell in love and that was it."

Lara said, "But maybe your feelings are actually a reliable guide to what is best for you. I mean, I have only a bird's brain, and my only option is to rely on my feelings and hope that my feelings lead me to do what a rational being would consciously do too."

"Maybe you're right. Maybe I should trust my feelings a bit more," reflected Sita.

Sita then said, "I thought that when you searched for a mate you would be looking for the strongest and best looking male. That way your offspring would be strong and good looking too. I was taught by my elders that males show off their quality to females, and you just have to choose which one is the best."

Lara replied, "Oh no, that would be a waste of time. Sure, there are a few males who are ill or unable to fly straight, but for the most part, the males are all the same in terms of intrinsic quality. There's no point in looking for a best male. What separates the males for me is whether we see the world the same way, whether we can intuitively cooperate."

Lara added, "Another thing that helps in looking for a mate is having fun together, just playing. When we sing together, when we dance together, well, then, I just feel good inside—I feel pleasure. And when we play together, we get to know each other's body rhythms. I can feel how he moves, when he's happy and when he's distracted. To play together we have to be fair with each other, because if we're not, the playing stops and then I feel bad. So that's how I find a partner: I ask myself, do we speak the same language? Do we have the same priorities about how to build a nest and raise our first chick? And can we have fun playing together? I hope I find my Mr. Right someday.

"Anyway," said Lara, "as I get older, I won't have to spend so much time talking every day. The older couples who have already had an egg together don't talk much with each other at the beginning of the season. But when their egg has been laid, they talk a lot when they switch off between foraging and incubating the egg. That's when I'll feel the most pleasure, talking with a partner on how to coordinate ourselves in a task we're both sharing. I don't feel as much pleasure now when I'm trying to find a partner as I will later on when I've found him."

Sita then advised, "As an elder, I say, just be patient. Your time will come."

Lara replied, "Yes, I guess so."

Sita concluded by saying, "Thank you for spending so much time with me."

Lara replied, "You're welcome." And as Sita glanced at the corner of the computer screen, she could see Elaros and Lara rubbing bills together and preening each other's feathers.

Agast now took the microphone and appeared over the webcam. He said to Ram, "As you can see, we have now achieved the goal of speaking with albatrosses. This is the first step toward speaking with animals from other species as well."

Ram replied, "This is breathtaking."

Agast looked over to Sita, who said, "Thank you so much for letting me conduct the interview with Lara. I am so grateful."

Agast replied, "At the end of this season, we'll return with a set of iBirds experienced in translation between albatrosses and humans."

Looking specifically at Ram, he added, "And sir, when we return, you can experiment with using an iBird to communicate with the hawk who has been patrolling your valley. Your albatrosses aren't patrolling the valley. They patrol the ocean. But hawks and albatrosses are not closely related and they speak different languages. Still, we'll have to hope that their languages are similar enough to permit communication."

"Yes," said Ram, "I can't wait to try. Is it time to end this call? You've given us so much to look forward to."

Agast answered, "Over and out."

When the video feed on Midway had closed, Agast turned to Sutik and said, "I wish science always progressed this smoothly. We've had a steady progression of small successes to get to this point. It's so unusual not to pursue a bunch of dead ends along the way."

"Yes," said Sutik, "and we had reliable funding during the project, plus the advantage of close contact with the funder. That way we could reassure the funder—namely, Ram—of our progress and get a reading on whether he was happy with our direction. This relationship has been rare and special."

Agast said, "Well, let's call it a day's work here, collect our iBirds from the field, turn in for the night, and begin again tomorrow. In several weeks we'll be able to wrap this season up."

Ravan's Sister

The expedition's return after its previous season was an unbridled triumph. Lak, Sita, and Ram prepared the best feast they could imagine fit for their life in the valley.

Agast, Sutik, Atri, and Sarab were elated. They had achieved what generations of people had forever dreamed of doing: actually conversing one on one with animals. Sure, they had only spoken so far with a few individuals of just one species, but they had attained a proof of concept that they could extend to other species as well. They journeyed to their home encampments to spend the night catching up on sleep.

The next day, the expedition members kayaked from their encampments to Awaawapuhi Valley for the luau. As soon as they arrived, the revelry began. There was no strategy meeting prior to the meal, just fun and good cheer from the first instant they clambered ashore at the beach and climbed the rope ladder to the valley floor.

At the end of the meal, Agast tapped on a gourd and one of the party blew a clarion call with a conch shell to get everyone's attention.

Agast began by saying, "I propose a toast to Ram, Sita, and Lak for their vision in proposing this project in the first place and then commissioning it!"

Everyone clicked their cups and glasses with one another, shouting, "Here! Here!"

Agast continued, "And as a gift to sustain you as you begin your own conversations with animals here in the valley, we are leaving with you the iBird, Elaros, whom Sita spoke through as the interpreter robot during her conversation with the albatross named Lara a few months ago."

Sita spoke up. "Oh, yes, I'll never forget. What a wonderful gift."

Ram then said, "And I trust you will continue looking more deeply into albatross culture at Midway while we pursue our goal of meeting the animals here."

"Yes, I was hoping you'd say that," said Agast.

"Indeed," said Ram, "and be assured of my continued financial backing. Rarely does a philanthropist have the opportunity to fund a project with such clear implications for so many academic and commercial interests."

Ram added, "Is Elaros comfortable, if that is the word, with his staying with us to assist in our activities?"

"Yes," said Agast, "he's fine with it. He has briefed his replacement iBird to continue the relationship that had been developing with Lara."

"Well, fine then, we gratefully accept Elaros and will be putting him to good use immediately. Now, let's everyone get back to partying."

The next day, after the expedition members had left to return to their encampments, Ram and Sita took Elaros to the narrow end of the valley, which was farthest from the ocean. This was where the hawk, Jat, shared a nest with his mate.

Pointing to a nest in a tree, Ram sent a Bluetooth radio message to Elaros, saying, "There is the nest of the hawk I would love to develop a relationship with. We're hoping to learn what he sees during his regular patrols of our valley."

Eventually, Ram and Sita saw Jat soaring over the treetops. After circling, Jat flew down to his nest and settled in.

Ram said to Elaros, "Try to see if you can communicate with him."

Elaros waddled up to the base of the tree that harbored Jat and bowed to him and then arched his neck up at him with a cooing sound.

Jat looked down at Elaros as though wondering what in the world an albatross was doing trying to talk with him. Didn't the bird realize they were in different species and their languages were barely intelligible to each other? But Elaros persisted, and eventually, Jat flew down from his nest to stand on the ground directly in front of Elaros. He flapped his wings and uttered a cawing sound.

Elaros radioed back to Ram, "Our languages are pretty different, but he does seem willing to engage."

That encounter began what would be many months of Ram, Sita, and Elaros working to refine their language skills at talking with the hawk.

After a year the communication had progressed to the point where Ram could put the question to Jat that he had wanted to ask ever since he had come to Awaawapuhi Valley years ago: "Will you help us? Will you report to us if you see signs of Ravan or his henchmen?"

Speaking though Elaros, Jat replied, "I'm glad to help. I'll report back what I see. This forest has been infested with Ravan's crowd many times and sometimes Ravan himself. I have my own reasons for wanting to be rid of him. His helicopters obstruct my daily flight path as I look for food. Their noise makes prey harder to find and interferes with family life back at our nest. I'm happy to ally with you against them. I will keep an eye out. And if you and your brother happen to leave Sita alone and unprotected in the base camp, I will try to protect her."

"Thank you," said Ram. "I will forever be in your debt."

One day, Ram said to Sita, "I wonder if I could ever learn to speak directly to animals without having to go through Elaros as an interpreter robot. I doubt I could ever speak directly with birds, but I was wondering if I could someday speak directly with, say, monkeys. A good chunk of my genome consists of primate genes, and I feel I have an intuition for what a simian society might be like. Although I couldn't chatter like a monkey or make many of the sounds they do, I feel I could perform many of their gestures. And if I could speak by myself, however haltingly, to a monkey, perhaps the monkey could learn to speak with me too. I mean, we might be able to meet halfway between monkey and human languages. Elaros, or some other translator robot, could help get us started. But rather than be an interpreter, he might function more as a tutor to get us talking the same language and then disappear from the scene when he was no longer needed."

Sita replied, "That's an ambitious goal. Who knows, though—the time may come to try that idea out for real."

One day during the tenth year of Ram's exile, Jat was flying his usual circuit over the Awaawapuhi Valley and its adjacent cliffs when he noticed unusual signs of human activity in the canyons above the valley.

Jat flew to the base camp and located Elaros. He also saw Ram and Sita near their hut reading. Ram was teaching himself the habits of monkeys. Sita was teaching herself how compose music on her iPad with the latest update to GarageBand. Lak was standing near Sita, tending to the equipment—making sure Ram's bow was well strung, its arrows straight, his machete sharp, and the kayaks seaworthy.

Through Elaros, Jat said to Ram, "There's activity in the valley from Ravan's crowd. I can't see the details yet, but be on guard."

Lak's attention perked up. "Ah, some action at last," he thought.

Later that day, a shapely woman in her twenties with jet black hair and dressed in a black cocktail dress with a black purse carefully descended into the valley along the nearly impassable path from the helicopter landing pad used by Khar for his parties. The woman wore a pendant with the curious cave art that Ram had first seen in his encounters with Tata, Marich, and Ravan's thugs in California years ago.

Ram looked up, surprised. He noted the view of the woman's deep cleavage afforded by her dress and remarked to Lak, "An item like that seems a bit out of place here."

Lak smiled at the understatement.

The woman sauntered up to the trio and inquired, "Who might you three be, dressed like geeks yet possessing weapons like a bow and arrows and machete?"

Ram stood and said with a sense of self-importance, "I am Ram, CEO designate of the Apple kingdom. This is my brother Lak and my wife Sita. We're staying here during a period of fourteen years to honor my late father's promise. At the end of that time, we will return to Apple and I will assume my position as CEO. And whom might you be? What is a beautiful woman such as yourself doing here?"

The woman slithered seductively over to Ram and said, "I'm Shurpana, sister of Ravan and his two brothers, Khar and Dush, who live on this island. I'm visiting from Vegas, where I live."

Then, lightly grazing the back of her hand over Ram's groin, she purred, "I wonder if we could step into the woods, big boy. I could get to know you better and show you a good time. I'm looking for a husband and think you'd do wonderfully."

Ram and Lak were taken aback.

Nodding toward Sita, Shurpana continued, "You needn't bother anymore with that scrawny wretch. I can take you to heights of pleasure beyond what you could ever imagine."

Ram chuckled, saying, "Oh beautiful Shurpana, I'm already married, and surely you wouldn't want to be my second wife."

Then, directing a wink toward Lak, Ram said, "Why don't you try my younger brother? He's handsome. Take him."

Shurpana turned her attention to Lak, who was fingering his machete. Looking at him, she shook her breasts and wiggled her pelvis, saying, "You'll certainly do well enough. How about a walk in the woods?"

Lak winked back at Ram and said, "Why settle for me? As my wife you'll be a social second best to Sita. You should hold out for my older brother. He'll soon dump his granola girl for a sexy number like you."

Shurpana nodded and turned back to Ram, saying, as she pointed at Sita, "Why are you bothering to keep that loser around? Come with me. I'm the winner here."

Shurpana then advanced on Sita, flashing her long, sharp, red-painted nails.

But before she could reach Sita, Ram shouted, "Stop!"

Shurpana paused.

Ram said to Lak, "We're wasting time joking around with this trash. Hack her with your machete but don't kill her. That's sure to send a message to Ravan."

Lak swung his machete and loped off one of Shurpana's ears and gashed her nose and cheek. She ran, bleeding and screaming, back up the path and clawed her way up the rocks and gravel to Khar's helicopter landing pad.

Sita watched and was saddened. Although this violence was committed in her name, she didn't feel honored. She wondered if mutilating the face of Ravan's sister would needlessly antagonize Ravan, making them all vulnerable to his revenge in the future. And Sita had mixed feelings about the woman herself. She knew that craving love was no crime, though the woman had sought it in the wrong way. Sita grieved as she empathized with the woman's evident desperation.

Ravan's Brothers

Shurpana eventually reached Khar's helicopter landing pad in a clearing above Awaawapuhi Valley. There she threw herself, exhausted and bloodied, at Khar's feet.

Khar was seated with his brother Dush, accompanied by his burly henchmen. They all wore clothes or tattoos with the archaic cave drawing used by Ravan as his company's insignia. Khar was shocked.

He growled, "Who's done this to you? Tell me, and I will pronounce their death sentence. Who would have the gall to injure a person of my own flesh and blood? Tell me who it was. I'll pull each limb from their body. I'll drag their barely living remains through thorns and brambles. Once finally dead, I'll leave their remains for scavenging animals."

Shurpana gathered her senses and answered her furious brother. She said, "When I went exploring the valley floor, I ran into two young men, one with matted hair, who acted like geeks but had physiques like athletes. They introduced themselves as Ram and Lak, the CEO designate of the Apple empire, and his brother. And with them was a young woman with perfect features whose beauty shone like the moon. Because of her, I was attacked and mauled as you see me now. Khar, my brother, please kill them. Please avenge the atrocity they have committed against me. Kill them all. Bring me their blood. I want to drink it, especially the blood of that woman, whom I detest."

Khar stood up and said, "I'll send some men to take him out."

He nodded to three men, who were standing by, and gave them three empty canteens. Khar said to them, "Kill the three residing in the valley and bring back their blood in these canteens."

Khar's three henchmen then descended the steep path into the valley.

Eventually, they encountered the trio. Ram and Sita had resumed their reading. Lak was near Sita, attending to the gear.

When Ram saw the henchmen arrive, he said to Lak, "Take Sita away and stand guard. I'll get rid of these thugs. I've been wanting to do this for years. I'm glad the waiting is finally over. I know you're anxious to get at these guys yourself, but I need to be sure that Sita is okay. Please take her somewhere safe."

Lak then hurried away from the yard in front of their hut with Sita. He brought her to a cave in the cliffs surrounding the valley. There he took up his station.

Ram stood up. He grabbed his bow with its quiver of arrows.

Facing the henchmen, he said, "I've sworn to eliminate the world from the likes of you. If you want to live, run away now and never return. Otherwise, stand here and watch me take you out."

Khar's three henchmen looked at Ram and laughed. "One against three?" they thought. "No way!"

One of the henchmen said to Ram, "You idiot. You don't stand a chance. You've angered Khar, our boss. Say your final prayers. Forget bragging about your strength."

The three henchmen then fiddled with their holsters, trying to draw their pistols. But before they could fire, Ram shot an arrow through the heart of each, killing them on the spot.

Shurpana, watching through binoculars from the landing pad above the valley, was astonished. She ran crying back to Khar.

Khar looked at her in surprise. "What's the matter?" he asked. "I've sent three of my men to take care of those pseudogeeks. What happened?"

Shurpana replied, "I watched the whole thing through binoculars. Ram killed your men in an instant with his bow and arrows, before they even had a chance to draw their guns. You were too confident. Why don't you go down there and handle this yourself?"

Khar stood up and said, "Who do these guys think they are, messing with me and my people? I'll kill them, decapitate their corpses, and collect their blood for you to drink."

Shurpana replied, "That's what I was hoping to hear. I'll watch through binoculars from here."

Khar asked his brother Dush, "How many of us can squeeze into the helicopter?"

Dush replied, "If we take the seats out, we can fit six, so it's you and me plus four of our men. That's double the number who went after Ram last time."

Khar said, "Good, let's make it happen."

Khar, Dush, and four of their henchmen piled into the helicopter, which took off, leaving their lieutenant, Akam, behind to stay with Shurpana.

The helicopter shook in flight from being overweighted. A rainsquall blew in that threw the helicopter dangerously close to the cliffs that bordered the valley.

The henchmen looked scared, but Khar laughed. "Hey, team, no worries. We'll gonna land soon and have us a good time knocking off these geek wannabes."

When the helicopter had landed on Ram's pad, Khar and two of the henchman advanced on Ram, who awaited them with his bow and arrows. Lak remained guarding Sita in the nearby cave. Dush and the other two henchmen held back in case they were needed.

With lightening speed, Khar's two henchmen approached Ram, pulled guns from their holsters, and fired. The bullets bounced off the implanted boron nitride shield surrounding Ram's heart. Ram fell backward from the bullets' impact, but as he fell, he fired back two arrows that pierced the hearts of the two henchmen, instantly killing them. Ram was beginning to get seriously angry.

Dush and the remaining henchmen were shocked that their comrades had been killed without laying a hand on Ram. They looked at Khar, fear in their eyes.

Khar said, "This guy is pretty good, but still no match for us. We outnumber him, and we're tougher."

To Dush he said, "Would you take our remaining men and bring this guy down? You will outnumber him three to one."

"Sure," replied Dush.

But before the two remaining henchmen could move against him, Ram fired two arrows, killing them on the spot. Then Dush himself drew his pistols. Firing with both guns, he charged at Ram. Again Ram fell back as the bullets ricocheted off his implanted shield. Again he managed to fire off an arrow as he fell, piercing Dush's heart. Then Ram pulled out a broad razor-tipped arrow and fired it at Dush's neck, severing his head from its body. Dush's head rolled around on the ground. His headless torso spouted blood into the air, spattering Khar, who still survived.

Khar was beginning to feel real fear. Ram had killed all his men, including his brother. Now it was up to him to annihilate Ram. He felt Shurpana's eyes on his back looking through binoculars from the cliffs above.

In a flash, Khar drew his guns and fired at Ram. But instead of aiming at his heart, he aimed at Ram's arms and legs and the sides of his body and face. Ram felt the bullets enter his flesh and graze his skin. The wounds hurt, and Ram fell back. As he fell, Ram shot an arrow at Khar. But the arrow missed his heart and embedded itself in Khar's right shoulder. Then Ram regained his footing even as Khar was stumbling backward from the arrow's impact.

As Khar was falling back, Ram declared, "I'm here to punish you for persecuting geeks throughout the valleys and encampments of this island, for corrupting industry and politics, and for the evil you symbolize. As you have lived by violence, you shall die by violence."

Khar replied, "Bullshit. I'll wipe you out just like I've taken out the other wimps living around here."

Khar tried to lift his right hand to fire, but the wound to his shoulder slowed him down, giving Ram time to send off another arrow. This time the arrow found its mark, piercing Khar through the heart and killing him instantly.

Ram then called out to Lak that all was now safe. Lak brought Sita with him to rejoin Ram in front of the house.

Looking around, Lak saw Khar's dead body and said to Ram, "Nice work."

Then Sita looked at Ram and said, "But you are wounded, my love. I will get some antibiotic ointment and bandages right away."

Ram said, "Thanks. The wounds will heal soon using the stem cells implanted under my skin."

Sita ran off to get the supplies and quickly returned to bind her husband's wounds.

Meanwhile, Lak looked at Khar's helicopter and asked, "What are we going to do with this thing?"

Ram replied, "We'll give it to Agast for him to ferry out to Midway. They can use it there to get around to the other cays and widen their study area."

Lak replied, "Good idea."

Ram then FaceTimed Agast, Sutik, Sarab, and Atri and told them that they were now free of Khar's harassment. He asked them to pass the word on to Valmiki, Bhar, Guh, and others living along the North Shore and elsewhere on the island. He also told Agast that he was now the proud owner of a helicopter.

Agast said, "Thanks. And I'll take care of reporting Khar's death to the police. I'll say he met with an unfortunate accident. Some of my people are licensed helicopter pilots, so we can collect the helicopter. And I'll also take care of the paperwork getting the helicopter ownership papers transferred to me now that Khar is dead."

Ram said, "Okay."

Lak then concluded with, "And I'll take care of burying what's left of Khar, Dush, and their henchmen."

Ravan Decides

Shurpana and Akam watched from atop the cliffs as Ram destroyed Khar and his henchmen.

Shurpana then called a cab and set off on her own to make her way to the Lihue airport. There she took a plane back home to Vegas.

Meanwhile, Akam tried to make contact with Ravan to describe the carnage that had spelled the end of his two brothers, their associates, and their helicopter business.

After a while, the signal from his phone was routed with Tor through proxy servers and URL anonymizers and eventually reached Ravan's hidden command center.

This was the first time Akam had ever summoned the courage to call Ravan directly. He had never seen him in person and didn't know the secret location of Ravan's headquarters.

But Akam could now see Ravan very well on his phone's screen. Ravan was dressed in pressed black trousers, with crocodile leather shoes and belt. He wore a skin-tight black T-shirt with exposed shoulders. His trademark cave-drawing insignia was emblazoned on the shirt in red. His torso was buff and covered with tattoos extending from his shoulders to his wrists. A cigarette dangled from his mouth, and his face sported a sardonic grin. A jaunty gangster hat topped his head. He wore a pistol in a holster on his right hip.

Akam thought Ravan was in some type of control room. He was surrounded by video screens, switches, dials, and red and green pilot lights. Pin-up pictures of girls wearing shiny red lipstick decorated one wall. Ravan's environment of metal and red light struck a jarring contrast with the earth tones and greenery on Kauai where Akam was.

Akam could make out other people in the background, each also wearing a black T-shirt emblazoned with Ravan's company insignia. Akam recognized one of them as Ravan's eldest and most powerful son, Ind.

Ravan said to Akam, "What's up?"

Akam replied, "Bad news, very bad. Your two brothers here in Kauai have been killed in a fight, and your helicopter business is now gone. Of all your contingent, only I survived, and that was because I was told to watch the fight from afar, so I wasn't physically at the battle myself."

Ravan flew into instant anger. "Who did it? I'll kill 'em."

Then, alluding to his immunity from arrest or prosecution, Ravan shouted, "No one can challenge me and get away with it—not the police, the governments with their armies, the CIA or MI5, or any other authority. Tell me the name of the SOB who killed my brothers. And don't worry, my anger is at them, not you."

Relieved to hear it was safe to continue, Akam replied, "It was a guy called Ram, who is big, strong and apparently has bullet shields implanted under the skin around his heart. He's the son of Das, the former CEO of Apple. He's living on the north shore of Kauai with his wife and brother. Someday he's supposed to return to Apple to inherit his father's CEO slot."

Ravan retorted, "I don't get it. How could one guy knock off all my people? He was grossly outnumbered. Was he helped by his brother? Did they set up an ambush that my people got trapped in somehow?"

Akam replied, "No, this guy knocked off all our people single-handedly when they charged at him. He had no help. There was no ambush."

Ravan was pissed. He spat on the floor of his control room and said, "No way I'm going to let this stand. I'm coming out there myself to finish this guy off."

Akam took a deep breath, gathered his courage, and said, "Sir, I wouldn't do that if I were you. This guy's not easy to bring down. When he's mad, he's a well-aimed cannon. He could do a lot of damage. Why not leave things as they are? You're still sitting pretty. Messing around with Ram will put everything you've got at risk. Your chances of beating him are about the same as you getting elected Time Magazine's Most Admired Man in America."

Although Ravan was pissed, he was paying attention.

Akam continued, "But listen, I have an idea. This wife of his, Sita is her name, is a real knockout. I mean, a really good looker, a true jewel. She's got to be worth a lot to Ram. I say why not get to Ram by kidnapping Sita? Then you've got him by the balls. You can demand he get off your case and leave your syndicate alone. And maybe you can keep the woman as a hostage or even another mistress."

Ravan thought about this and said, "I like it. Let me work on it from this end."

Ravan decided to seek out Marich for some help. He knew Marich had tangled with Ram some years ago and thought that his experience would come in handy. So Ravan left his secret control room and went to the hanger on his estate where his all-black, stealth, radar-invisible private jet was kept. He ordered the pilot to fly to the Monterey airport in California.

Once at Monterey, he had the driver of his jet black four-wheeler take him to the rugged and desolate canyons of the Santa Lucia mountains east of Greenfield. They drove past Arroyo Seco into the Ventana Wilderness of the Los Padres National Forest and later arrived at a remote cabin in the oak woodlands. Marich came out to greet them. He was a relic of his former self. Grizzled, he walked dejectedly, with the stooped shoulders of a defeated man.

When Marich saw his former employer among the visitors in the jeep, his pulse quickened.

"Welcome, sir," he said to Ravan. "What brings you here? Can I be of service?"

"Nice to see you again," said Ravan. "Yes, you can be of service. If I recall correctly, you've had a run-in with this guy called Ram some years ago. Am I right?"

"Yes," said Marich slowly, treading water.

After a pause, Ravan continued, "Well, he's now struck directly at my family. I've got to eliminate him. The idea I'm working with is to kidnap his wife, Sita, and get at him that way. Can I have your help on this?"

Marich sighed and said, "I wouldn't go there if I were you." He stood up and started pacing back and forth, shook his head, and said, "This guy is really something else. You're playing with fire when you go after him. He's smart, principled, and relentless. You have more to lose than to gain by taking the battle to him. My advice is to stay home, enjoy your wives, and let Ram enjoy his."

Ravan asked, "Why are you so certain that he should be avoided at all costs?"

Marich answered, "Because of the run-in I had with him years ago. I was a big deal then. I had my people, and we did whatever we wanted with the geeks in the Santa Barbara hills. We had fun, and we had swagger. He was just a boy then, and still he and his brother took us out—three of us, including my lieutenant, Subah. Ram warned me not to mess with the geeks again or he would personally chase me down and kill me once and for all. I live now because of his mercy. I've learned my lesson. That is why you see me now living as a hermit in penance for what I did back then. I still see images of Ram in my nightmares. In my mind he lurks in the shadows at night."

Ravan thought for a while about what Marich had just said. He reflected that although he had immunity from arrest and persecution from police or military, he did not have immunity from a private militia, which is what Ram and his brother effectively were. If anyone was to knock him off, it would be someone like Ram.

Ravan replied, "Okay."

He climbed back into the jeep, returned to the airport, and flew back to his secret headquarters. He wasn't convinced that he couldn't deal with Ram, but he felt his motivation wasn't strong enough yet.

Meanwhile, Shurpana, who knew the location of her brother's secret headquarters, flew from Vegas, where she had been recovering, to join up with Ravan. She intended to entreat him to pursue Ram.

Ravan was in his command center, accompanied by his senior henchmen. When Shurpana arrived in his presence, Ravan saw her and asked without much tact, "What happened to you? You look terrible."

Shurpana replied, "Ram instructed his brother to do this to me, your sister."

Ravan slowly nodded.

Shurpana continued, "How can you let them harm me this way? You're losing control of your syndicate. If you allow Ram to get away with this attack on your sister, you'll be seen as weak, and you'll soon be knocked off by one of your ambitious underlings."

Some of Ravan's henchmen stirred uneasily. She continued, "If you want to stay in charge of your syndicate, you've got to avenge me."

Shurpana added, "And another thing—Ram's wife, Sita, is with him. Her beauty is hard to describe. Her dark eyes and hair contrast with the golden luster of her body. Her breasts, hips, and thighs are exquisite. She shines like a goddess. With her thin waist and delicate limbs, Sita is beyond compare. I have seen no woman like her on the face of the earth. Any man who embraces her would enjoy unimaginable delight. She would make you a worthy consort, which you deserve, oh brother and chief of the most powerful syndicate on earth."

Ravan's mind was captivated. He was sure Sita would be attracted to him if only she had the opportunity to see him and witness his power and wealth firsthand.

Reading his mind, Shurpana seized the moment, saying, "Why not go and see her beauty for yourself? Snatch Sita from Ram. Then, as he grieves, go on to defeat him and his nasty brother."

Ravan was convinced. Already angered by Ram having killing his brothers and ruining his helicopter operation in Kauai, now here was his own sister, disfigured and humiliated, standing before him in the presence of his staff. Ravan took this personally. He especially could not permit the sharp and taunting words Shurpana uttered in front of his henchmen to go unanswered. He had to prove his power. And above all, he was beginning to lust for Sita. So Ravan resolved to return to Marich's cabin and press him into service. This time he would refuse to take no for an answer.

Sita Kidnapped

Marich heard the sound of a vehicle snaking its way to his cabin before he saw it. When the jet black four wheeler broke into view, he rolled his eyes and sighed, fearing what was coming.

Ravan hopped out of the jeep and strode up to Marich, who asked simply, "What brings you here again?"

Ravan replied, "I want you. Now! I'm going after Ram and want your help. I want to kidnap his wife."

Marich hardened his jaw and spoke through clenched teeth, "You don't know what you're doing. You haven't researched this. You don't know his strength. You're living in an echo chamber, surrounded by lackeys who tell you what you want to hear."

Ravan replied, "Bullshit. This guy Ram has been banished by his father from Apple. He's a disgrace to all CEOs. He had my sister assaulted. He threatens all of us. With his wife gone, his spirit will evaporate, and I'll easily knock him off."

Marich replied, "Bullshit yourself. Ram was not banished against his will for any act he committed. He voluntarily agreed to live in the forest to protect his company's integrity. And with or without his wife, he's a force to be reckoned with. Remember, he and his brother took out me and my men in Santa Barbara before he had even met Sita. Oh Ravan, please stay at peace in your estate. Treasure what remains of your family and your assets."

Ravan replied, "If I want your advice, I'll ask for it. For now, I want you to obey my command, or I'll have you killed for insubordination."

Marich knew then he was a dead man, one way or the other. Marich's face whitened, knowing he would surely die, as would Ravan himself, if they did actually mount an attack on Ram and his allies.

So, throwing caution to the wind, he said, "Lust blinds your mind. You're impervious to advice. But okay, I'll come. I'd rather die in battle than at the hand of your executioner. I make you this prediction, though: by kidnapping Sita you will destroy yourself, all your family, your friends, and our entire syndicate."

Oblivious to this ominous prediction, Ravan replied, "Good man, I'm glad to have you onboard at last."

So Marich grabbed a T-shirt with the Ravan Syndicate insignia from the back of a dresser drawer and climbed into the jeep. They sped away to the Monterey airport, where Ravan's jet awaited.

Once Ravan and Marich arrived in Kauai, they rented an SUV and drove to a B&B on the West Side that was relatively close to the trailhead of a difficult and rarely used path that descended the cliffs into Awaawapuhi Valley.

Marich inquired locally to see if any of the hunters had seen an albino wild boar or sow. One of them had. Marich offered the hunter and his friends ten thousand dollars to trap any albino pig they could find, preferably a sow with a cute piglet. The hunters knew where to look in the Na Pali forest. Within a day they came back with a sow and a darling little albino piglet that had not yet been weaned.

The lead hunter asked Marich, "Now that we've found you an albino sow and piglet, I'm curious as to what you plan to do with them. You're not going to experiment with drugs on them, I hope?"

"No, no, nothing like that," Marich lied. "My boss is going to propose to his girlfriend, who happens to be camping at the moment in the Awaawapuhi Valley with her brothers. She loves animals. My boss wants to hike down to the valley. As a surprise he wants to offer her a cute pet piglet as an engagement gift along with the engagement ring."

"Huh, that's different," grunted the hunter.

Then Marich handed them ten thousand dollars, and the hunter and his friends nodded their thanks.

Marich continued to the hunter, "Would you like to make some more money?"

"Sure," the hunter replied.

Marich said, "There are two things you'll need to do—one easy, one hard. The easy first: in a couple of days, simply return the sow to where you trapped her. One grand for that."

The hunter replied, "Okay, what's next?"

Marich said, "Now the hard job. Can you locate and rent a military-grade Zodiac with a well-maintained 50 hp motor? After my boss proposes and gives his fiancée her pet, he'd like to take her back with him for a sumptuous dinner and recreation, if you know what I mean."

Marich winked at the hunter knowingly. The hunter snickered.

Marich continued, "So, he would like you to take the Zodiac and wait offshore from the beach at the base of Awaawapuhi Valley. He'll call you when they're ready to leave. They'll descend the rope ladder to the beach. Then you pick them up and take them to Port Allen, where they'll have a car and driver waiting."

The hunter replied, "Yes, we have military-surplus Zodiacs around the island that have been reconditioned. They've been outfitted with big engines for landing on remote beaches and taking divers to offshore reefs. I'm sure I can arrange this."

Marich said, "We're proposing fourteen grand for this, so fifteen grand all together. Sound fair?"

"Yes. Generous, actually. When do you want us to do this?"

"The day after tomorrow," replied Marich, "and my boss will be the one to pay you directly when you drop him off at Port Allen. I'll call in the morning to let you know when we're heading off to Awaawapuhi Valley so you can know when to head out with the Zodiac."

The hunter replied, "Good, consider it done."

Later in the day, Marich took the sow with her piglet and used his cell phone to record sounds the sow made calling the piglet to nurse. He also scanned the Internet to download recordings of Ram.

The next day, using his tablet, he extracted the audio of Ram's voice for a suite of syllables to synthesize into words. He also filtered out the piglet's squeals, leaving only the sow's grunts in the audio from the pigs. Then he prepared two recordings for playback, one of the sow calling its piglet to feed, the other of Ram plaintively calling out the word help.

Marich then went to a drugstore to purchase some golden-blond hair dye and some gold sparkles. While at the drugstore, Marich also purchased a pet-carrier to transport the piglet, a bottle of short-duration sleeping pills, a small screw-top plastic bottle, and a box of first-aid supplies. Next he drove to an auto supply store and purchased a can of carburetor starter fluid. Then he drenched some cotton from the first-aid kit with the carburetor starter fluid, thus making a compress soaked with ether. He stuffed the cotton into the small plastic bottle, screwed the top back on, and gave the bottle to Ravan.

When the day to kidnap Sita arrived, Ravan made sure he was clean-shaven, with freshly cut, blow-dried hair. He dressed for the occasion in pressed tan slacks with a pressed Hawaiian shirt and collar. His sleeves covered most of his tattoos, and his shirt carried the label, *Hawaii Park*

Service Volunteer. He sported a green day pack with a small tripod hanging from a carabiner, a camera with macro and telephoto lenses in the side and back pockets, and a water bottle in a holster on his hip.

Prior to leaving their B&B for the valley, Marich applied the blond dye to the top of the piglet's head, around its ears and neck, along the top of the piglet's back, in a ring at the base of each leg, and on its tiny tail. He added the sprinkles to the piglet's ears, cheeks, and tail. The piglet looked stunningly cute in white with blond and gold accents. Then Marich gave the piglet a sleeping pill and placed it in the carrier. He called the hunter to say that the time had come to bring the Zodiac around to the beach and wait offshore.

After these preparations, Marich and Ravan descended the steep path into Awaawapuhi Valley. Ravan carried the piglet. Marich lugged a portable boom box in addition to his iPad.

Once they arrived near the valley floor, Marich instructed Ravan to carry the piglet and sneak along the base of the cliffs to the mouth of the canyon, facing the ocean.

As Ravan quietly crept past the trio's encampment, his footsteps were masked by the sound of the trade winds blowing through the vegetation. Ravan made sure to keep out of sight of Ram and Sita, who were again seated while reading, and Lak, who was again servicing some equipment while standing near Sita.

Aware of Lak's presence, Sita stole a glance at him. She couldn't help noticing his strong forearms and the athletic coordination of his movements as he sharpened the machete blades with his grindstone. Sensing her gaze, Lak glanced over at Sita, who blushed and turned away.

Meanwhile, Marich climbed back up the path halfway to the top of the cliffs and then veered off the path about fifty yards into the bush. There he set up his tablet and boom box.

Marich called Ravan to ask if he had reached the mouth of the canyon yet and whether the piglet had awakened from its sleeping pill.

Ravan replied that he had reached his station and that the piglet was beginning to stir. He aimed his cell phone's camera at the piglet to show Marich that it would soon be awake.

Marich said, "Okay, give me ten more minutes and then release the piglet. Put her on the trail leading to Ram's encampment."

After ten minutes, Ravan released the piglet, which sprang out of its carrier and scurried off in the general direction of the trio, who continued their reading and tending to equipment.

Sita was wearing, as she often did, the lei of colorful shells bestowed on her years ago by Anasuya when they first visited Atri's encampment.

The trio heard some rustling in the brush and looked up to see the cute little piglet, cheerily wiggling its tail, bounding into the clearing where they were seated.

Sita exclaimed, "Oh, look at that! What a little darling."

Ram remarked, "Unusual colors. It must be an albino. That's rare."

Lak added, "Unusual markings too. I've never seen an albino animal with gold streaks and gold flecks."

The little piglet scampered up to Sita, tail wagging. Sita reached out to pet it. It squealed happily and then continued bounding all around the encampment's clearing.

Suddenly, off in the distance, the trio heard the sound of a sow calling its litter to feed. The piglet's ears immediately perked up. It then ran off in a bee line directly to its mother's call, presumably looking forward to a morning meal.

Sita then jumped up in excitement, saying to Ram, "Oh, please go and gather that darling piglet. I'm totally captivated by it. It would make a wonderful pet. We don't have any children, and a pet would be a wonderful addition to our family. It would be so nice to love and cuddle."

Lak said, "Remember Jat's warning that some traffic from Ravan's group has been spotted. We can't assume that everyone from his gang has been killed off in our recent battle with them. I suspect this little strange-looking piglet is really some kind of trap."

Sita insisted, "Oh, no, that lovely, darling, cute little piglet can't be a vehicle for evil and deceit. It's a tiny innocent baby."

To Ram, she repeated, "Oh please, go and fetch it for me."

Ram said to Lak, "What can I do? The lady has her heart set on it, and I respect that. I must go and fetch it. But I will bring my bow and arrow in case I encounter one of Ravan's henchmen. Please stand guard here while I'm gone. And remember, Jat is nearby to help if needed."

Ram took off after the piglet, knowing that with the piglet's head start, it would take some time to catch up.

The piglet continued scampering up the path leading out of the valley. Marich paused the playback, and the piglet became disoriented, not knowing which way to go without the sound of its mother's grunts. The piglet easily ran around in the brush, under branches and over rocky outcroppings, making it difficult for Ram to keep up.

As Ram was thrashing around in the bush chasing the golden piglet, Marich decided the time was right to play the synthesized call for help from his speaker. He kicked some nearby rocks on the steep slope and started a small rockslide. Then, over noise of the falling rocks, he clicked the play button on his tablet and a plaintive call in Ram's voice calling "Help!" rang out into the valley three times.

Hearing falling rocks and then his own voice made Ram do an about-face. He could see, on an overhang in the distance, none other than Marich, the very person whose life he had spared many years ago. Marich was wearing a Ravan-syndicate T-shirt. Ram saw immediately he'd been tricked. Lak was right. He placed an arrow in his bow and shot at Marich. The arrow flew unerringly and pierced Marich's heart, killing him instantly. Ram left the body unburied where it fell to be consumed by scavengers. He then started back to his encampment, all too aware that it might take an hour or more to return.

At the encampment Lak and Sita heard the rockslide followed by what sounded like Ram's cry for help.

Turning to Lak, who stood unperturbed, Sita cried, "Did you hear that?"

Lak nodded.

Sita continued, "Then why aren't you rushing up the hill to help him? He could have a broken leg or crushed his skull."

Still Lak remained unmoved.

Sita lashed out, saying, "Oh, now I know what's going on. You want to possess me for yourself. You're happy to leave Ram to die on the cliff face, exposed to the sun, to be picked apart by ants and beetles."

She broke down in tears.

Lak was shocked at her words and said, "Your husband is surely not in danger from a rockfall. He knows his way around the cliffs like a mountain goat. He'll soon return once he's figured out what sort of trick Ravan is up to with that decorated albino piglet."

But Sita's fear bordered on hysteria.

She continued to attack Lak, saying "You've wanted me all along and have concealed your true intent. But I'll never give in to your lust. I would sooner die than to be without Ram. After Ram, how could I ever sleep with an ordinary and evil man like you?"

Stung, Lak replied, "What a conceited and hurtful thing to say. Your words pierce me like a heated bullet. You've been like a goddess to me, an ideal. I've never wished to know you carnally. I'm already married. I miss my wife's sweet caresses. I'm encouraged that our ordeal here in the forest should soon be over. I'm sure the piglet is a trick and it's dangerous for me to leave you alone. But you insist in the most hurtful terms possible. So I will go and check out where the call for help seems to come from. But I fear you won't be here when I return."

Lak then took off up the trail to the top of the valley heading in the direction where the call for help seemed to come from.

As soon as Lak departed, Ravan walked into the encampment.

"Hi," he said cheerily, "I was in the area photographing wildlife and heard some commotion. Is there anything I can do to help?"

Sita was weeping and nodded noncommittally.

Ravan was noticing Sita's beauty and continued, "Please permit my saying, and as others must have told you before, you are a truly gorgeous young woman. I suppose living here in the forest agrees with you. You radiate both health and competence. What brings you here, if I may ask?"

Sita stopped crying and her face lit up somewhat. Looking at Ravan, she thought him a nature photographer volunteering to supply the forest service with photos for their publications.

Sita replied, "Let me first get you something to drink." She walked into her cabin and emerged with a glass of cool water with a slice of lemon. Ravan noticed her graceful movements and was stunned by her beauty. He was determined to snatch her for his own.

Sita sat with Ravan and explained, "I am Sita, adopted daughter of Janak, the CEO of Microsoft/IBM in Seattle. I am married to Ram, the CEO designate of Apple in Silicon Valley. Along with his brother, Lak, we are living here until a trial period has ended, when we will return to Apple. My husband and his brother are off foraging and will return soon with fruits and vegetables. Rest here, and when they return, you three can strike up a conversation. Now it's my turn to ask questions of you. Who are you and what brings you here? Are you a nature photographer?"

Ravan decided to reveal his true identity. He stood up and opened his Hawaiian shirt, revealing his black T-shirt with his syndicate's insignia and displaying his many tattoos. He proudly declared, "I am Ravan, CEO of a diversified syndicate, the most powerful on earth. I am above the law. I have a splendid palace in the Caribbean. Now that I have seen you, I feel I stand before the most beautiful woman on earth. I've now lost interest in my other wives. Come with me and be my first wife, above all the others. You'll live in splendor in my palace with all the diamonds, art, music, and servants you can possibly desire. You can roam the world's bustling cities and resorts. I have villas and penthouses everywhere. You'll always be safe, accompanied by my staff and protected by my personal guards. Oh, come away with me, my beautiful darling!"

Sita was taken aback. "Not a chance. I'm married to Ram with an unshakable vow. Ram is bold, strong, virtuous, true to his word, and devoted to me. How dare you covet me? You are a criminal, no better than a jackal. How dare you approach me, disguised as a nature photographer, with such an evil purpose?"

Her temper rising, Sita shook like a sapling in the storm. She continued, "And if you abduct me, where will you go? Ram will hunt you to the ends of the earth. And he will kill you. Your power is pathetic compared with Ram's. You are a common crow compared to a majestic eagle."

Ravan persisted, describing the unlimited opulence of his palace and the lavish hideouts he owned across the planet. All would be hers, he assured her, if only she would come with him. He concluded his entreaty with, "Forget Ram, he's already lost everything and lives in fear in the forest here. It's your good fortune that I, Ravan, have come to rescue you and am here in person to seek your love. Accept me, oh Sita, and abandon the worthless Ram."

Sita spat out, "Go to hell." Then Sita saw Jat flying over and gesticulated wildly toward him, beseeching his help.

Ravan became furious and said, "Look at me, oh proud lady. I command resources on the seas and the dry land. With my hospitals and medical staff, I can forestall even death itself. I am a husband fit for you, oh beautiful charmer. I promise to take good care of you and never to bring you displeasure. You deserve a life better than scratching for a living in the forest. Give up your infatuation with Ram, who'll soon be dead. Instead, come with me to be the queen of my palace."

Sita was obviously not going anywhere willingly. So Ravan quickly took off his backpack, unzipped it, reached in for the ether vial, and pulled out a wad of ether-drenched cotton. He grabbed the delicate Sita and pressed the cotton over her nose and mouth. Soon Sita's body went limp.

Ravan then called on his cell phone for the Zodiac. He heard the outboard motors start up. The Zodiac made for the beach.

Ravan gently placed Sita over his shoulder, but not before accidentally dislodging her shell lei. It dropped, unseen, on the ground.

Ravan then headed to the mouth of the valley where the rope ladder to the beach was coiled. He uncoiled the ladder and threw it down over the side of the cliff. Ravan gestured to a huntsman to come to the base of the rope ladder. Then Ravan climbed down the ladder with Sita draped over his shoulder. At the bottom Ravan handed Sita to the waiting huntsman.

The huntsman asked what had happened. Ravan replied, "She was overtaken by emotion and surprise. I'm bringing her back to a hotel suite I arranged for our vacation here. When she wakes up, she'll be overjoyed."

The huntsman shrugged and helped settle a limp, unresponsive Sita into the base of the Zodiac.

Ravan called his jet pilot and instructed him to drive to Port Allen to pick them up and take them to the airport for a quick getaway.

Meanwhile, Jat, the Hawaiian hawk, continued surveying the situation from above. Seeing the emergency develop, he flew to the encampment and roused Elaros. He needed to speak to Ravan to get him to stop. Elaros came to life, his circuits activated by the sound of Jat's squawk.

Jat said to Elaros, "Ravan is abducting Sita while Ram and Lak are midway up the slopes at the other end of the valley. Ravan's getting away with it, and we have to stop him."

Elaros waddled over to the mouth of the valley and looked out at the scene below where the huntsmen were getting ready to shove off from the beach.

Jat spoke to Ravan through the directional speaker lodged in Elaros's bill: "Hey you, Ravan, I am Jat, the guardian of the valley here. Let Sita go! Take her out of the Zodiac. Put her on the beach and leave."

Ravan looked around. The voice was coming from what looked liked an albatross perched near the top of the rope ladder. But the hawk flying overhead was swooping up and down as though it were the source of the commands.

Through Elaros, Jat called out, "I am Jat, the hawk you see flying above you. My voice is from the albatross, who is translating for me. If you carry Sita away, Ram and his friends will come after you and kill you and all your family and associates. Then they will commandeer your palace and all your possessions. You are nothing but a thief and a criminal. You who are a CEO yourself should not steal the wife of another CEO. You violate all the moral codes of your status. You should be ashamed of yourself. Now, again I say, release Sita! It's not too late to save yourself from the certain ruin that will result if you go through with this kidnapping."

Ravan replied, "Get lost, dumb bird."

Jat then dive-bombed Ravan and the huntsmen. The huntsmen cringed and covered themselves as best they could, even as they bled from the scratches gouged in their flesh from the talons of the hawk.

Ravan fought back, but the hawk attacked again and again, scratching Ravan's skull and breaking open the flesh on his arms with its sharp beak.

Ravan staggered over to his backpack, unzipped it and pulled out a knife. As Jat kept attacking, Ravan slashed back wildly. Eventually he nipped Jat on some of his primary flight-controlling feathers, causing Jat to lose his precision aerodynamic control.

In his next dive-bombing foray, Jat veered too close to Ravan's knife. Ravan slashed one of Jat's wings, slicing it off near the base, leaving only a beating and bloody stump. Jat careened to the side with the remaining wing. But Ravan slashed at the other wing too, severing it from Jat's body, leaving the bird to crash into the water. Jat's writhing body bobbled in the waves as hungry fish nibbled at it. But before the fish could submerge Jat's body in the water's depths, it washed ashore. Along with his body, the waves deposited spatters of Jat's blood on the shore, where it mingled with fragments of seaweed and broken shells. Still, Jat was clinging to life as Elaros watched. With nothing left to do, Elaros wandered back to camp.

Ravan called out to the huntsmen, "That's over now, so let's get going."

So the huntsmen fired up the Zodiac's outboard engines and they sped off to the dock at Port Allen. When they arrived, Ravan's pilot was there to meet them. The pilot and huntsman gathered Sita's still limp body into the jet black SUV. Then Ravan payed the huntsmen and thanked them for their work.

The pilot asked, "Where is Marich?"

Ravan replied, "Ram got him. His SUV is still up there. Call the car rental guys and tell them to retrieve the car from the top of the valley. Tell them the driver exited the bottom of the valley with us. Give them my credit card number and tell them to bill me for the extra pickup charges. We need to get away clean."

The pilot drove them to the private jet terminal at the airport. They pulled up alongside Ravan's black stealth jet and loaded Sita into the plane. The pilot then dropped the SUV at the nearby car rental agency and walked back to the private jet terminal. The jet was already fueled. The pilot started the engines and took off to the east without bothering to ask for runway clearance or file a flight plan.

Sita slowly regained consciousness. She rubbed her eyes and looked around. Then she saw Ravan and clenched her fists.

Ravan said to her, "Don't be afraid, and don't be angry. I will provide for your every wish."

Sita replied, "Go to hell. You have no shame, drugging me and then kidnapping me. You are a coward. You steal the faithful wife of another. People throughout the world will scorn you, revile you, and spit at the mention of your name. Go to hell, I say again. You will never possess me."

After about seven hours, the plane landed at a tiny airport with no tower and one runway (with weeds sprouting through the cracks in its pavement) surrounded by jungle.

Out the window, Sita saw the words *Bienvenido a Isla Colón, El Aeropuerto de Bocas del Toro* on a faded sign on a shack that served as the airport terminal. She also saw monkeys in trees surrounding the airport watching the black stealth jet as it landed. Sita surmised she was in Central America somewhere.

Sita then reached in her belt pouch and pulled out her iPhone. She was relieved to find it connecting to a signal. She checked that her Find My iPhone feature was still activated, knowing that Ram would be looking for her on his laptop as soon as he discovered her missing.

When Ravan saw her with the iPhone, he grabbed the phone, turned it off, and put it in his pocket so she couldn't call for help. But he apparently didn't realize that the phone had already transmitted its location to the servers and could be traced.

The door to the airplane opened, and a mechanic climbed in the plane. He said, "*¡Hola!*" and then in English, "Sign here and give me your credit card. Then we'll begin the refueling."

The pilot signed and handed him a credit card. Seeing an opening, Sita threw her empty belt pouch out the open door onto the runway.

Ravan shouted to Sita, "Why did you do that?" Then he hollered to one of the mechanics on the ground, "Grab that pouch!"

But before the mechanic could retrieve it, a medium-sized white-headed monkey scampered across the tarmac, snatched the pouch from the asphalt, and scurried off into the trees, barking and squealing as it ran.

Ravan then shrugged, saying, "Shit, there it goes. Oh well, doesn't matter."

Sita smiled.

After the refueling was completed, the monkeys in the surrounding forest watched the black stealth jet take off to the east, heading out to the Atlantic Ocean.

About five hours later, Ravan's plane landed on the private runway of his palace on one of the islands in the Caribbean.

After landing, Ravan's pilot taxied the black stealth jet into an underground hanger while henchmen pulled camouflage material over the runway.

Ravan's headquarters was a gated estate occupying ten acres on the island's coast. It featured beautiful views of the ocean, with private formal gardens and swimming pools whose water flowed over the edges facing the ocean. Fountains decorated the center of the pools. Near one side of one of the pools was a ballroom with a stage for musicians. Near the other side was a dining room with a center section containing a large table with seating for dozens of people, and small dining alcoves dotted the walls overlooking the gardens and ocean. The floor was marble. The large windows opened to the sea breeze, obviating any need for air conditioning. The tables were mahogany, and the chairs rattan, with seat covers in native quilting. The oil paintings on the stuccoed walls were drawn from around the Caribbean—from Haiti, Jamaica, Guadeloupe, Trinidad, and Guyana.

After pulling into the hanger, Ravan's palace staff came over to greet him.

Ravan gave a despondent Sita over to his maids and said, "Take good care of her, making sure she doesn't come in contact with any of the men in the palace. Give her every item of enjoyment she desires—jewelry, gadgets, pets, anything. Anyone who displeases her will have to answer to me."

Ravan then summoned his security staff to meet in an hour in the estate's executive suite.

Ravan began by praising the staff for the wonderful work they had done so far on all the various tasks they had been assigned around the world.

Then Ravan said, "I have another task. Gather any information you can about Ram and his brother Lak. Seek them out and spy on them in person if you can find them. Use any technology you need, but be sure to observe them yourselves—don't delegate. Be sure to make your own observations and form your own judgments about Ram's tendencies and capabilities. Study films, social media, his writings. Anything. But be careful. He's dangerous. He's already inflicted substantial damage on me, my relatives, and our syndicate. I feel a rage against him burning my insides, a rage that will only be stilled when I have killed him myself."

Accordingly, members of the syndicate's security staff began attempting surveillance of Ram and anyone or anything associated with him.

Meanwhile, Ravan came again to Sita's quarters. He tried once more to impress Sita. He bragged of his power and derided Ram. He gestured toward the palace and its grounds, which were planted in native vegetation. He pointed out the wildlife—the parrots, the pearly-eyed thrasher, the ground lizards, tree lizards, and the monkeys.

He said, "All this can be yours. Just say the word."

But Sita retorted again, "Go to hell. How dare you abduct me? Stop your boasting. Once Ram has killed you and rescued me, your wealth will evaporate and your palace will become a museum to your humiliation."

Sita's stinging words and continued obstinance aroused Ravan's anger. He could feel the hair on his body standing up.

He said to Sita, "Oh, beautiful lady, here is my warning. I warn you that if you've not acceded to my entreaties after one year, I shall have you executed and your remains fed to the hungry sharks that patrol the coast."

Then, as he stormed out of her quarters, he told the attendants, "Alternate sweet words with fearful threats. That way you'll tame this lady like you would a wild animal."

"Her mind will gradually change," Ravan thought. If not, then, by God, he really would put her to death when the time was up.

Sita went out from her quarters into the grounds. She sat among some trees and broke down weeping. With the vision of Ram in her mind, she eventually drifted off into a restless sleep.

Ram Pursues

Ram charged back to his camp as fast as he could, bounding over rocks, crashing through vegetation, and hurtling over gullies. His mind was filled with foreboding.

As he ran he encountered Lak coming toward him.

Ram grabbed him and shouted, "What have you done? Have you left Sita unguarded? I've just killed Marich. The piglet, the sounds of a rockslide, and the fake call for help, all was to lure us away from Sita. We've been tricked. Why did you leave Sita alone?"

Lak replied, "I didn't leave her willingly. She sent me away. She accused me of not going to your aid because she said I secretly wanted to keep her for myself. I was shocked and hurt by the accusation and her cutting tone. I tried to convince her that you knew your way around these hills and would never provoke a rockslide."

But Ram became angry, saying, "You idiot, how could you take Sita's accusation seriously? There was obviously no truth in it. My order should have been more important than hers."

Ram and Lak ran back to the camp. When they arrived they saw no sign of Sita. The trade winds blew through the leaves, but the birds were eerily quiet. Everything looked normal and not normal at the same time, as though all of nature stood in shock at the violence just wreaked against it.

Ram was beside himself. He wailed out loud, "She's gone, she's gone." He shouted to the skies, to the trees, to the wind, "Where is she, where is she?" But they offered no clue. The camp was empty.

Ram thought, "How will I explain this? What will I say to my mother, to her father? They will blame me for losing Sita and call me a liar for not living out my time of exile. I shall never return to Apple. Barat's mother can gloat, her plot fulfilled. I'll ask Lak to return to Apple and pledge his allegiance to my brother."

Ram fell to the ground, crying, "With Sita dead, I'll die too. But there's no place for me in heaven. I failed to protect my gentle and loving wife, and now I face an eternity in hell."

Lak saw his brother's agony. He approached Ram and said, "Don't despair. They can't have gone far. It's been less than an hour since Sita has gone. We'll find her."

Ram composed himself and looked around. Elaros had wandered back to the camp and now was watching as the humans decided what to do.

Ram called over to Elaros, "Ask the birds in the trees which way they went."

Elaros asked. The birds pointed and replied, "There! Toward the ocean at the mouth of the valley!" Elaros added, "I saw that too."

As Ram and Lak were taking their first steps down the path toward the rope ladder, they stumbled across Sita's shell lei that had dropped from her neck during Ravan's abduction.

"Oh, my God," said Ram as he went to his knees to pick up the fallen shell lei he had almost crushed underfoot.

Ram and Lak then broke into a run down the path toward the rope ladder. Elaros waddled not far behind. From the top of the cliff overlooking the beach the brothers could see signs of a fierce struggle. Blood was everywhere.

Ram gulped and wailed piteously, "My Sita is surely dead. All is lost."

Then Ram became seriously angry.

He shouted, "What the hell is going on here? I've tried to be kind and thoughtful during my life. I've tried to treat all people with respect. And what has it gotten me? My loving wife stolen from under my nose, now brutally murdered. Enough of being honorable. I've had it. The world will now see a different Ram. I too can be brutal and uncaring. I too can be a law unto myself. I too can wreak havoc on the world to demonstrate my power. I will start by dumping all my stock at Apple and selling all of Apple's trade secrets to Samsung. The stock market will crash, and it will be worse, much worse than the Lehman Brothers collapse of fifty years ago. I will bring my kingdom and all who depend on it to bankruptcy. That will cascade to bankrupting the whole US economy, and that in turn will bankrupt the world's economy. Then Ravan will be reduced to a pauper like everyone else in the world. Like them, his life will be given over to groveling in the dirt like worms."

Lak was worried. He had never seen Ram act from spite. He said, "Oh, my brother, don't forget who you are. You are kinsman to all humanity.

You're related to all those whom you threaten to hurt by casting them into bankruptcy. By hurting them, you only hurt yourself. You say you have no reason to live anymore. But all your kinsmen do not deserve to suffer from your wrath. They are blameless. Even more, they love you, for you are their blood relative. In a fit of wrath, do not harm those whom you love and who love you. Be calm and consider with me what to do next."

Lak continued, "We don't know yet whether the blood is Sita's. It could be from Ravan himself or one of his henchmen. We don't know. If a leader like you acts impetuously, it sets a bad example that inhibits other leaders from maturing in the future. If we keep our heads clear, I'm sure we'll find Sita somehow. She's too valuable for Ravan to kill. Yes, we'll find her somehow. I'm sure of it."

Ram calmed down and thanked Lak for sticking with him through his moment of rage. One after the other, the brothers descended the rope ladder to the beach. They walked up to the water's edge to take a closer look at the blood-soaked seaweed.

There they came upon the quivering body of Jat, still alive, but barely. The brothers gestured to Elaros, who was watching from the cliff at the top of the rope ladder, to join them. Unable to fly, Elaros glided down to the beach and waddled up to the brothers.

Jat raised his head, spat out blood, and began to speak. Through Elaros, he said to Ram, "Oh Ram, Ravan has stolen your wife and has done this to me. I tried to assist Sita. I flew to her defense. I fought with Ravan. I did my best, but he lashed back with his knife and severed my wings. Now I will die."

Ram picked up the dying hawk and stroked his head. Ram faced the ocean, looking at its horizon, and cried, "I feel sorrow everywhere. I'm exiled to a remote jungle, my loving wife is stolen, and now my first friend from the animal kingdom has been slain after trying to help me. I don't see how I can go on from here."

Then, looking down at Jat cradled in his hands, he asked, "Do you know which way Ravan went? Where did he take Sita?"

With his last breath, Jat replied, "Around to Port Allen, in a fast Zodiac. I have faith you'll catch him.

And then Jat's neck went limp and his head drooped.

Ram gently placed Jat's body on top of a boulder near the beach and said to Lak, "This bird has laid down his life for the sake of my Sita. It's clear that souls who practice virtue are found even in the lower species of life and not just among humans. Jat was a moral being. I was blessed to know him."

Ram asked Lak to grab some driftwood to build a funeral pyre. The brothers placed the body of Jat on the pile of wood and set it alight. They watched the fire burn in silence, listening to the sound of waves breaking gently on the sandy beach, the rustle of wind in the leaves, and the chirping of geckoes. When the fire had extinguished, Ram collected the remains of his friend and placed the ashes in the small leather pouch he always carried.

Ram said to Lak, "To complete the proper burial of our friend, we'll scatter these ashes on the ocean."

The brothers returned to the empty camp. After clambering back up the cliff, Elaros eventually waddled over to join them. Ram and Lak sat down, staring at the ground in front of them.

After a while, Lak said, "Well, we've got to get to work. I'm guessing Ravan hightailed it to Port Allen and grabbed a van to the airport to make their getaway."

Ram replied, "Yes, we've got to find out where they went. I'll call the control tower now."

Ram dialed the Lihue airport and asked to speak to an air controller. When connected he asked, "Has any private jet just taken off?"

The controller replied, "Yes there was one—took off about an hour ago."

Ram said, "May I ask where it went?"

The controller replied, "You may ask, but I don't have an answer. The pilot didn't file a flight plan. He just looked around and took off on his own. I'd like to slap a violation on him for taking off without runway clearance. The problem is that the private jet had a stealth design and we couldn't track it by radar. It's invisible to us. So, it was outta here, and I don't know where. Sorry I can't be of more help."

Ram thanked him for taking the time to speak with him and then hung up.

Ram said to Lak, "Looks bad. Ravan took off, and the control tower doesn't have a clue where he went. He could be anywhere in the world. He could have flown west to Asia or east to America—anywhere at all."

Lak replied, "I have an idea. Turn on the Find My iPhone app on her tablet and maybe her location will turn up."

"Okay," said Ram as he grabbed Sita's iPad.

"Do you know her PIN?" asked Lak.

"Yes," said Ram, "same as mine, 0616"

Lak looked quizzical.

Ram answered, "Our wedding date."

Ram opened Sita's iPad, tapped on the app, and entered the PIN. Sita's last location popped up on a map.

Ram said, "Too bad. Her last location is the Lihue airport. Let's wait a while. Maybe a new location will turn up when their plane lands somewhere to refuel. Now let's get ready to leave."

Ram FaceTimed Agast to tell him the tragic news. Agast said he'd alert the others and they'd kayak over right away to bid them good-bye.

Agast asked, "Do you know where they've taken her? Do you know where you're going?"

Ram replied, "Not yet, but we'll scour the planet if we have to."

Agast replied, "Well, you may know by tomorrow when we arrive to say farewell. I'll ask Atri to bring an assortment of new translator robots we've made since the last time we met. Once you know where you're going, you can select translators for the animals in the region to which you're headed. That way, you can call on local animals for help. It might be hard to find allies among the local people because they may report back to Ravan, whereas the local animals won't be on Ravan's payroll."

"Great idea, and thanks," said Ram.

Several hours later, Ram checked again on Sita's tablet for a GPS location readout from her iPhone.

He exclaimed, "Hey, here it is! Her iPhone reports being in Panama, at a place called Bocas del Toro on the Caribbean coast near the border with Costa Rica."

Lak said, "Okay, at least we know we've got to go to the Americas and not to Asia. Any more info about this place?"

Ram replied, "Yes—it's pretty remote. The airport has one runway, no taxi lanes, and no control tower. But it's for real. It has an airport code and is served by two commuter airlines. Can you book us two tickets to go there tomorrow?"

"Will do," responded Lak.

The next morning, kayaks from all the encampments that the trio had visited pulled onto the Awaawapuhi beach. They clambered up the rope ladder to join Ram and Lak as they were about to depart.

Speaking for all, Agast said, "We're devastated to learn of Sita's abduction. If there is anything we can do to help, please don't hesitate to ask. Do you know yet where you are going?"

Ram replied, "Ravan's jet headed east. Sita's iPhone reported a location in Panama near the Costa Rican border. So that's where we'll go first."

"Okay then," said Agast. "Common vertebrates there, in addition to birds, are monkeys, bats, and small lizards. You should be able to find allies among the monkeys."

Ram nodded.

Agast continued, saying, "Sita confided in me that you were personally interested in someday speaking directly with monkeys rather than going through a translator. We've built a robot that we call a tutor rather than a translator. We've named this iMonkey Ceroc. It will guide both you and the monkey you're interacting with to develop a shared language."

Ram nodded again. Ceroc had the appearance of a medium-sized gray monkey, with a beard and face that conveyed age and wisdom.

Ram said, "Thanks so much for all your help over the years. I know I speak for all three of us when I say that we will always treasure our time here on the North Shore of Kauai. After we've gone, please offer our camp to some other group of geeks seeking a home in which to heal and innovate."

Agast said, "I have two last gifts for you. Here are some nonibars, energy bars I have made from local ingredients. They contain honey and noni in a base of taro. The honey gives you sugar for immediate energy, the taro gives you carbohydrates for longer-lasting energy, and the noni juice makes your mouth pucker and gives you a jolt in case your attention is flagging. I also have included a bundle of arrows made with a tropical hardwood from South America we call massaranduba, or bulletwood. It will pierce body armor. Now, be careful and succeed."

Agast and the other visiting geeks gathered up Elaros, then hugged Ram and Lak, headed to the ladder, climbed down, and got into their kayaks to return to their camps.

Ram and Lak were already packed except for their new iZoo tutoring robot. Lak disassembled Ceroc while Ram fetched a large backpack. Then Lak gently wrapped the robot parts and carefully packed them into the backpack. He also packed a solar battery charger for Ceroc as well as for their cell phones.

The brothers then carried their gear down the rope ladder to their beach, inflated their two kayaks, loaded their gear, and pushed off the beach on their way to Port Allen. They placed their machetes, as well as Ram's bow and arrows, within easy reach should they be needed.

They paddled southwest past Sutik's robotics encampment at Nualolo Beach then past Agast's natural history encampment at Milolii beach. Continuing on, they gradually made their way increasingly south down the west side of Kauai. As they rounded Makaha point, a kayak darted out from the shore hidden in the brush of Puu Ka Pele Forest Reserve.

A large, tanned man with rippling muscles approached. A grizzled face accompanied his forbidding physique. Despite his fierce presentation, both brothers immediately noticed his pained expression and sorrowful eyes. Before they had time to react, the man threw lassos, one after the other, and roped the brothers. Then, hand over hand, holding both ropes at the same time, he hauled them and their kayaks up against his.

Lak wiggled his arm free from the lasso and started swinging his machete at the man, shouting to Ram, "Make your getaway now while I keep him busy. And remember me once you've rescued Sita and returned to Apple."

"No way," said Ram, "I'm not leaving you. Hang in there. We'll take this guy out."

But the man pulled the brothers even closer to him and growled, "Who are you? You're dressed like geeks, but you seem athletic. And you're carrying weapons. I'm hungry and I'm going to kill you and steal your provisions."

Now Ram sighed, looked up, and shouted to the sky, "What next? One tragedy after another. Now we're threatened with death before we can even start to search for Sita."

Lak shouted back, "All this guy has on us is the ropes! We slash through these and get at him." He lashed out at the man's hands that gripped the ropes holding their kayaks against his kayak. Lak's sharp machete sliced the man's hands at their wrists, leaving him with two bleeding stumps.

The man pulled back, knowing that he was now the one about to die. He said, "So, who are you anyway?"

Lak replied, "We are the sons of Das, former CEO of Apple. We've been living in Awaawapuli Valley. But my brother's wife has just been abducted."

"By whom?" asked the man.

Lak replied, "Ravan."

"Ah," said the man. "In return for some advice, I want you to finish me off and cremate me in a proper burial."

Ram replied, "Not until you explain what you're doing here yourself."

The man replied, "My name is Kaband. I was once a banker for Goldman Sachs. Every day when I came to work, I had to step over the bodies of homeless people sleeping on the doorsteps of my company's building. They were dirty, and they stank of urine. I felt they should clean themselves and try to make a living instead of being a public nuisance, sponging off the public. They made me angry. So I kicked them, again and again, day after day. Finally, some police made videos of my brutality toward the homeless and charged me with assaulting them. I was convicted and sentenced. I lost my job. But I escaped before I could be sent to jail. I came here to live out my days in penitence for how cruel and inconsiderate I had become."

"Okay," said Ram. "As you requested, we'll put you out of your misery and cremate you. But first, what is this advice you've promised?"

Kaband replied, "Do you know where you're going to find your wife?"

Ram replied, "The only lead we have is that Ravan's plane touched down in Panama, in the eastern corner near Costa Rica on the Caribbean side."

Kaband replied, "Then you're in luck, so to speak. There was an encampment of geeks studying tropical folk medicines in that region of Panama. Matang was their leader. I believe he's died and is survived by his chief scientist, Sabara. She'll be able to help you. Now, do what you promised and be done with it."

Ram nodded to Lak, who drew his machete and thrust it through Kaband's heart. Kaband died immediately. The brothers then pulled onto shore and unloaded Kaband's body. They gathered driftwood, built a bon-fire, and cremated the body. Hours later, after the fire had cooled, Ram collected some of the ashes from the body and put them in a vial. The brothers then pushed off back to sea, leaving Kaband's kayak on the beach for any passerby to claim as their own.

Once out to sea, Ram emptied the vial in the water, saying to Lak, "Now that's finished. Too bad he had to end that way. He repented and did seem to be seeking redemption for his wrongs."

Lak nodded, and the brothers continued their paddle on to Port Allen.

When they arrived at a public boat landing at Port Allen, they hauled out their gear, deflated their kayaks, and hailed a taxi. Ram asked the driver to take them to the airport. An hour later the brothers arrived at the airport curb and, with the driver's help, unloaded their gear.

As Lak was paying the driver, Ram asked, "Would you like to keep our inflatable kayaks? We're not going to need them anymore."

The driver's face lit up as he said, "Sure. Some of the youngsters at my church would love to have them. Just leave them with me, and I'll take care of it. Do you need a receipt?"

"Nope," replied Ram, "have fun."

The taxi driver smiled, got back in the car, and drove away.

Lak got in line at the check-in counter. When his turn came, Lak collected the tickets he had booked—Lihue to Los Angeles with Hawaiian Airlines; on to San Jose, Costa Rica, with American; and finally to Bocas del Toro with Nature Air, a Costa Rican commuter. The brothers were looking at about twenty hours of flying time and a total trip time of about thirty hours.

The agent checking their baggage said, "I hope you can sleep on air-planes."

The brothers nodded, and Lak added, "No problem."

Ram in Panama

The trip was uneventful, though long. As the tiny commuter plane circled in its initial approach to the Bocas del Toro airport, the brothers could see out their windows low-lying coral islands and mangrove trees along the shore. The pilot called their attention to the small marine station of the Smithsonian Institution near the shore and to an inland section of forest that included a botanical garden.

After the plane landed, the brothers emerged, stretched their legs, and waited at the side of the plane for their luggage. When it appeared, they collected their gear, obtained some local currency from a rusty ATM outside the airport, and trudged into the town, which they had seen from the air was walking distance from the airport. At the edge of town, they came to a sign in the front yard of a house that read on one line *¿Cansado? B&B Aquí* and on the line below *Tired? B&B Here.*

They put their luggage down by the side of the road. While Ram waited, Lak climbed the rickety steps to the front door and went in. He pushed a little bell on the check-in counter and a lady came in from the kitchen.

She smiled and said, "*Bienvenidos, soy la dueña.*"

Lak replied, "*¿Tiene una habitación grande?*"

The lady nodded and wrote down the price. Lak paid for one night by credit card.

After thanking her, Lak motioned to Ram and the two of them carried their gear upstairs to a large room with a veranda, two beds, and a bathroom. The brothers plopped down on the beds and immediately went to sleep for the night.

The next morning they awoke, showered, and went downstairs for their breakfast.

At breakfast, Lak asked the proprietor, "*¿Dónde está el campamento de Matang?*"

The proprietor replied, "*Junto al jardín botánico.*"

Then, after eating triple portions (and agreeing to pay extra), they set off to find Sabara at Matang's encampment. They walked to the botanical garden on the outskirts of town, where they found an old hut with corrugated tin roof and peeling green paint. Ram approached the front door and knocked gently.

An elderly Panamanian lady emerged, and said, "*¿Sí?*"

Ram replied, "*Buenos días. ¿Podemos hablar Inglés, por favor?*"

She replied, "*Sí, sin duda.*"

Ram was relieved to hear that she spoke English and said, "*Gracias, señora.*"

The woman introduced herself as Sabara, the former chief scientist at Matang's tropical folk-medicine encampment.

She said, "Since Matang died, I'm the only one who's stayed on. I'm getting on in years, and this will be my final resting place. And who are you?" The brothers introduced themselves and described where they had been living for the last ten years.

Ram continued, saying, "We are here because of a tragedy. Ravan, whom I'm sure you've encountered here, has kidnapped my wife, Sita. The last sign of her was a cell phone signal from the Bocas del Toro airport. We've come here to begin the search for my wife. We intend to rescue her and to destroy Ravan in the process."

Sabara replied, "Yes, I've encountered Ravan. And yes, I will help you. What do you need?"

Ram replied, "First, we need to find out where Sita is. Even in these days of cyber surveillance and satellite monitoring, no one knows where Ravan's palace is or where his control center is. And then there is the matter of finding information that we can trust—that hasn't been planted by someone in cahoots with Ravan, if you get my drift."

"Yes, I see that finding trustworthy allies poses a problem. Do you have any work-around for this?" Sabara asked.

"My friend, Agast, whom you may know, suggested that we somehow enlist the help of animals and of monkeys specifically. The idea is that monkeys would be innocent of contact with Ravan."

Sabara replied, "Yes, I know of Agast, although I haven't met him personally. He's an expert geek on animal natural history. It's like him to suggest animals as allies. I would agree the monkeys would be innocent of human corruption. They may sometimes be deceitful dealing with one another, but probably not when dealing with you—at least not yet. Initially, there would be no payoff for deceiving you. Who knows whether that initial trust would last, though. Anyway, have you any method for communicating with monkeys?"

Ram replied, "Another friend, Atri, has developed a series of robots over the last ten years that can translate between animal and human language. He's supplied us with a robot specifically designed to communicate with monkeys."

Sabara replied, "Yes, I've heard of Atri too. An innovative robotics geek. It's interesting that you've managed to combine his skills with Agast's."

Ram added, "And as an ace in the hole, personally, my father designed my own genome before I was born to contain 10 percent genes from primates, including monkeys. So I'm guardedly optimistic that I'll eventually be able to talk directly with monkeys myself without going through the translator robot. In fact, the robot has been designed more as a tutor than a translator."

Sabara replied, "Okay, that's novel. It might work. Do you know how Ravan arrived here with Sita?"

Ram answered, "The control tower back in Kauai reported a black stealth jet that took off soon after the time we estimate Sita was kidnapped. The pilot didn't file a flight plan. The control tower people assume the plane was Ravan's."

Sabara replied, "The monkeys around here undoubtedly noticed an unusual plane like that both landing and taking off. I think asking them if they saw the plane is a good idea. I guess what would be most helpful at this stage is for me to brief you on the monkeys around here."

Ram replied, "Thanks, that would be great."

Sabara said, "Two types of monkeys are common, and three others are either hard to spot or not so common. I've been watching them for years, mostly in the national park on Bastimentos Island, a short water taxi ride from here. For an island, it's pretty big—over twenty square miles—and it has lots of wildlife. I've also shared observations with the folks from the Smithsonian marine station nearby."

She then pointed in the direction of some of the small islands the brothers had seen from the plane.

"Yes, please go on," said Ram.

Sabara replied, "Here's how I like to think about what I've observed. Imagine each monkey species as a sector in the forest's ecological economy. And a social group is a firm within its species' sector. Take the larger of the common monkeys here—the mantled howler monkeys. They're the ones whose males make a loud roar you can hear as far as a mile away. They're pretty big, primarily black in color, with males up to twenty pounds and females up to fifteen."

She continued, "That species comprises the sector in the forest's economy that consumes plant products. They are vegetarians. They eat leaves, lots of leaves, plus some fruits and nuts. They're the only monkey in Central America that eats up to three quarters of their diet in leaves. They spend lots of time just sitting around while their saliva and stomach juices break down the leaves. Leaves are abundant all year round, but low in energy and hard to digest."

Ram said, "With you so far."

Sabara continued, saying, "Howler monkeys usually come in firms of about ten to twenty and up to as many as forty. Basically, each firm of animals is in the business of producing offspring. If a firm succeeds in making offspring, its members prosper through natural selection. I've also found that the way monkey firms are organized mirrors some of the ways human firms are organized."

Ram said, "Really? Please keep going."

Sabara continued, "Take the howlers again. They have no specific breeding season and reproduce year round. When a young mantled howler, male or female, approaches sexual maturity, it leaves the firm it was born in and goes job hunting in a nearby firm. The adults within a firm usually cooperate with each other, but they fight like the dickens with other firms. Each firm has its own franchise area, often around a hundred acres. But the franchise areas of adjacent firms can overlap. So if a firm encounters another firm when wandering around its franchise area, a big fight breaks out."

Sabara glanced at Lak and back at Ram and asked, "Heard enough?"

Ram replied, "No, keep going please." Lak nodded in agreement.

Sabara went on, saying, "A howler alpha male is like the CEO of his firm. And like the CEO of a human firm, he must make sure that the compensation paid to his subordinates is sufficient to keep them from bolting and joining another firm. The compensation is paid by making sure a subordinate gets some opportunity to reproduce. A CEO male gets to sire most of the firm's offspring himself, but the other males often get to sire some of the offspring too. If the subordinates don't get enough opportunity to sire, they can leave, in hopes of joining another firm, or maybe even go independent and try to start a firm of their own."

Sabara looked over to Ram, who nodded.

She continued, "Howlers are not touchy-feely, and not much grooming takes place. But some does. Grooming among adult males involves a higher ranked male grooming a subordinate male, which I interpret as an effort by the employers to keep their employees happy. Now, a CEO always faces the threat of a management challenge. If a young male leaving from another firm comes in and knocks off the CEO, he purges any existing infants to bring the females into estrus so he can mate with them to have offspring of his own. The females thus in effect give up their existing young to produce new offspring who can mature in an environment favorable to the new CEO rather than try to raise their previous young in an unsupportive environment."

Ram asked, "How about the other monkeys?"

Sabara replied, "The other common monkey is the white-headed capuchin, or organ grinder monkey. Not only is it a frequent companion of street musicians, it's also been trained—because of its intelligence—to assist paraplegic persons. It has a white skin on its face and white to golden fur on its head down to its shoulders and upper arms. Even though it's a smaller monkey, its brain is larger than the howler's. Males can get up to eight pounds in size and females a bit over six. Their name comes from the Capuchin friars, whose headgear looks like the monkey's head coloration."

Ram asked, "And what should we remember about these monkeys?"

Sabara replied, "Well, first, they work a different sector than the howlers do. They eat fruit and insects, not leaves, and they forage mostly in the canopy, not the ground. They don't compete much, if at all, with howlers. The two types of monkeys can even be seen occasionally feeding peacefully in the same trees. Also, juvenile capuchin and howler monkeys sometimes play together. So, they could work jointly as allies with you if needed."

Ram said, "Yes, that's good to know. Please go on."

Sabara continued, "Capuchin firms are organized differently from the howlers'. The firms consist of about fifteen to twenty monkeys. They don't reproduce year-round, but rather, only in the dry season, from December to April. So that means a whole year's offspring production is up for grabs in a narrow window of time."

Sabara paused in her narrative. "Do you want anything to drink? The midday heat will soon be with us."

"No, thanks," said Ram. "Not yet, at any rate. Please continue."

Sabara resumed, saying, "Now think about corporate raiders. Their modus operandi is to take over a company with little debt and low-priced stock. They buy all the stock, take the company into debt, and pocket the proceeds. To prevent this, the company has various defenses. Well, in capuchins, the females who are about to give birth at the beginning of the reproductive season are a target for male corporate raiders. The raiders band together to kick out the firm's males and kill any infants who have already been born. They then mate with the females and produce offspring of their own."

Sabara asked, "Can you guess what the female defense strategy is?"

Ram replied, "I'll bet the female capuchins team up against the raiders."

Sabara replied, "Exactly, the females stick together. Females do not leave the firm they are born in. So all the females wind up being related to each other in a matriline—you know, a great-grandmother, grandmother, mother, and daughter all living together. Being related evolutionarily incentivizes the females to cooperate with each other. Also, the females groom each other. They share reciprocal pleasure, which builds trust and coordination. So the females wind up cooperating a lot, not only in defending against raiding males who would kill their offspring, but also in parenting. A mother carries her baby on her back for the first four weeks of its life, and other females pitch in and carry the baby for two more weeks."

"How about the males?" asked Ram.

Sabara replied, "Can you guess the male defense strategy against raiders?"

"They probably cooperate too," Ram replied.

"Yes, here's how it works. Like in howlers, there is an alpha male, the CEO. He can remain CEO for a long time, up to fifteen years. He sires most of the young. When a raiding band arrives, the CEO helps the females defend against the raiders, presumably because he's sired most of the offspring that are in jeopardy of being killed by the raiders. Okay so far?"

"Yes. It's pretty complicated, but please continue," said Ram.

Sabara continued, "Now, the other males are like junior management. To coordinate and build trust with one another, they sleep touching each other, play together, and share homosexual sex. They don't groom each other like the females. By cooperating they can ward off raiding bands. Okay?"

"Yes, keep going," said Ram.

Sabara continued, saying, "So, unlike the females who stay their whole lives in the firm they were born in, the junior management males move in bands from firm to firm several time during their lifetime (though, as I mentioned, the senior management males can stay with one firm for a long time). The long residence time of the CEO means that most females share him as their father. So the females, overall, are related through their matriline and also share the same father. So, females are a tightly knit core of relatives within a capuchin firm."

Ram remarked, "This is much more intricate than the albatross social structure we've been working with back in Kauai. And we thought that was pretty sophisticated. But this is in a different league altogether. Anyway, you said there are other kinds of monkeys around here that we should know about too. What's the story with them?"

Sabara replied, "Another species is the tiny monkeys called red-crested tamarins. They live mostly in central and eastern Panama and toward the Pacific coast, not here on the Atlantic coast. But twenty years ago some were being kept as pets in one of the lodges on Bastimentos Island. They escaped and established a breeding colony in the island's forest. They are really tiny—both males and females weigh only one pound each, and the males and females share the same appearance. Their backs are covered in black fur with yellow patches. Their undersides are whitish, and their heads are covered in reddish fur with a conspicuous triangular patch of white that points down at their noses. They eat bugs, tiny fruits, nectar, and, curiously, the sap and gum that flows from cracks in the bark of trees. They're sort of like squirrels, but instead of running up and down tree trunks like squirrels do, they move horizontally, leaping from branch to branch in the canopy. Unlike all the rest of the native Central and South American monkeys, tamarins do not have prehensile tails."

"Yes," said Ram, "they do seem quite a bit different from the rest of the monkeys here."

Sabara replied, "Now, here's what's especially interesting about them. A female typically mates with two brothers who help her raise the young. Think of a wife with two husbands who are brothers and who all live together and raise their children jointly. In fact, this type of family occurs in Tibetan families who live near the border with India. Tamarins reproduce year-round—although mostly during the rainy season of April to June—and their group size is usually only three to five individuals. So you can think of these social groups a comprising a family firm, a Mom and Pop with Junior type of company."

Sarara looked over at Ram and Lak to ask, "That covers three of the species around here. Should I mention the other two you may encounter?"

Ram and Lak nodded approval.

Sabara continued, "There is one other type of monkey that is as big or maybe even bigger than the howler. It's called the black-handed spider monkey, and it's an endangered species. It's very arboreal, with arms longer than legs. These monkeys support their entire weight with a prehensile tail they use as an extra limb and which has a palm-like pad at its end.

These monkeys also have a vestigial thumb and long, strong, hook-like fingers. They swing from branch to branch like Tarzan. The fur on their back is brownish, their underside pale, their hands and feet black, and they have pale fur, like a mask, surrounding their eyes and extending to their chin. They often weigh twenty pounds, which is as big as a howler can get. What's especially interesting in these monkeys is that the females have a large protruding genital organ that from afar resembles a male organ. Because of this, people often mistake the females for males. The typical firm includes about thirty monkeys, and they occupy a huge home range of over 2,000 acres, which is ten to twenty times more area than the howlers' home range. They can travel over a mile a day swinging from branch to branch."

Ram looked surprised, and Lak whistled.

Sabara continued, saying, "These monkeys, like the howlers, are vegetarian, eating ripe fleshy fruit and some leaves but not nearly as many leaves as the howlers do. They're said to be very smart. They're pretty rare. I don't see them often and don't know so much about them. I do know that females leave the firm they were born into while the males stay behind—the opposite of the capuchins."

Looking at Lak, whose was becoming impatient, Sabara said, "Hang in there, one more species to go."

Lak replied, "I'm fine. Please keep going."

Sabara said, "The last species is another you're not likely to see. It's called the night monkey because it's nocturnal. These monkeys are pretty small, weighing about two pounds—bigger than the tamarins and smaller than the capuchins. The fur on their back is brownish, their underside is yellow, and the hair on the back of their hands and feet is black, but you can't really see all that in the dark. They're monogamous, a rarity among monkey species. A typical group consists of an adult pair, an infant, and a couple of juveniles. Like the tamarins, a firm of night monkeys is also a Mom and Pop and Junior family firm. So, that's it, a complete rundown on the monkeys around here."

Ram replied, "Thank you so much. You've given us a lot to absorb. I can't wait to meet these monkeys now that you've given us such insight into their lives. Now may I ask, where do we go from here? How would you recommend we search for allies among these monkeys, allies who will help us find Sita and then help us rescue her from Ravan?"

Sabara thought for a while, stroked her chin, and replied slowly, "Well, I guess if I were you I'd look for a monkey who's had roughly the same experience you've had. You need to find a former CEO from one of the monkey firms who's lost both his position and his wife. I don't think you'll find an exact parallel, but hopefully, you'll find enough in common with some monkey that he will empathize with your situation and agree to help, perhaps in return for some help from you."

Ram replied, "Okay, but where do we start? You've spent decades watching these monkeys. Could you suggest a monkey who might have had experiences similar to mine?"

Sabara thought some more and said, "Yes, I think I have a candidate. There's a howler monkey whose name might be Sugriv or something like that. What I know is that when other monkeys say syllables that sound like *soog* and *riv*, he looks up from whatever he was doing, so I assume Sugriv is his name. Now, what's interesting about him is that he was once the CEO of his firm. He has a brother whose name I think is Val. One day I saw Val attack Sugriv and drive him away. Val then took over the firm, including Sugriv's wife, who remained with the firm. Sugriv now lives by himself in mangrove thickets. I'm guessing that if you developed a relationship with Sugriv and helped restore him as CEO of his firm, he would help you in return by canvassing the other monkeys for information about where Ravan is now hiding."

"Okay, we'll seek him out. Can you suggest where we should start looking?"

Sabara replied, "I'd start with the path from Salt Creek on Bastimentos Island that leads into the jungle. Pitch your tents in there and you're sure to be visited by many monkeys, including Sugriv. There you can try to communicate with him, and hopefully build a relationship that will prove mutually beneficial."

Ram then asked, "And what about all the other monkeys you've introduced us to? Can we somehow employ their talents too?"

Sabara answered, "Yes indeed. They all bring special skills and insights to the table. The spider monkeys can quickly traverse huge distances through the jungle; the night monkeys, with their night vision, can offer an awareness of what goes on in the dark; the tiny tamarins can pick up hidden clues that bigger monkeys would overlook, as well as offer advice on how to successfully cooperate with one another; and the capuchins are clever, wily, and adaptable. They'll all be resourceful foot soldiers in your cause. But I'd start with Sugriv and the howlers. He would be the one to help enlist the support of the other monkeys. And the howlers, I should add, have long been formidable players in human affairs. Long ago, the

Mayans worshipped howler monkey gods as patrons of artists, musicians, sculptors, and writers, with all of those roles serving as a metaphor for the creation of mankind. Even today humans regard howlers with respect. Howlers usually get along just fine with humans, but if someone offends one of them, the howlers piss and throw shit at them, usually hitting their targets with uncanny accuracy."

The brothers made eye contact and chuckled.

Ram replied, "Thank you ever so much for all your advice. We are eternally grateful."

Sabara replied, "You're welcome. And now I'm tired. I think I'll lie down and get some rest. However, I have one small request."

"Certainly, just ask," answered Ram.

Sabara asked, "Could you please tuck me in? I've been lonely here."

Ram replied, "Of course, we'll tuck you into bed to help you feel all comfy. We're honored you asked."

So Ram and Lak followed Sabara into her sparsely furnished hut. She lay down on her bed and the brothers pulled the covers over her, kissed her on both cheeks, and set the mosquito netting. She sighed contentedly and then drifted off into sleep.

Then her breathing stopped. Ram and Lak looked at each other and knew her time had come. They closed the curtains in Sabara's hut and walked back to their B&B. There they told the proprietor that Sabara had just peacefully passed away. The proprietor then called the undertaker and the village priest to make preparations for a proper funeral and burial.

The next morning, the brothers gathered their gear, walked to the docks, took a water taxi to Bastimentos Island, and disembarked at the beach near the tiny village of Salt Creek. They hiked past a few small wooden huts and up a path into the jungle. There they cleared a spot for their tents and prepared to wait. They heard monkeys above them all around. They heard the throaty roar of howler monkeys, the squeals and barks of capuchin monkeys, and the bird-like chirping of tamarin monkeys. They occasionally caught a brief glimpse of monkeys darting among the leaves in the canopy overhead. The brothers knew they were being watched.

Lak unpacked and assembled Ceroc, making sure its battery was charged. Ram peered into the jungle for a better look at the creatures who were related to him almost as closely as he was to his human first cousins. Soon, he hoped, Sugriv would show himself.

Meeting Monkeys

Sugriv was one of the monkeys watching from the canopy as Ram and Lak trudged up the Salt Creek path into the jungle. He was a twenty-pound, full-throated howler, ferocious in his jet black fur. Sugriv was accompanied by his companion, advisor, and chief lieutenant, Hanuman, who was slightly smaller at seventeen pounds.

Hanuman had mostly gray fur, with black skin on his face and ears, and white fur on his haunches. He was not a howler. He was a green vervet monkey whose ancestors originally came to the New World from Sudan. He was part of an African monkey diaspora accompanying the African human diaspora. Hundreds of years ago, slave traders (and sometime the slaves themselves) had brought local monkeys with them as pets.

Hanuman's own parents were brought as pets from somewhere in the West Indies to Panama. Hanuman's mother escaped her cage while pregnant and took refuge in the rainforest. She gave birth and soon died because there was no firm to employ her. But her baby joined in with the play of howler and capuchin juveniles. When the juveniles gradually stopped their playing and joined their own firms as adults, Hanuman was allowed to stay on with the howlers. He was adopted by the howlers, eventually becoming Sugriv's chief lieutenant because, as an outsider, he was no threat to take over the CEO position himself.

Sugriv and Hanuman watched the brothers from their perch high in the canopy. The brothers were dressed as geeks but looked uncommonly athletic.

Sugriv said, "I'm worried they've been enticed here somehow by Val. Perhaps Val littered some old stolen coins on the path here to lead them on. Perhaps he's inviting the men to bulldoze our last habitat in order to search for more coins, for buried treasure. I have found refuge in this mangrove thicket, lousy with water, mud, and roots below instead of a proper forest floor. Without this fragment of forest, I will die."

Hanuman replied, "I too fear men and their genocidal instincts, but I see no sign these men come with evil intent. They seem sad and worried. I'll look closer."

Sugriv replied, "Be careful, my friend. Be very careful. I look forward to hearing what you find."

Ram saw that the monkeys gathering in the canopy overhead were mostly howlers. He reached for Ceroc, turned on its power switch, and pressed the button to activate the howler sign language option.

For decades, people had been communicating with apes using American Sign Language (ASL), pioneered for use with humans who were deaf. Although apes and humans could communicate in this way, monkeys and most other nonhuman primates didn't adapt to ASL. A breakthrough came a couple decades later when researchers figured out that monkeys had their own sign language. Researchers found they could communicate with monkeys if they learned monkey sign language (MSL) rather than trying to make the monkeys learn ASL. Knowing this, Sutik had programmed Ceroc with several dialects of MSL. On one hand, Ceroc was able to talk with humans verbally, and on the other hand, it could use sign language to speak with the monkeys. Ceroc could also tutor humans in MSL so they could learn to talk directly with monkeys, and it could help the monkeys understand what humans were trying to say.

As Hanuman dropped down to the ground from the canopy and approached, Ram rose up with a welcoming smile and offered his hand. Hanuman was surprised. A human had never before offered him a hand in friendship. Hanuman gazed at Ram and felt a strange sensation of familiarity—and with a human! He noticed the regal epaulettes with their simian blue embedded in the skin on Ram's shoulders. Hanuman could barely stop himself from grabbing Ram's hand in return while blurting out a greeting call in howler dialect.

As Hanuman watched, Ram gathered Ceroc in his arms. Hanuman saw what looked like a toy monkey, well built and realistic. Hanuman heard Ram say some words to the creature and saw its hand and fingers begin gesturing. It was actually speaking, speaking directly to him in his sign language! It also uttered a universal call of supplication.

Hanuman was shocked.

Then he signed back to the monkey-like object and Ceroc translated verbally to Ram, saying, "Hello, what brings you to our jungle fragment? What makes you so sad?"

While Ram was composing an answer, Hanuman decided to take a chance and disclose his own identity.

He signed to Ceroc, "I am Hanuman. I am the executive assistant to Sugriv, the former CEO of the howler firm in this region. Sugriv takes refuge in the nearby decrepit mangrove thicket because he was displaced by his brother in a boardroom coup. His brother, Val, took over all the company's assets, and he took Sugriv's wife, Ruma, to be his second wife. Now Sugriv is looking for partners to regain control of his company and reclaim his wife. Again, I ask, what brings you here?"

The brothers looked at each other and grinned.

Lak said, "This is a lucky development. This monkey who says his name is Hanuman is exactly whom we were hoping to meet up with."

Ram nodded and added, "And notice the clarity of his hand signals to Ceroc. He seems well educated, if I may put it that way. His dignity connotes an air of high-class breeding. Let him know why we're here."

Through Ceroc, Lak replied to Hanuman, telling him briefly of their travails since leaving Silicon Valley and how they lived for years in the forests of Hawaii only to lose Sita to a kidnapper. Lak explained how they followed Sita's trail to Panama and met up with Sabara, who urged them to get in contact with Sugriv.

Lak concluded, "We're hoping to ally ourselves with Sugriv. What do you think?"

Through Ceroc, Hanuman signed back, "This sounds promising. Both the CEO you serve and the CEO I serve have had similar wrongs inflicted on them. They should indeed find each other as welcome allies. Come, I will take you to Sugriv."

Hanuman guided them off the path into the mangrove thicket and away from their campsite. After going a distance, they heard, and then saw, a large howler monkey high in the canopy. Hanuman called out and a huge, formidable jet black howler descended a vine and dropped to a small spot of dry ground amidst the sinewy roots of the mangrove trees.

Hanuman then briefed Sugriv on what Lak had told him.

Sugriv turned to Ram, and through Ceroc, signed, "I am honored that you wish us to be allies."

Like Hanuman, Sugriv intuitively sensed a kindred spirit in Ram, a brother, and noticed the sign of rank glistening on Ram's shoulders. They immediately bonded.

Sugriv extended his hand, and Ram extended his own. They shook hands and then embraced.

Through Ceroc, Sugriv added, "May we be allies forever!"

Ram was beginning to get the hang of the sign language that Ceroc was using to communicate.

To Ceroc, Ram said, "Let me try to speak directly with Sugriv by myself."

Ceroc replied to Ram, "Go ahead, and I'll add any clarification that's needed."

So Ram moved his hands and fingers to sign to Sugriv, saying, "Now that we're allies, my machete is your machete, my bow your bow. I will seek out and kill the one who displaced you as CEO."

Ram looked over to Ceroc to see if he had signed correctly. Ceroc nodded approval.

Expecting that the message would have come from Ceroc, Sugriv turned his attention to Ram, surprised, and signed back, "Thank you. Once I'm restored to my firm, I'll have the assets to help you in the search for your wife. Until then, it's just me and Hanuman here in the mangroves. The two of us alone can't do much to support your mission. But when I'm restored, I pledge to search for your Sita across the surface of the earth, and from its bowels to the vaults of heaven."

Sugriv continued, saying, "Let's sit here to eat. Hanuman is going to collect some food for us."

The three of them sat on mangrove roots springing up from a dry patch along the forest floor. Then Hanuman dropped from the canopy carrying a handful of roots, fruits, and edible leaves.

As they were eating, Sugriv mentioned that one of his capuchin allies had brought him a belt pouch collected at the airport that might belong to Sita. He added that the capuchins regularly traveled to the city of Bocas del Toro by hitching a ride on the water taxis. The tourists were always amused by taking along a monkey as a passenger, and so the boat operators tolerated their riding along.

Sugriv asked Hanuman where the pouch was. Hanuman scurried up into the canopy and returned a few minutes later with the pouch.

When Ram saw it, tears came to his eyes.

Lak said to Ram, "That confirms it. Sita was here. This is concrete evidence confirming the electronic signals from her iPhone, which is all we had to go on before."

Ram nodded and, turning to Sugriv, said, "Yes, that pouch is hers. The villain who kidnapped her is called Ravan. Can you tell me where he took my wife?"

At the mention of Ravan's name, Hanuman looked up and scowled. Ram saw Hanuman scowl and resolved to ask him why later.

Sugriv replied, "We monkeys don't know where Ravan lives either. But we'll surely find where he's taken your wife. We have a worldwide network of monkeys we can call upon."

While the foursome was sitting on the mangrove roots allowing their food to digest, Ram asked Sugriv, "How exactly did Val manage to depose you as CEO of your firm? I want to know his strengths and weaknesses before confronting him."

Sugriv explained, "Val and I are the two sons of the former CEO, Rik. When my father died, Val, as the elder, automatically became CEO. I remained subordinate, standing by his side. Then one day a hunter named Dundub arrived in the forest where our firm is headquartered. He was looking to take some bushmeat. He grabbed at a woman from our firm. Val went to attack him, and the hunter let go of the woman. Then I joined Val and we attempted to drive the hunter out of the forest. We chased him a long distance. At one point I became separated from Val. Then I heard a shot echoing through the jungle. I looked, but I could find no one. Then I heard an outboard motor start and saw a boat speed off, heading in the direction of the mainland. I searched and searched, but could find no trace of Val. I returned to the firm and explained what had happened to everyone."

Ram said, "Sounds bad. What happened next?"

Sugriv continued, "The board members of the firm asked me to serve as acting CEO for one year. If, after that time, Val had not reappeared, then they would install me as the permanent CEO. Well, the year passed, and still no sign of Val. So the firm's board installed me the permanent CEO. But then, as luck would have it, Val did return. It turns out that he escaped from captivity on the mainland. There he attacked Dundub and gauged out his eyes and broke his hands at their wrists. After torturing him, Val left Dundub for dead, and indeed Dundub eventually died of his grievous wounds. Then Val found his way back to a launch that was coming to our island. He hid among the crates and, when the boat arrived on the shore, jumped off and ran back to rejoin our firm."

Ram remarked, "Your brother seems like a serious opponent."

Sugriv replied, "Yes, he is. And when he saw that I was now the CEO, he became enraged and drove me away, keeping all the firm's assets. He also took my wife, Ruma, to be his second wife. As long as I live here as a refugee among the mangroves, Val leaves me alone. But if I should venture into his firm's territory, he will surely kill me on sight."

Ram then reassured Sugriv, saying, "I promise I will make short work of Val."

Sugriv replied, "Well, my friend, I appreciate your willingness to take Val on, but I wonder if you're really a match for him."

Ram answered in surprise, "Are you kidding? Taking him out should be a piece of cake."

Sugriv replied, "I'd love to think so, but Val is a huge howler, and no one could beat him in battle. In fact, Val once killed a two-hundred-pound mountain lion ten times his size. Could you even do that?"

"Sure," said Ram, "but I won't. They're rare and endangered."

Sugriv replied, "Anyway, we don't have a mountain lion on the island at the moment, but we do have a gargantuan three-hundred-pound black male jaguar that escaped from one the lodges. It's a hundred pounds heaver than I estimate you are, and it's also a hundred pounds bigger than a mountain lion. A male jaguar needs 10,000 acres for home range, so he lives comfortably in our Bastimentos Island with its 14,000 acres of area. Can you defeat a jaguar?"

Ram replied, "Yes, I could easily take him down with my bow and arrow, but I won't. A jaguar is also rare and endangered, and I don't want to kill one. But I'll tell you what I will do instead—I will subdue it with my strength. Take me to the jaguar."

Sugriv shook his head and said, "Okay, as you wish."

So, Ram and Hanuman guided the brothers to the den where the jaguar slept. Ram and his brother climbed a tree.

Ram shouted down to the sleeping jaguar, "Hey, wake up." The jaguar stirred, rubbed his eyes with a paw, stood up, and looked around. He saw Ram in a tree overhanging his den shouting at him. The jaguar roared.

Ram jumped down from the tree onto the jaguar's back. He grabbed its neck in a headlock and wrestled with the large cat. After two hours of writhing around on the ground, back and forth, the jaguar began to tire.

Then Ram started stroking its head. Eventually the jaguar began to make a purring sound with each exhalation. Ram gradually released the jaguar. They faced each other warily.

Then Ram began backing away, and Lak swung down to the path to join him. The jaguar watched them go and made no move to follow.

From the branches above, Sugriv called down to Ram, "I'm truly astonished. I'm now convinced that you'll indeed be a match for Val. So let's go find him and be done. With you as my ally, I'm now optimistic for the future."

"Fine," said Ram, "I suggest you challenge him to a fight. When I get a clean shot at him, I will kill him with a well-placed arrow."

"Sounds like a plan," replied Sugriv. "Let's go."

So Sugriv, Ram, Hanuman, and Lak headed into the interior of the Bastimentos Island forest reserve to find Val. When they arrived at the trees where Val and his firm usually slept, Sugriv let out a huge roar, the kind of terrifying roar, heard for miles, that only a huge howler can produce.

The roar startled Val, who had been resting after his morning breakfast of tender leaves. Val looked over to see where the roar was coming from and saw his brother perched on a major branch of the adjacent tree. He saw that his brother was challenging him.

Ram, standing on the ground below, couldn't see Val in the canopy overhead. He heard Val grunt and saw leaves and branches come crashing to the ground as the huge monkey swung himself over to where Sugriv had issued his challenge. They ran up and down branches, jumping from tree to tree. Ram could discern that Val was pummeling Sugriv. Eventually, Sugriv fell down out of the canopy and landed with a thud near Ram.

Ram could see Sugriv was hurt and bleeding.

Sugriv signed to Ram, asking, "Where were you? You were supposed to help me. Instead you stood by and did nothing while Val beat up on me!" Sarcastically he added, "Some kind of ally you make."

Ram replied, "I'm sorry, I couldn't tell you apart. You're both huge monkeys and from a distance look identical to me. I couldn't shoot an arrow at the monkey I thought was Val without running the risk of hitting you instead."

"Pretty lame excuse," grumbled Sugriv.

"Anyway," replied Ram, "let's try again. This time wear something to identify you."

Lak reached into the vegetation at the edge of the path and pulled out a long thin vine. He wrapped the vine around Sugriv's neck and tied its ends in a square knot with an extra twist so it wouldn't come undone.

"Good," said Ram, "now I can tell you apart from each other. Go on and challenge him again. I'll be there for you."

Sugriv was doubtful. He hesitatingly returned to the tree next to where Val was now reclining while Ram hid in the underbrush. Sugriv sounded a mighty roar and dared Val to come out again to fight.

Val could not believe his ears. He wondered to himself, "Hasn't my brother learned anything? Does he really want to be beaten up again?"

Val's first wife, Tara, was nearby. Her intuition told her something was amiss.

She said to Val, "Don't respond to Sugriv. His challenge doesn't make sense. He could not be speaking for himself alone, because you can easily beat him up, as you've already shown. He must have found some sort of ally to help him."

Val paused as he gazed at his beautiful wife.

She continued, "Our son, Angad, reports to me that Sugriv had just joined up with some humans. Angad says they're powerful. Angad says the humans talk with Sugriv using our sign language. It seems they've mastered our code of conduct. Do not go out and fight Sugriv again. Instead, please make peace with him. Welcome him. He shouldn't be your enemy. You once were the best of friends. It should be so again. And if you befriend him, he will bring the humans along as allies with him, so they will now be on your side too."

But Val was resolute, and he said to Tara, "My honor has been challenged. How can I hold my head up high before you and the other members of my firm if I back down from a public challenge? Don't worry. I'll kill him once and for all, and we won't be annoyed by him anymore."

Val jumped to the branch on the adjacent tree where Sugriv was perched. The two of them began to fight again. And as before, Val slowly but surely began to subdue Sugriv, who was losing strength as blood oozed from his wounds and broken nose. Sugriv, looked around with desperation for Ram, imploring him with his eyes to come to the rescue.

Ram placed an arrow in his bow, pulled back the string and sent the wooden shaft screeching through the air until it buried itself in Val's back. Val fell forward, lost his footing, crashed through leaves and branches to the ground, and landed with a loud thud. But he did not die.

He looked Ram in the eye and signed to him, "Is this your code of combat? Gang up to prevent a fair fight? Shoot an unsuspecting fighter in the back?"

He spat out some teeth that had broken when he landed headfirst on the ground, saying, "You disgust me. How could you do this? How have I hurt you? I've never attacked you. I was in a fair fight with my opponent. You hid in the bushes like a common thief to shoot me in the back. Disgusting. You are a fake. Your virtue is a pretense. I can't understand why you did this. You couldn't kill me for bushmeat, for that's a crime in this land. I am a mere monkey living here on leaves and fruits. You will go to hell for this!"

Val felt his strength ebbing away. He wished, oh he wished, he had taken Tara's advice.

Ram responded to Val's condemnation, saying, "You're not pure as the white foam of ocean waves. You stole your brother's wife. It was not enough for you to take your firm's assets back from him, even though he was only stewarding your company in your absence. The firm was yours to possess, but not your brother's wife. Therein lies your sin. And for that I attack you because I am your brother's ally."

Ram continued, "As to sneaking up on you from behind a bush and shooting you in the back, that is the way a hunter stalks his prey, that is the way it always has been and always will be."

Val then replied in a broken voice, "So you have two codes of ethics. It's okay to sneak up and shoot a mere animal in the back, but you wouldn't do that to another human. You are a hypocrite. But I let that pass."

Turning to Sugriv he said, "Brother, forgive me for taking your Ruma as my second wife. Now, please, I implore you from the bottom of my heart, look after my own wife, Tara, and my son, Angad. Their destiny is in your hands."

Val then lost consciousness and breathed his last breath.

Looking down from the canopy, Tara and Angad saw their husband and father dying. The other monkeys from their firm saw their most recent CEO now dead on the ground. They all wailed piteously. Their howls filled the forest air, causing birds to stop chirping. All came to see what calamity had befallen their monkey neighbors.

Sugriv began to have second thoughts. He said disconsolately, "I have caused my brother to be killed. This is surely wrong. Two wrongs do not make a right. He never killed me when he had the opportunity. He banished me to the mangroves, but he did let me live. How can I assume control of the firm now that I have lost the moral high ground? How can I stand by while Tara and Angad howl bitterly because of me? What, oh what, shall I do?"

Hanuman crossed over to where Tara was sitting on the ground by her late husband's body.

He signed to her, "All of us die eventually, oh gentle lady. Val has come to the end of his allotted time. Do not grieve. Carry on."

Unconsoled, Tara murmured, "I see nothing left to live for."

Seeing what she had signed, Ram signed back to Tara, "Don't think your life worthless. Creation yields happiness and distress one after the other for all beings. Joining your husband in premature death won't change this inevitable cycle. In time, after you've mourned the death of your late husband, you'll come to enjoy Sugriv's protection. And your son, Angad, will be respected as the CEO designate in training. Your role now is to join Sugriv's household and attend him as his second wife. He will then protect and treasure you accordingly."

Ram turned to Sugriv and said, "Prepare according to your custom for dispensing with the body that once was Val."

Sugriv replied, "Our custom avoids leaving the body on the ground for scavengers. We'll bring the body to the den of the great jaguar whom you fought. We will leave the body there so that the greatest carnivore of the forest can eat without killing any of our vegetarian brethren."

Ram nodded his approval.

Ram turned again to Tara and signed, "Don't grieve the dead body that was your husband. A dead body is a collection of inert chemicals. The real person, the person to whom you were connected, is his soul, not his body. Only our ignorance attaches us to another's corporal presence, calling that physical manifestation our husband, son, or friend when we are actually connected to their souls. Our souls are immortal. Your bond to Val is eternal, living forever, even after his body disappears. Do not grieve."

Ram looked over at Sugriv and indicated that the procession to the jaguar's den should begin. The monkeys picked up the lifeless body that had been Val and carried it through the canopy to the jaguar's den. Ram and Lak followed them on the ground. When they arrived at the jaguar's den, the great cat awoke, stood up, and looked at Ram but did not move. The monkeys then cautiously descended from the trees and gently deposited Val's body on the ground. The monkeys ascended back into the canopy, and Ram backed away slowly, keeping an eye on the jaguar. The great cat remained still. Eventually, the monkeys and humans were far enough away from the jaguar's den that they could be sure the great cat was not pursuing them and that their task had been completed.

Once the monkeys and humans had returned to the grove where Sugriv's firm was headquartered, Ram signed to Sugriv that he and Lak would remain in a cave in the forest for the coming months until the rainy season ended. The brothers dismantled Ceroc, placing the parts in their carrying case for possible future use. They would fish and eat fruit and leaves. After the rain they would resume the search for Sita. Meanwhile, Sugriv was reunited with his wife, Ruma, and he re-assumed the position of CEO of his firm.

Search for Sita

As the months passed and the rains subsided, it became clear that Sugriv was taking no action to live up to his part of the alliance.

Ram asked Lak what to do. "Why hasn't Sugriv been in touch with us? It's time to get going. Each passing day further risks the life of my Sita. Nothing good can come of waiting."

Lak tried to reassure him, saying, "Don't worry yet. We'll find her."

Ram tried to relax. He looked around at the flowers coming into bloom, at the colorful bees and butterflies hovering around them—he listened to the dawn chorus of birds and watched at dusk as the sky filled with flocks of bats. Despite the local beauty, he missed the encampment back in Awaawapuhi Valley where he and Sita had lived happily for the last ten years. He didn't like living in a dark cave while it rained day and night, seemingly without end.

Although he sorely missed Sita, Ram's anger toward Ravan was growing daily. He fumed at the arrogance of this man who abducted his wife. Ram was impatient to show the world that no one could get away with such theft directed against him.

Ram said to Lak, "Where is Sugriv? I helped him. Is he now going to forget all about me? Is he just forgetful or actually evil? Does he take me for granted? How can he be so ungrateful?" Ram's anger was rising. "I think he's just lolling around all day after eating the tender leaves where he now lives, rubbing his tummy while his wives fawn over him."

Ram then added to Lak, "Go to him. Tell him that, just as I killed Val, I can kill him too. Tell him I won't tolerate duplicity."

Ram's anger was contagious. Lak told Ram, "He's become a traitor. I will go now and kill him myself."

Then Ram calmed down and said to Lak, "Don't kill him yet. Be gentle to begin with. After all, Sugriv is but a monkey. Perhaps you can awaken in him a sense of duty by starting out in a conciliatory way."

Lak stroked his chin in doubt, saying, "I wonder if we should let him off easy just because he's a monkey. He should still honor his word."

Then Lak strode off in the direction of the trees where Sugriv lived with his firm, determined to kill the lazy slob if he didn't live up to his promise.

Meanwhile, back among the trees, Sugriv was indeed lolling around with the members of his firm. Seeing this, Hanuman was getting worried himself. He could tell that Sugriv wasn't about to take any action on Ram's behalf.

Hanuman approached Sugriv, who had been dozing, and advised him, "You have regained your CEO position and the spoils that go with it, but you won't prosper for long without attending to your friends and allies. You promised to help Ram rescue Sita from her kidnappers. It's shameful if Ram should have to come here himself to ask you to honor your promise after all he's done for you."

Sugriv awoke with a start.

To both Hanuman and Angad he said, "You're totally right. I've let myself slip. Please summon my other allies among the monkeys—summon the CEOs of the capuchins, spider monkeys, night monkeys, and tamarins. Together, we'll hatch a plan to find Sita."

But after Hanuman and Angad left to find the other CEOs in the forest, Sugriv climbed over to where he had been reclining and went back to sleep in the company of his wives, Ruma and Tara.

Once Hanuman and Angad had brought the other CEOs to Sugriv's domain, they all heard Lak approaching along a path on the forest floor. Angad dropped down to the ground to meet him.

Lak, who had by now picked up some monkey sign language himself, began quietly by saying, "Son, please tell your father that I have arrived to see him."

Angad scrambled up a tree, awoke Sugriv and told him of Lak's arrival. Sugriv snapped to attention. He told Angad to immediately bring Lak some sweet, ripe fruits—watermelon and mangoes. Sugriv peered down from his branches at Lak on the forest floor and could see he was angry.

Sugriv said to Tara, "Go down to Lak and try to calm him. He will not continue to be angry in the presence of a lady."

So Tara dropped down from the canopy and approached Lak, saying, "My dear, it's wonderful to see you again after so many weeks. You seem out of sorts. Is there anything I can do to help?"

Lak replied, "My brother and I are angry with Sugriv. He's more interested in lolling around after gorging himself than fulfilling his promise to us. We want you to remind him of his solemn obligation."

Tara replied, "Please forgive him. He is, after all, but a monkey. Of course he's fallen victim to the temptations of food and sex. Even wise geeks among the humans have sometimes been overcome by desire. What could you expect of a mere monkey?"

Lak replied, "Not so fast. I prefer to hold the CEO of a major firm of howlers to a proper standard of ethics rather than slide down the slippery slope of accepting immoral behavior. Tolerating immorality among you monkeys devalues you, rendering you subhuman and not entitled to human rights. Look at your advisor, Hanuman. He shows no sign of shirking his responsibilities, and he adheres to the highest of ethical standards."

Tara appeared taken aback.

Lak continued, saying, "Tell Sugriv to accompany me. Together, we shall speak with Ram."

Tara ascended to the canopy and told Sugriv what Lak had said. Sugriv then descended from the canopy to join up with Lak.

He apologized, saying, "Please forgive my transgressions. I am devoted to Ram and to honoring my promises."

Sugriv then gathered the other monkey CEOs, and together they set out with Lak to join up with Ram.

When the delegation of monkeys met up with Ram, Sugriv prostrated himself on the ground and begged forgiveness.

Ram raised him up, seated him on a log next to him, and said, "A wise CEO allocates effort to ethics, profit, and pleasure, in that order. He who neglects the first two in favor of the third wakes up one day after falling, as though asleep, from the treetops down to the ground. The CEO who honors his commitments gains great ethical merit. The time has come for you to earn ethical merit."

Sugriv replied, "Again, I'm sorry for not attending to my promise. Please let me make it up to you now. I have brought with me the CEOs of the monkey firms living in our neighborhood."

Sugriv then introduced Sush of the capuchins, Nal of the spider monkeys, and Maind of the tamarins, as well as the secretive Nil of the night monkeys.

Sugriv said to Ram, "All these CEOs have agreed to assist in rescuing your wife from her kidnapper. What do you want them to do?"

Ram replied, "First we have to find Ravan's secret hideout. When we know where that is, we can formulate detailed plans for how to extricate my wife from his clutches."

Sugriv assigned the CEOs to search in different directions. He sent the spider monkeys to travel south through the forest canopy. He explained to the other monkeys that they should make their way to the Boca del Toros airport and stowaway in the wheel compartments of the little planes that landed there. For their short flights, the little planes never reached dangerous altitudes. Then, after the little planes went on to land at the big airports, they should hop off and stowaway in the luggage compartments of the giant planes that went very far away. Sugriv knew that this would allow the monkeys to reach all the regions of the earth.

He added, "I want you to return in a month and report what you've found."

As it happened, the night monkey found his way by airplane to southeast Asia, the capuchin to Africa, and the tamarin to South America, while the spider monkey sped, hand over hand, through the canopy to Central America.

Sugriv said to Angad and Hanuman, "I would like you to scour the east coast of this land where we live. Ravan's black stealth jet was last seen heading east out to sea. I believe your search will have the best chance of all of finding out where he's gone."

Ram heard that exchange and approached Hanuman. He could see Hanuman was itching to get going.

Ram said, "Here is my ring. If you find Sita, please give this to her. I hope this will reassure her and let her know that we are soon coming to her rescue. Now, let me teach you the human sign for hello."

Ram demonstrated the salute-like sign of ASL. Hanuman repeated it back.

Ram resumed speaking to Hanuman in MSL and signed "fine."

Then Ram handed over his wedding ring of flowing gold and platinum to Hanuman and added, "On you rests my main hope for finding Sita. I pray you will succeed."

Hanuman slipped the ring on his finger and replied, "I will succeed, and I will surely give this to Sita. I am loyal to you as my CEO's ally. Also, I have my own reasons for wishing to eliminate Ravan. You saw me scowl when you first mentioned Ravan's name?"

Ram nodded.

Hanuman continued, "Part of his syndicate is devoted to harvesting vervet monkeys such as myself. He traps them and sells them as slaves to drug companies. The drug companies infect my brothers and sisters with debilitating and painful human diseases. Then they inject my suffering brothers and sisters with experimental drugs that rarely work as cures. The drug companies' conduct is crude and barbaric. I have sworn to put a stop to their slave trade in monkeys if I ever get the chance. Now you have given me that chance. I will succeed. You will soon be reunited with your Sita."

The assembled monkeys then headed for the airports or other points of departure, optimistic and enthusiastic about their mission.

But after a month, the monkeys straggled back to Bastimentos Island and reported to Sugriv. The night monkey had found no trace of Sita in southeast Asia, and the capuchin had found none in Africa. Neither the tamarin in South America nor the spider monkey in Central America had discovered anything either.

Meanwhile, Angad and Hanuman scoured the ports and fishing villages along the Atlantic coast of Panama, asking among the local monkeys if they happened to know where Ravan lived. Although some had seen Ravan's black stealth jet on occasion, none knew where he came from or where he went.

Out of desperation, Angad and Hanuman sought out a small inter-island freighter, the kind that could reach islands lacking a deep-water port for container ships. These tiny vessels had old-fashioned cargo holds with booms to hoist nets filled with cargo boxes on board. Security was lax among the informal longshoreman, allowing Angad and Hanuman to board unnoticed and to remain out of sight during the short voyages from island to island.

The boat left Panama and headed east, eventually docking at a city Ram would later tell Hanuman was Port of Spain, Trinidad. Hanuman and Angad hopped off the boat and looked for local monkeys around the port to ask if Ravan lived on this island. They found no monkeys to speak with, so both reboarded the boat.

The boat headed north to dock at a port that Ram later told Hanuman was St. George's, Grenada. Here they had better luck. A parrot perched on the shoulder of a dockside worker said monkeys lived in the interior jungle of the island. Hanuman and Angad looked each other in the eye and knew they had to check out a possible lead."

After the pair shimmied down a rope tying the boat to the posts at the dock's edge, they scurried into town and hitched a ride on a banana truck that drove into the mountains. When they entered the jungle of the Grand Etang National Park, Hanuman and Angad hopped off the truck once it stopped to let some pedestrians cross the road. As they swung themselves into the nearby tree canopy, they felt a sense of home after so many days mousing around villages and ports and riding on boats and trucks.

Once among the trees it wasn't long before Hanuman and Angat could discern the calls of their brethren. The monkey sounds were strange to them, but monkey sounds nonetheless. They traveled through the trees in the direction of the calls and came upon a firm of beautiful multicolored arboreal monkeys.

The fur on the back of these monkeys was the color of rust, and their legs, arms, and tails were dressed in black, contrasting with the cream-colored fur on their chest and face. The CEO had a scrotum painted in blue, like the blue of Ram's epaulettes. His wives had pendant nipples. Hanuman noticed that, like him, their tails were not prehensile. (Since childhood he had envied his friends, the howlers, as they did acrobatic tricks with their prehensile tails, tricks that he dare not attempt.) The monkeys here stuffed food into cheek pouches, reminding him of a human with whose cheeks were puffed out with air. Hanuman surmised these monkeys, though strangers to him, were nonetheless distant relatives who originally came from the same place his ancestors had. Ram later told him that humans called them mona monkeys. They, like Hanuman himself, originally came with the human slaves in the late 1600s to these islands from western Africa—in the case of the mona monkeys, perhaps from somewhere near the Congo.

Hanuman and Angad approached the monkey firm. In the universal gesture of supplication, they bowed low. The mona monkeys could see these new strangers were not a threat.

The mona CEO then signed in his local dialect saying, "You're not from around here. Who are you and where did you come from?"

Hanuman could understand enough of their dialect to respond. He explained they were from the mainland and their mission was to find the kidnapper of their friend's wife. He asked, "Have you seen the black stealth jet the kidnapper uses?

The Mona CEO replied, "Yes, we see it, but we don't know where it's based. We don't hang out much near the ocean by the airport. We stay up here in the jungle in the center of the island. Still, you've come a long way. Come join us as we eat."

Hanuman and Angad then spent the rest of the day and most of the next lolling around in the trees where the mona monkeys lived. They loved the succulent fruits and tender leaves that the forest in Grenada had to offer. Some of the mona monkeys also visited a parking lot along the road where tourists gave them bananas and other fruits which they stuffed in their cheeks. They invited the their visitors to join them, but Hanuman and Angad declined, having had enough contact with humans during their travels so far and happy to be spending time in the trees.

After a while Angad said to Hanuman, "I think we should stay here. I am afraid to return to Sugriv empty-handed, and we're late too. His clear instructions were to take a month, no more. I'd rather simply remain here in the hospitality of these monkeys than go home to an uncertain future."

Hanuman responded, "Don't worry. Sugriv is a good-hearted monkey. He wouldn't punish us when we did our best to carry out his commands."

Angad replied, "I don't share your regard for Sugriv. After all, he caused my own father, Val, to be dishonorably killed and now has taken my mother, Tara, as his second wife. And even after Ram had rendered him the great service of reinstalling him as CEO, he still needed prodding to honor his promise to help Ram. I don't see how Sugriv could ever really be kind to the son of his former enemy. Indeed, I think he's only looking for Sita from fear of Lak and not out of a sense of obligation to Ram himself."

Angad then withdrew from Hanuman's side and swung himself to the trees where the mona monkeys were resting. There he lay down on a nearby branch.

Suddenly the monkeys heard a rustle below on the jungle floor. A large bird was crashing through the underbrush, a bird that appeared to be a hawk, but a hawk walking, not flying.

The mona monkey's CEO signed to Hanuman that this bird was called Sampat. He was a great hawk who had once flown too high and too long in the open sun in the hot tropical air. His wings overheated, singeing his primary feathers and damaging the follicles where his feathers would regenerate. His follicles had since healed and his feathers regenerated, but Sampat was still reluctant to take wing again.

Hanuman wasn't sure if he could speak with a hawk, but he tried anyway to sign to the hawk to see if it would respond.

The hawk observed Hanuman signing to it. The hawk unfolded its wings and flapped them, apparently in an invitation to say more.

Hanuman hoped the bird could raise and lower its wings, extend or withdraw them, and hop up and down in ways that resembled his own sign language, albeit in a different dialect.

So Hanuman tried out a couple of symbols. He pointed to the sky and signed sky. Sampat raised his wings and pointed his bill to the sky. Hanuman pointed to the ground and signed ground. Sampat pointed his bill at the ground and scratched the surface with his feet.

His excitement growing, Hanuman wondered if he might talk with the bird by making a dictionary translating between the bird's signs and his signs. He spent the rest of the day and much of the next day working with Sampat to develop a shared set of terms.

Toward the end of the second day, Hanuman wished to go beyond vocabulary building and to start a conversation.

He signed to Sampat, "You resemble the great hawk whom I'm told gave his life in protecting my friend's wife."

At this, the hawk began screeching, calling, and wailing. It went on this way for over an hour, and the nearby animals came by to see what the disturbance was.

Eventually the hawk looked at Hanuman inviting him to sign.

Hanuman obliged, signing "Was the great hawk who died helping my friend a relative of yours?"

Sampat signed back, "Yes."

Hanuman continued, "Was he perhaps your younger brother?"

Again Sampat signed back, "Yes."

Continuing, Hanuman signed, "Before you hurt your wings, did you fly over the many islands in this ocean?"

Sampat signed back, "Yes."

Hanuman then took a deep breath and asked, "Do you know where my friend's wife's kidnapper lives?"

Sampat enthusiastically signed back, "Yes! Yes! Yes!"

Hanuman became really excited. "At last, the break we've been looking for," he thought to himself.

Angad saw what was going on and came over to look.

Hanuman then asked the bird, "Where?" and pointed to the south. Sampat signed, "No."

Hanuman then went around the compass. South-southwest? No. Southwest? No. West-southwest? No. On he went until he reached north-northwest.

At last, Sampat signed, "Yes." He signed it twice again for emphasis.

Hanuman then asked how many islands away. Sampat jumped up and down nine times. Hanuman asked again for confirmation. And again Sampat jumped up and down nine times.

So now Hanuman knew that Ravan was nine islands away from where they were in a north-northwest direction. Hanuman bowed to the bird in the universal symbol of thanks.

During his conversations with Hanuman, Sampat found himself using his wings much more than he had since his injury years ago. Sampat thought that perhaps by some miracle he could fly again, and in any case, he should not be afraid to try. He flapped his wings as he had in days of old, and lo and behold, found himself becoming airborne again for the first time in many years.

He dipped his wings toward Hanuman to say thanks. Sampat hoped that Hanuman could discern how grateful he was to be flying again on his own two wings.

Indeed, Hanuman knew he had accomplished two good things—the great bird had gained the confidence to fly again, and he had learned where Ravan was.

Hanuman next turned his attention to how to get to the correct island.

Angad said to Hanuman, "As a howler, I'm too big to stowaway in the wheel compartment of the small low-flying interisland planes that fly around here. Meanwhile, the tramp freighter we took here is heading back to Panama, not farther out in the ocean."

Hanuman didn't know how to respond. He felt that Angad might be shirking his duty to act.

Then the monkeys heard yet another crash on the jungle floor beneath them. A shaggy black South American spectacled bear with white rings around its eyes lumbered into sight. The mona monkey CEO signed to Hanuman that this bear was called Jamb. He had escaped from a private zoo on the island that catered to tourists.

Hanuman shimmied halfway down a tree to engage the bear. He signed to the bear, "Hello."

The bear leaned back on its haunches and, with its front paws, signed back, "Hello. You're not from around here."

Hanuman signed his name to Jamb and said he was looking for the kidnapper of his friend's wife.

Jamb said, "I saw you arguing about who should be the one to travel up the island chain to the place where your friend's wife is being held."

Both Hanuman and Angat nodded in agreement.

Speaking to Hanuman, Jamb continued, "You should be the one to go north. You are small enough to fit in the wheel compartment of the planes around here, and because you're a vervet yourself, you'll blend in with the monkeys on the other islands north of here."

Hanuman, perhaps reluctantly, nodded affirmatively.

Jamb concluded, "Good. All of us who wish to see evil destroyed have pinned our hopes on you."

Hanuman turned to Angad and asked, "When I find Sita, what should I do? Should I try to infiltrate Ravan's estate and free Sita? I could guide her to the airport so she can fly back to the mainland where her husband is waiting."

"No," replied Angad, "Sugriv was clear that our task is to return and report back to him on Sita's location. Then he and Ram can decide on the next steps."

"Okay. I will simply locate her and give her Ram's ring as reassurance."

Hanuman then hopped on a banana truck headed to the side of the island where the airport was located. He waited at the edge of the runway until a propeller-driven plane landed. It had four letters on it: *L-I-A-T*, signifying the airline whose small planes fly short half-hour hops among the islands. Hanuman ran over to the plane while luggage was being unloaded. He swung himself onto the plane and squeezed himself into the wheel compartment. He was now ready for his journey north to find Sita.

Hanuman Finds Sita

The pilot started the engines, and the propellers began turning. The plane taxied to the end of the runway as the two propellers started whirring and throbbing. The plane lumbered down the runway. Just as it seemed the plane would run out of pavement, it gradually climbed into the air, inch by inch, foot by foot. The wheel assembly folded into the wheel compartment. After the assembly came to rest, Hanuman peered around the tire and stared down at the moving ground below.

The plane left the island that Ram would tell him was called Grenada and headed out to sea. Through a gap where the wheel compartment covers joined, Hanuman peered down at the islands below as the plane flew on. After flying over tiny islands that Ram later said were the Grenadines, the plane landed on the first large island it came to. Ram would later tell him this one was called St. Vincent. When on the ground, Hanuman jumped down, looked around, and, finding no monkeys to talk to, jumped back on board to curl up again in the wheel compartment.

The plane took off and went on to a second large island, where, once again, it landed. Ram said this one was called St. Lucia. Then the plane landed at the third large island, Martinique; the fourth, Dominica; and then the fifth, Guadeloupe. The plane passed around a large volcano spewing smoke on the sixth large island, Montserrat. The plane skipped over the seventh large island, Nevis, and then landed on the eighth large island, St. Kitts.

He jumped off the plane once again, and at last Hanuman saw some monkeys to talk to. He ran over to where they were perched on the rocks near the airport's edge.

Hanuman was excited. These monkeys looked like him. These were his brothers and sisters. And they spoke his language fluently—no need for sign language or deciphering strange dialects here. The local monkeys gathered around Hanuman as he approached.

One asked, "Did you really arrive on the plane that just landed?"

Hanuman embraced the speaker, saying, "Oh brother, I've been searching for you all my life. I've come such a long way."

The speaker answered, "Welcome home. Will you stay with us?"

Hanuman replied, "I'd love to, but I'm looking for the kidnapper of my human friend's wife. The kidnapper uses a black stealth jet. Does he live here?"

The speaker replied, "No, he doesn't. But you're close, just one more island away. We monkeys have been on the island you just flew over, as well as on this island, for hundreds of years. But we've just colonized the next island, the one where your kidnapper lives. If you get back on the plane and continue flying in your same direction just one more island, your journey will be over. Good luck."

Hanuman replied, "Thank you my brothers, I hope to return someday to visit."

At that, he hopped back on the plane and squeezed into the wheel compartment. The plane took off and soon landed in the center of the ninth large island Hanuman had seen since he first climbed aboard the plane, the island that Ram was to call St. Eustatius. It was late afternoon.

Hanuman jumped out from the wheel compartment. Here too he could readily see monkeys on the ground and perched on boulders. He ran over to some who were lingering by the edge of the airport. They were indeed vervet monkeys, just as he was.

Hanuman asked a monkey who looked like the CEO whether a black stealth jet was based here. The monkey answered, "Yes, it's here."

Hanuman continued, "Does the man who owns the jet live here too?"

"Yes, he does," was the reply.

Holding his breath, Hanuman brought himself to ask, "And did he recently bring a captive human woman here in that black stealth jet?"

And the monkey replied, "Yes, he did."

Hanuman was elated.

He asked, "Can you direct me?"

"Yes," the local CEO vervet replied as he pointed in a northwest direction. "Head over there until you come to a bay that faces the ocean."

Ram was later to tell Hanuman that the bay, located on the Caribbean side of the island, was called Jenkins Bay.

Hanuman scurried off in the indicated direction. As he crossed between two small hills, the remnants of ancient volcanism, he came to a bay that opened out toward a beautiful blue ocean. On the shores of the bay, Hanuman saw a large estate surrounded by a tall stucco-coated brick wall topped with barbed wire and broken glass. The estate was similar to many of the gated communities Hanuman had seen in his travels. Over the wall he saw a large estate house with a widow's walk on the roof, private formal gardens, swimming pools, decorative ponds with fountains in their centers, and several smaller buildings, gazebos, and sheds.

Night was approaching, so Hanuman decided to wait until morning. He climbed into a nook among the branches of a tree outside Ravan's estate to spend the night.

Hanuman awoke at dawn and noticed a tree branch that hung over the wall. He crept out along the branch and dropped down into the grounds of Ravan's estate. He then crept into the large estate building next to the swimming pool and saw the equipment from a rock band lying on the stage of a ballroom. He looked into another room with double doors leading to a grand kitchen. He peered into the kitchen and saw a large walk-in freezer. In the dining room, a table was set with plates and wine glasses. On closer look, the plates still had food on them, a dessert course, left over from the preceding night. The glasses were half filled with a sweet-smelling amber wine. A bowl in the center of the table had some chocolate candies in it. Hanuman helped himself to the candies, being hungry from his long cold journey in the wheel compartment. He continued to a room with couches and armchairs on a marble floor. Here he found people sleeping, snoring. The men, wearing black T-shirts with the syndicate insignia, were sprawled about alongside women in sheer cocktail dresses with plunging necklines. But Hanuman did not think Sita was not among them.

"Where is Sita?" he wondered.

He kept searching. He saw a set of stairs leading down to a garage. Downstairs, he found two four-wheel-drive jeeps, one with a machine gun mounted on a turret behind the front seats. Beyond the jeeps he saw an open door. Passing through, he encountered Ravan's black stealth jet. Near the jet was a door opening into a room with printing equipment. It was printing wide strips of green paper, the kind of paper Hanuman saw people carrying in their purses and wallets. Along the wall he saw cabinets filled with guns, rifles, grenades, and what looked like coils of ropes. He saw a funny suit hanging up, big enough to cover a human's whole body, that included a mask with a tube leading from the nose to a can. And beyond the jet he saw another door that led to stairs descending some-where, perhaps as far as the edge of the ocean or onto the cliffs bordering the ocean. But he didn't have time to explore further.

Hanuman felt he was getting closer, but he said again to himself, "Where is she? Where is Sita?"

Hanuman retraced his steps and climbed back up the stairs into the room where people were sprawled about, sleeping off their drunken stupor. He saw the door to a room he hadn't explored yet, a door leading to a bedroom. A large man was snoring on a huge bed accompanied by two young women, one sleeping next to him on either side. Hanuman surmised the man was Ravan. His pressed black trousers, trademark black T-shirt, crocodile leather shoes and belt, and pistol holster were draped over a chair. His torso was buffed, and his tattooed shoulders, biceps, and forearms contrasted with the white silk sheets. But Hanuman wasn't looking for Ravan, not now.

Hanuman again asked himself, "Where is Sita?"

Hanuman then went outside and searched the grounds. He bounded down the hill to the beach and looked around. Nothing. He looked again. This time he detected a small gazebo in a clearing halfway up the hill near a grove of trees at the edge of the estate. He scampered up the hill to the gazebo.

Hanuman saw a gorgeous, statuesque dark-skinned woman in rags with a tear-stained face. Grim attendants in trademark black T-shirts sat on lawn chairs nearby keeping an eye on her. The gorgeous woman was sitting at a table in the early morning sun, trying to read a book. But she kept looking away, stopping to sob and wail, before resuming her half-hearted attempt to read.

Hanuman surmised this woman must be Sita, as she was clearly not another partygoer. She was a distraught prisoner, dressed without regard for style, with tattered clothes loosely covering her emaciated body.

Hiding behind a bush, Hanuman wondered how he should approach Sita. But then he heard an alarm radio blaring in Ravan's bedroom followed by a loud yawn, a raucous burp, and the murmuring of the women who had been sleeping with him. Ravan soon came striding out of the house. He went directly to Sita at the gazebo.

Ravan stared at Sita sitting at the table in the gazebo. She didn't look up at him or notice him in any way.

Ravan entreated her, saying, "Come be with me. You're the most beautiful woman in the world. Yet your youth is wasting away. See all I have to offer you here. I will treasure you forever. I ask you to become my wife, the first among all of them. Throw off the rags, shake off your grief, and come have some fun with me."

Still not looking at him, Sita replied, "Go to hell, I say again and again. Kidnapping the wives of others is not the way to earn a woman's love. How could I leave my husband after all the loving moments we've shared? I am as inseparable from Ram as sunlight from the sun. Release me, make peace with Ram, and ask his forgiveness. If you continue to keep me here, it's only a matter of time until Ram comes to destroy you, your family, your entire syndicate, and all you stand for."

Ravan snarled back, "Oh, woman, if you were anyone else, I would have you killed. But my love for you prevents that—for now. I will not hurt a hair on your head while I await your free and open choice to join me as my first wife, displacing Mandara, a modest woman, who would become my second wife. I leave you now. But remember, I've given you a year to accept my offer. You have only a few months left before I offer your flesh to the sharks you see lurking offshore."

Sita rejoined, "Go to hell, I say."

Ravan seethed and spoke to the attendants guarding Sita, "Continue to soften her up in whatever way you can. Remind her of the advantages of hooking up with me and help her forget her time with Ram."

At that, he stomped back to the grand house on his estate.

The attendants then started in on Sita, cajoling her, needling her, and scoffing at her love for Ram. Eventually, Sita just gave herself over to nonstop crying. She fell to the ground outside the gazebo and sobbed uncontrollably. The attendants just shrugged and resumed sitting on the chairs, where they watched Sita's agony with amusement.

One of the attendants said to another, "I don't think this is going to end well."

The other just nodded in reply.

After a while, the attendants got up to go to the main building to collect their lunches before returning to their posts guarding Sita. With the attendants briefly gone, Hanuman spied his chance to make contact with Sita. He scurried from behind the bush where he was hiding and ran up to Sita.

Sita didn't know what to make of this monkey that had boldly approached her. She was used to seeing monkeys scampering around the rocks and occasionally climbing the trees, but they always kept their distance and bounded away when she tried to get close to them. Of course, she could tempt them to come closer by leaving some food nearby, but then the monkeys would only dart in, grab the morsels, and quickly withdraw. This monkey did the opposite. He approached without the temptation of food, sat by Sita's side, and gazed with kindly eyes at her tear-stained face. He put the palms of his hands together over the top of his head and bowed low to Sita in the universal gesture of respect and supplication.

Sita was amazed, and with her hands gestured for the monkey to rise. Hanuman then tried to convey that he had been sent by Ram. He stood up straight and tall and, with his arms and legs, gestured as though he was marching. He pointed toward the horizon far away.

Sita knew right away this wasn't just another ordinary monkey. She knew the monkey was trying to communicate.

Hanuman then tried the ASL hand signal for hello, making like a salute. Sita knew only a few ASL signs, but this one wasn't hard to figure out.

So she signed hello back to Hanuman.

Hanuman then grinned and uttered some squeals of joy, knowing he had made contact.

Hanuman then removed the ring Ram had given him and gave it to Sita.

Sita could barely believe her eyes. This was the first sign from Ram she had received in nearly a year's captivity.

She rose up joyously and embraced Hanuman, saying, "Thank you, thank you."

Hanuman could tell that he had brought Sita great happiness and that made him happy as well.

Hanuman then gestured as though to indicate that Ram was coming. He pointed toward the horizon and then, with his hands, indicated that someone far away was coming here. Sita made a sign of a knife across her throat and pointed to Ravan's estate house. Hanuman surmised that Sita was telling him she was in danger and would soon be killed.

Sita wanted to continue conversing with Hanuman, but the sound of the attendants returning intruded on them. Sita quickly slipped Ram's ring on her index finger, removed her own ring from her ring finger, and gave it to Hanuman. Hanuman bowed low to Sita and put her ring on his pinky finger to give to Ram, confirming that he had indeed found Sita and made contact with his loving, waiting wife.

Hanuman's Havoc

Hanuman withdrew from Sita and looked about. He wanted to explore Ravan's estate before returning, hoping to test its strength and find its weaknesses. He also wanted to begin the attack against Ravan.

Hanuman trashed the garden nearest to him, pulling flowering bushes up by their roots, knocking over trellises with flowering vines, kicking dirt into the goldfish pond, and overturning lawn tables and chairs.

The security personnel, all wearing those trademark black T-shirts, became alarmed. They wondered what was going on. The monkeys living throughout the island were perhaps pests now and then, but never dangerous or malicious. What was going on here? Seeing the security personnel, Hanuman slushed saliva around in his mouth and let the froth drip from his lips.

The personnel then pulled back away from him. "He's got rabies," one shouted. "He's a mad monkey. Be careful he doesn't bite you, or you'll catch it too."

Earlier, as the attendants were returning from the house with their lunches, they saw Sita apparently communicating somehow with the monkey. The monkey had scurried off as the attendants arrived at the gazebo where Sita was seated.

They asked her, "Who was that monkey?"

She replied, "I have no idea. He came over here and hung around for a while. You're the ones with spy cameras and high-tech security gear. Don't you record monkeys? Or is it only humans you care about?"

The attendants fell silent and resumed their posts guarding Sita.

One of the security men ran to Ravan, who was eating breakfast, and told him a mad monkey was loose in the garden, destroying the plants and making a mess.

Ravan spoke sharply, saying, "Well then, trap or kill him somehow. Why are you wasting time talking to me? Take some initiative and get rid of the crazy monkey before he does any more damage."

Some security personnel then tried to corner Hanuman and to poke him with sticks, but Hanuman was having none of it. He felt driven to avenge the deaths of his vervet monkey brothers that Ravan's syndicate had captured and sold into slavery for drug tests. He jumped on the men and bit and scratched those he could get his hands on, gouging out the eyes of some and breaking the noses of others. He even pulled the flesh from the cheeks of one man, revealing his skull bones. The security henchmen fell back, injured, maimed, and defeated.

Through a window of his house, Ravan witnessed the debacle unfolding in his garden. He ordered his burly West Indian chief of security, Jambu, to put an end to it.

But as soon as Jambu came out of the house, Hanuman scampered up to the roof of the compound's main building and began pulling clay tiles off the roof, throwing them on the ground and through skylights.

Jambu tried to follow the monkey, climbing up a ladder to the roof himself. He pulled out his pistol and took a shot at Hanuman.

The bullet grazed Hanuman in the temple. His blood began pouring from the wound, staining the fur around his face and head a shiny crimson red.

Vines of bougainvillea were growing on a tall wrought iron trellis extending up the side of the house to the roof. Hanuman grabbed a bar of the iron and swung it at Jambu, hitting him in the head. Hanuman then banged the security chief on the head and neck until his skull was broken. Hanuman rolled the writhing body off the roof. It crashed onto the thorns of rose bushes in the garden below.

Ravan then ordered some other security guards to take up the attack, but they cowered in fear of the mad monkey and wouldn't obey orders.

So Ravan said, "Shoot him." But Hanuman danced around on the roof so quickly and unpredictably that no shot could hit him. Their attempts to kill him merely tore up the roof and broke more tiles.

Ravan turned to one of his younger sons, Aks, and said, "Go get him."

Aks, a diminutive version of his father, ran out of the house to pursue the monkey.

Hanuman then jumped down from the roof, ran to a tree, climbed it, and taunted the newest human to pursue him.

Aks took a shot with his pistol and grazed Hanuman on his other temple. The newly released blood intensified the red staining on Hanuman's fur, giving him the appearance of a devil come straight from hell.

Hanuman was getting angry now. Before Aks could react, Hanuman leapt out of the tree down onto him. Hanuman ripped at Aks's ears, gouged his eyes out, bit off his nose, and pulled the skin off his cheekbones and jaw. Then he grabbed Aks's bleeding head in both hands and gave it a jerk, breaking his neck, and let the body collapse on the ground

Ravan, now filled with grief as well as rage, turned to his eldest and most powerful son, Ind, a younger carbon copy of him, and said, "Surely you can take out this wild and crazy monkey."

"Yup, leave him to me," Ind replied.

Ravan looked with pride and affection as his favorite son strode out to face the mad monkey

Ind went outside to face the monkey. He shot again and again, missing each time, as Hanuman hopped around. But Hanuman couldn't find an opening to drop down on Ind as he had against Aks. The two had come to a momentary standoff.

About to reload his pistol, Ind paused and thought a bit. He reached into a special pocket on his holster and pulled out a bullet that split into pieces when fired—buckshot from a pistol. He loaded, aimed at Hanuman in the tree above, and squeezed the trigger. One of the bullet fragments hit Hanuman, who fell to the ground, momentarily stunned.

Seeing the monkey down on the ground, a crowd of security henchman who had been holding back ran up and grabbed Hanuman. The monkey feigned fear and pretended to be groggy.

The security henchmen dragged Hanuman into the house and set him before Ravan. One said, "Whip the monkey and roast him alive. I haven't tasted fresh bushmeat in ages."

Hanuman knew the man he was now facing was the notorious Ravan. The archvillain looked large and powerful but also intelligent. Hanuman wondered how the world would have been different if only Ravan had taken a path of virtue instead of evil.

Observing Hanuman, Ravan was inquisitive. He held up his hand for the henchmen to stop molesting the monkey. Ravan looked closely at Hanuman and wondered who he was. He saw Sita's ring on Hanuman's pinky finger and surmised Sita had given it to the monkey. Somehow the monkey must be a messenger from Ram, perhaps an animal trained to do Ram's bidding.

Hanuman gestured to Ravan. He pointed in Sita's direction and then motioned to the sky, suggesting that Ravan should free Sita.

Ravan was annoyed. He said, "Such insolence. My curiosity is satisfied. Kill the monkey."

At this point, Vibish, one of Ravan's brothers, and his chief counselor, interceded. "One never kills an ambassador. This monkey was apparently sent by Ram to make contact with Sita. That makes him an ambassador and eligible for diplomatic immunity."

Ravan replied, "Nonsense. This monkey is not an innocent ambassador. He killed one of my sons and my security chief. He maimed many of my security personnel."

Vibish persisted, saying, "But he was only acting out of self-defense. It's in the nature of monkeys to tear down gardens and wreak havoc on peoples' possessions."

Ravan retorted, "Well which is it? Is the monkey like a human ambassador, entitled to diplomatic immunity, or is the monkey to be excused as less than human and not entitled to diplomatic immunity?"

While Vibish pondered this dilemma, Ravan continued, "Okay, I accept your advice not to kill him. Still, he needs to be taught a lesson. Monkeys are fond of their tails, so I say let's set his tail on fire. Let him prance around with his tail in flames, and if he survives that, let him return to wherever he came from, dragging his mutilated tail in shame."

Ravan then instructed some of the remaining security guards to set Hanuman's tail aflame. The henchmen wrapped some rags around the monkey's tail and tied the wrapping with wire-mesh cord. They took him outside the house. They poured kerosene over the rags, fastened a dog's leash around Hanuman's neck, and then lit the rags with a cigarette lighter. Then they paraded Hanuman with his tail all aflame around the estate grounds.

From her vantage point at the gazebo near the edge of the estate, Sita could see that Hanuman's tail was on fire. She was worried and made a wish that he would not suffer much.

Hanuman was not groggy. He was biding time and building his strength. He suddenly pulled the leash away from his handlers and undid the buckle holding the leash around his neck. With his tail still on fire, he hopped back into the house through an open window, setting the curtains on fire. Then he bounded back outdoors and set the bungalows, garages, and bushes on fire. Soon a large part of the estate was ablaze. Chaos and turmoil were everywhere. Sirens began to sound, and the roar of fire trucks was heard coming up the road to the estate.

Hanuman decided at this point that he had seen and done enough. He went to the swimming pool and dipped his tail in it, extinguishing the flame. He pulled the rags from his tail to restore his regular balance. Then he washed the blood from his face and head. It was time to hop back on a plane to retrace his steps and return to Ram.

"What about Sita?" he suddenly thought. "Is she okay? Has she been hurt in all the confusion from the fire I've started?" Hanuman berated himself for letting his anger against Ravan get the better of him. "What if Sita's been harmed? I'll never forgive myself."

He looked over to where he'd left Sita by the grove of trees near the gazebo next to the estate's tall, barbed-wire-topped wall. He saw she was fine. She waved to him. He was relieved.

He scurried through a gate that had been opened to let the fire trucks in and proceeded to the airport for his return journey to report back to Ram.

Collecting an Army

Hanuman retraced his steps, leaving Jenkins Bay, passing between the small hills on either side of the road, and headed toward the airport.

After a short wait, a plane like the one he had flown in on, but coming from the opposite direction, landed. He ran onto the tarmac and jumped into the wheel compartment.

The plane took off and landed, took off and landed, again and again. Finally, after counting nine big islands, Hanuman hopped off the plane in the familiar airport of Grenada.

As before, he ran to the road and waited until a truck overloaded with bananas came by. When it stopped at a pedestrian crossing, he hopped on it, ran up to the top of the pile of bananas where he was out of sight, and waited. As the truck traversed the passage around the island's central mountain, it came to the Grand Etang forest. There the truck stopped at another pedestrian crossing. Hanuman saw his chance and jumped down. He ran toward the surrounding forest and climbed a tree. Once he'd found a perch, he heard the familiar calls of mona monkeys. He knew that Angad would be waiting with the local monkeys for his return.

Hanuman moved to the sound of monkey calls. There he found Angad, who wanted a full report.

Hanuman told Angad that he had found Sita and showed him the ring she had given him, He also reported that he had done some damage to Ravan's estate.

Angad was overjoyed about the progress and happy to know that Sita was alive and uninjured. But he was alarmed to hear that Sita was in imminent danger.

Angad blurted, "Sita's in danger, so I say let's go and attack Ravan now. A lot of us monkeys can hop on planes, one by one, and eventually, there'll be enough of us in the woods outside Ravan's estate that we can attack and defeat him."

Jamb, the spectacled bear, spoke to Angad. "No," he said, "you originally told us your uncle, Sugriv, didn't commission you to kill Ravan or bring back Sita. You told us you've only been asked to locate her and report back on her whereabouts. I'm sure Ram has vowed to rescue her himself. If we rescued Sita on our own initiative, assuming we could even succeed, which is not obvious, we would deny Ram the chance to honor his own promise."

Angad cooled off and reluctantly agreed. So he and Hanuman signed their thanks to the mona monkeys for their hospitality.

The pair then proceeded to retrace their steps. They hopped on a banana truck that took them to the harbor. There they found that the tramp steamer that had originally taken them to Grenada was going back home. So they re-boarded the boat and hid onboard until it arrived back at Bocas del Toro. They disembarked and caught a water taxi to Angad's home island of Bastimentos.

Angad and Hanuman were exhausted but elated to arrive home. Angad pointed to some of the fruits in Sugriv's domain as well as to some fermented honey in a beehive. Angad gestured to Hanuman to join him in gobbling the fruit and slurping the fermented honey. Soon they were drunk and carrying on like frat boys. They were throwing rolled balls of beeswax at one another, squealing, shouting, and laughing.

One of the howlers in Sugriv's firm was patrolling the firm's borders and saw the monkeys roughhousing and disturbing the other animals. He reported back to Sugriv, saying, "The good news is, Angad has just returned with Hanuman. The bad news is they are up to mischief, gobbling your fruits, chugging your fermented honey, and kicking up a ruckus."

Sugriv replied, "Oh, this is such good news. I mean, not the misbehaving part, but the celebrating part. They wouldn't be celebrating if they had failed in their mission. Go and tell them to come to me and report."

The howler on patrol returned to where Angad and Hanuman had been messing around. He found them sobering up. Now, they were up in the trees pissing on the plants below.

The patrolling howler grimaced and tried to overlook this childishness. He said, "Sugriv is anxious. He's waited three months for your return. And Ram is beside himself with grief and worry about Sita. The other monkeys, the ones who went in other directions, did not find Sita. You are our last hope. You must come right away and make your report."

Angad and Hanuman followed the patrolling howler back to where Sugriv, Ram, and Lak were waiting. Sugriv came down from the tree branch where he had been perched to join Ram on the ground. Hanuman approached Ram, placed his palms together over his head, and bowed.

Hanuman signed to Ram, "Sita has been found." Then he removed Sita's ring from his pinky finger and gave it to Ram.

Tears dripped from Ram's eyes. He signed, "This is so wonderful. Please tell me everything."

With a nod from Angad, Hanuman launched into an account of everything that had happened: their catching a boat to an island with monkeys that lived in the canopy of the jungle and then hopping into the wheel well of a plane that took him nine islands away to another island with many monkeys like him that lived near the ground among rocks, boulders, and brush. He told them of Ravan's estate and how Sita was imprisoned there. He related how he had burnt down much of the estate, but had still not explored all of it, and that some parts were surely still intact.

When he had heard all this, Ram was overcome with joy. He went to Hanuman, embraced him in a huge hug, and kissed him on each cheek, saying "You've been a great friend. I will repay you somehow, someday. For now please accept my eternal friendship."

Ram then withdrew from the group to ponder what the next steps should be.

After a while, he called to Lak to discuss a plan. He said, "Could you go back to town in the water taxi to a place where you can get Wi-Fi and cell phone access? I'd like you to see if you can charter a C-130 transport plane for us. I'd like to assemble an army of our monkey allies and fly to where Ravan's estate is. Once there we'll demolish not only his estate but also his control center. We'll kill any henchmen who won't surrender. We'll rescue my wife. But it all starts with getting our army to the target site to begin with, and a C-130 will do just fine. It can land anywhere. It holds about ninety people, so I'm assuming that translates to about 300 monkeys. With an army that size, we can take out Ravan. And we might be able to recruit some more monkeys on Ravan's island, where I'm sure he's not loved. That would add even more monkeys to our strength. And when you're in town, find out where that tramp steamer Hanuman took stopped and where the island-hopping flight goes that Hanuman used. That way you can reconstruct where Hanuman went and find out exactly where Ravan is located. Then make arrangements for a chartered C-130 to take our army to Ravan's island. Finally, can you take the carrying case with Ceroc's parts and post it back to Sutik, care of general delivery, and have it held for pickup at the Hanalei post office? Then email him to expect it."

"Yeah, sounds good. Lots to do, but I can do it," replied Lak.

Ram said, "Great, and do you still have the passwords to my e-broker and e-bank accounts? You'll have to sell some of my stock to raise the funds to pay for this. Also, I forgot to mention—in Panama, weapons are available. Can you procure some of those weapons that Vish taught us to use years ago?"

"Yes, I remember," replied Lak. "I'll look around and see what I can find. I'll also look for some ceramic body armor and digital-thermal imaging scopes."

"Yeah, that ought to do it," said Ram. "Our army will mostly be monkeys, but you and I might need a little more than the machete and bow and arrows we've made do with in recent years. Ravan and his henchmen will be fighting back with serious weapons of their own, and we'll have to be prepared. We can start with our trusted bow, arrows, and machete and switch to heavier stuff when needed. And by the time we get to his estate, Ravan will probably have repaired the damage Hanuman caused, so we'll have to start all over to demolish his facility. Oh, while you're at it, see if you can pick up some heavy-duty backpacks for us to carry the weapons in. We'll need to haul them to our point of attack."

"Yes, I can do all you ask," replied Lak.

"Wonderful, I'll see you in a few days when you return," said Ram as he waved to the departing Lak.

Ram then called out, "Wait, I just thought of two more things. Can you go online to my assets page and find the tissue-culture lab where the supply of our stem cells is being cultured? If I recall correctly, Vasis transferred some stem cells from storage at our mothers' homes for growth in a tissue-culture lab. Have the lab send us a large quantity of our stem cells packed with liquid nitrogen in Styrofoam containers by overnight courier."

"Okay," said Lak, "I'll do that. What else?"

Ram continued, saying, "Do you think you could find some nerve-gas antidote auto-injector kits, you know, with atropine and pralidoxine chloride? The syndicate boss Saddam Hussein, when he was president of Iraq, used the nerve gas sarin against his Kurdish citizens decades ago. About twenty years later another syndicate boss, Bashar al-Assad, also used sarin against citizens when he was the president of Syria. So we might expect that Ravan could use them against us too."

Lak replied, "Shouldn't be too hard to get the anti-nerve gas kits. You can get 'em online and from army surplus stores."

Ram replied, "Thanks, that should provide us with the medical supplies we'll probably need, although I hope we won't."

While Lak was off making arrangements and getting provisions, Sugriv began assembling an army. He contacted Sush of the capuchins and Nal of the spider monkeys as well as the Nil of night monkeys and Maind of the tamarins. These were the CEOs who had originally assisted in the search for Sita. To these he added his trusted howler fighters, Gaj, Gav, Gand, Rish, and the tenacious tamarin, Dwivid.

Sugriv asked them, "Now that Hanuman has found Sita, we're looking for volunteers to fly in a plane to Ravan's island. Together with Ram and Lak, we're going to destroy him and his syndicate. Any takers?"

The CEOs and howler fighters each responded, saying in their own way, "Count us in. It is our code to help a brother, and Ram is our brother. How many of us do you need?"

Sugriv replied, "Twenty from each of you plus twenty howlers from my firm makes one hundred from our island. Then we'll collect some more volunteers from the other islands closer to Ravan. The plane will hold about 300 of us, so altogether, we'll be bringing a large force."

The CEOs squealed and jumped about in excitement.

Lak returned from town and reported to Ram, saying, "Success. I have managed to charter a C-130 to transport our expeditionary force of monkeys. It was expensive."

Ram asked, "How expensive?"

Lak replied, "I found a firm descended from one called International Air Response that for decades has supplied C-130s for charter to foreign-aid organizations and oil-spill remediation tasks."

Lak continued, saying, "I got the firm's CEO on my cell phone. I asked him for a quote on a flight from Bocas del Toro to the Lesser Antilles. He said, 'That'll be one million.' Then he paused, and asked, 'What's the cargo?' I said, 'Three hundred monkeys.' He said, 'Then it's two million. It'll take a week to clean the plane.' I told him that our monkeys are real clean, but he still insisted on the two million, so I had to agree. I sold off some of your stock and paid him, half now and half when he shows up at the Bocas del Toro airport with the plane."

"Good work," said Ram, "really good work."

Lak said next, "I also found out where Hanuman went. I found the tramp steamer. The crew remembers two monkeys disembarking on Grenada. Then I checked the LIAT island-hopper flights going north from Grenada and counted nine large islands to the north-northwest. That took me to St. Eustatius. It's just beyond St. Kitts and Nevis. Those two islands both have had lots of monkeys on them for a couple hundred years. The monkeys have now spread next door to St. Eustatius too. So I'm guessing we'll be able to recruit lots of allies there in addition to those we fly in with."

Ram asked, "Anything else?"

Lak answered, "Yes, I did manage to get some guns and ammo on the black market. Got a sniper rifle, a half dozen AT4 disposable light antitank weapons, and some top-notch ceramic body armor. Lot's of this stuff is available around here from all the local rebellions, insurrections, and drug wars always going on. I also got a pair of sharp, well-balanced knives good for throwing and a pair of Glock automatic pistols. I've put all the armaments in a crate along with two heavy-duty backpacks, all of which I left in a storage locker at the airport so that I didn't have to lug the stuff over here. I also picked up ten nerve-gas antidote kits. You can pack them in with the stem cells in our medical supplies chest."

Ram nodded and said, "Thanks, good job."

Then he asked, "When is the C-130 due to arrive to pick us up?"

Lak said, "It's arriving tomorrow during the day sometime. They will refuel and overnight at the airport to be ready for us the day after tomorrow in the morning. The stem cell cultures should arrive tomorrow too. We can pick them up at the counter at the courier's office in town.

Ram then briefed Sugriv.

The next day Sugriv gathered all one hundred monkeys from Bastimentos Island and brought them to the water-taxi dock. Lak flagged down a water taxi and arranged to pay the operator to transport the monkeys to shore. Then Ram and Lak—with their bow, arrows, and machete—along with all the monkeys climbed aboard the water taxi and, a few minutes later, hopped out on the shore. The monkeys crossed through the woods to the outskirts of the airport, where they spent the night. They could see the C-130 waiting for them on the tarmac. Ram and Lak went to the B&B where they had stayed when they first arrived at Bocas del Toro. The brothers slept in a bed for their first time in many weeks.

The next morning at the crack of dawn, Lak went to the storage locker to retrieve the crate with guns, ammo, and backpacks. Carrying the nerve-gas antidote kits with him, Ram went to the courier's office in town to collect the stem cell cultures. They were packed in big Styrofoam containers for insulation to keep them cold. Ram added the antidote kits to the container and exited the courier's office.

Lak, Ram, and the monkeys then met at the C-130. Lak paid the pilot the balance of the charter price, and they all walked aboard the cargo ramp into the cargo bay, lugging the gun-and-ammo crate and Styrofoam container with them.

Hanuman remarked to Ram, "Sitting inside a big plane sure is better than holding on for dear life scrunched inside the wheel well."

Ram patted him on the back and said, "You've arrived, my man, you've arrived."

Ram went up to the cockpit and instructed the pilot to fly to Grenada and to wait there for two hours while they collected some more monkeys. The pilot gestured to Ram to sit in the copilot seat next to him. The pilot composed a flight plan on his laptop. The pilot then started the four propeller engines and called the tower for permission to take off.

The tower radioed back, "Have a good flight." The C-130 lumbered down the runway, bound for the Lesser Antilles.

After a couple of hours, Ram and the pilot could see the cloud-covered mountains of Grenada off in the distance ahead of them. The pilot radioed for permission to land. In they came, and then they taxied onto a waiting area on the tarmac. As soon as the pilot opened the cargo door, Hanuman scrambled down the ramp, hopped the fence surrounding the airport and hopped on a passing banana truck. Half an hour later, he was back in the Grand Etang forest, looking for the CEO of the mona monkeys.

Hanuman asked the CEO to solicit twenty volunteers to join the army to defeat Ravan. He didn't need to remind them how Ravan's syndicate had been capturing monkeys to sell into slavery. Twenty monkeys immediately jumped up and down, squealing and calling in anticipation. Even Jamb the bear offered to join. Hanuman said to them, "We've no time to lose. The plane's waiting. Let's go."

The twenty mona monkeys plus Jamb scurried out to the road through the Grand Etang and waited for a truck heading in the direction of the airport. As luck would have it, an empty banana truck pulled up at a pedestrian crossing. All twenty monkeys plus Jamb clambered onto the truck's flatbed. When the pedestrians had crossed, the truck started up again in the direction of the airport with the driver none the wiser.

When the truck neared the airport, it stopped at another pedestrian crossing. At Hanuman's hand signal, the animals clambered back onto the ground. From there Hanuman led the animals to the fence surrounding the runway. The monkeys swarmed over the fence, and some stopped to assist Jamb, pulling him up by the paws from above and pushing his behind from below. Once Jamb toppled over the top of the fence, all the animals ran to the cargo ramp of the waiting C-130 and scurried up inside the cavernous cargo hold. Lak looked at his watch and said to Ram, "Perfect. That took an hour and forty-five minutes. Let's go."

Ram then instructed the pilot, "Our next stop is St. Kitts. We'll also wait there for two hours and collect some more monkeys to join our army. We may not need the full two hours, however. There are over 50,000 monkeys on that island, and we've only got space for 180 more—and that's not counting the bear we've had to squeeze in too. We should be able to recruit pretty quickly."

The pilot nodded, uploaded his flight plan, asked permission to take off, and off they went.

They flew past volcano after volcano. In about another two hours they came to island number seven since leaving Grenada, a perfect conical volcano. The pilot said, "That's Nevis. Beautiful isn't it?"

Ram nodded, saying, "Great, and that's St. Kitts coming up next?"

The pilot nodded, saying "yup" as he started his descent.

After getting permission to land, the pilot put his C-130 down on the runway, pulled to the waiting area, and opened the cargo door.

Hanuman ran down the ramp and immediately saw his brothers and sisters watching from the scrub vegetation and exposed boulders near the airport. He hopped the fence and ran over to them. The CEO of the vervet firm whose franchise was around the airport embraced him, saying ,"Welcome back, brother."

Hanuman replied, "Thanks. We're on our way to the next island to destroy Ravan and his syndicate. We'd looking to recruit 180 monkeys from here to join up with us. Can you put out the word?"

"Sure," replied the vervet CEO, then he let out a loud call.

Soon several hundred vervets came by to see what was up. Hanuman explained that they were looking for 180 monkeys to join up with them. Lots of hands shot up and lots of monkeys began jumping up and down, chattering. Hanuman counted out the nearest 180 and pointed to the plane, where Sugriv was waving to them from the cargo ramp. The new recruits ran to the fence, clambered up and over it, scampered to the plane's cargo ramp, and bounded onboard.

"Wonderful," said Hanuman to the vervet CEO, "thanks so much."

The CEO replied, "For many years, even generations, we've wanted to put Ravan out of business. His black-shirted henchmen are the ones who regularly capture us with traps and dart guns. They store us in tiny cages. They squirt fluids into our skin that make us feel bad, make us itch, and make us break out in sores. They're horrible humans. We could assemble many thousands of monkeys to join your army with a little more time to get the word out. Let me know if you need any more help."

"Thanks, I'll let you know," replied Hanuman, who embraced the vervet CEO before climbing the fence to join Sugriv in the cargo hold.

In the cockpit Ram said to the pilot, "Everything's okay here. Now on to our final destination."

The pilot responded, "Okay, we're off to St. Eustatius. This will take only a few minutes."

After the pilot had uploaded the flight plan and received clearance, the C-130 took off.

As soon as the plane reached an altitude of 1,000 feet, they could clearly see St. Eustatius nearby. It had a relatively small extinct volcano at its south end and two small hills at its north end bordering a bay with a large beach. As the plane neared it, Ram could see on the bay what looked like the buildings, bungalows, a swimming pool, decorative pools, and watered lawns of a wealthy estate. It faced the beach, and the entire complex was nestled between the scrubby vegetation of the adjacent hills.

Ram called Lak into the cockpit, pointed, and said, "That looks like Ravan's place, according to Hanuman's description."

To the pilot Ram said, "Can we invite one of the monkeys to join us here in the cockpit for a few minutes?"

The pilot nodded. Lak turned through the cockpit door and motioned for Hanuman to join them. Hanuman came in and Ram pointed to the estate bordering a beach on the northwest corner of the island.

Hanuman signed, "Yes, that's it," grinned, and returned to his seat.

The pilot brought the plane in for its St. Eustatius landing. He opened the cargo door and all 300 monkeys (plus one bear) scampered down the ramp, to the amazement of some local vervet monkeys. Ram and Lak, with bow, arrows, and machete, dragged the weapons crate and stem-cell containers down the ramp as well. Hanuman pointed to a road leading to the north of the island and gestured to the monkeys to head over there. They swarmed over the fence next to the road, bringing the bear as they went.

Once over the fence, Hanuman approached some of the local monkeys who had been watching to ask who was the CEO. The monkeys pointed to a wise elder vervet nearby. Hanuman walked up to him, introduced himself, explained their mission, and asked for help in recruiting volunteers to join their army.

The CEO replied, "Yes, we have a common cause with you. Ravan and his black-T-shirt-wearing henchmen are a constant danger to us, trapping us to send in cages to wherever they've come from."

Hanuman replied, "Wonderful. Can you get 700 of your brothers to join us at the knoll along the road leading to the gate outside Ravan's estate?

We'll bivouac there while we organize our assault on Ravan's estate. We've brought 300 monkeys plus a bear, and with your 700 that will give us an army of over 1,000. We have some heavy firepower too." He gestured to Ram and Lak, who were standing by the weapons crate.

Hanuman continued, saying, "With your recruits and our contingent, I'm confident we can defeat Ravan now and forever."

The local vervet CEO said, "Will do. I'll put the word out and we'll get 700 monkeys right away, and even more will follow later."

He went off to round up the local recruits, who soon began arriving in small groups to join up with Hanuman and the rest of the monkeys.

Meanwhile, Lak went back onboard the plane to thank the pilot for his excellent service. Lak said, "We'd like to call on you for the return flight once our expedition has been completed. Would that be okay?"

"Sure," replied the pilot, "same terms?"

Lak nodded.

"Then okay," the pilot said. "Nice to pick up two million for a day's work. Most of it goes to me as an independent contractor and the rest to the company. I'll fly over to St. Martin now to overnight and refuel. I'll fly home to Arizona tomorrow."

Ram said, "Great, see you again in the near future."

Lak disembarked to join with Ram, who was waiting on the tarmac by the weapons crate. They watched the great C-130 taxi back onto the runway and take off on its journey home.

Ram and Lak then hefted the weapons crate and stem-cell containers on their shoulders, stacking the bow, arrows, and machete on top. After clearing customs at the F.D. Roosevelt Airport, they walked out through the airport gate. Once out of sight of the airport, they opened the crate and loaded the weapons and ammo into the backpacks. Ram carried his bow and the arrows. Lak carried the sniper rifle and machete. They left the empty weapons crate under a tree near a bus stop for people to use as a make-do seat while waiting out the island's frequent rain-squalls.

As Ram and Lak approached the vicinity of the syndicate estate, a white SUV with blue horizontal stripes on the side and Police emblazoned across the door screeched to a stop next to them.

A man in shorts and a white uniform jumped out and demanded, "What you doin' here? You can't just fly in and camp in the bush. And why all these monkeys around you? Are you feedin' 'em or something?"

Ram approached the officer, saw the name tag under his badge, and said, "Officer Samud, we're not going to camp in the bush. We're here to question the owner of the estate ahead on this road about a missing woman who happens to be my wife. We mean no harm or disrespect."

The police officer replied, "Then you both go to the police station and give the officer your passport numbers and how to get a hold o' you if we want to."

Ram's face was beginning to show anger, and Lak pulled him aside, saying, "Cool it. Even if he's being an officious prick, don't get him angry. And don't get angry yourself. We're counting on you to keep your head."

Ram nodded and turned back to the officer. "Yes, sir, we'll do that. But first, can you tell us anything about the owner of the estate here? We'd like to prepare for our interview with him."

Officer Samud replied, "The owner's name is Ravan. He's secretive, so we don't know much about him. He gives money to our charities on the island. He gives to our hospital, our schools, and our facility for unwed mothers. So we don't ask too many questions. We just hope he's on the level. We hope he ain't into drug smugglin' or nothin' like dat. But so far we got no problem with him."

Ram replied, "Thank you, officer. We'll immediately comply with your instructions." With that, the officer climbed back into his car and sped away.

Ram and Lak set their items by the side of the road and hiked to the police station near the airport. They gave the officer there the information that had been requested. Then Ram and Lak headed back up the road to join up with Hanuman, Sugriv, and their army of monkeys, ready to plan their assault against Ravan's estate and syndicate headquarters.

Ravan Declares War

After dousing the flames Hanuman had started with water and foam retardant, the firemen withdrew their firetrucks, leaving the bungalows and ancillary buildings on the estate in smoldering ruins and much of Ravan's central house a water-damaged wreck.

Ravan went to his control center, got on his secure Internet connection, and summoned his syndicate bosses from all the major cities around the world to an emergency council of war.

As though attending a papal conclave, they all arrived the next day in their private jets. Some were fat, others thin, some tall, others skinny, some black, some brown, and some white, but all disembarked wearing their trademark black T-shirts and black baseball caps. The local monkeys had never seen so many private planes parked around the airport in hangers, waiting areas, and even on the grass. Throughout the day, Ravan's security personnel ferried the visitors in jeeps to Ravan's estate.

Ravan was at the estate house when everyone arrived. After all were settled in their guest rooms, Ravan called them to the executive conference room in an undamaged wing of the estate's main house.

Ravan was apprehensive. He knew it wouldn't be long until Ram and his brother arrived, perhaps bringing their dangerous monkey with them.

As soon as everyone was seated, he began, "We're facing a serious enemy. As you know, Ram and his brother have already inflicted damage against our syndicate. And this mad monkey of his has just killed my youngest son, Aks, as well as my chief security guard, Jambu. He also destroyed much of my estate, which I had thought safe from incursions. I will have to import workers from the mainland to repair the damage because there aren't enough local skilled tradesmen. So I now ask your advice on how to proceed. He who acts without soliciting and considering advice is certain to fail."

One of the strongest and most successful of Ravan's syndicate bosses, Pragast, who was from Crimea, spoke up, saying, "That monkey launched a surprise attack on you. Now, if it was me, if he had come and fought like a man—I mean, fought face to face—I would have maimed his sneering face and killed him with my bare hands."

Virup, a syndicate boss from North Korea, piped in to brag, "I can hunt that monkey down and kill all the monkeys in the world. Just give the word."

Another syndicate boss advised trickery instead of brute force. He suggested that once the monkeys were located, they should be infiltrated by sending a human disguised as Ram's brother, Barat, in among the monkeys. Then they could attack the monkeys from both the inside and the outside.

One after the other, every syndicate boss around the conference table spoke up to brag that he could single-handedly defeat Ram, Lak, and Hanuman, and also destroy all their allies and associates. Even Ravan's relatives and the syndicate hit men who had been silent so far joined in, including Mahap, a half brother from Sudan; Mahod, a half brother from Hollywood; Durmuk from Northern Ireland; Pratap from Corsica; Vidumal from Los Angeles; Sharab from Nigeria; Supar from Pakistan; Vajram from Chechnya; Vajrad from Yemen; Dhum from Colombia; Durd from the Vatican; Kamp from Miami; Sonit from Uganda; Praj from Syria; Saran and Sard, security guards; Vidyu, the counterfeiter; Yupak, the physician; Ravan's younger sons, Trishir, Devant, Naran, and Atik; and also Nikum and Kum, who were Ravan's nephews, sons of Ravan's brother, Kumb—all of them nodded approval.

All but Vibish, that is, who demurred. Although a younger brother of Ravan, Vibish was a favorable social mutation within Ravan's nefarious family lineage. He was not inclined to gangster interests or behavior. Through study, he had become a geek of history in his own right.

Vibish said, "May I remind all of you how strong Ram and his associates are? Don't take them lightly. Let's review all they've done to us so far. Ram and Lak defeated Marich's mother, Tata, and banished her to Chechnya. They killed our powerful lieutenant Subah and defeated Marich. Later they killed Marich during Sita's kidnapping. They maimed my sister Shurpana's face. They killed my brothers, Khar and Dush, and now add to that what Hanuman has just done, which was to kill Jambu, our chief security guard here, and Aks, my nephew. Don't underestimate them."

Turning to face Ravan, Vibish said, "My brother, my dearest Ravan, please return Sita to Ram before it's too late, otherwise we'll witness the total destruction of our syndicate and we'll perish like moths in a flame."

Ravan's body language revealed his dislike for what Vibish was saying. But to be circumspect, Ravan told his conclave of syndicate bosses, "Much has been said on both sides. I suggest we sleep on this matter. I'll announce my decisions in the morning."

The next morning Vibish went to Ravan's bedroom to urge restraint. He earnestly repeated his arguments, suspecting that his brother would lose a conflict in which he would be outmaneuvered by Ram and outnumbered by a seemingly endless supply of his monkey allies.

But Ravan only replied, "Ram is a wimpy daddy's boy. He's no match for me. And there's no way I'll give up Sita. Once I kill that goody-goody, Sita will come to my side. See, I will wind up the victor. But if I took your advice, all I would end up with is disgrace. A surrender would completely discredit me as the CEO of my syndicate, and I would be no better off than if I actually lost my fight with Ram, which isn't gonna happen. So your approach has nothing to offer me. I reject it."

Vibish nodded and withdrew, leaving Ravan to finish getting dressed.

After all the syndicate bosses had finished their breakfasts, Ravan reconvened the conclave in the executive conference room. Vibish sat next to him at the conference table.

Ravan began by saying, "You have all become rich and powerful under my leadership. However, our entire firm, with all its assets, is now threatened by Ram for sake of reclaiming Sita as his wife. But I cannot give her up. I admit it: I am pierced by the shafts of love. I can have no one else. And Sita has promised to marry me after a year has passed. I need only hold out a couple months more until she is mine. I regret putting our firm at risk, but for me personally, I know I have no other choice."

Vibish heard this and knew immediately that Ravan was mistaken. He wondered, "Does Ravan really believe that Sita will willingly become his wife if he happens to defeat Ram? If Ravan does believe this, my brother is seriously deluded."

Another of Ravan's brothers, Kumb the Killer, angrily confronted him, shouting, "Did you bother to ask our advice before abducting Sita in the first place? No. You just acted on impulse alone. You shouldn't have done that. But, fortunately for you, I'm still on your side. I'll kill Ram and Lak for you."

But Kumb knew he wouldn't easily be able to deliver on his promise. Though once big and strong from a disciplined weight-room regime, Kumb was now a heroin addict who spent most of his time in a medically supervised drug stupor. His attending doctors arranged to have him come to his full senses only one day every six months. By coincidence, the day of this conclave happened to be the one day in the current six-month period when Kumb was fully conscious and capable. But to back up his promise when the time came to face Ram in a battle, he would somehow have to be awakened from the coma of his drug and somehow summon back his former strength.

Mahap, Ravan's half brother living in Sudan, then spoke up to ask, "Why haven't you simply forced yourself on Sita and taken her for your own? She can't escape."

Ravan inhaled and said, "I've never spoken about this before, but here is my reason: As you know, I became CEO of our syndicate by forcing out my weakling half brother, Kuber. He was obsessed by wealth, which was fine by me. But he was dumb. As an example, it was he who introduced the hated mongoose to this island to control the feral chickens and rats. Anyone could have told him the mongooses would go on to kill native birds, endanger our pets, and damage the livelihood of the poultry farmers—pretty stupid, but that's the way he was. It hurt our syndicate's reputation on this island. Anyway, after I forced him to resign as CEO, I banished him and his son, Nalak, to Saba, the tiny rocky island just northwest of here. Before they left for Saba, I felt entitled to force myself on Nalak's beautiful wife, Rambha. But before leaving for exile on Saba, Nalak confronted me about the evil I had done to his wife and indirectly to him as well. I felt guilty and ashamed. After all, Nalak was my nephew and I was wrong to hurt a kinsman. And the tears of his wife seared my memory. I resolved then and there never again to force myself on a woman."

Hearing this, Vibish felt a tinge of sorrow for his evil brother. Ravan had just revealed a conscience buried underneath the bravado. Ravan wanted to win Sita's hand but only by defeating Ram. He did not want to acquire her by rape. Yet, Vibish predicted to himself, ironically, by following his conscience, Ravan would guarantee his ultimate destruction without yielding his desired prize.

After his revelation, Ravan's bravado returned. He continued bragging at length about his strength and invincibility.

Once Ravan had finished his latest boastful harangue, Vibish addressed him before the entire conclave, saying, "Sita has become an obsession with you. Her sweet smile, gorgeous face, slender neck, and graceful, athletic physique have beguiled you, made you lose all sense of reason and perspective. I implore you, stop before our complete destruction becomes inevitable."

But the syndicate bosses were with Ravan. They shouted and hooted at Vibish, saying, "Bring 'em on! Let us at 'em! We want to take it to Ram now—no more waiting. We want at him now!"

Ind, Ravan's eldest and strongest son, said to Vibish, "Uncle, you've become a weak bookworm. I am strong. I too can defeat Ram with his fawning groupies in a flash." He snapped his fingers.

Vibish responded, "You're merely a boy. You don't comprehend Ram's power. You just don't get it."

By this point Ravan had heard enough. Putting his foot down, he pronounced, "Enough! I hereby declare war on Ram, his associates, and his descendants from now and forever more."

The syndicate bosses thumped their fists on the conference table in applause.

Turning to Vibish, Ravan added, "You've become a disgrace to our whole syndicate and our family."

Vibish retorted, "And you, my dear brother, are deluded. I've tried to advise you in your best interests, but I've failed. I leave you now. I will not remain to be insulted."

Vibish pulled off his black T-shirt and placed it at his spot on the conference table. Vibish then left the estate's grounds, called for a taxi, and went to a B&B to spend the night while thinking about what to do with the rest of his life.

Army Prepares

Vibish spent the night at the B&B sleeping fitfully, tossing and turning. He was trying to avoid a simple choice between good and evil. He thought to himself, "Help Ram or help Ravan—I've already abandoned evil, but how can I affirm the good? What about loyalty to my syndicate? It has employed me all my life. What about loyalty to my family? Doesn't loyalty mean anything? I don't want to be a traitor. Can I just hide somewhere?"

Vibish pondered his dilemma as he climbed the stairs down from his bedroom on the second floor of the B&B to join the other guests at breakfast in the main dining room. The B&B matron's West Indian family was sitting at the table nearest the kitchen. The matron brought out mugs of steaming hot coffee to the guests, all tourists from the mainland and Europe. She also spoke to her children as she passed them on her trips to and from the kitchen.

Vibish overheard her saying to her eldest boy, "In soccer today, you play hard but you don' kick the other guy even if dat ref ain' lookin'. Game over, you still gotta live wit dat other guy. You hear? World's small place. Time to do good short. You hear?"

"Yes, Mama," said the boy.

And Vibish knew then and there what he had to do. He gathered his things and gratefully settled his account at the B&B. He retraced his steps from town back to the outskirts of Ravan's estate, the site he used to call home. As he neared the estate, he left the road and stepped into the scrubby woods. He threaded his way through the acacia thorns and sharp limestone boulders lining the exterior of the barbwire-topped wall surrounding Ravan's estate. Along the way Vibish saw small groups of local monkeys arriving from the woods. In time he lost count of the monkeys he saw—300, 500, maybe as many as 1,000 monkeys had assembled. While one monkey may not seem dangerous, at worst little more than a pest, 1,000 of them was another matter.

Vibish's heart began to beat faster as fear gripped him. "This must be where the assault will come from," he surmised.

A big howler monkey dropped down to the ground from the low canopy above and confronted Vibish. The monkey pointed toward the road and gestured fiercely toward the town, which Vibish surmised meant, "Get the hell out of here."

Vibish gestured back, pointed at the estate's wall, stuck out his tongue at it, banged his fist against his palm, and ran his finger across his neck in the universal signal to stop.

The howler paused and shook his head, but then he decided to bring the human to Sugriv. The howler pulled on Vibish's shirt, leading him through the bush to Sugriv. Seeing that the human wanted to communicate, Sugriv asked the attending howler to summon Ram to translate, along with Lak and Hanuman.

When Ram and Hanuman arrived at Sugriv's side and saw the human, Ram asked, "Who is this guy?"

Sugriv replied, "I don't know, looks suspicious. Ask him."

Ram turned to Vibish, "Who are you? What do you want?"

He replied, "My name is Vibish. I am Ravan's younger brother. My brother has abducted Ram's wife through trickery and brought her here. Although I kept asking him to release her, he kept refusing. So I left him. I have come to seek Ram's protection. Are you Ram?"

"Yes," replied Ram.

Turning to Sugriv he translated what Vibish told him and asked Sugriv, "What do you think we should do with him?"

Sugriv replied, "I think it's a trick. How could we ever trust a human who's double-crossing his brother? More likely, he's a spy for his brother. I think we should kill him."

Sugriv looked around at the other monkeys that had gathered to watch, and asked, "Should we kill him?"

The other monkeys all nodded, chattered, and squealed in agreement. All but Hanuman, that is.

Ram turned to Hanuman and asked him directly, "Do you think we should kill him too?"

Hanuman replied, "No, I don't discern any deceit in his tone of voice, expression, or bearing. I think we should accept him as an ally. What do you think?"

Ram replied, "Having heard all of you, I find I agree with Hanuman. I think this guy is for real and he can be of considerable help to us."

Sugriv replied, "But think of the downside. If he sells us out, our cause is defeated and your Sita rots in Ravan's prison."

Ram said, "I think we can still defeat Ravan even if we are betrayed. Ravan will know soon enough we are here. Moreover, a principle is involved. One must always accept the overture from an enemy. Only then can one realize a mutual gain. If the enemy defects, then we defect as well, having lost only our initial investment. But if the enemy becomes our friend, we're both better off living in peace."

Hearing Ram's wisdom, Sugriv replied, "Okay, I see your point. Let him stay."

Looking out at the other monkeys who had been listening in, Sugriv saw they approved too.

Ram turned back to Vibish, saying, "Welcome, brother."

Vibish fell to his knees in relief, and Ram raised him up.

Vibish said, "I have been insulted and cast out by my older brother, Ravan. I have come to you, abandoning my family, friends, and home. My life is now in your hands."

Ram replied, "You're safe now. But tell me about Ravan's army. Who are his personnel?"

Vibish replied, "His chief generals are his cunning eldest son, Ind, followed by his powerful brother, Kumb, and his ruthless syndicate bosses, Pragast from Crimea, Virup from North Korea, and Mahap from Sudan. Others too are strong and experienced. Ravan must have well over one hundred gangster henchmen who arrived here with their bosses from abroad. Combined with his resident security guards and enforcers, his total force must be about 1,000."

"Okay," said Ram, "I think we can match that. If you have been honest in your reporting' I will reward you with control of Ravan's estate and all the syndicate's other assets once I have defeated him. I shall not return home until I have obliterated Ravan, his sons, his kinsfolk—besides you—and all his gangster accomplices."

Vibish replied, "For my part, I'll give you whatever help I can."

Hanuman then asked Ram to translate some further questions for Vibish.

Through Ram, Hanuman asked, "Tell me about Ravan's estate. I saw the buildings, bungalows, and other surface structures. I saw a large kitchen with a walk-in deep freeze. I briefly checked out the garage and saw the black stealth jet and the jeeps, including the one with a machine gun. I also saw an open door leading to stairs descending to somewhere in the cliffs next to the ocean. Have I missed anything? Where do the stairs go?"

Through Ram, Vibish replied, "You've only seen half of Ravan's estate. He had to keep his control center secret, which isn't easy with all the satellite surveillance and Internet eavesdropping these days. So Ravan built his control center underwater, invisible to satellites, on a geologic formation called the Saba Bank. He keeps the control center offline except for brief, random occasions when a periscope is raised. The periscope has an antenna on it that connects with the Internet via satellite link that is filtered through proxies and URL anonymizers. Our proximity to the Saba Bank, which is a huge underwater plateau, is actually why Ravan chose to build his estate here on St. Eustatius in the first place."

Ram and Lak looked at each other and arched their eyebrows. This was a curve ball.

Through Ram, Hanuman asked Vibish to continue. So Vibish said, "The Saba Bank is a big deal. It's about thirty-five miles long and twenty miles wide. Around 1,500 square miles are shallower than 150 feet and reachable by scuba divers. The bank starts about fifteen miles due east of us. That's the windward side of the bank, which is the shallowest part. This windward side is the most heavily fished and is occasionally used by ships as an anchorage. The whole Saba Bank has been an official national park of the Netherlands for the last fifty years, and dropping anchor there is illegal, but still sometimes boats still do it. The bank possesses a fabulous diversity of marine life, from fishes to sponges to coral to algae—you name it, everything."

Ram asked, "I've never heard of it before."

Vibish replied, "Well, that's the point—it's like a secret even though it's actually public knowledge. Marine conservation geeks know about it, but almost no one else does, which makes it a great spot for Ravan to build an underwater control center. The Saba Bank is at a hinge point between Puerto Rico and the Lesser Antilles. The underlying rocks on Puerto Rico go back to the age of dinosaurs, so maybe the rocks underlying the Saba Bank are that old too."

Ram was listening intently.

Vibish continued, "The Saba Bank must have been a huge island in the last ice age. A gigantic 400-pound rodent used to live on Anguilla and St. Martin to the east of us. I'd bet the Saba Bank used to have a great terrestrial fauna of its own too. But the sea level rose, and the ocean flooded the Saba Bank, killing its terrestrial fauna and paving the way for the coral covered platform Ravan could appropriate today for his secret hideaway."

Ram asked, "How should we knock out this underwater hideaway?"

Vibish replied, "Ravan built his control center on the leeward side of the Saba Bank, away from any fisherman or anchoring ships. It's near the western tip of the plateau in an inconspicuous rise called Small Bank. It's about fifty miles from here. Ravan contracted with a company originally founded by an entrepreneur, L. Bruce Jones, who has been building luxury underwater residences and luxury submarines for about fifty years now. Ravan bought two of those submarines and had each of them outfitted with tiny CUTIE II torpedoes."

Lak was listening with rapt attention.

Vibish said, "He included an underwater dock at the control center so up to two subs could tie up there in complete secrecy."

Vibish now pointed and asked, "And you see the cliffs on either side of the beach?"

Ram nodded.

Vibish continued, "Ravan blasted a large cavern into the cliffs on the right side of the beach and had a dock built for two subs there too. Although this dock is at the water's surface, as many as two subs can tie up there in secret because it's inside the cave and invisible from the air. Ravan typically stations one submarine at the control center and the other here at the dock. These submarines ferry people and supplies back and forth on the hour's journey between the control center and the dock. When one goes outbound the other returns inbound, although sometimes, if need be, both subs are at either the control center or dock."

Lak jumped in to ask, "Do you think Ravan will hole up in his control center?"

Vibish nodded.

Lak said, "In that case, I guess we'll wind up having to commandeer one of the subs and go after him there."

Vibish nodded again.

Hanuman tugged on Ram's arm for a translation. As Ram explained what Vibish had just told him, Hanuman's eyes widened.

Hanuman said to Ram, "I didn't know that living underwater was possible for anything but fish. I'll tell Sugriv. We'll have to prepare our howlers so they aren't freaked out by the whole idea of going underwater."

Hanuman then asked Ram to inquire about the best way to attack the estate.

Vibish responded, "I suggest that you have the monkeys swing in over the walls on vines and drop onto the estate grounds. To do this you'll have to collect vines from throughout the woods, tie them together into ropes, and fasten them onto the trees beyond the perimeter of the wall."

Ram translated to Sugriv and asked, "Would that be possible?"

Sugriv nodded yes.

Ram turned back to Vibish. "Please continue."

Vibish said, "I suggest that half of the monkeys be stationed in the trees ready to swing into the estate on vines and that the other half assemble outside the gate. Then you somehow blast the front gate open. That will make the security guards rush to the front gate. As the guards approach the gate, the monkeys in the trees should swing over the fence and drop onto the grounds. The security guards will then have to turn around to chase the monkeys. When they do, that will be the signal for you and your brother, plus all the remaining monkeys and the bear, to rush through the gate and continue the attack. At that point all your force will be inside and engaged in the combat."

Ram, Lak, Sugriv, and Hanuman looked at each other and nodded agreement.

Ram said to Vibish, "Thanks. Sounds like a good plan to first get the estate and then we'll follow up at the underwater control center. To begin we'll need to secure the kitchen and unload the Styrofoam crate with our stem-cell and medical supplies there. It's a pain to tote that cumbersome box around even though it's pretty light."

While the attack on the estate was being planned, local vervet monkeys continued to arrive outside the estate grounds in small groups, doubling the initial size of the expeditionary force.

A security guard named Suk noticed the buildup of monkeys. He called Ravan, who was working offshore in the control center. Ravan's face appeared on the video screen.

The guard said, "Sir, a huge number of monkeys is amassing outside our estate walls. I fear they're planning to attack us somehow. Their numbers are already enough to overrun us, and more are joining every hour."

Ravan replied, "Gather some fruit and water from our galley and bring it to them as a sign of our friendship. When you find the monkey CEO, signal to him somehow that I've done him no harm. Why should it matter to a monkey that I have carried off Sita?"

So Suk went to the kitchen and returned pulling a cart piled high with bananas, mangoes, and mountain apples as well as jugs of water. He asked the guards to open the front gate just wide enough to let him through. Suk pulled the cart with all the food out on the road in full view of all the monkeys perched in the scrubby trees and on top of ragged limestone boulders.

But instead of rushing down to the cart to gobble up the fruits, the monkeys ran over to Suk and grabbed him. They dragged Suk into the woods and deposited him at the feet of Sugriv. Ram, Lak, and Hanuman remained nearby looking on. The monkeys began banging on Suk with sticks.

Suk caught sight of Ram and pleaded with him, "Can you get these monkeys to stop? Please! My name is Suk. I am only an emissary. I bring only food and an offer of peace."

Ram asked Sugriv, "Can you ask your monkeys to stop hitting Ravan's emissary? If we want our emissaries to be safe, we have to permit our enemy's emissary to be safe too."

Sugriv replied, "Okay, I'll ask my monkeys to stop." He gestured to the monkeys to back off.

Sugriv asked Ram to inquire as what Suk wanted. Through Ram, Suk relayed Ravan's offer of nonaggression between them.

Sugriv retorted, "Although Ravan hasn't brought direct harm to me personally, his syndicate, and that includes you, has profited by selling my brothers and sisters as slaves. Now Ram has become my ally, and you have done direct harm to Ram. Because of this, I'll pursue Ravan. I'll destroy him and his whole organization. Tell that to your boss."

The monkeys released the defeated Suk, who slunk back through the estate gates to report to Ravan.

Sugriv then appointed the spider monkey CEO, Nal, as the architect of a system of vines they would use to swing into Ravan's estate when the time came to attack.

Nal organized the monkeys to search for vines throughout the forest. He taught them to look especially for groves of old trees where vines and other epiphytes are found.

As more monkeys arrived at the bivouac and the system of vines gradually took shape, Ram became increasingly excited and optimistic. Each day brought him closer to Sita. It also brought him closer to revenge against Ravan. He couldn't wait to start the attack. Ram's war of revenge was assuming a dynamic of its own, increasingly detached from its original purpose rescuing Sita and protecting humanity from exploitation by Ravan's evil syndicate.

Dirty Trick

Suk returned to the estate building and called Ravan in his offshore control center.

When Ravan's face popped up on the communicator video screen, Suk said, "Sir, I've been to see Ram and the monkeys. I found the monkey CEO, who was with Ram and his brother."

"Yes, continue," said Ravan.

"The bottom line is that the monkey CEO and Ram have become inseparable allies. There's no way the monkeys will back off, leaving Ram and Lak to fight us alone. And their numbers are huge, with more arriving every hour. May I speak frankly?"

"Go ahead," said Ravan.

Suk continued, "I seriously think you should return Sita while there is still time. The force Ram has put together with his monkey allies seems invincible."

Ravan replied, "Bullshit. We can take out a bunch of monkeys. You're a wimp. Go back and get me a better estimate of their numbers. Find out who their generals are and whom Ram listens to. This time take Saran with you for help. Disguise yourselves as local boys looking to trap some chickens in the bush to take home for dinner."

Suk went to the quarters housing the security personnel, found Saran, and told him of Ravan's orders. They dressed and went through the estate gate. They bushwhacked into the scrubby woods to gauge the number of assembled monkeys. They were astonished at the numbers they encountered.

Before long, Vibish detected the pair wandering about. He gestured for some monkeys to drag the pair before Ram. The monkeys started beating the pair with sticks. Terrified, the pair appealed to Ram for help. Ram interceded.

Suk asked Ram, "Once again, sir, please spare our lives. Ravan sent us to estimate the size of your army."

Ram replied, "Go ahead and look around. Vibish will show you anything you wish to see. Then report back to Ravan that he can't win and should stand down."

Vibish then grandly swept his hand in a 180-degree arc. He also pointed specifically to Sugriv and the other leaders of the howlers.

Vibish said, "Our army of monkeys includes five species from Panama plus many vervets from this island. The biggest are the howlers from Panama." He added matter-of-factly, "Give it up. You don't have a chance."

Suk and Saran crept back to the estate and called Ravan, who was still working in his offshore control center.

Saran said, "Sir, it's hopeless."

Ravan was furious. "Nonsense, the monkeys beat you up and broke you. That won't happen to me. I'm strong. I'll not bend. I'll come to the estate myself, and you can point out the leaders of the monkeys to me."

Ravan climbed into the submarine waiting outside his control center and, less than an hour later, arrived at the dock by his estate. He disembarked, ran up the stairs to the garage, and through the garage to the estate. There he met up with Suk and Saran, and together, the three climbed the stairs to the widow's walk on the roof. From this vantage point, Ravan could look into the scrubby woods beyond the estate walls.

Saran pointed to some trees, saying, "See that huge monkey? That's Sugriv, the CEO of the howlers from Panama. The massive one next to Sugriv is another howler, Angad, his nephew, who is being groomed as his successor. Next to him is a fierce night monkey, Nil. Finally, there is Hanuman, the vervet monkey whom you've already met."

Near the monkeys Ravan could also see Ram and Lak. There was no doubt in Ravan's mind that Ram and his allies were planning an attack in the near future.

Ravan ordered yet another security guard, Sard, to reconnoiter among the monkeys. Yet again Vibish quickly saw the intruder poking around in the woods. Once more monkeys beat the spy with sticks before dragging him before Ram. And once again, Ram ordered his release and return to Ravan.

Sard straggled back through the estate gate, entered the estate house, and found Ravan.

Like the spies before him, Sard reported, "No way we're gonna win this one. Whether we die in defeat or live to fight another day is in your hands."

Ravan said through clenched teeth, "We fight."

Still, Ravan reflected on the unanimous reports from his emissaries and his security guards sent to spy on Ram and his monkey allies. "Maybe I can try another tack," he said to himself.

Ravan summoned his chief counterfeiter, Vidyu, and said to him, "I want you to make a counterfeit US passport for Ram, complete with an embedded microchip, a photo, and a visa from Panama with official arrival and exit stamps. Can you do it? Do you have the facilities here?"

"Sure," replied Vidyu, "that's a lot easier than counterfeiting the hundred dollar bills that we produce in our engraving room downstairs. Four hours okay?"

"That would be great," said Ravan as he gave Vidyu a pat on the shoulder.

Four hours later Vidyu came to deliver the fake passport. Ravan took a look at it and gave Vidyu a high five, saying, "Great work. You're a true artist."

Vidyu beamed and withdrew to return to his work in the engraving room.

Ravan gathered up the passport and went out into the garden looking for Sita. He found her sitting in her usual spot by a grove of trees near the estate wall.

He came up to her and said, "My dear, take a deep breath. I have some news of your husband, or former husband, I should say. My forces led by Pragast have sought him out and finally killed him. As proof I bring you now his passport."

Handing the passport to Sita, he continued, "As you can see, his official passport has his picture and stamps from his recent travels to Panama on his way here to try to take you back. Please think about this. Ram is no more, and I still offer you my hand. Come and be my wife."

Sita looked at the passport and the picture of her husband. She wailed in grief and agony. She would not look at Ravan. She ran from him and stepped behind a tree in the grove, as though to hide, even though the tree was too small to shield her from view. She embraced the tree and spoke to it, as though it were the body of her beloved Ram.

She cried out, "What now? We weren't supposed to end up this way. Where did our future go that was once so bright and promising? How can I go on?"

To Ravan, she said, "Kill me now, you dog. Kill me or I'll kill myself. There's no reason to go on."

Sita continued wailing as Ravan looked on, uncertain how to console her and feeling any attempt at consolation would be rebuffed.

Then a security guard came up to Ravan and said, privately, "Pragast has assembled our forces and awaits your word on when to begin the attack on Ram and his monkey allies. Come take charge now."

Ravan nodded, turned away from Sita, and strode back to the estate house to meet with his assembled forces.

Sita let herself collapse to the ground at the base of the tree she had been embracing. She lay on the ground gasping and sobbing. Gradually, she began humming a lament she had composed during her long, lonely agony.[1]

From the window of her room in the estate house, Vibish's wife, Sarama, saw Sita lying on the ground beneath the trees where she usually spent her days. Sarama had seen Ravan come to Sita and hand her a small booklet. It must have contained something devastating because she saw Sita collapse in grief.

Sarama went out of her room and approached Sita. Sitting on the ground next to her, Sarama said, "Whatever Ravan just gave you, don't take it seriously. I saw him speaking with his master counterfeiter and suspect they concocted a fake document to show you as proof that your husband has been killed or captured. What did he give you, if I may ask?"

Sita handed Sarama the fake passport.

Sarama instantly said, "Oh, this is child's play for them. Don't believe it. This doesn't prove your husband is dead. Vidyu can counterfeit a passport in a few hours."

Sita remained on the ground. Sarama sat near her, holding her hand. Sita gradually stopped crying, afraid to let herself believe that Ram was still alive. As the women sat together, they heard the preparations for battle begin. They saw the jeep with its mounted machine gun being wheeled out of the garage.

Sarama turned to Sita and asked, "Is there anything I can do to help?"

Sita replied, "Can you find out somehow what Ravan is planning to do to me? Do you think he would kill me before Ram could rescue me, just to prevent Ram from ever getting me back again?"

Sarama stood and said, "I'll see what I can find out." She then returned to the estate house.

____

[1] Music score of Sita's Lament is included near the end of the book. Free download of audio available at Ram-2050.com.

Once back inside the house, Sarama saw that Ravan was conducting his final council of war in the executive conference room prior to the upcoming battle. She went to a nearby room to listen in.

Soon Sarama returned to Sita and said, "I don't think he will kill you before or during the attack. He wants you alive, for himself. But I overheard Ravan's mother. She visited the war council just to exhort Ravan to return you to Ram. But Ravan wouldn't respond to even his mother's advice. He will no more part with you than a miser will let go of his treasure."

Hearing this, Sita resolved to wait patiently in the safety of her room in the estate house while anticipating Ram's rescue.

Meanwhile, Ravan continued addressing his council of war. His chief henchmen, who had been so confident of success in their last council meeting, were now afraid, and their fear showed on their faces.

Seeing this, Ravan declared, "I've heard all the reports of Ram and his prowess. I see monkeys clamoring in the trees around the estate. But I tell you, their strength is overrated. We can easily take Ram, and defeating a gaggle of monkeys is no big deal."

Then Malay, the elderly counselor who was Ravan's maternal grandfather, spoke up. "Oh, Ravan, my grandson, do not pursue this battle. There are many ways to deal with a hostile enemy. War is one way, but only recommended when the enemy is clearly weaker, military success is certain, and diplomacy has failed. Otherwise, the likely costs outweigh the benefits. Try to reason with Ram. Try to make an alliance. Give Sita back. The outcome of battle is always unsure. There must always be a loser. I know you to be intelligent. Negotiation can be a win-win strategy for both parties. And here's something else to consider: Your immunity is only from government militias, police and army, not from private militias like the army Ram has assembled with his monkey allies. They have every license to defeat you. I recommend you negotiate now. I recommend you avoid the beginning of a war."

Ravan retorted, "Why do you say that? As I have said many times now, Ram is nothing but a weak daddy's boy. Our machine gun will mow down any attacking gaggle of monkeys. So shut up."

Hearing this, Malay got up from the council table. He returned to his room to await an outcome to the ensuing battle.

Ravan returned his attention to the battle plans. He stationed his chief henchmen at key spots around the estate grounds and buildings and awaited the onslaught.

War

Ram could see that Ravan's emissaries had failed to dissuade him from continuing his hostilities. War seemed inevitable. So Ram sent monkeys to inspect the preparations Ravan had set in place.

From their positions in the trees the monkeys spotted the Crimean commander in chief, Pragast, standing in the center of the estate behind the main gate, as well as Ravan's half brother, the Sudanese Mahap, and the American Mahod standing toward the left of the estate. They also saw Ravan's elder son, Ind, toward the right of the estate, and Ravan himself in the center.

Ram then placed the howler CEO, Sugriv; the spectacled bear, Jamb; and Vibish on the road facing the gate, ready to rush in once the gate was blasted open. Ram placed the night monkey CEO, Nil, and the howler CEO designate, Angad, in the trees on the left, and the vervet Hanuman in a tree on the right. Ram and Lak stationed themselves at the head of the attacking force, ready to seek out Ravan once the battle began.

As the monkeys moved into position, Ram's anger toward Ravan grew. He reflected that Ravan's entire syndicate, along with all his family members, were certain to perish because they were commanded by a mean-spirited, lustful, and stubborn CEO.

As Sugriv moved into position, he could see Ravan in the distance, in the center of his estate, surrounded by security-guard groupies. Incensed at Ravan's self-confident pretentiousness, Sugriv didn't try to restrain himself. He sprang from his tree over the fence into the estate and ran to confront Ravan. Sugriv growled and jumped on Ravan.

The syndicate boss shouted, "You fuckin' animal. Get away from me."

They wrestled, but neither was able to overpower the other. Then Ravan reached for his pistol. Seeing that, Sugriv suddenly pulled back, hopped up to the roof and scampered across it to the end nearest the forest, where he leapt to an overhanging branch.

Ravan was annoyed, thinking, "Goddamned animals. At least my allies are humans. And it's a human I aim to defeat, Ram." Disgusted, Ravan retired to his offshore command center to be advised of the war's progress.

When Sugriv returned to the woods, Ram embraced him in welcome.

But Ram followed up, saying, "It was irresponsible of you to go running off to confront Ravan. You're a CEO. A CEO should never act rashly. Many depend on you. If anything had happened to you, what would become of them? What would become of me and our plans to rescue Sita? Please don't be so impetuous again."

Sugriv replied, "I'm sorry. I lost self-control seeing Ravan surrounded by his fawning groupies. It won't happen again."

Ram patted him on the back reassuringly.

The monkeys continued taking their positions around the estate. As Ram saw the battle preparations approach completion, he thought he'd try one last time to avoid all-out war. He sought out a scrap of paper he had packed in with his supplies.

He took a pen and wrote a note to Ravan, saying, "I am Ram. My army is poised to attack. I now offer you one final chance to avoid certain defeat. Return my wife, and we will withdraw."

Ram gave the note to Angad and asked him to deliver it to Ravan. Angad climbed into the trees, moved along a branch, and dropped onto the estate grounds. He gingerly approached Ravan and handed him the note.

Ravan read the note and became furious. He reached out to grab Angad. Some of his surrounding security guards reached out as well. But Angad was a fierce howler and couldn't be restrained. He pulled and twisted free, jumped up to the roof, and followed the same path back to the forest that Sugriv had taken earlier that day.

By this point Ravan was beginning to get a bad feeling about the entire enterprise that was about to begin. He felt a pang of fear grip his stomach. He said to himself, "If I am defeated, then so be it. But I will never of my own free will give up Sita."

Angad returned to the woods and reported back to Ram, saying, "Ravan would not consider our olive branch. He and his guards tried to take me prisoner. But I escaped and returned to report back to you."

Ram replied to Angad, "Thanks for trying. Now we can attack with a clean conscience, knowing we did everything possible to avoid the violence and bloodshed that is about to begin."

Turning to Sugriv and all the other CEO's, Ram declared, "That's it. Let's go."

Ram and Lak reached into their backpacks and each pulled out a suit of ceramic body armor, a disposable AT4 antitank gun, a knife, and a Glock automatic pistol. After strapping on their armor, knives, and pistols, they aimed their AT4s at the front gate to Ravan's estate.

On Ram's nod, they fired together. The front gate splintered. Its jagged pieces flew into the air and fell among Ravan's security guards, causing them to break ranks and run for cover. Tossing their spent AT4s to the side of the road, Ram and Lak—as well as Sugriv, Jamb, and Vibish, trailed by dozens of monkeys—began to march through the gaping hole left by the AT4s.

The security guards and syndicate hit men could see Ram and his army approaching. They regrouped and rushed forward to meet their enemy. As the syndicate forces and Ram's army were about to collide, Ram bellowed out the howler attack call.

At this signal, the monkeys stationed outside the estate's wall swung in on vines, hollering as they came, and landed around the entire perimeter of the estate grounds. As the guards and syndicate hit men turned to see what the commotion was, they lost their focus on Ram, Lak, and the army arriving through the front gate.

Then the gunner on the jeep's machine gun turret pivoted and started spraying bullets. He aimed at the monkeys rushing into the interior of the estate grounds from the perimeter where they had landed.

Hundreds of monkeys fell. Some fell wounded, spouting blood on their enemies. Some died immediately, their entrails spilling over the mowed lawn, while others lost limbs that came to litter the intricately designed walkways of Ravan's estate.

But some monkeys escaped the withering barrage of bullets and reached the security personnel and hit men. These monkeys jumped on their enemies, biting ears, ripping cheeks, and gouging eyes. Other monkeys reached the machine gunner, overpowered him, dragged him to the ground, and stomped on him, pulverizing his corpse. They then overturned the jeep, crushing its machine gun. The grounds were soon covered in a mire of flesh and blood.

As the battle continued, the initial formations dissolved into a general melee. Angad, the howler CEO designate, squared off against Ind, the syndicate's CEO designate; Hanuman, a vervet, against Sharab, the Nigerian; Vibish against Supar from Pakistan; Lak against Dumuk from Northern Ireland; Nal, the spider monkey CEO, against Pretap from Corsica. Then four henchmen attacked Ram. Lak turned away from Dumuk to decapitate Ram's attackers with his machete.

The battle waged on. Maind, CEO of the tamarins, leapt like a squirrel onto the back of Vijram from Chechnya, biting him on the nape of his neck. Vijram tried to slap the tiny monkey away but Maind continued working his way around to the front of Vijram's neck, severing carotid arteries as he went. Nal, the spider monkey CEO, killed Nikhumb, Ravan's nephew, the son of Ravan's brother Kumb; Sush, the capuchin CEO, sneaked up and strangled Vidyumal, the hit man from Los Angeles.

When they could briefly get away from the fighting, Ram and Lak located the kitchen's walk-in freezer. They deposited their medical supplies there on a top shelf and returned to the battle. They were sure their supplies would be safe there because none of Ravan's security personnel would think to check on the freezer's contents during the conflict to come.

As casualties and carnage accumulated, vultures arrived to peck at the fallen bodies, hermit crabs climbed from the shore to scavenge scraps of flesh, and stray dogs, cats, goats, and pigs arrived to graze upon the body parts and lick at the ponds of blood. Ameiva ground lizards joined the scavenging, as did Alsophis snakes, who poked the corpses for maggots to eat. Flies buzzed around the stinking flesh, and ants carried tiny morsels to their nests. Anolis lizards descended from the trees to dart at the flies and lap up ants. Then sparrow hawks and pearly-eyed thrashers flew in to gobble up lizards. The entire scavenger ecosystem enjoyed a holiday feast at the awful expense of fallen monkeys and humans.

As night fell on the battlefield, Ram and Lak—with help from Nil, the night monkey CEO—looked around for syndicate henchmen hiding out in structures and plantings around the trees. Ram could see almost as well in the night as Nil could because of the bush-baby genes he had been endowed with. Lak too could see well at night because many of his mammalian genes came from nocturnal species. Together they crept about the estate, surprising security guards, hit men, and other syndicate henchmen, and slitting their throats one by one. Eventually, they could find no more enemies to attack, so they sought a place to sleep until the battle resumed in the morning.

Throughout the day and early evening, Ram and Lak had stood together, often back to back, protecting one another and killing countless enemies. Ram felt strength and confidence when he sensed Lak's back pressing against his. He felt exhilarated during the combat even as he was appalled at the destruction. His coordination with Lak reminded him of their teamwork as children under their father's tutelage. Despite the raging battle, Ram found his physical contact with Lak rekindled happy memories and pleasant sensations from the innocent days of their childhood camaraderie. He realized how precious and irreplaceable his dear brother was to him.

Ram and Lak lay down on the ground near the pavilion with its grove of trees where Sita habitually spent her time. Ram slept fitfully. In his mind he kept seeing dead, wounded, and mutilated friends and allies. In his mind, he could hear their deafening cries of agony.

The morning's sun illuminated an estate littered with mangled bodies—half-eaten, partially gnawed bones and body parts, pools of coagulated blood, and fragments of flesh were everywhere. Ram vomited in revulsion.

But he couldn't quit. More fighting lay ahead. Ravan's surviving henchmen regrouped and rushed at Ram and Lak, who, back to back, rebuffed them again as they had the day before. Henchmen fired bullets at the brothers from their pistols, but the bullets bounced off their ceramic armor. Neither brother fell from a bullet's impact, as each was propping up the other, standing back to back. Instead of falling, the brothers fired back with their own pistols. And when henchmen came close enough, Lak decapitated them with his machete.

Meanwhile, Angad fought again with Ind, who eventually tired and retreated to the main estate house. Seeing Ind withdraw, the surviving monkeys hooted and chattered in joy.

Feeling ridiculed, Ind decided on a different tack. He summoned one of the security guards.

He told him to go to the armory in the garage and find the closet labeled *Active Ropes*. The heat-seeking ropes, made by Mechanical Python Inc, consisted of a linear array of contracting motors enclosed in a flexible fiberglass sheath. The head of the rope contained a control center that released the motors.

Ind said, "Make sure the ropes' batteries are fully charged."

The security guard returned with two coils of the active ropes. Ind took them, left the house, and approached Ram and Lak, who were still standing back to back, battling syndicate henchmen.

Ind hollered to the henchmen, "Stand back. Get away from them!" The henchmen backed off. Ind twirled a rope like a lasso and then threw it at Ram; he did the same with the next rope and threw it at the other brother. The heat sensors in the ropes detected their bodies, and the ropes slithered toward them in a flash. They coiled around the brothers and started squeezing.

Ind gloated as he saw the brothers losing color and becoming weaker. He then left the battlefield in search of his father to tell him that Ram and Lak were now defeated.

The monkeys saw their human leaders now bound in the ropes, helpless and seemingly near death. They wailed and beat their breasts.

Vibish heard the wailing, saw the fallen brothers, and came running. He said to anyone who would listen, "Ind can't win a fair fight. He has to resort to a goddamned gadget."

Vibish could see that Sugriv, the howler CEO on which all the monkeys depended, was about to give up.

Vibish shouted out said to anyone who could hear, "Victory is never easy. Heroes aren't derailed by setbacks. They go on. They exert themselves even more."

Vibish then took his shirt off and poured water from his canteen onto it. With his shirt he wiped Sugriv's eyes and stroked him to reassure him.

Then Vibish took Sugriv to look closely at the brothers. Ram and Lak were bound with so many coils of active rope that their bodies were scarcely visible. Jamb, the spectacled bear, ambled to the side of the brothers to take a look. Together, they examined the brothers.

Vibish held his hand in front of their mouths and pointed to their heaving breasts. He declared, "Ram and Lak are still alive."

Sugriv and Jamb understood and found fresh hope within themselves.

Garud Saves Ram

Ind went to a video screen to speak over the secure link with his father, who was in the offshore control center. The remaining security guards and henchmen clapped with joy.

When Ravan's face appeared on the screen, Ind reported, "Father, I have captured your two worst enemies. They lie bound in our mechanical pythons where they are slowly and painfully suffocating."

Ravan was elated. He sprang from the chair at the desk where he was working, saying, "Wonderful, this is such wonderful news. I'll come and join you now at the estate house."

When Ravan arrived at the estate house, he summoned Trijata, who was a maid to Sarama, Vibish's wife.

He instructed her, "Find Sita in her room and take her to the balcony on the roof to see the dying bodies of her husband and his brother. Then she'll realize she has no choice but to accept me as her new husband."

Trijata went to Sita in her quarters and led her to the widow's walk. From the rooftop, Sita gazed out over the field of carnage, dried pools of blood, and the ecosystem of scavenging animals. There she also saw her husband bound up with his brother in coils of rope, apparently dead.

Sita was shocked. She cried, "How could this happen? Ram and Lak are smarter and stronger than anyone the syndicate has to offer. Their mothers, Kausha and Sumitra, will be devastated. Not only their mothers, but all of Apple will crushed. I foresee a run on Apple stock. I foresee a stock market crash, and all will suffer, retirees and widows the most. And if Ram and Lak can be killed as they have been, which was unthinkable to me, then now I conclude that any calamity must be considered possible."

But Trijata, like her mistress, was favorably disposed to Sita. She gazed intently at the bodies of Ram and Lak and at Vibish and the monkeys who were standing about.

She said, "I don't think your husband and his brother are dead. If they were, Vibish and the monkeys would have abandoned their bodies or be trying to bury them. Instead, they're standing around expectantly, as though anticipating that the brothers will somehow recover from their wounds."

Sita replied, "I pray your words prove true. Please bring me back to my quarters, where I may rest and suffer in silence."

Trijata then accompanied Sita back to her room and left her there.

As the day of war came to an end, Ravan and his entourage began a victory celebration that lasted well into the night. Meanwhile, the monkeys watched over Ram and Lak throughout the night.

The next morning the monkeys keeping watch over the brothers gently awakened Ram. He opened his eyes and from the corner of one eye could see Lak lying bound and unconscious next to him.

He was stunned. He cried out, "What's this? My brother dead at my side? This is horrible. Absolutely horrible! Why should I go on trying to defeat Ravan now that my brother is dead? I can find another wife, but I've come to realize that I could never find another brother like him. From our fighting together back to back, I find the bond to my brother grows stronger daily even as the memory of my wife gradually withers. I now feel like giving up and following Lak to be with him in heaven. It's my fault that he is dead. I wish I'd never boasted that I would kill Ravan and install Vibish in his place. I can't do it—I can't go on."

Turning his gaze to Sugriv, he continued, "Return with your monkeys to your home in Panama. Thank you for your service, but our mission is now aborted. Return home before there's even more bloodshed than we've already seen."

But Sugriv was having none of this defeatist talk. He was furious and said to Ram, "I will kill Ravan myself if you don't. I will rescue Sita if you don't. I will remain here until our mission is accomplished."

As Sugriv spoke, the shadow of a large bird passed over them. They looked up and saw a fish eagle, an osprey, circling on his daily route high above the ocean looking for food. The monkeys gestured to him, pointing to the brothers who were bound in the mechanical python. Having caught many fish and an occasional snake in the past, the eagle sensed an opportunity for a good meal in what seemed to be the large snakes wrapped around Ram and Lak. The great eagle dived on the mechanical python with its talons extended. The osprey severed the control module from the head of one of the active ropes, then dived again and severed the head module from the other rope.

Now the osprey could tell that the coils weren't snakes at all but were some human contraption. "Oh, well," it thought, "no free lunch here."

The ropes relaxed and uncoiled, freeing the brothers. Ram looked around. He was relieved and overjoyed to see that Lak was still alive.

Ram arose and faced the great bird. He bowed in the universal gesture of thanks, and signed to the eagle to ask its name.

The bird squawked what sounded like "Garud." He then raised his wings and bowed to Ram before taking to the air to resume his graceful circling over the ocean in search of food.

Throughout the night the stem cells laced under the skin of the brothers had regenerated their broken flesh and healed their lacerations. They now they stood ready for battle again. Ram gave the howler attack call, and the monkeys responded in kind, making a deafening clamor.

Battle Continues

The clamor outside awoke Ravan, who was sleeping in after a night of partying.

From his bed he summoned a security guard and asked, "What the hell is all the noise?"

The guard looked out the window and reported, "It looks like Ram, Lak, and that big monkey they call Sugriv are starting to attack us again."

Ravan turned pale and buried his head in his pillow. He knew this meant big trouble. It seemed Ram was impossible to stop.

Ram sent his guard to summon Dhum, a syndicate boss from Colombia.

He told him, "Go finish off Ram and his monkeys. It's embarrassing that this has been going on so long. I mean, they're just monkeys. Go kill enough of them to scare them away once and for all."

Dhum replied, "Consider it done."

Dhum gathered some remaining security guards and headed out into the estate grounds to confront the monkeys, who were jumping up and down, spoiling for a fight. The security guards were outfitted with Russian AK-101 automatic rifles. They advanced on the monkeys, spraying bullets as they pressed forward. The bullets mowed down the army of monkeys, and corpses started to pile up. Some monkeys made it through the withering rifle fire to maul some security guards, tearing flesh from their bones. But by and large, the monkeys began to falter, and eventually turned to run back through the front gate to the trees.

Hanuman watched his compatriots being routed. He picked up a heavy rock. He ran forward, darting from one pile of bodies to another, hiding behind them, until he was next to Dhum.

Out of the corner of his eye, Dhum saw Hanuman as he was about to leap. He aimed his AK-101 at Hanuman. Some bullets grazed Hanuman's side, but too late to save Dhum. Hanuman leapt upon Dhum's back and brought the heavy rock crashing down on Dhum's skull, killing him the old-fashioned way.

Brains oozed out of Dhum's broken skull, and blood spurted. The security guards saw that yet another of their leaders had been killed by the monkeys. They quickly retreated back to the estate house. The monkeys rejoiced, jumping up and down, clapping and chattering.

Meanwhile, word was spreading among the monkeys throughout the island that humans from the estate at Jenkins Bay were killing their brethren.

Monkeys dropped what they were doing and made their way to Ravan's estate to join the cause. Although the monkeys were rivals for food and territory in their habitat, opposition to Ravan's persecution elicited a unique degree of cooperation among them.

With their new and enthusiastic reinforcements, the monkeys dropped down from the trees and again poured through the front gate into Ravan's estate grounds.

When Ravan leaned of Dhum's demise, he hissed in anger like a cobra whose tail had been stepped on. He summoned another syndicate boss, Vajrad from Yemen.

He told him, "I want you to resume the assault on the horde of monkeys that keeps attacking us. Can I count on you?"

"Yes," replied Vajrad.

Vajrad gathered up another band of security guards from among the survivors. He grabbed a machete in addition to his AK-101. Waving his machete like a knight of old might have waved his sword, Vijrad led his guards back into the fight with the monkeys. The security guards again fired from the AK-101s, killing monkeys with wild abandon. Again, some monkeys survived the onslaught and managed to kill some security guards. But overall, the firepower from the guards overwhelmed the monkeys and they fell back again through the gate and into the trees for safety.

When Angad saw his army of monkeys falling back, he became furious. Like Hanuman before him, Angad grabbed a heavy rock and stealthily ran from pile to pile of corpses until he was near Vajrad. He jumped on Vajrad.

Before Angad could hit Vijrad with the rock, Vijrad shook him off, furious at the direct attack. Vijrad struck Angad with his fist. But Angad jumped back on Vajrad and managed to hit him in the skull, hard enough to knock Vajrad out briefly but not hard enough to crush his skull and kill him. Vajrad came to almost immediately. He attacked Angad again, and both traded blows until they fell to the earth in exhaustion. But of the two, Angad was the less exhausted. He saw a chance to grab Vajrad's machete. With one lunge, Angad decapitated Vajrad. The overjoyed monkeys spilled back into the estate grounds while the Ravan's security guards retreated to the house again.

As the security guards straggled back, Ravan was beside himself in anger. This time, he summoned Durd, the syndicate boss from the Vatican.

Ravan said to him, "Just do it."

Durd nodded and collected a band of guards from among those who were not hiding and still willing to stand up and be recognized.

In a now-familiar sequence, Durd advanced on the monkeys, who fell back. This time, Hanuman returned to the forefront to accost Durd directly. Hanuman picked up a huge branch to use as a club. Running between piles of monkey and human corpses, Hanuman reached Durd.

Before Durd could aim his AK-101 at Hanuman, the powerful monkey jumped in the air and brought his club down on Durd, splitting his head wide open. Again the monkeys cheered, grateful for leaders of such courage and martial skill.

As the security guards retreated from the battlefield, Ravan became increasingly exasperated.

Pragast, the Crimean chief syndicate boss, had joined Ravan on the widow's walk to watch Durd succeed. Instead, they found themselves watching Durd's defeat.

Ravan said to Pragast, "It's come down to us. You, Ind, Kumb, and myself—we're the only ones left who can take on Ram and defeat him. Pragast, my chief, can I ask you to put this matter to rest once and for all? Can I count on you?"

"Yes," said Pragast, "I'm emboldened by your confidence. I'll finish this matter now and for all time."

As Pragast was gathering a contingent of guards to join him in what Ravan hoped would be the final assault on the monkeys, Ravan's misgivings grew. He knew his immunity from retribution extended only to official enforcement units, not to private militias, and certainly not to militias comprised mostly of animals. Perhaps the matter would only end when he and Ram personally dueled.

Pragast advanced with his guards against the monkeys who had poured through the gate into the battlefield. This time the monkeys gathered rocks in advance. They pelted the guards with rocks even as they were ducking and dodging bullets from the security guards' AK-101s. Those monkeys who survived the volleys to reach the guards found their rocks had already injured many, allowing them to immobilize the guards more efficiently. But as before, the firepower of the guards eventually forced the monkeys to fall back.

Seeing his monkeys retreat, Nil, the night monkey, grabbed a rock in one hand and a small boulder in the other. Darting among mounds of corpses, he ran to Pragast. He threw his rock to one side of Pragast, diverting his attention. Then, coming from the other side, he jumped on the man. With the small boulder, he smashed Pragast's head, killing him instantly. The security guards had no choice then but to trudge back to the safety of the estate house along what were becoming well-trodden paths.

Nil returned to the woods outside the estate walls. Ram and Lak, who had been watching the battles from outside the gate, congratulated Nil on a job well done. From the outside Ram seemed increasingly hardened to the suffering all about him, but on the inside he tried to calm his thoughts as his stomach churned in disgust at the stinking corpses of former allies.

Ravan Engages

From his balcony Ravan had been watching the latest battle between his forces and those of Ram and his allies. He was appalled. He called his remaining syndicate bosses to the council table in the executive conference room.

He said, "Clearly, Ram and his allies are a force to be reckoned with. They have strength in numbers, and they are well led. They have defeated four of my most experienced syndicate leaders. The time has come for me to go personally into battle and defeat Ram. I will scatter the monkeys and take down Ram and his brother."

The syndicate bosses cheered and pounded the table, relieved that the burden of defeating Ram would no longer be carried by them alone.

Ravan gathered every last one of the remaining guards, which formed an army larger that the previous four bosses had been able to assemble. Ravan and his forces then marched out from the estate house back into the field of battle.

Once outside on the estate grounds, Ravan and his troops could see hordes of monkeys in the surrounding trees, as though the strife of the last few days had not diminished their numbers at all. They didn't realize that Ram's army of monkeys was being continually replenished with reinforcements from throughout the island.

Ram was keeping an eye on Ravan's estate house. He saw that Ravan's henchmen were organizing for another attack.

Ram turned to Vibish and asked, "Who are the people grouping to attack us this time?"

Vibish identified the various participants. Then he pointed to a large, powerful-looking man toward the rear of the attacking forces.

He said, "See that one dressed in pressed black trousers, crocodile leather shoes and belt, and a skin-tight black T-shirt with a cave-drawing insignia emblazoned in red?"

Ram nodded.

Vibish continued, "He's the one you're after. He's Ravan."

Ravan's gold jewelry shimmered in the sun. The jaunty gangster had his usual cigarette dangling from his mouth and sported his sardonic grin. He also had a Glock automatic pistol holstered on his right hip.

Ram exclaimed, "At last! I've waited so long for this chance to rid the world of him and the evil he embodies."

Preceded by Sugriv, the other monkey CEOs, and the new recruits, Ram and Lak headed directly toward the advancing phalanx of Ravan's security guards. As the distance separating the two opposing armies shrank, Ravan raced to the front of his troops. Ravan's forces intersected the army of monkeys, and Ravan waded into the midst of them, carving a path through them like a killer whale dividing the ocean waters of fish. As Ravan approached the monkey CEOs, Sugriv grabbed a huge rock and threw it at Ravan. Ravan laughed, pulled his pistol, and shot Sugriv, who fell to the ground, in pain but still alive.

The monkeys then rained rocks upon the guards, killing many by crushing their skulls and wounding others. The guards answered with their AK-101s and mowed down wave after wave of charging monkeys.

Fearing their own annihilation, the monkeys appealed directly to Ram to take over. Ram heard their call for assistance and began to make his way to confront Ravan personally.

But Lak interceded, saying, "Let me. I'd love to take the first crack at him."

Ram said, "Okay, go for it."

As Lak was plotting his approach to attack Ravan, he noticed that Hanuman was advancing toward Ravan and would arrive at Ravan's side before he did.

When Hanuman directly confronted Ravan, Ravan recognized him as the monkey who had killed his son, Aks. Hanuman jumped on Ravan and landed a blow.

Ravan reeled back but recovered. He said to Hanuman, "You landed one. Now take one from me." Ravan delivered an uppercut punch of his own to Hanuman and said, "Take that!" Then he added, "I don't have any more time to bother with you."

Ravan threw Hanuman off like a rag doll and strode forward, aiming to get closer to Ram, the primary target of his rage.

Ravan caught sight of the night monkey, Nil, among the monkey CEOs. Nil saw Ravan as well and ran up to bang on him with a club.

Ravan fired some bullets at Nil. Nil ducked out of the line of fire.

Then tiny Maind, CEO of the tamarins, leapt from behind onto Ravan and reached around his head, knocking the insolent cigarette from his mouth and ripping the T-shirt from his back. Ravan slapped Maind away and pressed ahead.

Ravan caught sight of Lak on the battlefield and headed directly for him. As he came within shouting range, he called out, "Today you die. You are nothing but your brother's bootlicker."

Lak replied, "Trash talk all you want. If you were really were a man, you wouldn't need to mouth off."

Each fired a round of bullets from their pistols at each other, but their anger toward each other was so intense that a moment later they were locked in hand-to-hand combat. Lak's boxer instincts and training clicked in. He danced around the villain, throwing an uppercut, then a body blow.

Ravan threw a kick at Lak and, braving his punches, closed in on the boxer, grasping him around the chest, pinning his arms to his body. They wrestled around on the ground, each hitting the other at every opportunity. Ravan seized his chance to choke Lak. He squeezed until Lak fainted.

Then Ravan got up and tried to drag the fallen Lak back to his house as a prisoner for interrogation.

Hanuman jumped on Ravan, choking him as he was dragging Lak.

Ravan eventually collapsed, releasing Lak's unconscious body.

Casting Ravan aside, Hanuman picked up Lak's body and brought him back in the woods to Ram.

Ram stroked Lak's face until he came to.

Ram said to him, "Now it's my turn. I'll especially enjoy destroying Ravan after what he's done to you."

Then he and Hanuman advanced together on Ravan, who by this time had regained consciousness himself.

As Ram and Hanuman approached, Ravan pulled his pistol and fired a volley at Hanuman. But as he was firing, he slipped on some coagulated blood and missed. Infuriated and offended that Ravan attacked Hanuman before attacking him, Ram fired off a volley that grazed Ravan. Ravan fell, not so much injured as exhausted.

Ram strode up to Ravan, who was lying on the ground. He ripped off Ravan's gold jewelry and said, "I can't kill you now. It's not right to kill a defenseless man. Come back tomorrow and we'll finish this off. I'll kill you then." Ram had by now completely assimilated the warrior's ethic, becoming increasingly oblivious to the goal of rescuing Sita.

Ravan climbed to his knees and then stood up. He limped back to the estate house with his surviving security guards, leaving the decomposer ecosystem to feast on the carnage.

Kumb Engages

Ravan retreated to the estate house, humiliated and depressed. "Why is this happening?" he wondered to himself as he waved his hand across the expanse of his estate grounds, littered with bodies and body parts. "I thought I had prepared myself against attack from all conceivable angles. I have immunity from all official armies and police raids. My syndicate is skilled. We manipulate banks and exchange rates, we have politicians on our payroll, we mess with the gene pools of our enemies, we take down our enemies' Internet, we plant our own propaganda in their entertainment, we distort their news sources, we tie up their court systems, we undercut their social trust, we inflame bigotry, and we amplify economic iniquity. Nothing is beyond us, I would have thought. But here we are being attacked by monkeys, by monkeys! It's so implausible as to be laughable. I must be living a nightmare. Never, never, in my wildest imagination would it have occurred to me to plan a defense against a marauding army of monkeys. I thought the monkeys living here were for the taking, like all the animals over which we humans have dominion. I think this war will never end, never stop. Our battle seems so primordial, good versus evil, innocent nature versus corrupt humanity. And I'm beginning to feel I'm on the losing side of this conflict."

Ravan then said to himself, "Well, I'm down but not out. I have an ace in the hole."

Ravan went to the clinic building adjacent the estate house and spoke to Yupak, his physician, saying, "I need you to awaken Kumb the Killer immediately from his heroin stupor. I need him now. I know it's been only several days since he was last awake, but I need him to lead an attack against the Ram and the monkeys."

Yupak replied, "I understand the need. Bringing Kumb out of his stupor will take some time, however. I'll administer naloxone intravenously to counteract the opiates in his system. That should begin to wake him up in minutes, then I'll have to continue to administer it for about twenty-four hours while the opiates slowly wash out of his system, until the naloxone isn't needed anymore. I'll continue feeding him intravenously during this period."

"Good," replied Ravan, "do it. I'll be working at my offshore control center in the meantime."

As Kumb was being treated, he showed the symptoms of opiate withdrawal. His body ached. He had diarrhea, fever, runny nose, sweating, shivering, vomiting, abdominal cramps, weakness, and even convulsions. He often cried.

Finally, Kumb was present enough in his surroundings to be fully cognizant. He asked, "What's going on? Why was I awakened from my pleasurable slumber?"

Yupak replied, "The syndicate is under attack from Ram and his allied army of monkeys. And we're losing. Ravan and all of us need you desperately."

Kumb got himself up out of bed. Still somewhat high from his opiate, he walked shakily to the main estate house to present himself to Ravan.

From the trees the monkeys saw a large, muscular man emerge from the clinic building and make his way to the estate house. They rushed to Ram and called him to come quickly. Together with Vibish, Ram came to the gate to see who the new opponent was.

Ram asked Vibish, "Who is Mr. Bodybuilder over there?"

Vibish replied, "He's Kumb, our brother. He's a killer. He enjoys killing. When excited, he takes pleasure in killing friend and foe alike. Ravan considered having him confined to a psychiatric hospital to live out his days there in a drug-induced stupor. But when locked away in the hospital, he'd be a security risk for us, as he could be given drugs to induce him to disclose syndicate secrets. So Ravan decided it would be better for Kumb to live out his days in a drug-induced stupor right here rather than in an updated version of an insane asylum. He's perfectly rational at times but irrational during his rampages. He's dangerous. Ravan's hoping that when the monkeys see Kumb in action, they'll run away from him they way they'd run from a mad dog."

Ram told the night monkey, Nil, to assemble the newly arrived reinforcements. Then they poured through the gate to await the next attack from Ravan's steadily dwindling forces.

Kumb arrived at the estate house and pushed the communicator video screen to connect with Ravan in his control center.

Ravan was overjoyed to see him, saying, "You see all the monkeys surrounding us? They're fighters allied with Ram and his brother. I've been unable through any means to defeat them. I turn to you, my beloved brother, as the only one who has the strength and prowess to deal with them."

Kumb replied, "You were warned. Now you reap the fruit of your rash and lustful theft of Sita. Had you followed my advice and those of other well-wishers, you wouldn't be in this mess."

Mahod, Ravan's half brother, the hit man from Hollywood, was listening in. He said, "But Ravan was right to steal Sita. The duty of each person is to secure their own happiness. Even virtue is only a means to secure happiness, to feel good about yourself. Because Ravan's theft of Sita was to realize his pleasure, he was right to do so."

Ravan retorted to Kumb, "Why lecture me now? This is the time for action not words. Whether I was wise in capturing Sita is beside the point in this crisis. Let's do what's needed now."

Kumb replied, "Don't worry. I gave my advice out of love. I will indeed set out to annihilate Ram as promised. I enjoy killing—this will be fun. I will bring you Ram's head as a trophy, and the bodies of his chief monkey allies will disintegrate into dust."

Ravan was elated, as he knew of no one who could defeat his bodybuilder brother.

Kumb strapped on a Glock automatic pistol and a throwing knife. He gathered some remaining security guards and strode forth to battle on the estate grounds.

When the monkeys saw Kumb, they were immediately intimidated and ran back to their trees.

Their spontaneous retreat was checked by Angad, who urged them on, saying, "Don't run! We can take them again like we have in their prior attacks."

But Kumb attacked by grabbing several monkeys. He ostentatiously banged their heads together, crushing both skulls simultaneously. This show of brutality frightened the monkeys, who again retreated to the trees.

Again Angad tried to rally the retreating monkeys, but to no avail.

One cried out, "We can't win this time. It's pointless to continue just to show our bravery. Life is dear."

But Angad, Sugriv, Hanuman, and all the monkey CEOs remained firm. The leaders reminded the retreating monkeys that Ram could defeat anyone and urged them not to be afraid. At last the monkeys regrouped to face Kumb.

The tenacious tamarin Dwivid hurled a sharp-pointed stone at Kumb, but Kumb ducked. The security guards fired their AK-101s at the monkeys. The monkeys threw rocks and clubbed the security guards. Casualties mounted on both sides.

Hanuman jumped on Kumb. But Kumb threw him off with a body blow that left the monkey almost senseless, and vomiting. The CEOs from all five Panamanian monkey species attacked Kumb from all sides. But Kumb cast them off, dismissing them with a wave of his arm.

Sugriv attacked Kumb with a club, smashing it across Kumb's chest. But the club simply broke in two. Kumb pulled his knife. As he raised his arm to throw it at Sugriv, Hanuman intercepted Kumb's arm in its throwing motion and the knife fell harmlessly to the ground. But Kumb rebounded and landed an uppercut on Sugriv, knocking him out cold.

Kumb dragged Sugriv's unconscious body toward the house to show everyone. But a brief rainsquall appeared, and the raindrops awoke Sugriv.

As he came to, he realized he was being dragged to the estate house. He bent his body and flipped over, then ripped off Kumb's right ear, bit off the tip of his nose, and clawed his side.

Kumb reacted in shocked pain, releasing Sugriv.

The monkey bounded up to the roof of the estate house, scampered across it, and jumped onto a branch to rejoin his fellow monkeys in the trees.

Kumb was excited now. He turned back to the army of monkeys and drew his Glock. He fired at the monkeys, killing dozens.

Then Lak interceded. Ever the boxer, in accord with his genes, Lak threw a punch at Kumb.

But Kumb ducked and pulled back, saying, "I see you're a skilled fighter. But I won't fight you. It's your brother I want."

Ram heard what Kumb said and shouted, "I'm over here." Ram pulled his gun and shot a volley of bullets at Kumb, some of which scored. Blood spurted from his wounds.

Kumb was now intoxicated with battle. Like a loose cannon, he fired off shots at friend and foe alike, killing both monkeys and security guards.

Vibish now tried to intercede. He interposed himself between Kumb and Ram.

Kumb said, "Move away, my brother. What are you doing here? I've always respected you, and I would never kill you. But you know that my nature is to wantonly kill all creatures. So stand aside."

Vibish replied, "I offered my best advice to our brother, but he wouldn't listen. He just kept insulting me, so I left and joined with Ram."

Kumb had by now come quite close to Ram.

Turning his attention from Vibish to Ram, Kumb said, "I am Kumb. I'm not an easy kill. I'm your executioner. Don't hold back. Give me your best. I'll still conquer you."

Ram simply drew his pistol and fired off another volley, wounding Kumb even further. Then, with another volley, Ram killed him. He gestured to Lak by drawing a finger across his throat; Lak drew his machete and sliced Kumb's head off. The force of the machete blow propelled the head onto the ground. It rolled to the front door of Ravan's estate.

Meanwhile, monkeys dragged Kumb's decapitated body to a cliff overlooking the ocean. They kicked it off the cliff to the waiting sharks below.

Still high on adrenaline from his victorious combat, Ram gave Lak a high five, and all returned to their bivouac by the trees outside the estate gate.

Sons Engage

The security guards trudged back dejectedly to the estate house. With the video communicator, one of the guards called Ravan, who was working in the control room of his command center.

Ravan answered the call expectantly, anticipating good news. But one glance at the crestfallen security guard on his video screen told him all was not well.

The guard said, "Sir, I'm sorry to have to tell you that your brother, Kumb the Killer, is now dead. Ram and his brother killed him. Also, Lak decapitated his body. The monkeys threw his body off the cliffs where sharks are now feeding. Your brother's head rolled near our front door, where it now sits, ghoulishly attracting flies."

Ravan slumped back in his chair at the news. He seemed to enter a catatonic state for a spell of time.

He eventually awoke to ask himself, "How?"

Then Ravan began muttering and whining in a grief-stricken voice, "What's the point of going on? My brother was like my second half, a part of me, and now gone, and leaving me alone before what seems to be the invincible force of Ram and his allies. What use is my syndicate or Sita or even life itself? I should have listened to my brother, Vibish. I should have learned by now that ignoring the advice of people who wish you well always leads to grief."

Hearing of Kumb's death, Ravan's younger sons, Devant, Naran, Trishir, and Atik boarded the sub to join him in his secret underwater command center. After disembarking, they went to Ravan.

Devant said, "Why are you feeling sorry for yourself? You are powerful, you are bold, and you'll be the last one standing. Now is the time for action. Don't cry in your beer. Send me, and I will destroy them."

Ravan's other sons were heartened by Devant's speech. They boasted of their power too.

Ravan arose, embraced his sons, and said, "Thanks. I'm counting on you. Go do it."

They left Ravan in his command center and boarded the submarine for its return trip back to the estate.

After disembarking, they went to the weapons store in the garage. Each strapped on a Glock and grabbed an AK-101. Then they rounded up the remaining security guards.

Ravan's sons decided on a change of strategy. Devant said, "Let's take it to the monkeys ourselves and not wait for them to take it to us."

Ravan's sons decided to group themselves within the house, out of sight of the monkeys, denying the monkeys the opportunity to prepare. On Devant's signal, he and his brothers, together with the security guards, poured out the front door of the house and ran directly through the estate gate to meet the monkeys at their bivouac in the woods outside the gate.

Naran fired a rat-a-tat-tat volley at the monkeys in the trees, carving a path into the monkey army.

Seeing his monkeys fall from the trees dead or wounded, Angad dropped from his tree directly in front of Naran. Angad screamed at Naran, deflecting attention from the monkeys in the trees to himself.

Naran fired his Glock at Angad, who ducked and weaved.

Angad jumped on Naran, dealing him a blow.

Naran struck back, temporarily dazing Angad.

Angad shook off the daze and came back with a combination—an uppercut followed by a jump onto Naran's back. Then Angad grabbed Naran's neck and strangled him.

Seeing their brother killed, Davant and Trishir and their uncle, Mahod, rushed Angad.

Hanuman saw the three henchmen ganging up on Angad and rushed to his aid, as did Nil, the night monkey, and Rish, a howler warrior.

Devant hit Hanuman, who fought back with a his own combination, striking first at Devant's solar plexus then jumping onto Devant's back. Hanuman grabbed Devant's neck and strangled him.

Then Hanuman turned on Trishir, wrestling away his AK-101 and banging his head open with it.

Meanwhile, Nil killed Mahod with a club and Rish killed Mahap by snatching away his AK-101 pounding him with the gun barrel, crushing his skull.

Ram was watching and remarked to Vibish, "That's five down, one more to go."

Then, seeing Atik off in distance, Ram asked Vibish, "Who's he?"

Vibish replied, "He's Ravan's bodybuilder son. He's nearly as strong and intimidating as Kumb was."

Then Vibish added, "This attack on us is unusual. They've come after us as a team of leaders rather than as a single leader, one at a time. Also, this attack is the first where they've tried to surprise us instead of trying to intimidate us in advance. This time they've taken the battle to us rather than let us move into position first. Still, our numbers and our teamwork will defeat them anyway."

Nil, the night monkey, and Dwivid and Maind, the tamarins, ran toward Atik and jumped on him. As Atik was swatting the monkeys away like flies, he saw Ram in the distance.

Turning from the monkeys as though minor annoyances, Atik challenged Ram, saying, "I don't want to bother with your pesky monkeys—I want you, if you have the courage to face me."

Lak overheard Atik's challenge to Ram and was furious. He interceded, placing himself between Atik and Ram.

Atik looked at him and said, "Boy, get away from me if you want to live."

Lak replied, "Talk all the trash you want. Whether I'm old or young is irrelevant. I'll kill you now."

Lak fired a round from his Glock. The bullets missed as Atik dodged. Lak fired again and winged Atik.

Atik said, "Good shot," and fired back with a burst from his AK-101, winging Lak as well.

Lak and Atik fired at each other, hiding behind the trees and limestone boulders in the woods, but neither could score a direct hit.

Lak knew he'd need to try a new tack. Timing when he thought Atik would peek, he threw his knife.

Atik didn't hear any sound so looked again to see where Lak was, but the knife was already on its way and buried itself in Atik's eye socket.

Lak ran up and finished the job with his machete, severing Atik's head and throwing it on a heap of recently killed monkeys.

Yet again, the security guards retreated, having to run back through the gates, across the battlefield of the estate grounds, and back through the door into the estate house. They glanced at the severed head of Kumb as they went in.

The monkeys congratulated Lak, jumping up and down, and he went to join Ram, who gave him another high five.

Gas and Flames

Ravan was becoming desperate as he sat in his command center. Ind, his eldest son, came by submarine to cheer him up, saying, "I know this battle isn't going well for us. But I can turn it around. I've already defeated Ram and his brother once with the active rope. I can defeat him again. Just give the word, and I'll put a stop to this nonsense."

Ravan replied, "Finish the job this time." They both boarded the commuter submarine to return to the estate.

Upon arrival, Ravan went to the rooftop balcony to watch. He was confident—after all, Ind had already defeated the brothers once before, he could surely do it again.

Ind knew that simply increasing the quantity of brute force used against Ram and his allies wasn't working. A qualitatively different attack was needed. It was time for sarin.

He went to the armory in the garage and donned a Level A hazmat whole-body suit. He grabbed a belt with pockets stuffed with sarin-filled grenades and a grenade launcher.

In his spaceman-like suit, Ind slowly stepped across the estate lawn strewn with the relics of the days' conflicts, through the front gate, out the driveway, and toward the bivouac in the woods where the monkeys, Ram, and his allies were encamped.

Ind took a position on the side of the road across from the bivouac where he could see monkeys. He fired a sarin-filled grenade across the road into the woods. It exploded, releasing gas.

With little wind in the woods to disperse the gas, the cloud of gas remained concentrated and dangerous. It slowly rose up from the ground into the canopy. As the gas cloud intersected the space occupied by the monkeys, they squealed in pain as their noses began running and their eyes constricted. They had trouble breathing. Some drooled and some even vomited with nausea.

Crossing the road and entering the edge of the woods at a clearing, Ind saw the monkey high command.

He fired another grenade across the clearing to a spot under the trees where Sugriv, Angad, and Rish, the howlers; Dwivid, the tamarin; Nil, the night monkey; and Jamb, the spectacled bear, were perched. They all fell from their trees with a thud and lay writhing on the ground.

Ind continued on like a serial killer on the loose, looking for Ram and Lak. A few minutes later he found them on the ground near the trees where the monkey high command had been stationed.

Ind fired his third grenade, which threaded its way through the trees to explode at their feet. Ram and Lak immediately keeled over, writhing in pain as gas fumes hung in the air about them.

The exertion of simply moving from the estate house across the lawn and into the woods was causing Ind to overheat in his heavy whole-body hazmat suit. He knew he had to return to the estate house and to take the suit off or he would die of heat stroke.

He said to himself, "I've got 'em this time. Now I can go back. I can tell my father I've killed the leadership of Ram's army and Ram himself. I can tell him the war is over. Meanwhile, I've got to get out of this suit or I'm going to die myself from the heat."

Ind exited the woods and walked to the estate driveway, then on through the estate gate, across the lawn, and back into the house. As soon as he was inside he ripped the suit off and sat down to cool off.

His father, who had been watching from the rooftop balcony, came downstairs to welcome his son home.

Ind told his father, "Good news! Ram and Lak are defeated at last. Our syndicate is victorious. Tomorrow, after the gas has dispersed, I'll revisit the woods where Ram and his allies were camping out and mop up any who manage to survive the night."

Ravan clapped Ind on the back and said, "Well done, my son!"

Ravan and the remaining security guards in the estate house began to celebrate. They broke out the champagne and began splashing it over one another.

However, not everyone was felled by the sarin that Ind had shot into the woods. Vibish and Hanuman happened to be upwind of the sarin grenades and were unaffected.

Vibish knew that his nephew had used nerve gas on them. He also knew that he would need to apply the antidote within fifteen minutes to save those affected by the gas.

Vibish gestured to Hanuman with his hand, making the shape of the box of medical supplies and pointing in the direction of the walk-in freezer at the estate. He waved his hands to indicate that Hanuman should fetch the box and bring it to him. He rapidly clapped his hands to indicate that Hanuman should go quickly.

Hanuman got the message right away. He climbed up a tree, traveled hand over hand to the branch that extended out near the estate house's roof, crawled out on the branch, and jumped onto the roof. He scampered across the roof to where the kitchen was.

The kitchen staff was gone, busy celebrating. Hanuman let himself in through an open window and ran to the freezer. He opened the door, spotted the Styrofoam medical-supplies crate hidden away on a top shelf, and grabbed it.

He could hear the syndicate staff celebrating and saw that everyone was busy partying. He decided to risk returning by running out the door from the kitchen that opened onto the lawn. (Carrying the bulky Styrofoam box would have made returning via branches and trees nearly impossible anyway.) So he scurried out the door, over the lawn, and through the gate.

One of the syndicate partygoers saw him running with the crate but dismissed him as a mere animal scavenging among the litter of war.

Hanuman charged up to the bivouac where Vibish was waiting impatiently. Vibish looked at his watch. Hanuman had managed to make the round trip in ten minutes. That gave him five to administer the antidotes.

With his knife, Vibish cut through the fiberglass tape holding the box shut. He grabbed the ten nerve-gas antidote autoinjector kits inside.

Vibish immediately injected both Ram and Lak, who were lying on the ground. They had stopped their writhing but were still breathing. The antidote worked almost immediately.

Ram and Lak opened their eyes and raised their heads to look around.

Vibish left Ram and Lak to recuperate on the ground. He made his way to the fallen monkeys. He had enough injector kits left to administer to the five fallen monkey leaders plus Jamb. He then had two left over and injected the nerve-gas antidote into two other monkeys who were lucky enough to have fallen nearby. Then he returned to Ram and Lak.

Ram said, "Thanks. You saved our lives."

Vibish replied, "That was a close one. But the credit for saving your lives goes to Hanuman. Hanuman is the hero. He ran to retrieve the medical supplies in ten minutes, leaving me the relatively easy task of administering the antidotes in five minutes. That was enough time to take care of you both as well as the monkey CEOs who had been felled, plus two other lucky monkeys nearby. Are you recovered enough to think about our next step?"

Ram replied, "Yes. I feel I'm getting stronger by the minute. Lak and I have stem cells that were seeded throughout our bodies by medical doctors after we were born. I feel the stem cells already starting to repair my gas-damaged nerves."

Holding up his hand out to Vibish, he said, "See, the shaking is almost gone and the pins-and-needles feeling is disappearing. We should be better by nightfall."

Turning to Lak, Ram said, "Up for a nighttime raid on the syndicate estate? Try to finish them off while they're celebrating their illusion of victory?"

Lak replied, "Yup."

Ram continued, "One other thing. I'm going to ask Vibish to administer some of the stem cells from the medical-supplies crate to the fallen monkeys. That way the monkeys can heal their nerves just as we have with our built-in stem-cell layer. I'm going to draw on my own stem-cell supply for this. Is it okay to draw on your stem-cell supply too? When Vibish is done, I'll ask Hanuman to return the Styrofoam crate back to the walk-in freezer in case we need it again."

"Sure," replied Lak. He added, "I'm surprised you ask. Not long ago you viewed monkeys as less than human. When you killed Sugriv's brother, Val, you shot him in the back. You justified this by saying he was a mere animal. For my part, I wouldn't let Val's wife, Tara, excuse Sugriv as merely an animal when he was going back on his promise to help us. So now you're willing to blend human cells with their human genes into animals? To make them one with us in body as well as spirit?"

Ram replied, "That was then, this is now. Our monkey allies have fought with us, have died with us. I've seen that they're moral creatures even as we ourselves are, regardless of how our personalities and bodies differ. They deserve to be recognized as first-class citizens in our moral community. They've earned it. They've earned access to our life-saving facilities. And if we absorb their cells and genes into our bodies, it's only fair that we provide cells and genes from our bodies for them."

Lak nodded. "Well, brother, I see we now agree. Anyway, we should return our attention to the battle before us."

Ram then called to Sush, the capuchin CEO and surgeon.

Ram said, "Here's how to apply the stem cells to the fallen monkeys. You open one vial plus one compress per monkey. Pour the contents of the vial onto the compress and apply the compress to any open wounds you find. Tape the compress over the biggest open wound. The cells will migrate from the compress through the wound into the body. They will seek out damaged nerve cells and transform themselves into new nerves to replace the damages ones. Can you do it?"

"Yes, gladly," replied Sush.

Sush then went to the five fallen leaders and to Jamb. They were awake now. Sush explained that this medication came from the humans and would help heal their wounds.

After tending to the CEOs, he moved on to the two lucky monkeys who had been given gas antidotes.

Ram approached Nil, the night monkey, and asked if he was feeling better.

Nil responded, "Yes. I'm up to about 90 percent now. I'm ready."

Ram said, "I suggest we counterattack during the night when Ravan and the rest of the syndicate are partying. Can we do that?"

"Yes," said Nil, "I think that's a good idea. I'll assemble our surviving veterans and add some new recruits that have arrived over the last several hours."

Meanwhile, Ram asked Lak to build a bonfire. Ram told Sugriv, "Let's attack tonight and set fire to the estate."

Once the monkeys had assembled, Ram asked them each to gather a fallen stick from the woods and to place one end in the bonfire. Soon each monkey had a stick with one end glowing red with heat.

Hanuman spoke up, "What about Sita's safety?"

Ram replied, "Oh, yes. Can you point out her quarters so that the monkeys can avoid torching the area where she's likely hiding from the conflict?"

Hanuman gestured to the area of the estate to be avoided and looked around at the other monkeys to be sure they understood. Then Ram gave the signal to Sugriv.

With Ram and Lak at his side, the great howler CEO led his troops and Jamb through the gate into the estate grounds. The monkeys torched the various structures and gazebos they encountered on their march to the main estate house.

The roar and crackling of flames awoke Ravan from his drunken slumber.

He wondered to himself, "What's happening? Surely this can't be the monkeys again. I thought Ind killed most of them. Weren't those few still alive left lying on the ground, writhing in pain?"

Pulling on his silk robe, he ran out of his bedroom to look. Security guards were milling around, confused. One said to Ravan, "It's the monkeys again, sir."

Ravan caught sight of his nephews, Kum and Nikum, sons of his now-deceased brother, Kumb.

Ravan said, "I promote you both to take the place of our syndicate bosses who have been slain. Can you step up in their places and repel this latest attack from the monkeys?"

The nephews nodded their assent.

Ravan added, "Then hurry up. Here they come."

Monkeys were pouring into the estate house, going room to room, fighting syndicate members and setting fires.

Hand-to-hand combat was everywhere amidst the smoke and flames as Kum, Nikum, and the guards tried to restrain the monkeys from setting more fires. In the melee Angad, the howler, killed Kamp, the hit man from Maimi. Maind and Dwivid, the tamarins, teamed up to maul Sonit, the hit man from Uganda; Yupak, Ram's physician; and Praj, the hit man from Syria. The fire cast their fighting silhouettes upon the crumbling walls.

Kum then interceded against the Maind/Dwivid team, kicking them with his boot.

When Angad saw Kum attacking his diminutive but fierce tamarin allies, he joined in, pulling Kum away. But Kum fought back, tripping Angad and pinning him to the ground with his boot.

When Ram saw Angad losing strength, he directed Jamb, the bear, to attack Kum.

But Kum fired a pistol shot at Jamb, winging him and forcing him to back off.

So finally, Sugriv himself came forward to challenge Kum. They gradually pursued each other out of the flaming house to the cliff's edge overlooking the ocean. There Sugriv lunged at Kum, pushing him off the cliff into the ocean.

The sharks detected blood in the water. But before the sharks could arrive, Kum pulled himself onto a small rocky beach.

In the moonlight, Sugrive could see that Kum was still alive. Sugriv climbed down to the beach along steps carved into the cliff's wall. He picked up a boulder from the beach and slammed it down on Kum's breast, crushing his ribs. At that, Kum's heart stopped beating once and for all.

Nikum could see that his brother had been killed. He started down the steps to the beach. He would corner Sugriv there and kill him in revenge.

Sensing his intent, Hanuman jumped in Nikum's path. Yet Nikum, nearly twice the size of the monkey, simply picked Hanuman up, tucked him under his arm, and started to carry the monkey back to the still-burning estate house.

But Hanuman spun free, grabbed Nikum's neck, and twisted it violently, snapping Nikum's spinal cord. Hanuman threw the screaming Nikum off the cliff into the school of sharks that had gathered in the waters below.

Ind Beheaded

As dawn broke, Ravan, still at the burning estate house, could see that his nephews, Kum and Nikum, had been killed. He located Ind among the other syndicate defenders in the estate house.

Ravan confronted him, saying, "Twice you've told me Ram was killed and he wasn't. Now you must really succeed. Use whatever means necessary. I'll be in the control center if you need me."

Ind looked around the estate house and, in the morning's light, saw a mess: ruins, debris, monkeys everywhere clapping in joy, and Lak and Ram looking triumphant.

In disgust, Ind picked up an AK-101 lying on the floor and started spraying bullets in the general direction of the monkeys and the brothers.

In response, Lak picked up an AK-101 himself from a fallen guard and was about to return fire, but Ram restrained him, saying "Random gunfire will kill the innocent women running from their burning quarters. We shouldn't kill innocent creatures unnecessarily. You should specifically target the syndicate bosses and their hit men. I will now attack Ind directly."

Seeing that Ram was personally about to attack him, Ind pulled back from the fighting into a corner of the house that was still quiet.

Thinking about how to proceed, Ind wondered whether another trick was worth trying. He reviewed how his fragmenting bullet had brought down Hanuman for a time, how his active rope brought down Ram and Lak once, and how his sarin brought them down again. A trick worked each time, better than any brute force did, even though each time his targets escaped or were rescued. Now he needed to come up with a new trick, pronto. An idea hit him in a flash.

Ind told a security guard to bring him his rape doll, the sex toy he used to satisfy his rape fetish. He told another guard to fetch him one of Sita dresses from the closet in her room. A few minutes later, the guards returned. Ind dressed the full-size solid latex mannequin in Sita's dress and pushed the buttons to program the doll to scream, "No, no, don't hurt me."

Then Ind dragged the screaming doll out to the area where most of the fighting was occurring. In full view of the combatants, he drew his knife and raised it over the doll, about to strike.

Hanuman saw what he took to be Sita's imminent murder. He groaned and slumped in despair. Then Ind pulled his Glock and hurriedly fired a shot at Hanuman. The bullet missed.

Ind returned to making threatening gestures over the screaming latex doll. Then he raised his hand high over his head and plunged the knife into the doll over and over again. The doll was manufactured to scream in agony and squirt artificial blood when punctured.

The monkeys saw Sita's apparent murder and were fooled.

Ind said to them, "Give it up. What you were fighting for is now lost."

Hanuman felt he now had no choice but tell the monkeys to withdraw, saying, "Let's regroup with Ram. We'll ask him how to proceed after this tragedy."

Hanuman located Ram, who was outside the burning estate house, standing on the roof of one the gazebos that had not caught fire. Ram was directing monkeys to places where security guards and hit men were holed up.

Hanuman jumped up on the gazebo roof and told Ram the terrible news that Ind had murdered Sita. Ram wilted at the news, sliding off the gazebo roof and collapsing on the ground.

Lak came up to Ram and said, "I see no justice in the world. Why bother being honorable, ethical? If good and bad comes equally to the ethical and unethical, why bother being ethical? If the world were just, Ravan would long ago have succumbed to his excesses while you would be enjoying your days with Sita. Destiny moves according to its own will, which we seem powerless to influence."

He joined with Ram in wailing while Ram buried his head against Lak's shoulder.

Vibish arrived and asked Lak what was the matter.

Lak briefed him.

Vibish thought a while and said, "I think it's another trick. Ravan wouldn't allow Sita to be killed. He still lusts for her. She's worth more to him alive than dead. Killing her doesn't make sense. It must be a trick. Deception is the syndicate's hallmark. Ind must be hoping he can throw your armies into disarray prior to a counterattack."

Ram opened his eyes and asked Vibish, "Say again?"

After repeating his logic, Vibish added, "That's not to say Sita isn't in danger. We have to work fast to rescue her because the situation here is deteriorating into chaos. Anything could happen."

Ram looked over at Lak and said, "You've wanted to get at Ind for some time. Can you find him now and take him out?"

Lak replied, "I'd love to. Glad you asked."

Hanuman, Lak, and Vibish left the gazebo where they had found Ram and went together in search of Ind. They surprised him near one of the other gazebos on the estate grounds.

Hanuman started in on Ind, jumping on him. Ind threw him off and reached for his Glock to shoot him.

Lak intervened, shouting, "You wimp, are you afraid to take on someone your own size?"

Ind pivoted away from Hanuman and stared at Lak.

Seeing Vibish standing next to Lak, Ind said to his uncle, "You're a disgrace to our family and the entire syndicate. You've done great harm by siding with Ram and his allies. You're a traitor. You don't know the difference between right and wrong."

Vibish replied, "Bullshit. You and your father are the ones who've lost the distinction between right and wrong. One should always abandon an evil relative as one abandons a sinking ship."

"Bullshit yourself," replied Ind. "I'll now have to kill you along with your monkey allies."

Lak was listening and jumped in, saying to Ind, "You're nothing but a thief and a coward. If you were a real man, you'd fight like one, rather than resort to pathetic trickery. How about it, you and me, mano-a-mano?"

Ind threw down his AK-101 and Lak unstrapped the holster with his Glock and set down his machete. Lak and Ind started to circle each other warily, like boxers. Monkeys gathered to watch on one side of the makeshift arena, syndicate guards and hit men on the other.

Ind moved in on Lak, dancing with his feet, faking punches, occasionally coming close enough to touch Lak's body, but always staying far away. Then Lak closed in and staggered Ind with a right hook to the side of his head. Ind responded by head butting Lak and grabbing hold of him with both arms to stop him from inflicting any more damage.

Lak pushed Ind away and then hit him with another right hook, followed by a three-punch combination. Next Lak hit Ind with a right overhand that knocked him to the ground. Ind got up and tried to bounce back in the fight with isolated punches to Lak's body. Lak countered with an uppercut and right hook that again sent Ind to the ground.

Ind got to his feet. Lak closed in again, trying to knock him out. But Ind survived, lying on the ground with a broken jaw and his left eye swollen shut.

Vibish, who was watching the fight, felt the entertainment was over. He gestured to the monkeys to resume their offensive against the syndicate guards and hit men.

Hanuman added, "Go for it. What you see is all that's left of our enemy."

Lak then retrieved his machete and beheaded Ind on the spot. Seeing Ravan's powerful son and successor dead on the ground took all the remaining fight out of the syndicate's security guards and hit men. Most dropped their weapons and ran away. They flew past the glowing embers of what had once been a grand estate house, through the front gate, and out the driveway. From there, they dispersed throughout the island.

The monkeys clapped, roared, and jumped up and down. Together with Hanuman and Vibish, Lak returned to the gazebo where Ram was.

Ram got down from the roof where he'd been watching from afar. He gave everyone a high five, saying, "You've done the Lord's work, and you've won. Congratulations! Ind's death cripples Ravan's ability to continue. The end is now in sight."

Turning to Lak, Ram embraced him, saying, "Thank you. You're a wonderful brother. My bond to you is eternal."

Lak returned the embrace and added, "In our victorious exhiliaration, let's not lose sight of rescuing Sita."

Ram said, "With each passing battle, the vision of my lovely Sita grows ever more remote."

Lak said, "Well brother, let's press on."

Last Gasp

One of the hit men who still remained rummaged around in one of the still-undamaged sections of the estate. He found a functioning video connection to Ravan's control center and called in. He reported that Ind had been killed fighting Lak. He added that Ind had put up a great fight, a credit to his father and the syndicate, but ultimately was defeated by Lak's superior boxing abilities.

Ravan cried out in a eulogy for his dead son, "You were a wonderful son. You alone came close to defeating our enemies where all my other leaders failed. You alone approached the battle with intelligence and cunning where the others approached with merely bravado."

Ravan continued wailing, "Your mother, Mandara, will be crushed, devastated, and may try to take her own life in grief. Oh, what perverse destiny has brought your end before mine. No father should outlive his son. Oh, Ind, how could you leave me here alone while Ram and Lak still live?"

In his grief, Ravan could think only of revenge. He said to himself, "My son tried to trick Ram by pretending to kill a latex image of his Sita. Now I will do the real thing. I will strike back at Ram. I will kill his dearest possession."

Ravan boarded his waiting sub and returned to the smoldering estate. Ravan disembarked and climbed the stairs from the dock to the garage. He went to the armory cabinets in the garage and drew out his own tempered, shining machete. Then he went through the smoldering remains of the main section of his estate house and headed for Sita's quarters, which were still largely undamaged.

Sita heard Ravan angrily tramping down the hallway leading to her room. She shrank back in fear, knowing the abuse he was capable of. She knew he was gruff and violent with his wives, disrespecting them in public, demeaning them in private. She knew he enjoyed berating his staff in front of coworkers.

Looking out a window, Sita saw him carrying his personal machete, its silver surface gleaming in the sun. She thought, "Why didn't I try to escape when Hanuman first alerted me that Ram was on his way? Why was I content to remain here? I could have tried to wait for him in town, under police protection. Why was I so trusting that Ram would succeed in rescuing me from the most sinister force on earth?"

As Ravan neared Sita's quarters, Supar, the hit man from Pakistan, placed himself in Ravan's path.

Ravan said, "Get out of my way."

Supar replied, "But sir, I've come to dissuade you from an act that will surely make matters worse. Our situation is pretty bad already—killing Sita is pointless. No good will come from it. You'll be condemned by everyone. You'll lose the allegiance of your staff, your bosses, your hit men, everyone. You'll lose control of your syndicate immediately upon killing Sita, unarmed and vulnerable as she is. You'll be branded as a coward in your own ranks. By killing Sita, you defeat yourself. Instead, turn your rage on Ram and Lak. Defeat them, not yourself."

Ravan paused and listened. He said to himself, "Okay, Supar is right. I'll first kill Ram and then deal with Sita. Then she'll come around to me."

All about him Ravan could hear women wailing who had lost their husbands and sons. He was at his wit's end. His eyes were crimson, his cheeks flushed. Like a losing gambler driven to bet everything in hopes of a final win, he convened the last of his surviving bosses and hit men in the ruin of the executive conference room. The conference table still stood but was charred from the fire. Ravan's henchmen were clearly terrified of proceeding further.

To cover his fear, Ravan bragged, saying, "I myself will now kill Ram and Lak. I myself will avenge our fallen kinsmen and fellow workers. I will mow down any remaining monkeys. Their corpses will nourish generations of carrion feeders."

Ravan gathered the remains of his troops and stormed out of the estate, through the gate to the monkeys' bivouac. With his AK-101 he sprayed bullets up at the monkeys, killing some, but mostly just knocking leaves out of the canopy.

Sugriv was furious to be facing yet another attack. He hurled large rocks at Ravan and his henchmen, dispersing them like a shower of hailstones falling upon a flock of birds.

Virup, the syndicate boss from North Korea, struck back at Sugriv, firing a burst of bullets from his AK-101, which caused Sugriv to throw himself on the ground to avoid being hit. With Sugriv on the ground, Virup grabbed his machete and struck at him, opening a gash in his leg.

Regaining his senses, Sugriv jumped up onto Virup and pounded on him with his fists. Virup died of brain hemorrhaging as blood oozed from his eyes, ears, nose, and mouth. Meanwhile Angad eliminated Saran, the security guard who had spied on the monkeys early on and warned Ravan of their strength.

Ravan, looking beyond his devastated army, searched for Ram. Seeing him in the distant woods where scrubby trees grew amongst huge limestone boulders, Ravan ran toward him, accompanied by two guards, bypassing Lak on the way.

Ravan fired his Glock at Ram. A bullet struck, then bounced off Ram's ceramic body armor. The impact pushed Ram backward, causing him to career off a huge limestone boulder. As he was falling backward, Ram fired at Ravan but missed.

Lak caught up with the combatants. He fired at Ravan but hit a guard accompanying him.

Vibish joined in as well. Firing at Ravan, he too merely disabled the other guard accompanying Ravan.

Then Ravan saw Vibish. He turned to fire at his brother.

But Lak cut him off. Firing first, Lak's bullet grazed Ravan, causing him to miss his shot at Vibish.

Ravan seethed and, through clenched teeth, growled to Lak, "You may have saved Vibish but now you will die yourself." Ravan fired a round from his Glock and scored. Several bullets bounced off Lak's body armor, driving him backward and making him trip over exposed tree roots. As he fell, Lak hit his head against a huge limestone boulder, which knocked him unconscious.

Ram immediately ran to aid his brother. Indifferent to the danger posed by Ravan, he gently lifted Lak's unconscious body from the side of the boulder and laid him on the ground upon a thick bed of dry leaves. He then called Hanuman and Sugriv to come and help.

Ram said aloud to all who could hear, "This attack on my brother is the absolute last straw. I shall now kill Ravan or die trying. I shall rid the world of evil personified."

For the first time, Ram fought aggressively. He fired a round at Ravan. He pressed his attack. He ran for cover from boulder to boulder. He fired again and again. Ravan was forced to duck every which way, backpedal, and give ground.

Eventually, Ravan turned and ran. He ran to the burning estate, to the garage, and grabbed his body-armor vest. Then he ran down the stairs to the dock where the submarines waited, found an open hatch, and jumped in. He hit the ignition switch, gunned the engine, and shot forth from the cove, then pointed the nose of the submarine down, heading to the safety of his underwater control center on the leeward side of Saba Bank.

Ravan Routed

Ram went back to check on Lak, who was being looked after by Hanuman and Sugriv. The gash on his skull where he fell looked serious, as if it might need stitches.

Looking at Lak, he grimaced, saying to himself, "Without Lak fighting with me, without sensing him behind me, beside me, I feel lost. I feel my strength dissolving. I know I should go on to defeat Ravan on my own, but if I succeed, I'll feel no joy if Lak isn't with me. He's followed me through thick and thin. If he dies, I'll soon die too. It's inevitable. I depend on him so much. If he dies, what will I say to his mother, Sumitra, when I return? What will I say to my brothers, Barat and Shat? They will all accuse me of not protecting him. I'll never be able to face them." Ram buried his face in his hands.

Hanuman signed to Ram, "Be patient. I'll call our surgeon, Sush. I know the walk-in freezer wasn't damaged in the estate fire. I'll fetch the medical supplies."

Hanuman bounded across the estate grounds to the remnants of the estate kitchen, where the walk-in freezer was still standing, unharmed by the flames and fighting that had surrounded it. Hanuman entered and retrieved the Styrofoam container, again hidden away on a top shelf, and brought it to Lak.

Meanwhile the capuchin Sush had been located. He was now by Lak's side. Sush opened the medical-supplies crate and removed the vial with Lak's stem cells, as well as some smelling salts. He applied a compress of stem cells to Lak's wound, supplementing the stem cell layer Lak already possessed. Then he held some of the smelling salts under Lak's nose. Lak snorted and awoke. The wound to his skull was now healing with astonishing speed.

Lak said to Ram, "Though barely conscious, I think I heard through my haze you saying that you might not continue fighting Ravan if I died.

Brother, remember, you have vowed to kill Ravan and given your word that you'd install Vibish in his place. Then the syndicate can reform and become an honest corporation. Regardless of whether I'm alive, you must keep your promise."

Ram said to himself, "Lak's right. I do have to finish this job." He grabbed his bow and reached into the supply chest for the bulletwood arrows and nonibars that Agast had given him when they had set off from Kauai, seemingly an eternity ago. He had saved these supplies for this final, all-important conflict.

"What, no guns?" asked Lak.

"No," said Ram, "I heard Ravan take off in a sub to his underwater control center. We've got to follow him there to finish him off. If we use guns, our bullets will puncture the walls of the underwater structure, making it flood and trapping us below water to drown. We'll just have to finish the job the old-fashioned way, with my bow and arrows, and your machete"

Ram asked Vibish, "Do you know how to operate the submarines?"

Vibish replied, "No, but my assistant, Matal, does. He's a brilliant pilot and navigator, both above and below water. I hope he's still alive. Wait here while I go look for him."

Vibish ran to the ruins of the estate house to search for his assistant. He investigated the area where his own quarters had been and found them relatively unscathed.

Matal saw Vibish looking for him and came out of hiding.

Vibish embraced him and explained that they needed a pilot to take a sub to attack Ravan at his command center on Saba Bank.

Matal said, "I'm your man."

Vibish replied, "Great. Hurry, we can't waste time—we have to chase Ravan now. We have to prevent him from getting too much of a head start. I don't want him having enough time to prepare a defense."

Vibish brought Matal back to the bivouac and introduced him to Ram.

Ram said, "Welcome. Let's get going."

So Ram and Matal—accompanied by Vibish, Lak, Hanuman, Sugriv, Andag, and Jamb—all ran to the estate garage and down the stairs leading to the dock, where they climbed into the hatch of the remaining sub tied up there.

Matal checked the gauges, confirmed that the tanks were full, hit the ignition switch, and pulled away from the dock. Then he pointed the submarine down into a dive and turned on the sonar. They could hear the sound of Ravan's sub up ahead.

Ravan was also listening on his sonar and heard the other sub start up and put to sea. Ravan then cut his engine to let his sub sink, anticipating that Ram's sub would pass over him. Once it did, he could fire a torpedo, destroying Ram's sub and all his warriors with him.

Matal was chasing Ravan's sub at full speed. When he heard Ravan cut the engine, his sub was already speeding through the water too fast to stop. Reversing his engine would only make matters worse, alerting Ravan to their exact location.

As Ram's sub passed over Ravan's sub, Ravan fired a torpedo.

Matal heard the whoosh of the torpedo being discharged into the water. He took immediate evasive action, diving and turning sharply to port, away from the Saba Bank, south into the Caribbean. The maneuver worked. The torpedo sped by, passing harmlessly up to the surface, where it sputtered, stopped, and eventually sank.

Meanwhile, Ravan started up his engine again and headed for the control center.

Ram asked Matal to get Ravan on the sonic underwater telephone.

When Ravan answered, Ram said, "It's Ram here. You're proud of your military assets, but they will not save you. You're a shameless coward. You stole my Sita behind my back. If you'd tried to take her in my presence, you would already be dead. Now your time has come. I will kill you now."

Ravan replied with a sneer, "Go to hell," and hung up the phone.

Matal navigated along the southern flank of the Saba Bank until he could see Small Bank up ahead. He spotted the control center and steered to the remaining slot at the underwater dock.

Ram asked Vibish, "What's the layout inside the control center?"

Vibish quickly diagrammed the locations, relative to the entrance portal, of the main control room, equipment room, conference room, bathrooms, bedrooms, and kitchen storage center.

As soon as the sub docked, Ram asked the others to remain on board to avoid confusion in the confines of the control center. Ram then stepped through the portal into the command center carrying his bow, arrows, and a nonibar. It seemed pitch black. To hide in the dark, Ravan had turned off all the lights at the master switch and drawn the shades over the portholes. Ram waited while his eyes adjusted to the dark. Eventually, his bush-baby-enhanced retinas picked up some blue light peeking around the shades at the portholes. This was enough for Ram to proceed. Ravan was nowhere in sight.

Ram made his way along a corridor, moving sideways, keeping his back to the wall to minimize his profile. He headed to the main control room. He felt around, sensed nothing—listened, heard nothing. Then he went on to the equipment room. It was small and hot from the equipment, no place for a person to hide. He sensed the conference room was empty too. But the kitchen—aha, maybe there.

Ram thought he heard a noise. He raised his bow and fitted it with an arrow. But no, he couldn't make out Ravan's presence, if indeed he was even there.

Ravan surmised that Ram was pursuing him by crawling and feeling his way. Ravan decided he would ensure Ram's defeat by first tiring him out. If Ram continued crawling almost blindly from one end of the underwater compound to the other and then back again, over and over in his pursuit, he would surely tire. Then he would be easy prey once the master light switch was turned on.

Ram felt he was in a maze. In the dark he crawled from room to room, drawn by the slightest sound, the briefest glimmer of light, the suppressed cough. Back and forth, from the control room to the equipment room to the kitchen, two times, three times, countless times. Hours passed by.

Ravan knew the rooms and the furniture in them like the back of his hand. He had the advantage. Meanwhile, Ram knew if he showed himself, Ravan would attack—with a knife, a machete, or even a bullet if he was desperate enough to risk flooding his command center.

Ram was starting to tire and to lose his sense of direction. He couldn't remember where he had just been. Was he checking a room he'd already checked? He couldn't recall.

Ravan's cat-and-mouse tactics in the dark were causing Ram to lose his edge. He reached into his pocket and felt for the nonibar. He pulled it out, unwrapped it, and gobbled it down. He felt a jolt of energy and a sting in his mouth as his lips puckered. He sent a grateful thanks to Angast for giving him the lifesaving energy bar.

Finally, Ravan slipped. In the kitchen. Some cooking oil had dripped on the floor that the kitchen help had neglected to clean. Ram heard Ravan hit the floor hard. For once, he knew exactly where Ravan was. He drew an arrow from his quiver.

Ravan hit the master light switch and the flood of light temporarily blinded Ram. Ravan seized the moment and threw a knife across a kitchen counter at Ram. It bounced off Ram's body shield.

Ravan then ducked and darted toward another side of the kitchen. Ram couldn't get a clean shot.

Then Ram noticed a gong hanging from the ceiling. He figured it must be used by the cook to tell everyone when the meal is ready. Ram took his knife and threw it at the gong. It sounded with a large clang.

Ravan stood up and ran toward the noise with his machete raised, ready to hack at Ram. In doing so, Ravan came into Ram's full view.

Ram was ready, bow loaded with Agast's bulletwood arrow. He let the arrow fly. His aim was true. The arrow penetrated Ravan's body armor and pierced his heart. Ravan fell dead.

Ram went to the portal to let Vibish and the monkeys have a look around while Matal remained with the sub. Ram led his allies to the kitchen, where the body of Ravan slumped on the floor with a bulletwood arrow through his heart.

Vibish gave Ram a high five, and the monkeys clapped and jumped up and down. They playfully jumped on Ram as he embraced them all at once. Then Ram went to the kitchen refrigerator to see if any food was available, as the food at their bivouac had been simple and sparse. A glimpse at fresh fruit brought squeals of joy from the monkeys, and the goodies were passed around.

While the monkeys were eating their well-deserved feast and looking out the portholes at the marine life outside the control center, Vibish was gazing at his brother's dead body.

With broken voice, he said, "Oh, my brother, how have you come to this? You've always had such energy, such initiative, and now you lie here, soon to be stone cold. This is the very fate I had predicted. Why didn't you listen? Lust, greed, and anger are one's mortal enemies. I miss you so much. It seems the sun has fallen. The moon has extinguished. Our syndicate is no more. All is lost."

Ram placed an arm around Vibish to console him, saying, "Live by the sword, die by the sword. That has been your brother's way. You should not mourn for him—this is the natural passage for someone on his path."

Lak added, "His spirit lives on, even as the body decays. Think ahead, to his funeral. Then think ahead to your taking command of the syndicate, how you will reform it to become a force for good, not evil."

Ram retrieved his arrow from Ravan's corpse. Then he and Vibish picked up the body and brought it through the portal into the submarine. Ram called the monkeys, who clambered aboard for the journey home.

When they all arrived back at the estate dock, Ram thanked Matal for his seamanship. Then he and Vibish carried Ravan's body out to the remains of the estate's living room and set it down.

Hanuman went to Ram and asked, "Can we now fetch Sita so she can join you in this climax of victory?"

Ram replied, "No, let's wait. I have other matters to attend to first."

Ram was uncomfortable. He worried that he would no longer recognize Sita—his memory of her had grown so remote during the battles. He wondered if she would still love him, what he had become. The war's violence had changed him and he knew it. Could he still be a loving husband? And then there was the matter of her having lived nearly a year under the control of Ravan and his syndicate. Had she disclosed Apple's secrets somehow? He doubted she knew any secrets to disclose, but he also knew people would talk, would suspect. He decided to deal with more immediate matters and postpone rejoining Sita as long as possible.

From their quarters, Ravan's wives could tell the noise of battle had stopped. They looked out the windows and saw the body of their husband. They came out of their quarters to gather around Ravan's body.

Mandara, Ravan's principal wife, was especially distraught. Her face paled at the sight of her husband's dead body.

She gulped, nearly choked, sobbed, and said over the body, "I can't believe my eyes. You who struck terror into the hearts and minds of countless men and women around the world are now slain by a young man who seems little more than a jungle hippie. There must be more to Ram than meets the eye. Only a remarkable young leader could do this to you."

She continued wailing over her husband's body, and then said, "Although you had great discipline and powers of concentration, you weren't able to control your most base of emotions, your lust. And you chose to dishonor a young woman who is the very emblem of chastity, modesty, and grace. In chasing your obsession for Sita, you visited destruction upon yourself, your family, and your syndicate."

Mandara couldn't stop. "And now you leave me alone with no place to go. What have I done to deserve this fate? I was always your devoted wife, nay, even your servant. Why did you crave Sita? My life's become useless just because I couldn't satisfy you. Although we partied and danced in the best clubs among the best resorts in the world, I'm now condemned to live as a grieving widow and pauper. The fortune of a CEO is so fleeting."

Then, seeing Ravan's brother, she cried, "Here stands the noble Vibish. Ravan, you ignored his wise advice, and you now lie dead on the ground. Sinners reap the results of their sins, and the virtuous reap the results of their virtue. Your brother now will enjoy your former assets while you burn in hell."

Then Ravan's other wives gently led Mandara away.

Ram pulled Vibish aside and whispered to him, "Do you want to do something with Ravan's body? It's uncivilized to let him lie here, soon to be picked at by hermit crabs while flies deposit eggs on his eyeballs."

Vibish replied, "What can I do? I'm conflicted about him. Yes, he was my brother, and once we were close. But I can't overlook his cruelty to people and to animals, his merciless pursuit of money, and his sinful lust."

Ram replied, "You may condemn his flesh, but his spirit lives on. A proper burial is a ritual that hastens his soul to its next life, which is sure to be more virtuous than this one has been. The spirit is always worthy of respect—it is eternal and good and pure. I don't know what happened to his body in this life to pervert it so, but freeing his spirit from this body will offer him a chance for redemption in a future life."

Vibish looked down at Ravan's body. He knew Ram was right. He said to himself, "Ignorance is a property of the body, not the spirit. Ravan's sins, which proceeded from ignorance, end when his body ends. The spirit doesn't carry the sins from one body into the next. I will prepare a ritual cremation."

Vibish went to the woods several times, returning each time with a bundle of sticks. He lashed some sticks together to make a bier. He also piled sticks together on the beach to make a pyre.

With Ram and Lak's help, Vibish placed Ravan's body on the bier, and together they carried it to the pyre.

Ravan's old grandfather, Malay, accompanied them.

Lak emptied some charcoal lighter fluid on the sticks and lit a match. The bonfire burned brightly, the dry wood crackled in the flames, and the black smoke of Ravan's body wafted into the trade winds.

Malay said aloud to the black smoke, "May the gods have mercy upon your soul."

Meanwhile, Sita knew the fighting had ended and suspected that Ram was victorious.

She said to herself, "What's going on? Something doesn't seem right. Are they burying Ravan? What's so important about how Ravan is buried? I thought this war would lead to my rescue. Yet here I am, stuck in my quarters as though I were still imprisoned. I don't accept that honoring a dead body speeds its former spirit to a new and better life. I think honoring the corpse of an evil man dignifies his evil and does nothing for his spirit."

She hoped her situation would improve, but girded herself for any eventuality.

Sita's Torture

After Ravan's cremation, Ram and Lak wondered how to go about installing Vibish as the new CEO of the syndicate.

Ram asked Lak, "Do we have the authority to install Vibish as a CEO? The syndicate is not a public corporation. No board of directors appointed its CEO. The syndicate was a closely held private firm owned by Ravan and his relatives. It had franchises distributed across the globe. Now Ravan, the franchise leaders, and the bosses have all been killed, as has Ravan's immediate family."

Lak replied, "We're corporate raiders, literally, and we have de facto control of the syndicate now. So we can install whomever we wish to take over."

Ram replied, "Maybe, but I'm not sure anything we do would last, because we don't have legal standing to appoint the syndicate's new CEO, even though we defeated them in physical battle. I think the syndicate's ownership still legally resides somehow in Ravan's family, in his grandfather and in Vibish, regardless of what we say or do."

"Yes," responded Lak, "that's probably true. Who gets to be CEO then, Malay or Vibish? Or are they going to fight it out between themselves to be the new CEO?"

Ram replied, "I suspect old Malay doesn't want the position. So here's an idea, a way to make conferring CEO authority on Vibish appear official and as publicly honoring Malay's wishes: Let's invite Malay to witness and endorse an installation of Vibish as CEO. I'll devise an oath of office."

Lak went to fetch Malay and told him of the plan. Malay agreed. Ram fetched Vibish and told him that they wished him to say a pledge in front of his grandfather. He agreed as well. Ram waved to Hanuman to join them. The five of them gathered on the beach below the still smoldering ruins of the estate and near embers from the bier where Ravan's body had been cremated.

There, with Malay, Lak, and Hanuman looking on as witnesses, Vibish placed his hands, palms down, upon the hands, palms up, of Malay.

Ram said to Vibish, "Repeat after me. I pledge—"

"I pledge—"

"—to manage the syndicate—"

"—to manage the syndicate—"

"—for the betterment of its owners—"

"—for the betterment of its owners—"

"—while promoting the general welfare—"

"—while promoting the general welfare—"

"—and the health of its employees."

"—and the health of its employees."

"So help me God."

"So help me God."

Ram said, "By the power I have assumed as the victorious raider of the syndicate, I appoint you as the new CEO."

One after the other, Ram, Malay, Lak, and Hanuman shook Vibish's hand.

Vibish said, "I appreciate the dignified way you've handed over control of the syndicate, a marked contrast to the uncivilized carnage we've participated in to get to this point. My first act will be to take the syndicate public and raise funds to rebuild the destroyed facilities. I'll recruit respected executives to manage the franchises. The syndicate will become a public business-services company, offering Internet security and financial management expertise. I'll re-purpose the control center as an underwater hotel and restaurant. It will feature a playground for children and guided underwater ecotours for adults."

Ram said, "Excellent. I see you're already planning ahead."

Knowing he couldn't procrastinate any longer, Ram turned to Hanuman and said, "Please locate Sita and tell her the news of our victory."

Hanuman found Sita still in her quarters in a relatively unaffected section of the estate house. He went up to Sita and gestured to her by clapping his hands and pointing in Ram's direction.

Sita felt this confirmed her impression that Ram had been victorious. She gestured, pointing in Ram's direction, that she wanted to go to him.

Hanuman shook his head. Putting his hands palm down, he moved them up and down to indicate, slow down, wait. Hanuman then pointed to the few surviving hit men about the estate grounds and drew his index finger across his throat to suggest killing them.

Sita shook her head. She didn't know how to sign to the monkey everything she wanted to say, so she just went ahead and spoke.

She pointed at the surviving hit men, shook her head, and said. "No, they were just following orders. I have brought my suffering upon myself. I should not have craved a cuddly pet back in Kauai. I should not have sent Ram to fetch that cute piglet. I should not have suspected Lak of any romantic interest in me. That said more about me than him. I should never have insulted him, sending him away to find Ram. And after I was kidnapped, I should have tried harder to escape once I was brought here. I won't dwell on the offenses of others, but will, to the best of my ability, conduct myself virtuously. I will not return evil for evil. I will strive to show compassion for the bad choices of others because no life is free of mistakes."

Hanuman didn't understand all that Sita said but did understand her grace and sense of mercy for Ravan's defeated henchmen.

Hanuman took leave of Sita, returned to Ram, and pointed to Sita's quarters. He signed to Ram that Sita wished to rejoin him as soon as possible.

Ram called Vibish to his side and said, "Can you go to Sita and ask her to bathe, set her hair, wear her most dignified clothes and jewelry, and then join me? I assume that Ravan bought some clothes and jewelry for her so she wouldn't still be wearing the jungle clothes she had on when he kidnapped her. I'll go on to the command center and receive her there. While waiting for her, I'll explore the equipment and communications facilities there."

Vibish nodded and went to see Sita, telling her that she should bathe and dress in the finest clothes and jewelry she had and then meet Ram in the command center.

Sita replied, "No way! I want to see him now."

Vibish answered, "These are Ram's wishes."

So Sita did as she was instructed. She bathed and dressed. She gathered her attendants about her to form a procession and moved regally in the direction of the passageway to the dock to board the submarine that would take her to the command center.

Vibish called Ram to say Sita was on her way.

Ram replied, "Is she coming alone?"

"No," Vibish replied. "She has her attendants with her."

Ram said, "She should come alone. Tell her to set her attendants aside. Our encounter might be difficult, and I don't wish to have any witnesses to gossip about us." Ram then continued to distract himself by poking around at the control center's state-of-the art gadgets.

So at Vibish's direction, the attendants peeled off and stepped aside, leaving Sita to walk alone to the departure stairs. As she went, the surviving hit men whistled in obvious admiration of her beauty—they had only seen her lying on the grass under the trees, wearing rags as she wept.

Vibish called Ram again and reported that the remaining hit men on the estate were whistling at his wife.

Ram replied, "I'm sure she'll deal with it."

By herself, Sita descended the stairs to the dock where a sub was waiting to take her to meet Ram. Vibish, Lak, and Hanuman followed behind.

When Sita arrived at the command center and disembarked through the port, Vibish conducted her to Ram in the control room. Ram looked at her without smiling.

Sita was radiant—her face shone like the moon at the sight of her husband. But her face soon fell as she saw Ram's grim demeanor.

Ram felt he should embrace her, hug her, show his love for her. But for nearly a full year, Sita had been in the house of the world's most notorious gangster. She may have slept with him. If she had, people would take that in stride. More importantly, Ram knew she may have disclosed corporate secrets. Ram knew that Apple was paranoid about new-product leaks. The need for purity with regard to disclosing corporate secrets had been impressed upon him since he was a child. He knew he would be criticized throughout the financial media if he failed to pursue corporate policy and properly vet Sita upon her return. And stockholders would surely rebel if they suspected Sita had leaked secret products under development.

Ram took a deep breath and declared to Sita, "Now that I have killed Ravan, my objective in this war has been attained. I have demonstrated to the world that no one can steal from me. However, you have lived for a year in the house of the most devious crook in the world. The world will know that for nearly a year you were in a position to disclose Apple's corporate secrets to someone who could fence them to corporate espionage brokers. Ravan may have even have drugged you to place subcutaneous bugs under your skin. You may have had to sleep with him to save your life. That is of no matter. What matters is that Apple's corporate secrecy may now be corrupted. Therefore, I regret to inform you that our relationship must be ended. You may go wherever you wish. You may find a home with my brothers or remain here with Vibish and his wife while he rebuilds. As beautiful as you are, you're sure to find another husband."

Sita was stunned. In shock, she shrank, shamed by her husband's distrust. Eventually, gathering her senses she said, "Why do you speak to me as though I were a gold-digging corporate spy, a Silicon Valley call-girl about to tattle on you to my pimp? If you still distrust me after all we've been through together, how can trust ever be possible between two people?"

Sita continued, "Are you really telling me you went through all these labors, oversaw the death and destruction of so many people and animals, just to establish a reputation as someone who can't be stolen from? Have you forgotten your bond of kinship with all of humanity, your love for all peoples everywhere, your love for me? Have you transformed into nothing but a warrior automaton, a heartless killing machine. Have you descended to the way of the street, to gang warfare, where every slight evokes a violent counterpunch? Is rescuing me an incidental side effect of delivering a knockout blow against Ravan, someone who dared cross your turf? How trite, how small you've become, a broken god. While defeating the world's greatest hoodlum you've become infected with his values."

Weeping now, Sita turned to Lak and said, "I haven't disclosed corporate secrets to Ravan or anyone else. Ravan did try to intimidate me, yet didn't lay a hand on me physically. I haven't slept with him or anyone else. I know the drill. Use your enhanced interrogation methods. Go ahead. As testament to my honesty, I wish to be tortured. If I survive the torture, you will know I have spoken the truth."

Lak was angry. How could Ram act this way? There were no grounds whatsoever for suspecting Sita's honesty. Ram was entertaining a remote possibility. Lak looked over at his brother.

Ram said, "Go ahead, prepare to waterboard her. I'll direct you. If she survives that then I'll take her back."

Lak went to the area in the command center where the washing machine and cleaning supplies were located. He found a large pail, a small pail, and a plank of wood. He filled both pails with water and brought the three items out to Ram. In the control room, Lak rigged the plank so that one end was in the water of the large pail, and the other end of the plank was inclined up at fifteen degrees.

Sita looked at Ram and said, "I am innocent." Then she lay down on the plank and put her head on the end of the plank toward the water while her feet were raised above her at the other end of the plank.

Ram said to Lak, "Here's what to do. For thirty seconds, pour water onto her face. Let the water run into her mouth and nose. The water will stay in her head, filling her throat and sinuses with water. Don't worry—her lungs won't fill up, so she won't asphyxiate, but she'll feel the sensation of drowning. After the thirty seconds, stop pouring the water and ask Sita if she disclosed any secrets. If she says no, repeat. If she maintains her innocence ten times, then we can all agree that Sita is indeed innocent."

Lak held the small pail of water. He glanced at Ram. Ram nodded. Lak inhaled in a deep breath and poured water on Sita's face. She gurgled and screamed. Lak counted slowly to thirty and stopped.

He asked Sita, "Did you spill a secret."

"No," she spat back.

Lak picked up the pail again. He closed his eyes, knowing now where to pour. He couldn't bear watching Sita in pain, realizing he was the cause. After counting to thirty again, he asked again, "Give them any secrets?"

Again Sita spat back, "No."

Eight more times Lak administered the torture. He thought how excruciating this was. Killing enemies in battle was easy, mauling an opponent in the boxing ring a snap. This was hard, very hard.

Ram felt terrible. He began to tear. But he wouldn't intervene to stop the waterboarding.

He said to himself, "What have I become? Maybe she's right. Maybe I have lost my heart, descended to the level of a street hoodlum. If I will waterboard my own wife, what won't I do next? Do I have any sense of morality left? I need to rethink myself. I need to regain a sense of who I am."

When the ten tortures were over, Lak helped the sputtering and choking Sita off the plank.

She stood up ramrod straight, looked Ram in the eye, and said, "I have not disclosed any secrets. So there."

Ram breathed a sigh of relief. Slowly his joy built as he allowed himself to believe that he would be able to accept Sita back as his wife after all. If the stockholders were not satisfied with this test of honesty, then nothing would satisfy them.

He said to Sita, "I love you. Please forgive me. I felt I had to do my duty. Please come back to me."

Sita paused while she calculated her options. Should she stay with Ram knowing that if he feared stockholder gossip now, he might again, if he stood by while she was waterboarded once, he might do so again? "This is not the man I married," she thought. "The war has changed him."

Sita continued considering her options. She thought, "But where would I go if I leave him now? Going to live with Ram's brothers or Vibish are not viable options—I would still be in his sphere of influence."

Sita concluded, "I will stay with him for now and see how events unfold. I will be prepared to move on if need be. I will love Ram as my husband, but not unconditionally as before."

Sita relaxed and sidled up to Ram, who put one arm around her. He grabbed her in both arms and pulled her face to his for a long, endearing kiss.

Ram then said to Hanuman, "Please find the capuchin surgeon, Sush. Tell him that he may have the remaining medical supplies. He should apply them to as many fallen and injured monkeys as possible. That way our stem cells may save a few more of our brethren."

Hanuman replied, "Will do."

Ram then said, "Let's get back to dry land. I suggest we spend the night back in our bivouac, which served us well during the battle. Our fourteen years of banishment are now over. We can return to Silicon Valley."

Ram continued, saying, "We'll figure out the logistics of our return tomorrow. In the meantime, can you call the International Air Response folks? Get them to send a C-130 right away, hopefully tomorrow. Tell them we'll be retracing our route, returning the surviving monkeys to their habitats. Same fee as before. They should be expecting to hear from us."

"Right away," replied Lak. "It's exciting to be going home."

Ram Returns

In the morning, Ram approached Vibish and said, "Lak, Sita and I will now be returning home to Silicon Valley. I'm anxious to reassure my mother, Kausha, and to relieve my brother, Barat, from the CEO responsibilities at Apple if he wishes to pursue a different path. The C-130 that brought us here should be arriving later today. We'll retrace our steps, landing in St. Kitts and Granada to offload monkeys on our way to Panama."

"Then how will you get from Panama to Silicon Valley?" Vibish asked.

Ram replied, "I'm starting to think about that now."

Vibish said, "May I suggest that you take the syndicate's black stealth jet from Panama to Silicon Valley? Matal, our pilot, can have the plane waiting when your C-130 touches down in Panama. You can run across the tarmac and jump on board, and the monkeys who live there can hop the fence and melt into the forest."

Ram agreed that this was a good idea.

Vibish then asked, "Is there any final service I may provide?"

Ram replied, "Yes, as the new syndicate's first good act, can you arrange protection for our monkey allies?"

"Yes," replied Vibish, "I was thinking along the same lines. I suggest we give one billon dollars in trust to the Panamanian government earmarked for conservation of the monkeys' habitat, plus one hundred million dollars to Grenada to preserve the forest there. On St. Kitts, I'll shut down the monkey-harvesting business and its practice of selling monkeys to pharmaceutical companies. I'll also give one hundred million dollars in trust to protect the Quill volcanic park on St. Eustatius and another hundred million dollars to protect the volcanic park on St. Kitts."

"Excellent," said Ram. "That's generous. Those gifts make a statement that the syndicate will now become a force for good."

Seeing Ram and Vibish discussing plans, Sugriv approached to ask, "Would it be appropriate for us monkey leaders to come with you to your home? We'd like to see you installed as CEO. After that, we'd like to return home to our habitat."

"Yes," replied Ram, "we'd be honored if you and the other monkey leaders would join us in Silicon Valley. We'll all ride together in the C-130 as we discharge monkeys along the way to Panama. Then you and the other monkey leaders can accompany Lak, Sita, and myself when we board the black stealth jet in Panama for the flight to Silicon Valley. The stealth jet will then wait at the Silicon Valley airport until the ceremonies end. Then you can re-board the stealth jet, which will return you to your native habitats before continuing on to its hanger here in St. Eustatius."

Ram turned to Vibish to say, "We'd also be honored if you and your wife, Sarama, would accompany us as well. You can ride with us in the C-130 to Panama as well and then return home with Matal as he pilots the syndicate's black jet back here."

Vibish replied, "I know I can speak for my wife when I say we'd love to accompany you."

Vibish then called Matal to tell him the plans.

Ram next turned to Lak to say, "Remember Guh, the CEO of the software company on Kauai, and Bhar, the chief jewelry-maker geek from the Hanakapi'ai beach encampment on the Na Pali coast?"

"I remember them well," replied Lak.

Ram continued, "Please tell them to spread the news to the other geek encampments along the Na Pali coast—to Valmiki, Atri, Sarab, Sutik, and Agast—that we're all finally returning to Silicon Valley. Please thank them again for all the help they've provided over the years."

"Will do," replied Lak.

Then the sound of a large propeller-driven plane was heard circling overhead before landing.

Sugriv called out to all the monkeys and to Jamb, saying, "Let's get to the airport. We're going home!"

They didn't need to be told twice. All the monkeys plus Jamb ran, shuffled, or bounded—some with a limp—from the bivouac down the road to the airport. They piled over the fence and disappeared into the cavernous hold of the C-130 transport.

Ram went to get Sita and Sarama. Then they, along with Lak and Vibish, boarded the C-130 for the final journey with their courageous monkey and bear allies.

The C-130 touched down at St. Kitts and Grenada, discharging the animals who lived there. Ram and Lak gave each departing animal a hug before it ambled down the gangway to the ground. Hanuman, Sugriv, Angad, and the other monkey leaders remained onboard the C-130.

The C-130's last stop was the Bocas del Toro airport, where Matal was waiting in the setting sun with the syndicate's black stealth jet.

Lak paid the C-130's pilot, and then the people and remaining animals rushed out the gangway of the C-130, over to the stealth jet, and up the stairs to a well-appointed, corporate-style private jet.

Lak remarked to Ram, "Looks like our final leg is pretty cushy. We're not used to this anymore."

Ram replied, "Yup, no choice but sit back and enjoy."

Lak quipped, "Tough life, huh?"

Ram smiled and nodded back. Everyone bedded down for the overnight flight back to Silicon Valley.

The next morning the syndicate's black stealth jet landed at Moffett Field and parked next to the Apple company jet to symbolize the alliance between Apple and the reconstituted syndicate.

The passengers got out of the stealth jet to stretch their legs while awaiting clearance from the customs and immigration agents.

Ram said to Lak, "Before we go to our palace at Apple, we should send a messenger to tell everyone we've arrived. I didn't call ahead. Our appearance here might be an unwelcome surprise."

Lak replied, "Good idea. We should get a reading on what awaits us here."

Turning to Vibish and Hanuman, Ram asked them to take a cab to the Apple palace, telling them they should ask for an audience with Barat to personally tell him of their arrival.

To Vibish, Ram added, "Please look carefully at Barat's expression when you tell him the news that we're here. If you sense he's unhappy about our turning up, let me know. I'm more than willing to have him continue as Apple's CEO if he wishes. Please report back to me what your intuition is about how to proceed. In the meantime we'll simply wait here for you to return. We can easily keep ourselves occupied for the hour or so it will take you to ascertain whether we'll be welcomed back."

After the clearance formalities were completed, Vibish and Hanuman walked out to the road and hailed a cab. Vibish told the driver, "Please take us to the Apple palace at 1 Infinity Drive."

The cabby said, "I know where it is. Do you want to take that animal with you too?"

"Yes," said Vibish.

"Then the price is double what it says on the meter. I may have to clean up after him."

Vibish replied, "Okay, but don't worry about my monkey friend here, he's well behaved—better than many of your regular customers, I'll bet."

The cabby was noncommittal, saying, "Just go ahead and get in."

After the cabby discharged Vibish and Hanuman from the cab, they walked to the lobby at the entrance to the Apple palace, where they were met by a security geek. They identified themselves as messengers from Ram who wished to speak personally with Barat. The security geek looked dubious but called in the request anyway. To his surprise, Barat replied that they should be sent up right away.

Vibish and Hanuman were ushered to the guest quarters where Barat had been living as an ascetic since Ram's departure. Barat had left the CEO quarters vacant during Ram's absence.

Vibish introduced himself and Hanuman. He said, "I know it will be hard to believe, but Ram has learned to speak with animals, and especially with monkeys, primarily by using a kind of sign language. When Ravan kidnapped Sita, the monkeys helped Ram rescue her. The monkey you see before you, whose name is Hanuman, was Ram's principal ally."

Barat raised his eyebrows when Vibish mentioned that Sita had been kidnapped. He asked, "Is Sita safe now?"

Vibish replied, "Yes, and not only that, Ravan has been killed. Ravan was my brother, and I am now the CEO of the syndicate. I defected from his side and joined forces with Ram. Once Ram and his monkey allies were victorious, Ram installed me as the new CEO of the syndicate. I am redirecting the syndicate to be a beneficial presence in society. But enough about me. Ram, Sita, and Lak are waiting at the Moffet Field airport. They are wondering if they should return here."

Barat immediately replied, "Of course they should return here. I'm ecstatic that they've come home. Their banishment is now over. Ram should re-assume his position as CEO of Apple. I've had enough. I can't wait to hand over the reins. Are they ready to come here now? I can't bring myself to believe it! We've all been waiting for their return for fourteen long years. How many are in your party? Do you need several vehicles?"

Vibish nodded yes.

Barat then directed his chauffeur, Suman, to lead a caravan of six company limousines to the airport. The caravan should pick up Ram and his party and convey them home to the Apple palace.

Meanwhile, Barat called to alert Kausha, Ram's mother, to come from her home in the redwoods and Sumitra, Lak and Shat's mother, to come from her home in the desert. He also sent a messenger to Kaila, Barat's mother, in her quarters in the palace. He told them all that Ram had returned and was at this very moment in a limo about to arrive at the palace gate. Barat called Janak, Sita's father in Seattle, who offered to fly down immediately, bringing with him Urmila, who was Lak's wife and Sita's stepsister. Barat also called Kush, from Bangalore, who was the father of his own wife, Manda, and Shat's wife, Suta. Coincidentally, Kush and his daughters were visiting with relatives in Southern California. Kush was able to fly in on short notice with his daughters to the forthcoming reunion.

The caravan of limos from the airport arrived at the palace. Shat had joined Barat, and as Ram and Lak got out of their vehicles, the four brothers embraced for a long, long time.

After a while, Ram broke off from the hugs and gestured for Hanuman, Sugriv, and Angad to approach. Ram introduced them and briefly mentioned their vital role in the war to defeat Ravan. Barat embraced the monkeys one by one and said to each that he was now like an additional brother.

Meanwhile, Ram looked about and spied his mother. She held her arms out and Ram rushed to his mother's embrace. Kausha had aged and seemed emaciated from grief and worry. Lak too went to his mother, Sumitra, who also looked aged and weakened. But both mothers were clearly overjoyed to see their sons. Their faces radiated joy. Ram also greeted Barat's mother, Kaila, cordially.

Then Ram spotted his chief palace geek, Vasis, who was aged too but in good health. Ram walked over to him and bowed deeply in respect.

Ram went on to bow before Janak, his father-in-law. Janak was shedding tears of joy at Sita's safe return. Ram continued on to bow before Kush, the father of Barat's and Shat's wives, who was beaming with joy at seeing his daughters' extended family assembled after so long.

Barat disappeared for a few minutes. When he reappeared, he was carrying Ram's sandals. Barat had retrieved them from the executive conference room where they had remained these last fourteen years.

Barat said to Ram, "Here is the symbol of your company, which I've held in trust on your behalf. I hereby return the sandals back to you in their original condition. I return your company back to you in even better shape than I received it. The stock price, cash on hand, total sales, profit margin, and market share of the company, as well as the quality, health, and happiness of our employees and citizens, have all increased during your absence."

Ram replied, "You've obviously done a spectacular job. I knew you could. I had faith in you."

Barat asked, "Do you want to know how I did it?"

"Sure," said Ram, "please pass along your secrets for success."

Barat replied, "Actually, my secret was simple. I kept asking myself what you'd do in my place, and I went ahead and did precisely that. Thinking of what you'd do forced me to make decisions rationally, to prevent my ego from interfering, to have no proprietary stake in the outcome, and to view the decisions as yours to carry out rather than as mine to defend."

Vibish and the monkeys watched the love with which Barat and Ram interacted and were touched at the affection among them.

Kausha then said, "Your father left a hologram recording to be replayed upon your return. Now is the time to hear it, seeing as how our entire family is assembled."

Ram said, "This will be a tender moment for me, as I wasn't here when he died. Go ahead and play the recording."

Kausha then loaded the hologram in its projector, and a 3D image of Das appeared. He looked grim and weak but determined to have his say.

Das began, "My son, I know that when this recording of my final words to you is played, you will have returned from your banishment. I have grieved your absence. I realize my own culpability in causing you to suffer the sentence you have now lived out. I'm grateful for the sacrifice you've made. You've redeemed my promise. You've upheld the integrity of our company. You've earned the right to become my successor as CEO of Apple. Please assume the offer of CEO when it is made."

The figure in the hologram continued, saying, "I also thank my son, Lak, for his service in accompanying you. I forgive Kaila for her role in bringing about your banishment. Finally, I thank Sita for sticking with you through what must have been extraordinarily difficult conditions. And although I cannot peer into the future, I anticipate that in your struggles with Ravan, Sita may become involved, perhaps even captured. So to Sita, and I hope you are listening, if Ram should consent to your undergoing a vetting process upon being rescued, please don't think ill of him for this. Our procedure is to vet everyone who comes under the influence of Ravan's syndicate. I leave you now. Welcome home."

After hearing his father's voice and seeing his image, as though returned from the dead, Ram was moved to say, "My father has graced us with a fitting conclusion to the whole banishment episode. He challenges us to go forward from here, and I, for one, accept his challenge."

Keeping her thoughts to herself, Sita did not speak. She was unpersuaded that Das's policy on loyalty tests was wise.

Barat then escorted Ram and Sita to their former quarters, which had remained unoccupied during their long absence. He urged them to make themselves comfortable and to rest up for the CEO installation the next day.

Barat returned to the room where the rest were waiting and escorted Lak and Urmila to their quarters as well. Barat then led Vibish to a private guest room and the monkeys to a large guest suite that offered a panoramic view of the oak trees surrounding the palace.

The next day, Ram and Lak dressed themselves in proper business apparel for the first time in fourteen years. From there they went to the palace barber, where Ram had his dreadlocks cutoff and Lak received a fresh cut on his Mohawk.

Kausha, Sumitra, and Kaila joined Sita, Urmila, Manda, and Suta to assist them in dressing in more formally stylish outfits than they had worn in a long time.

Also in the morning, Vasis polled the board of directors and the principal geeks. All agreed that Ram should assume the CEO position immediately. With this consensus in hand, Vasis summoned all the directors and geeks to the executive room.

Once assembled, Vasis called Ram into the room. Sita and the other wives, their fathers, Kausha, and the other mothers, as well as the monkeys, came in to witness. Then Vasis administered the oath of office to Ram.

Ram placed his hands palms down on Vasis's upturned palms. Sita held a plaque for Vasis to read from. The transfer of power from Barat to Ram was over in about thirty seconds.

Word of the transition in leadership at Apple then spread. The public tweeted their enthusiasm and the stock soared.

The brothers—accompanied by their wives, their other relatives, and the monkeys—toured the Apple palace and grounds in jubilation, shaking hands and accepting congratulations from employees and citizens along the way.

After the palace tour was over, the entourage piled into limos, and Suman led them to downtown San Francisco. There the entourage walked along Market Street, starting at the Civic Center.

As they walked they accepted the congratulations of the independent app makers and web designers who contributed value to Apple's products.

When word spread about the impromptu parade on Market Street, the mayor of San Francisco came out to join them, ever eager for a photo op. The city council adjourned for the rest of the day, and the city council members, along with their staff, joined in.

As they walked by, the parade participants waved to drag queens on the balcony of the LGBT center, coming to rest at the plaza before the Ferry Building.

There they gobbled up salted pretzels and reveled in the joy of being home at long last.

The monkeys enjoyed meeting their compatriots who worked with the street musicians to collect donations from the listening audience.

Toward the end of the day, the entourage returned to the Apple palace. Each person returned to their quarters.

Ram and Sita were content. Surrounded by adoring relatives, they looked forward to a loving and prosperous life together.

Heaven on Earth

A day after the installation and ensuing festivities, Ram, Lak, and Sita went to the suite where the monkeys were staying. Vibish had already joined the group.

After Ram arrived, Vibish looked over to Hanuman, Sugriv, and Angad to see if they were getting impatient. Sugriv gave a sign with his hands that it was time to leave.

Vibish said to Ram, "We've all enjoyed seeing your extended family and your installation as CEO here. We also enjoyed the festivities afterward, but the monkeys are clearly anxious to return to their own families."

Ram nodded that he understood. He called ahead to have Suman line up the limos, and he asked Matal to be sure the black stealth jet was fueled for its flight home.

Then he turned to Vibish and said, "I'm relying on you to turn the syndicate around. Big job."

Vibish replied, "Count on me. I know the syndicate's system, and you'll see, slowly but surely, the evils the syndicate has been known for will disappear, replaced by good deeds."

Ram then approached Hanuman and embraced him, saying, "Brother, our genes and our bodies have melded. Future historians will forever intertwine our names. No one will write of Ram without writing of Hanuman and no one will write of Hanuman without writing of me as well. Our friendship will exemplify the ideal of people and animals working together. Thank you so much for all you've done."

Hanuman was stunned to learn the depth of Ram's gratitude. He had resigned himself to living a domesticated animal's role, to serve. He had anticipated remaining grateful for any treats he might receive in return. But Ram was different. This was equality.

Seeing that the monkeys were about to leave, Sita ran to her quarters and looked in her old dresser. It was just as she had left it fourteen years ago. She rummaged around in her jewelry drawer and pulled out her most precious item, a necklace of black pearls. She took it in hand and ran back to the room where everyone was assembled. Sita went up to Hanuman and placed the necklace around his neck. Hanuman knew instinctively that Sita had bestowed a great honor upon him. They hugged, and Hanuman reluctantly joined the other monkeys to leave.

Ram, Lak, and Sita escorted Vibish and the monkeys to Suman's limo for the short trip to the airport. There they met up with Matal, who was waiting beside the refueled jet. Vibish and the monkeys climbed the stairs to the plane, the door closed, and Matal fired up the engine. Ram and Sita watched as the black stealth jet took off, returning the monkeys to their native habitat and leaving them to begin a new chapter in their lives.

Later that day, Janak returned to Microsoft/IBM in Seattle, accompanied by Barat and Shat and their wives. The alliance between Microsoft/IBM and Apple remained strong as ever.

A month after the guests from Ram's CEO installation had departed, Agast, the chief geek of the conservation-biology encampment on Kauai, visited. Agast was wise. It was he who had helped in the research on how to talk with albatrosses. It was he who had thought to arm Ram with the nonibars that kept him focused while pursuing Ravan in the darkness of hideaway. It was he who gave Ram the bulletwood arrows used to kill Ravan his secret underwater control center.

Ram was glad to see Agast. He had questions that had been puzzling him for some time. After Agast had settled into his guest quarters, they met in Ram's office, seated in comfortable leather chairs placed around a coffee table.

After a while, Ram asked Agast the question that had been bothering him for a long time. "Can you explain Ravan? I don't get him. He was smart. Why was he so enamored of evil? He was stubborn about it, and wouldn't listen to advice—he wouldn't even listen to his brother, Vibish."

Agast replied, "Here's what I know. Ravan comes from a family marked by domestic violence as long as anyone can remember. You recall your early tangles with Tata, the Chechen gangster from that small town of Coyote, south of San Jose?"

Ram nodded.

"You had her sent back to Chechnya. And then there was her son, Marich, whom she cruelly abused—she even chained him up. Little wonder he wound up continuing in the family path. You eventually had to kill him back in Kauai."

Agast continued, "Ravan's clan has always consisted of angry people—angry at the world, at everyone, with no understanding of love. Their criminal activities always had a bit of meanness thrown in, always more violence than needed, always an underlying anger revealed. Always their modus operandi has been, 'just take it, baby, and then deal with consequences.'"

Agast added, "Domestic violence propagates intimidation, from parents to children and then onto their children. Evil begets evil."

Ram said, "Yes, Sita reports that Ravan tried to intimidate her."

"Indeed," replied Agast, "that's their style. And the family has always operated through bravado, not bravery. But their boastful individualism defeated them in the end. Your forces defeated their leaders one by one. You fought as a team. Their leaders each fought solo, as overconfident prima donnas. Thank goodness they never discovered cooperation. If they had, they would have beaten you with your courageous ragtag bunch of monkeys."

Ram stroked his chin, thinking.

So Agast continued, "I don't know how evil got started in the first place, its origin. I suppose some mystery will always remain, despite all our progress in science and technology. But while I don't know how evil started, I do see how evil is perpetuated. I think Ravan's family needed an intervention, but there was no one with the power to intervene. And now you have nearly obliterated them, a most extreme form of intervention. By defeating Ravan and his syndicate, you have benefited your entire extended family, the whole of mankind. And the whole of mankind is grateful. I would like to add that I am personally grateful too, because my encampment back in Kauai can now live and work in peace."

Then Agast blurted out, "And another point too: Evil is not inevitable. Even though evil is inherited through domestic violence, favorable social mutations can happen too. Vibish was a product of Ravan's family, yet he turned out virtuous. I don't know why. The origin of good in the midst of evil is as mysterious to me as the origin of evil in the midst of good. Anyway, the world will forever be in your debt for your accomplishments on the battlefield between good and evil."

Ram replied, "My dear friend, thank you for your kind words. I'll always treasure the memory of your gratitude."

Agast replied, "I take leave of you now. I came specifically to express my gratitude in person, and now can return home."

The next morning Agast returned by commercial airline to his home on Kauai.

Indeed, Ram had apparently fulfilled the life mission he was charged with when he was a young man still in Das's care. With Ravan gone and Vibish in charge of syndicate, the litany of evils for which Ravan was known did indeed gradually disappear. Stock market manipulation stopped, subprime extortionist loans stopped, Trojan malware stopped, Internet denial-of-service attacks stopped, Internet viruses disappeared, web traffic sped up, and the outcomes of athletic games stopped being fixed. Influence-peddling ceased, honorable people ran for office, political parties compromised, legislation was passed, trafficking in women and slaves stopped, kidnappings stopped, genetic engineering of mercenaries ceased, income disparity narrowed, and false rumors regarding race, religion, and sexuality ceased. The entire litany of evils the world had been suffering gradually disappeared. Could this be heaven on earth?

Sita Moves On

As part of his corporate responsibilities, Ram initiated two new product lines at Apple. One was the iZoo line of translator robots, starting with iBird and iMonkey, that were developed from his research in Kauai.

The other new product line was the iParel line of programmable *haute* fashion clothes. This product line was developed by Apple personnel in California under Barat while Ram was away. These clothes featured a style, color, and fit that could be modified for different occasions. The clothes could be programmed on a tablet to vary from formal to casual to sporty, and alterations could be made on the fly with an app on the wearer's Apple Watch. These clothes required research for Barat and the company to develop new materials that could stretch and change color at the beck and call of a computer program. With these new product lines, combined with the undying popularity of its venerable products, Apple's continued growth seemed guaranteed.

To all appearances, Ram was a great success, living the life he was designed to live. But ever since returning to Apple from his battles with Ravan, night after night he had bad dreams, recalling the horrors of mangled monkeys, their arms and legs twitching on the ground as scavengers picked at their remains. Ram kept these dreams secret, even from Sita. He feared the impact on Apple's stock should any word of weakness at the top of his firm's leadership leak out.

Meanwhile, feeling that her future was relatively secure, Sita restarted her ovulation schedule for the first time since leaving with Ram for their banishment to Kauai many years ago. After two years of exciting intimacy, Sita felt the stirrings in her belly. She was pregnant. She went through her days with a knowing Mona-Lisa smile.

One morning, she broke the good news to Ram. He was ecstatic. He gave her a big bear hug, clapped his hands, and exclaimed, "Wow! Wonderful! I've long hoped for this. Is there anything I can do?"

Sita had a ready answer, "Yes, my dear. Before I become heavy and lose my mobility, I'd like to see Kauai again. I'd love to revisit the Awaawapuhi Valley where we spent so many happy days among the birds and other animals. And I would like to stop in at some of the geek encampments to say hi to old friends and to tell them in person that I'm expecting."

"Sure," said Ram. "I'm sorry I can't accompany you at this time, but Lak will stay with you for the duration of your visit. You can leave as early as tomorrow on your vacation. A reunion with the forest geeks sounds like fun. Please say hello to them for me too. I'll call Suman now and have him get the plane ready and arrange for a helicopter on Kauai. I'm jealous, actually. Sounds like a great trip. Hurry home."

Ram gave her another hug, and she returned to her quarters to pack while Ram, joined by Lak, went on to the executive conference room for the day's meeting.

At the meeting, Ram called on his chief pubic-relations geek, Bhad, saying, "It's time, I think, for a status report. How are we being perceived among our stockholders and potential customers since I've taken charge? If I should be making any midcourse corrections, I want to know about it now and take appropriate steps."

Bhad spoke, "I regret to report that there's a problem."

Ram said, "Go on."

Bhad continued, "Samsung is launching a counter-line of products to our two new product lines. They're introducing cheap knock-off blue jeans with nothing but a programmable waistline—its style and color are fixed. This will steal business from our iParel line of programmable apparel. Moreover, they're naming their cheap knock-off pants the iJeans, which is a confusing play on our product name, the iGene, for our line of pocket DNA genetic decoders."

Ram scowled.

Bhad continued, "Not only that, they're introducing something marketed as the iGoat which is nothing but a smart lawnmower. Decades ago, the iRobot company developed a successful line of robotic vacuum cleaners, wonderfully smart appliances in their day. But the Samsung iGoat is nothing but the controller circuitry from a smart vacuum cleaner transplanted on top of a lawn mower. Samsung could have been made this fifty years ago. But they're making it now and naming it to confuse and interfere with our iZoo line of human-to-animal translators."

Ram asked, "What's the general reaction to this?"

Bhad replied, "Well, the shareholders are very happy overall with your leadership, but they're becoming upset about what looks like a leak of the main two product lines. They are wondering how Samsung could have heard about our new product lines in time to launch their counter-campaign of product disinformation."

Bhad paused and looked uncomfortable. Seeing this, Ram said encouragingly, "Go on."

Bhad continued, "Well, here's the problem. The buzz among the shareholders is that Sita may be the source of the leaks. The shareholders suspect her. They're wondering whether she divulged company secrets while still in Ravan's captivity. Ravan in turn may have sold the secrets directly to Samsung or perhaps to a corporate-espionage middleman, who in turn sold the secrets to Samsung. One way or the other, shareholders are tweeting that Sita is a security risk.

Ram said, "This is incredible."

Turning to the other geeks at the conference table, he asked, "Have you heard this too?"

They nodded.

One of them spoke up to say, "Bhad's report is accurate. These suspicions about Sita are circulating though the Twitter-sphere. Stock is being sold because shareholders fear the curtain shrouding our product development secrets is porous. The price of our shares is dropping as people bail out and buy other equities with less security risk. I don't need to remind you that when our stock drops, it's widows and retirees who depend on their Apple holdings for their livelihood who are hurt. Not us, who are wealthy enough to absorb stock fluctuations."

Ram turned to Lak and asked, "Did you know of this?"

Lak silently nodded his assent.

Ram then said, "I'm morally obligated to plug leaks. Otherwise many people suffer—not only our employees but our citizens and all those who depend on us for their livelihood through their stock ownership. But I don't know what to do in the specific case of Sita. After all, Sita has already submitted herself to waterboarding. Isn't that enough? She's obviously innocent. The leaks could be coming from many points in the development and manufacturing supply chains."

The geeks around the conference table remained silent. After a while one spoke up, "The stockholders, and the general public too, simply don't trust enhanced interrogation techniques. They know waterboarding doesn't work. They think the tortures are a ghoulish show that does nothing to prevent leaks. The suspicions won't disappear, I'm sorry to say." The geeks thought the next step was obvious, but no one wanted to speak it.

After several minutes of silence, Ram took a deep breath and said to the geeks, "I know where my duty lies."

Facing Lak, Ram said, "Sita is leaving on a vacation to Kauai tomorrow. I wish you to take her to Valmiki's history encampment at Hanakapi`ai Falls and leave her there. Don't linger. Just drop her off and depart."

Lak could scarcely believe his ears. This seemed so unjust. Sita had committed no infraction—she was as pure and virtuous as humanly possible.

Ram looked at Lak, seeing his incredulous expression. He uttered in a broken voice, "My mind's made up. Just do it."

Ram set his jaw, but could not disguise his anguished look.

The next morning Lak knocked on Sita's door, saying, "I'm to accompany you on your vacation today to Kauai."

Sita replied, "Wonderful! Won't it be great to see our old haunts again and meet up with our old friends?"

Lak nodded noncommittally.

Sita gathered a backpack with her personal items together with a basket of See's Chocolate Truffles she was bringing to the forest geeks.

Lak seemed somber.

Sita asked him, "Is anything wrong?"

Lak replied, "No, nothing's wrong. I'm just a bit preoccupied."

Suman drove them to the airport. He climbed into the cockpit while Sita and Lak took their seats in the passenger compartment.

Suman flew the Apple corporate jet to Kauai, whereupon they transferred to a helicopter. Lak instructed Suman to land first at Hanakapi`ai Beach.

Suman said, "It's a narrow spot, but I think I can."

After landing, everyone got out of the helicopter. Bhar was nowhere in sight.

Lak said, "He must be out with his group somewhere looking for shells for their leis."

Sita and Lak then walked to the water's edge and dipped their feet in warm waves as they broke across the sandy beach.

Lak said to himself, "I should just leave her here right now. Ram's clear instructions were to leave immediately and not dawdle. Sita need only walk up the trail to Hanakapi`ai Falls to be back with Valmiki and his encampment."

Lak could not admit to himself that he also felt ashamed, ashamed to tell Valmiki to his face that he was abandoning Sita.

Lak could think of no way to explain to Sita why he was about to climb back on the helicopter without her. He cleared his throat, nearly gagging. Beads of sweat formed on his brow, his face was ashen.

Sita saw Lak's discomfort and asked, "Oh, Lak, is there a problem? You look ill. Should we seek medical attention?"

Lak managed to choke out "Yes, sweet lady, there is a problem. I don't see any kind way to explain this. You see, there have been leaks about the new product lines Apple has been developing, and the shareholders are convinced you're the source of the leaks."

"What? That's ridiculous!" exclaimed Sita.

Lak continued, saying, "When Ram was informed of the rumors, he felt that to save the company's reputation he must be seen publicly plugging the leak. You're rumored to be the source of the leaks, tracing back to your time with the syndicate during Ravan's regime. Ram concluded that he needed to relocate you to somewhere far away from Apple, namely, back with Valmiki in his encampment. Ram took advantage of your planned vacation here to resettle you. I am to return alone."

Lak broke off, too pained to continue.

Sita was surprised at the timing and manner of this rude scheme to banish her. Ever since her reunion with Ram after Ravan's defeat, she suspected he might not stand up for her should rumors circulate doubting her corporate purity, her confidentiality concerning Apple's corporate secrets. She suspected her volunteering to be waterboarded would not permanently still any attacks on her loyalty." She covered her face with her hands and sank to the ground.

Then Sita said, "Why me? What sin did I commit that I should suffer so? What will Valmiki and his geeks say? Will they assume I did something to deserve this treatment from the hand of my powerful husband? Oh, Lak, do what you must, but first hear me out."

Sita pulled herself up and said, "Go return to Ram and say to him, 'I'm glad to remain here with Valmiki.' Say, 'I'm tired of unjust rumors, back-stabbing politics, and the life-in-a-cage that a CEO's wife must endure.' And to you, let me add that the happiest days of my life have been spent living close to nature here on Kauai. Do not grieve for me. I'll be fine."

Lak then turned. There was nothing more to say. In sorrow he climbed back in the helicopter with Suman for their trip back to Silicon Valley.

Two geeks from Valmiki's camp came down the path from Hanakapi`ai Falls to the beach to fish. They found Sita sitting on a boulder near the beach crying. They immediately recognized her as their beloved Sita.

One of the geeks ran up back up the path to Valmiki.

When Valmiki heard that Sita had been abandoned below at the beach he said, "She may take refuge with us. There's space in the women's quarters. Bring her here."

The geek returned to the beach, and together, the two geeks guided Sita back up the path to meet up with Valmiki.

Valmiki said to her, "My daughter, you are welcome. I'm so glad to see you again."

Sita's face lit up briefly, then clouded. She said, "Thank you so much. But I must tell you I am with child."

Valmiki replied, "That will be fine. We will care for you and your child. My home is your home."

As Lak was flying home with Suman, Lak spoke out loud of his sorrow. "It's amazing to me that Ram was able to eliminate the evil syndicate, to kill Ravan, and yet is powerless to quell the suspicions of the public and the shareholders without the sacrifice of separating himself from his loving wife. Ram was more pained by banishing Sita than he was at his own banishment. Why did he go along with the cruel words of the stockholder rabble? What virtue did he gain? Shouldn't he have stood up to them?"

Suman replied, "I once broached the subject of Ram's relationship to Sita with Vasis. He replied that marital difficulties go with the turf. The spouses of a CEO never have a partner to themselves. Their families can never be happy. The heavy burden of office falls on both husband or wife. Vasis even advised that separation is needed for a CEO to successfully execute the responsibilities of their job."

After the flight, Lak returned to the Apple palace to find Ram downcast and depressed.

Lak tried to console him, saying, "Take heart. Remember the eternal cycle. All gain ends in loss, all climbs in a fall, all union in separation, and life itself in death. The wise don't become attached to wives, sons, friends, or riches. All this you already know. Get over your sorrow. Go forward. What you've done will indeed satisfy the stockholders and put the rumors to rest."

Ram replied, "I sincerely hope so. There's nothing more I could do. Sending Sita away is the ultimate sacrifice. I will now immerse myself in my work and take happiness in my accomplishments."

The brothers embraced and retired for the evening.

Twelve years went by. Apple continued to prosper and the relicts of Ravan's evil continued to be snuffed out, as Vibish led the syndicate down new and honest commercial paths. Seeing the example Ram had set by banishing Sita, the leakers stopped. They hoped that if Sita had stayed, their leaks would be blamed on her and that her continued presence would signal a lax policy of cracking down on suspected leakers. With Sita gone, they were afraid they would be shown no mercy if caught.

To celebrate the success of Apple under his leadership, Ram convened a convention to be held in the main auditorium at the Apple palace. The convention would showcase new products and provide a hackathon for young students to show off their coding talent and 3D fabrication skills. Chief geeks from encampments around the country were invited to bring their most promising students with them to the convention.

Valmiki was among those invited to bring their especially worthy students. He was asked to bring promising members from his group and also from the other nearby geek camps to compete on behalf of Hawaii.

Unbeknownst to Ram, Sita had given birth not to one child, but to twins whom she named Lav and Kus. Both had a striking physical resemblance to their father, including the blue and red natural epaulettes on their shoulders.

Although both Sita and Valmiki had been up front with the boys that Ram was their father, Valmiki had raised them as his own sons. He taught them history, science, and culture. He also read to them from his ongoing work on the biography of Ram.

When the time for the event arrived, Valmiki flew to Silicon Valley with Lav and Kus. He took them to the Apple palace and registered them into the hackathon contest.

He told the boys, "If you're asked who your father is, answer that I am your father, not Ram. If they offer you money, a signing bonus to be their employee, turn it down. You're too young."

On the day of the fair, the boys exhibited an improved translator robot that could learn nuances of animal language that had previously defied human analysis. When the panel of judges visited their exhibit, the boys showed themselves skilled in the biotechnology of human-animal interaction. The hackathon judges were so impressed they awarded the boys first prize.

At the awards ceremony, Ram himself was present, along with Lak. Ram looked at the boys and remarked to Lak on their resemblance to himself. He also saw some of Sita's features in their statuesque bearing and inquiring brown eyes.

When the boys delivered their acceptance speeches, Ram perceived their grasp of subtlety, their ability to make complex issues simple. He saw how their conceptualizations would lead to fundamentally new products designed with an elegant simplicity promoting intuitive use. These boys would not produce yet more throw-away electronic trinkets.

After the boys' acceptance speeches, Ram went to the stage where they had been standing and shook their hands. He said, to them, "Excellent work. May I ask who you are, where are you from, and who your parents are?"

One of the boys replied, "We are the sons and students of Valmiki in Hawaii."

Ram replied in surprise, "Oh, I know him well. Excellent man."

Continuing, Ram said, "We're prepared to offer you both signing bonuses to join our team, to become employees and citizens with us here at Apple when you finish your schooling."

"No thanks," one of the boys replied. "Our father has asked us to decline any offers until we've grown older."

"I understand," said Ram. "Do keep us in mind when you're ready to sign."

After the awards banquet, the boys went outside, where Valmiki was waiting patiently. No one had recognized him. He took the boys and returned to Hawaii by commercial airline.

Hearing the name of Valmiki and seeing traces of Sita in the boys' appearance and manner made Ram long to see Sita again. He missed her so much and was so lonely for her. He wished her to return. He hoped that during her life of twelve years away from Apple, people would understand that she could not possibly now have any corporate secrets to disclose, even if she wished to.

"Surely," he thought, "the shareholders would not object to her returning now."

Ram summoned Bhad, the chief PR geek, and said, "Please invite Valmiki and Sita to return to our palace here. Send Suman in our corporate jet to fetch them. We have the annual company symphony featuring new compositions in the classical style coming up soon at Davies Hall in San Francisco. I would like to have Sita accompany me in public for all to see."

Bhad replied, "Wonderful. Seeing you both together will gladden the hearts of many who feel that Sita has been unfairly treated."

Sita and Valmiki arrived at the Apple palace the day before the gala concert in San Francisco. They brought the two boys with them. Once in the palace, they were shown to their guest quarters.

On the day of the concert, Ram went on ahead to the hall to inspect the arrangements. When the limo with Sita, Valmiki, and the young boys pulled up outside Davies Hall, Sita emerged to the flashes of cameras and clicks of cell phones. She was stunning in an ochre evening gown with large gold earrings. As she made her entrance to the reception hall, the crowd was hushed. She walked slowly and gracefully to Ram, who, without a word, took her on his arm as they went to take their place in the CEO's private box. The boys followed behind, along with some assistant geeks.

Valmiki hung back for a minute and gestured to Vasis. He said, "Here is the latest version of my biography of Ram. He authorized the biography and cooperated in its writing. It's based mostly on interviews with Ram when he, Sita, and Lak were staying with me, plus interviews with Sita during her time alone with me. Please add any insights you can to the narrative. I'll keep sending you the latest."

"Thanks," said Vasis. "This will be an invaluable ongoing record of these epic times for us here at Apple."

At the intermission, Ram and Sita emerged to the reception hall, where champagne was being served. Valmiki and the boys followed behind. Ram tapped on his glass, signaling for quiet, and gestured to Valmiki to speak.

Valmiki cleared his throat. In a clear and authoritative voice, he declared, "I am Valmiki, chief geek of the history encampment on Kauai. I testify before you that Sita has been staying with me these last dozen years. During that time she has had no contact of any kind with Apple. She does not possess any corporate secrets, nor would she ever disclose them if she did. To this I swear."

Ram then spoke up in a more definitive voice than people had heard him use in some time, saying, "I know in my mind and heart that Sita is now and has always been innocent and blameless. She volunteered to pass a torture test to confirm her innocence when I rescued her from Ravan. She accepted banishment for a dozen years. I have permitted these injustices and insults only to assuage the fears of stockholders' paranoid fears. I felt that reassuring these investors to prevent a sell-off served the greater good of the many who depend on Apple's prosperity, reflected in its stock price and dividends. I felt this greater good outweighed the suffering of two people—Sita, unjustly condemned to banishment, and me, unjustly condemned to loneliness without her."

Sita then spoke to the crowd. Her voice was quiet, but perfectly audible in the hushed hall.

She said, "I understand that people remain concerned about leaks of corporate secrets. Recognizing that reality, I know that if I were to return, I would still pose a problem for my husband, and for the Apple corporation as a whole. Why, you may ask? Because if I return, the leaks will begin again. And I will be blamed again. Why will the leaks return, you ask? Because those who do leak will feel emboldened knowing that I will be taking the blame, not them. And they will be right; I will be blamed, even though I am blameless. I've anticipated this situation and have come to a conclusion. I will not remain where my integrity is continually being questioned. Therefore, I have decided to return to where I was born. I will return to the furrows of plowed fields along the Upper Nile in Nubia where I lived a small child growing up."

Nodding to where her sons were standing, she said, "I hereby introduce my two sons to you."

Turning to Ram, she said, "You are their father. I hereby leave them with you to be raised by you from this time forward."

Sita gestured to Valmiki to accompany her. Together they left the reception hall, leaving Ram standing among the concert-going crowd, angry and distraught.

Valmiki purchased a one-way ticket from San Francisco to Aswan, Egypt. From there Sita traveled by horse-drawn cart to the village of her birth. She initiated her menopause, donned a headscarf, and lived the rest of her days in modesty.

Lav and Kus stayed with their father in the Apple palace. They attended public school and received supplementary instruction from Ram himself and from Vasis and the other chief palace geeks.

After Sita's departure, Ram thought often of her. In his loneliness he grieved for her. He could not bring himself to take another wife. He had a classic portrait painted of her on canvas and commissioned a statue of her to be carved. He placed the statue of Sita in the entrance hall of the Apple palace and had her portrait hung in the executive conference room.

Ram Dies

Decades passed for the Apple empire under the successful management of Ram and his three brothers. Vibish continued his reform of the syndicate. Honesty and shared prosperity waxed. Evil and social disparity waned.

Yet Ram continued to have bad dreams, as he had ever since his battles with Ravan on St. Eustatius. One night Ram had a particularly bad dream. He glimpsed a vision of a world without him, one he had left without taking time to say goodbye to the valiant monkeys who had assisted him during his life. He resolved to prepare for his death, properly and with grace.

Ram met with Lak that morning and discussed his dream. He said, "I know I'm becoming obsolete. My aspirations for our company no longer sync with what the market wants. I feel it's time to open fresh space on life's shelf. I'm wondering how to conclude my life with a suitable ending."

Lak replied, "I've been thinking along the same lines. I don't feel sorrow. Time is all-powerful, and my time to move on has come. I wish to return to Death Valley where I lived as a child. I wish to sit high upon a mountain overlooking great salt flats ringed by snow-covered mountains. I will fast until I slowly drift off to sleep in the cold of the night. I've arranged for childhood friends descended from the Timbisha Shoshone to let my body rest in a tepee before burying me in a riverbed. They will place my body in a cedar casket held together with wood dowels so my remains and casket may be recycled through the ecosystem."

Ram called his chief geek, Vasis, to tell him of Lak's decision.

Vasis consoled him, saying, "One should respect Lak's decision. One should appreciate his thoughtful approach to death and dying, his care to ensure that, though his act of dying, he brings comfort to the living."

So Ram acknowledged Lak's desire to go. He then said, "I wish to follow my brother's lead."

Ram called together his two remaining brothers. Ram said to Barat, "I sense my increasing obsolescence and know my time on this earth should come to an end. I wish to visit my friends among the monkeys to say good-bye before I die. Will you re-assume the duties of the CEO of Apple? You did such a good job many years ago."

Barat replied, "No. Absolutely not. I too have been contemplating my end of days."

Shat added, "As have I. Brothers, we have done so much together that I find it impossible to conceive of living without you both, hanging around in grief until I die myself. I'd rather we three left this earth together, joining our other brother Lak in union with the earth, wind, and seas."

Barat said to Ram, "I suggest you transfer the office of CEO to your two sons."

Vasis, who had remained silent while listening to this private moment, then added, "I'm sure the board of directors and the chief palace geeks will all endorse the move to appoint your sons to the CEO position. Such a transfer of power with no sign of boardroom conflict will instill confidence in our investors, many of whom were starting to get skittish and tweeting their anxiety. Although our stock has not fallen in recent months, it hasn't risen either, as people wait to see whom Apple's new leadership team will consist of. Let's pursue this further tomorrow morning."

That evening, Vasis polled the directors and chief geeks for their votes. The next morning he announced their unanimous support for appointing Lav and Kus as the new CEOs. The board also decided to split Apple into two divisions. One division would be an eastern branch for Asia and Europe, headquartered in Bangalore, India. The other division would be a western branch for North and South America that would continue to be headquartered in Silicon Valley. The directors observed that Apple's budget exceeded the national budgets of most countries in the world, and its employees exceeded the population of most countries as well. Splitting the company into two would promote the development of products that were more focused on local needs, as compared with the one-size-fits-all approach Apple had taken for decades.

Ram asked his mother, Kausha, now an old woman, to join the brothers and her grandsons in the executive conference room. Vasis administered the oath of office to Lav and Kus, while Kausha held the iPad from which Vasis read the oath.

Once Lav had assumed the position of CEO of the eastern division and Kus that of the western division, the four brothers departed the Apple palace for the last time.

Lak helicoptered to his mother's estate in Death Valley.

Carrying water but no food, he made his way to a lookout over the majestic great salt flats near Dante's View. There he took a deep breath and gave thanks for the fulfilling life he had led. Then he located an abandoned miner's shack. The door had a rusty padlock, but Lak crawled in through a crack in one of its weathered walls. After a week of fasting, Lak passed away. The next day his Shoshone childhood friends gathered his body for the green burial ceremony they had arranged.

The remaining three brothers accompanied Suman to the airport, where they boarded the company jet for a flight to the Bocas del Toro airfield in Panama.

There they met up with Hanuman, now an old and wise vervet monkey, along with many of the elder surviving howler monkeys, and Jamb, the spectacled bear, all veterans of the St. Eustatius expedition against Ravan.

Ram went to Hanuman and embraced him, saying, "We shall always be as one, my brother."

Hanuman replied, "You will always be in my heart. I will rejoice whenever I hear your name spoken."

Vibish had flown in from St. Eustatius in the black stealth jet to join the final farewell.

Ram said to Vibish, "You've done well."

Gesturing to include both Vibish and Hanuman, Ram declared, "The world in both its human and animal domains is in good hands through your combined leadership."

Ram then instructed Suman to fly on to Kauai. There they rented a helicopter. Suman piloted it to a spot offshore in sight of the great Na Pali cliffs.

Suman said to them, "I can't legally assist you in what you are about to do, but what I can say is this: if you jump and do not pull your parachute release cord, you will free-fall to the ocean waiting below."

One after the other, the three brothers stepped out the open door at the side of the helicopter for an exhilarating drop into the waves of the blue Pacific ocean. When they landed they were taken up by the Hawaiian shark spirit, Ka-moho-ali`i, becoming one with the animals under the sea.

Suman returned to Apple, sad at the loss of the brothers whom he had served so long, but resigned to their final choices.

Back at the Apple palace, Vasis was thinking of his own death too. He wanted to pass his position as chief palace geek to one of the younger geeks who had trained with him.

He convened his group of junior geeks and gave each of them a printed copy of the latest version of Valmiki's biography of Ram.

Vasis told them, "I'm giving you a printed copy because I don't want this manuscript finding its way onto the Internet just yet. I want you to read over the manuscript tomorrow. Then I want us to meet the day after tomorrow to discuss it."

When the time for the meeting came, Vasis opened by saying, "Decades ago Ram's father, Das, asked me to assist him in designing a perfect son. We considered his genome, his physical body, and how he should be raised. And back then I also briefed you all on the state of human reproductive technology. I hope your remember."

Some heads, those with streaks of white in their hair, nodded.

Vasis continued, "Our profession is regularly called upon to deliver human genetic design and reproductive services. Our new CEOs, Lav and Kus, might ask us to design their sons just as Das did so long ago. I want us to evaluate how good of a job we did—to find what we did right and what we did wrong so we can do an even better job next time."

Vasis then called on his heir apparent among the young geeks, asking, "What's your overview of Ram's life?"

Vasis junior replied, "In a nutshell, Ram forged a shared moral purpose between people and animals. He rooted out human evil. He defeated Ravan. Yet he failed in his home life."

Vasis said, "I agree."

Then Vasis asked of all the junior geeks, "I want you to speak up, in just a word or phrase from each, to say what worked."

The geeks noted that shared animal genes, shared genes from all of humanity, body armor, stem cells, raising the brothers to take pleasure in cooperating, the ability of the brothers to empathize with each other, and the lack of sibling rivalry among them—as well as Ram's big-data analysis of animal language, creation of translator robots, trusting animals, and including animals in the larger moral community—had all worked out well.

When the chatter died down, Vaisis asked, "And in a word or phrase, what didn't work?"

The geeks noted that Ram's relationship with Sita—including the way he put her on pedestal, didn't stand up for her against the rumors circulated about her, justified her suffering with a dubious appeal to his obligations to shareholders, and his overall inability to empathize with his wife as much as with his brothers—had not worked out well.

Continuing, Vasis asked, "Any ideas about why, in just a word or phrase again?"

A few geeks noted that Ram was not raised with a sister, and therefore had no experience with young women growing up. Others remarked that physical attraction was no substitute for the shared pleasure of cooperation and that Ram's lack of experience in relationships with the opposite sex had contributed to the failings in his home life.

Vasis then added, "Here's something else you wouldn't be aware of unless you had been living in close quarters with Ram, as I have been for many years. Ram came back from the wars a changed man. Until the day he died, he suffered from horrible dreams every night. He spoke with me about them. He said his dreams vividly recalled the death and carnage from his war with Ravan. During the war, his bond with Lak was strengthened by their fighting together. At the same time, his bond with Sita weakened. The war erased his memories of the pleasurable times when he and Sita jointly pioneered their research on communicating with animals. He returned from war physically victorious but emotionally broken. He lost his moral courage. He was no longer the man Sita fell in love with."

Vasis gazed into the eyes of the young men that comprised his staff and added, "You've not experienced war. What Ram went through to achieve his victory is an abstraction to you. I've never been in combat during a war either. But I can tell you, I have spoken to many veterans of the American wars. Those who fought in the trenches can remember vividly thirty, forty, or more years later who almost killed them and whom they killed. They can remember the faces of enemies they shot. In their dreams they can reach out and touch the wounds they inflicted and the wounds their friends sustained. They never forget. Ram experienced carnage beyond anything you've imagined. After his war with Ravan, he no longer had the moral courage he began with. You can't blame him. His indifference to suffering, to Sita's suffering, is a relic of the mental defense mechanism he constructed to see him through the war. Although Ram was the victor in the war against Ravan, he was a casualty of that war too."

Vasis continued, "And during the war, Ram lost sight of his immediate objective to rescue Sita. The war assumed a dynamic of its own, uncoupled from its original goal. Ram became obsessed with defeating Ravan to show the world that no one could steal from him rather than defeating Ravan to rid the world of an evil syndicate. At the end, by placing Vibish in charge of the syndicate, he did succeed in reforming it. But he never was able to connect again with Sita in the way he had when they first married."

The junior geeks fell silent. There was no shuffling around in their chairs.

Vasis continued, "Another sign too of his lingering stress from the war was his increasing isolation, his discomfort in social settings. His brothers became his only friends. Ram did his job, and Apple prospered. However, he had not really become as obsolete as he claimed. The truth is, he tired of his loneliness. Before he died, whom did he want to see? Not Sita, but the veterans he fought with, Hanuman, his closest friend, the survivors among the howlers, and Vibish, the only human, other than Lak, who joined him in the war. It's the war that killed him emotionally. I'm sure of it. It's the war that deadened his soul so he could passively watch Sita suffer her waterboarding and acquiesce to remedying impossible rumors about her integrity. I grieve that Ram's life, which began on such a celestial note, could collapse in tragedy."

Vasis's heir apparent spoke for the other junior geeks. "You have shared a painfully difficult insight. We're not old enough to have seen Ram before the war. We can't compare for ourselves what he was like before and after his war with Ravan."

Vasis then turned to his heir apparent and asked, "What, then, will you do differently?"

He replied, "I won't change a thing in your biological steps—the genes, body enhancements, and so forth. What I would change is his upbringing. I'd extend your methods that promoted cooperation among his brothers by devising some activities that involved both boys and girls, requiring them to cooperate. Then I would reward them both for doing so. That would build understanding and empathy between the sexes just like it did between Ram with his brothers. And I'd counsel any CEO to stay out of wars. As you've described all too well, although Ram destroyed evil, he paid an enormous emotional price—the loss of his loving and devoted wife. I realize some war can't be avoided—someone had to stop Ravan— but I would emphasize how winning a war is an illusion, an impossibility. Winning a war is a contradiction in terms."

Then Vasis junior looked around at all the junior geeks whom Vasis senior had assembled and said, "I see only men in our group. Shouldn't we begin by including women to join with us as palace geeks? And other unrepresented groups too? How can we learn to cooperate and empathize with diverse people ourselves without enjoying the pleasure born of accomplishing shared tasks with them?"

Turning to his surrogate father, Vasis Junior said, "We will build on what you've achieved."

The other junior geeks nodded, calling out, "Hear, hear."

The normally reserved Vasis gulped. He then said, "I call on you all never to forget our discussion today. There's much to be learned from the story of Ram."

Music Score

Sita's Lament

By Trudy Roughgarden

Acknowledgments

I thank Gwenn Seemel for the wonderful art that perfectly captures the main characters in the book and Trudy Roughgarden for the moving music composition that Sita sings while waiting to be rescued.

I thank Melinda Read, Trudy Roughgarden, and Virgil Zanders for suggesting improvements to the plot while reading the chapters as they became available.

I thank Susan DeFreitas and Vinnie Kinsella of Indigo Editing & Design for superb editorial improvements throughout the manuscript and for important developmental suggestions.

I thank Jessica Hardesty Norris and Jessica Glenn of MindBuck Media, and Julienne Givot of Both/And Media, for publicity and guidance during production.

I thank Fr. William Miller of St. Michaels and All Angels Episcopal Church in Kauai for his encouragement. I also thank my colleagues at the University of Hawaii—Megan Donahue, Flo Thomas, Jo-Ann Leong, Katya Sherstyuk, and Jonathan Goldberg-Hiller—for their stimulating discussions and hospitality.

I thank my husband, Richard Schmidt, for suffering the disruptions that come with being married to an author.

Finally, I gratefully acknowledge that my conjectured albatross conversation portrays ideas from my research on the evolution of cooperative social behavior supported by the John Templeton Foundation (Award ID 51473).

Biographies

AUTHOR

Joan Roughgarden is an evolutionary biologist and ecologist living in Kauai, Hawaii. She has carried out fieldwork in the eastern Caribbean and along the California coast. She works as a research scientist at the Hawaii Institute of Marine Biology, having retired as a professor from Stanford University. She has authored or edited eight nonfiction textbooks and monographs, the latest being *Evolution's Rainbow* (2004) and The *Genial Gene* (2009), both published by the University of California Press. *Ram-2050* is her first novel.

ARTIST

Gwenn Seemel is a French-American artist, painter, and portraitist living in Portland, Oregon. In addition to portraits, her portfolio includes an outdoor mural and the illustrations for *Crime Against Nature*, a book depicting conversation-provoking animals. Her website is gwennseemel.com.

COMPOSER

Trudy Roughgarden is a pianist and cellist living in Sunnyvale, California, where she performs, composes, and offers private lessons.